AFRICAN SKY

TONY PARK

Quercus

First published in Australia in year of 2006 by Pan Macmillan
This paperback edition published in the UK in 2014 by

Quercus Editions Ltd
55 Baker Street
7th Floor, South Block
London W1U 8EW

A CIP catalogue record for this book is available
from the British Library

PB ISBN 978 1 84866 617 7
EBOOK ISBN 978 0 85738 668 7

10 9 8 7 6 5 4 3 2 1

Printed and bound in Great Britain by Clays Ltd, St Ives plc

For Nicola

1

He knew he was about to die. He cried as much from frustration and anger at himself, as he did from the terror.

He heard the strange clicking noises of their language, a sound like a child learns to make early in life with its tongue and the roof of its mouth. He glanced over his shoulder. The two bushmen trailed him, about a hundred yards away. Small in stature, but more deadly than any big man he had ever tangled with. One held his tiny bow and arrow up at him and laughed at the way the white man ran, then stumbled.

The dry white salt stuck to his hands, stung his knees in the abrasions where he had fallen before. He was naked, except for his air-force-issue underpants. The skin on his back, face and arms was burned pink. He screwed up his eyes at the blinding whiteness of the saltpan. Earth merged with sky, the horizon lost in a shimmering heat haze that made his head spin when he looked at it.

He cried in the knowledge that he would die in this lifeless, blanched place. He bellowed, like the dying animal he was, a primeval cry of anguish at his stupidity. A desperate, futile plea for clemency.

He had no idea where his aircraft, his Harvard, was. In a matter of minutes he had gone from being an untouchable, privileged god of the skies to a hunted animal in the unforgiving white sands. His fear, born of the stories of his father and uncle, the only two to have survived the carnage of the first war's trenches from a family of six brothers, was to be trapped on the ground, pursued by an enemy who wanted to kill him. In the air, as a would-be fighter pilot, he felt himself more than a match for any German or Japanese airman. He was a good pilot, a damned good flyer. The instructors were spare in their praise, but he'd seen it in the small smiles and the odd wink after each phase of his training.

All that was for nothing now. He was on the ground, out of his element, a hunted animal.

They followed him, not even bothering to hush their voices as they would if they were stalking the wary gemsbok or the fleet-footed impala. He was just a man. Not agile enough to outrun the hunters, not smart enough to outwit them.

The hunters walked with the easy, loping stride of

men who must cover long distances on foot while expending minimal energy. Each wore a skimpy kaross made from the pelt of the black-backed jackal. They laughed as they chatted. Rarely, if ever, had either had to kill such a worthless prey.

'He runs like a child,' one said.

'There is no challenge in this deed,' the other added.

'The decision has been made. It was not ours to make.'

'Will we suffer for this hunt?' the second asked, his laughing checked.

'If anyone ever finds his body there will be nothing to point towards us.'

They were from another age. The two hunters, from the San people, known as bushmen to the whites who dismissed them as primitives, lived the same way as their fathers and grandfathers and those for generations before them had lived. Their bodies were slight, all muscle, without a trace of the fat that comes with an easy life. The hunters worked for every mouthful of food, every drop of water in the red-gold sands of the Kalahari Desert and the white-hot plains of the Makgadikgadi saltpans, places where other human beings died in a matter of days or hours. The noise above them, however, was from another world. They looked up in amazement, still unused to seeing one of the flying machines so close to the ground.

* * *

The pilot turned his blistered red face to the sun and held a salt-crusted hand to his eyes to shield them from the painful glare.

'Here! I'm down here!' His voice was tiny, lost in the emptiness. He hoped the man in the air could see his waving arms.

The Harvard was flying low, no more than seven or eight hundred feet, but the pilot pushed it into a shallow dive, until the spinning propeller was barely twenty feet off the shimmering saltpan.

The two San ducked instinctively, as though the flying machine would take off their heads. They turned and raised their bows and pointed them at the man they were stalking. He had stopped, to wave at the aircraft.

He looked again at the near-naked hunters, saw the bows and started to run again, all the while flailing his arms above his head to show the Harvard pilot he lived. He felt the beat of the engine in his chest. He had no idea where the aircraft had come from, but his tears now were of gratitude for his great fortune. He might yet live after all.

The shadow of the single-engine trainer raced across the flat surface, momentarily eclipsing the tiny dark figures.

The running man looked up and back at the Harvard, fervently hoping to see the undercarriage being lowered.

He hoped the pilot behind the controls knew the saltpan would make a perfect landing strip for his rescue. The wheels, however, remained up. He stumbled again, tripped and fell. He rolled onto his back as the aircraft overflew him. He saw the letters painted on the side of the aircraft.

'No!' he bellowed. 'No, no, no!'

2

From a thousand feet, where the martial eagle rode the hot current that rose from the baking white concrete and the shimmering black Tarmac, Africa looked scarred as never before.

In fifty years the white man had carved roads and railway lines through the Rhodesian bush, and built his towns and dug his mines, but, in truth, the British pioneers who had migrated north from the Cape had barely scratched the hide of the beast that succoured them. Until the war started, that was.

The great dry western lands, with their golden grasses and stunted acacias, were cattle country and had been for the best part of a century, since the Zulu impis migrated north, sweeping all other tribes before them. The sons and grandsons of the conquerors had become the Matabele – as feared and respected as their fore-fathers. They had fought the whites, in the same way the Zulu had defied the Europeans, and there were still a few gnarled and grizzled grey-hairs who remembered the rebellion of 1897. They had spilt the blood of Cecil John Rhodes' men and their women, before their families had suffered the inevitable consequences of making war with the settlers. Rhodes had given his name to the lands of the Matabele and those of their enemies, the Shona, to the east.

There was peace now between the Shona and the Matabele, and the blacks and the whites, but from the sky the soil of Matabeleland showed as a spear wound, fresh and red with the telltale signs of a new conflict.

The eagle let the air spill from beneath its spread wings and it dropped out of the path of the machine. It had learned how to avoid them – had to, if it wanted to survive. They were everywhere, belching their hot exhaust and assaulting the peace of the sky with the roar of their rotary engines. The metal bird's nest was below. When not flying, they hid in the rows of tin sheds and sat side by side in a most unnatural way on the concrete runways and taxiways that stood out like pathetic little Band-Aids on the freshly opened dirt wounds in the skin of Matabeleland.

In the distance was the town, Bulawayo. It had been the site of the vanquished Matabele king Lobengula's kraal. Gubulawayo, as the king had called it, meant place of death – where he had slain his foes. The killing was over, long dead with Lobengula, but more white men than ever before had come to this part of Africa to learn the way of the warrior and the eagle. To learn to kill. Some died in the process.

The eagle spied a duiker. The tiny grey antelope, no bigger than a small dog, darted from its hiding place in the meagre shade of a thorn bush, which had just been crushed beneath the steel tracks of a bulldozer. The bird of prey tucked in its wings and dived with a speed and accuracy that the pilot of the orbiting aircraft could never hope or dare to match.

Squadron Leader Paul Bryant watched the eagle streak towards the earth, but a cloud of dust stirred up by the dozer obscured his view of the kill. He loved watching the birds. Envied them. He turned away from the window at the sound of the man clearing his throat, then reluctantly sat down behind his desk. 'Yes, Wilson?'

'Seems another stupid bastard's bought it, sir,' the young pilot officer said. He was a native Rhodesian, with cheeks reddened by the last vestiges of acne.

'Who?' Bryant asked.

'Um, Smith, I think. No, sorry, Smythe. That's it. One of the Poms. Londoner, I believe. Short fellow. Second solo on a Harvard. The ops officer asked me to tell you, sir. Said you'd want to start the investigation. He was due back late yesterday afternoon but never arrived. There's been no word.'

Bryant closed his eyes for a moment and tried to place the missing pilot's face. It was hard – hundreds had passed through the flight training school since he'd arrived, but he made a point of meeting them all. He saw him now, and nodded to himself. He was mildly annoyed that the pilot officer, Wilson, had called the lost trainee a stupid bastard. The boy who'd delivered the news barely had his wings and hadn't flown an operational sortie. Hadn't earned the right to call anyone stupid. 'Shit. Two crashes in two weeks. That's a record even for this pilots' course. First the Canadian . . .'

'Cavendish, sir.'

'Right, Cavendish.' Bryant ran a hand down his face. 'Now this bloke.'

'We'll mount a search, sir?' Wilson looked down his nose at his superior officer.

Bryant reached into the desk's top drawer and grabbed a mint. He popped it in his mouth, bit hard into it. He knew some of the men called him a coward behind his back, but he had nothing to hide or prove to this boy. Boy? The pilot officer was only five years younger than he, maybe twenty-two or twenty-three, but the gap between them was like that between father and son. 'A-Flight will be following the same flight plan as the missing man today. They might see the wreckage. A bit of low-level won't do them any harm. Trouble is, he . . . Smythe might have been off course.'

'Shame for the silly bugger to come halfway around the world to Africa, only to die before he got to run onto the game.'

Bryant fixed him with a stare. His voice was calm, almost conversational. 'It's not a fucking game, Wilson. You don't "run on". We don't know if Smythe is even dead.' Anyway, Bryant thought to himself, if the pilot were a goner, it was better it happened to him here, in Africa, rather than him biding his time at some rain-soaked strip in England watching the bodies of his mates being hosed out of their kites after a mission.

Bryant closed his eyes to shake the memory and broke the contact with the junior officer. He'd let the door to his memory creak open and wished he hadn't. He didn't want their pity, these over-keen, wide-eyed pups who hadn't yet been there. He didn't want them mocking him. Didn't want to be the headcase crying in his cups in the mess.

'Yes, sir,' Wilson said, but he made no move to leave Bryant's office.

'Well? What is it, Wilson?'

'Um, just wondering, sir . . .'

'What?' Bryant looked up from a mountain of irrelevant,

yawn-inducing paperwork. It was getting warmer. September. The skies were still clear outside, no rain yet; not for another month, he reckoned. Good African flying weather.

'It's just that, well, I got my posting this morning, and I wanted to know what it's like, over there. What it's really like.'

Bryant saw the smile breaking at the corners of Pilot Officer Wilson's mouth. He closed his eyes again. Poor bastard. He was excited about it, too. 'Where?'

'OTU 10, in Buckinghamshire.'

The acronym stood for operational training unit, and this one was based near the village of Westcott. Bryant knew the place. Nestled in a patchwork of rolling green hills. Quaint country pubs, thatched cottages and pink-cheeked East End girls having the time of their lives ploughing fields for the land army during the day and flirting with pilots from the colonies at nights. Funerals under leaden skies. Marathon drinking sessions after each mission. The wailing klaxons and the trilling bells on the crash wagons.

He'd done his time in an OTU, converting to Wellingtons, and, before his second tour, in a heavy conversion unit, learning to handle four-engine Halifaxes – bloody death traps – and eventually his beloved Lancaster. He forced a smile for Wilson's sake. He'd been a carbon copy of the young pilot – keen, cocky, and overconfident, hungry for everything this new life had to offer and worried the war would be over before he got to England. He'd wanted to get his training over and get out of Rhodesia as soon as possible before his first operational tour, but now he'd be happy if he never saw England again. Despite the drudgery of his office job, Africa was suiting Paul Bryant just fine.

'It's what you wanted,' Bryant said.

'Yes, sir.'

'Be careful of wanting something too much, Clive.'

'What do you mean, sir?'

'It's not like here, mate,' Bryant said, opening the drawer again, taking out his packet of Woodbines. 'Smoke?'

'No thanks, sir, I don't.'

Bryant shrugged. 'Want to take a seat?'

'If you've got time, sir,' the younger man said.

Bryant inhaled deeply, looked out the window at the dry, yellow grass. An African labourer, sweating under the midday sun, scythed away with a *bemba*, a piece of iron bar bent like a crooked finger at one end and honed to a razor's edge. His arm moved in a long, wide arc. He made the back-breaking chore look effortless.

Bryant wondered how much he should say. 'You'll probably go straight to Wimpeys – Wellingtons. You know why they put you in Wellingtons, Wilson?'

'I imagine to get us used to a twin-engine kite before they let us graduate to one of the four-engine big boys, like a Halifax or a Lancaster.'

Bryant smiled. 'Yes, that's right. Gives you a chance to get used to working with a crew.' The real reason the OTUs used Wellingtons these days was that they were old, near the end of their operational lives, and it didn't matter so much if they were shot down or collided with another aircraft on the way into or out of Germany.

'But we'll be flying proper missions?' Wilson said, enthusiasm shining in his blue eyes.

'Yes, you will. And you'll be sharing the sky with other squadrons, operational squadrons full of men near the end of their tours. It can get crowded up there.'

'Sir?'

'One of the Lancasters in my old squadron was involved in a midair collision with a Wimpey from an OTU. The other kite was hundreds of miles off course. The pilot of the Lancaster had trained here in Rhodesia, when I did my elementary flight training. Jimmy Roberts was his name. On his last sortie, would have been going home afterwards. The Wimpey ploughed into Jimmy's fuselage, just aft of the mid-upper turret. Cut the Lanc in half. They all died. Thirteen men, from both aircraft. Try to be careful where you fly, Clive.'

Wilson nodded. 'The losses, sir. Are they as bad as some of the blokes reckon?'

Bryant shrugged. 'Numbers don't mean much, Clive,' he said. He dragged on the cigarette again. 'Live life.'

'Sir?'

He tried hard to think of something positive to say. Too late. The door had been opened wide. He took a deep breath and coughed. 'Live life, Wilson. Enjoy it while you can. Get rat-arsed tonight and hit the town. When you get to England, live every day like it's your last.'

'You make it sound like I won't be coming back, sir.'

Bryant smiled, and stubbed out his cigarette. He looked hard at the boy. He reckoned he could tell, during his tour, who'd make it and who would die. He'd been right more often than wrong. He was certain about Wilson. The boy had the look, the attitude, the cocky smirk, the swagger. He even wore his peaked air force cap at that rakish angle he thought made him already look like a veteran. 'You'll be fine, Clive,' he lied.

'Well, um, thanks, sir. I'd best be off. I'd like to talk more, if you have the time. Maybe over a beer or ten tonight?'

'I'll try to be there.' He searched the younger man's eyes to see if he were taking the mickey out of him. Bryant knew he drank too much, and he suspected the rest of the base was also aware of the fact.

'Thanks again, sir, for . . . for your words.'

'You're a good pilot. Do your job, look after your crew, and you'll all get home in one piece.'

'I hope so, sir. See you tonight,' Wilson said as he left, and shut the door.

He gave the young pilot officer a month in England. No more. Probably wouldn't even make it out of the OTU alive.

Bryant checked his watch. It was five minutes to eleven. Fuck it, he thought. Searches ran themselves once the operations room was alerted. He slid open the second drawer of his desk. He lifted the single sheet of blank paper that covered the Santy's gin bottle. Rarely did he take a nip before eleven. His hand shook as it closed around the smooth glass neck. He told himself it was the talk about Roberts and the severed Lancaster.

He started to lift the bottle, felt the saliva fill his mouth. The telephone rang. He put the bottle down and closed the drawer again. 'Adjutant, Squadron Leader Bryant,' he said.

'Flight Sergeant Henderson on the front gate, sir. I've two police officers here, sir.'

'God. Which pub have the trainees destroyed this time?' Usually the drunken brawls, property damage and car accidents happened on the final night of a course, not five days before graduation. While they were learning to fly, the student pilots tended to control their behaviour, lest they get kicked out of flight school and wind up as wireless air gunners, where they could look forward to freezing their balls off in front turrets or short lives as tail gunners.

'They won't say what it's about, sir. Should I send them through with an escort?'

That would have been the normal procedure. Bryant could probably have had a quick drink while he waited for the coppers to arrive. No, that wouldn't do. 'Don't worry, Flight. I'll walk down and pick them up.' The walk would keep him away from the bottle. He wasn't so desperate that he didn't realise he was developing a problem. That had to be a good sign, he told himself.

'Very good, sir.'

Bryant hung up. He took his peaked cap off the hook on the wall and opened the metal locker in the corner of his office. There was a small mirror on the inside of the door. His eyes were bloodshot. He adjusted his hat and gave himself what he hoped was a winning smile. 'Cheer up, you're alive,' he said to himself. The smile fell from his face and he shut the locker.

His office door opened onto the orderly room. Corporal Richards, the noncommissioned officer in charge of the base's daily paperwork war, looked up from his type-writer.

'Back soon. I'm going to the gate to pick up some

coppers. I'd call my lawyer now if I were you, Richards.'

'Very good, sir,' the younger man smiled. 'Should I burn the pictures of you and the goat, sir?'

'Get back to work or I'll have you horse-whipped.'

Outside it was another perfect Rhodesian flying day. It wasn't hard to see why they had picked this country to train pilots. It was the same with Australia. The empire needed airmen at an ever-increasing rate to make up for the losses over Europe and, to train flyers, you needed open spaces, empty skies and, preferably, a lack of enemy fighters.

Two students in RAF tropical uniforms, khaki tunics and shorts hemmed above sunburned knees, saluted him as they passed. The trainees marched, their arms swinging to breast-pocket height. Bryant walked casually. He couldn't remember the last time he had marched anywhere. He took the cigarette packet from his shirt pocket and lit one on the move. Oh yes, he thought, the last time he marched would have been at a funeral. He couldn't remember whose. Slow march, carrying the coffin. Bryant checked his watch and hoped the police wouldn't delay his lunch. Lunchtime was a highlight of his dreary, desk-bound day. A couple of bottles of Lion beer in the mess. Too many of his memories – all of them, it sometimes seemed – were linked to the death of someone or other.

He scanned the sky. An Oxford was on final approach to the main runway, its waggling wings betraying the trainee's nerves and inexperience. There was no sign of the eagle and he wondered if it had caught its prey. A ruddy dust plume from the dozer marked the site of the new taxiway. The twin-engine trainer bounced once then slewed down the runway. At least that one had landed safely.

'Cheer up, you're alive,' he told himself again.

'Squadron Leader Bryant,' a deep voice called behind him.

Bryant knew who it was and smiled at the man's formality. He turned and grinned. 'Is it worth me telling you again, Kenneth, that you can call me by my first name? You're not in the air force, man.'

Kenneth Ngwenya gave a small, pained smile. He lowered his voice. 'And I could tell you, again, that in a country where black men have to get off the footpath when they see a white coming towards them, for me to call you by your first name when there are others nearby would be bad for me and worse for you.'

'All right then, all right, get off the bloody pavement.'

Ngwenya laughed. '*Sawubona*, Paul,'

'And I see you, too, my friend.'

'Your Ndebele is getting better. Perhaps it's time you graduated beyond hello and goodbye.'

'You're like every schoolteacher I ever met, Kenneth.'

'Really?'

'Yes, a prick.' Bryant cut their laughter short with a glance at his watch. 'Where have you been all week? I've missed you pestering me for building materials and medicines.'

'The only reason I pester you is because you never say no. And the children appreciate it. I've been visiting my father; he has not been well.'

'I'm sorry to hear that. I hope he gets better soon. I'd love to stay and chat, Kenneth, but I've got the police waiting for me at the front gate.'

'Ah, I hope you enjoy your time in gaol. Is it about the woman who was killed last night?'

Bryant studied Kenneth's face. The man was as tall as he was, about six feet, with bright, alert eyes magnified by small rimless glasses that looked completely at odds with his powerful body. Ngwenya always seemed constrained by the dark suit, starched white shirt and black tie that he wore every day, no matter what the weather. Bryant had written, in one of his infrequent letters to his father in Australia, that Kenneth had the brain of a university professor and the body of a rugby player, even though Africans were barred from playing the game.

'What woman?'

Ngwenya's face was devoid of mirth. 'I am sorry to bring the news. I thought you would have heard by now. She was from here, Paul. White. One of the air force women. Some of the askaris' wives were talking about it this morning. It will be bad for us.'

Bryant swallowed hard. 'Us?'

'She was found in the township, Paul. Mzilikazi.'

'Who was it? Do you have her name?'

'No, sorry. I am worried about this.'

'So am I, mate. I have to go, Kenneth.'

'Of course. I'd like to see you, later, though, about some more building materials for the school. It's why I was looking for you.'

'I'll try to make time. Come look for me.' He clapped the African on one arm and nodded to him, then turned back to the guardroom. Bryant knew that Kenneth Ngwenya was a man driven by much more than his job as the sole teacher at the base's African school. He was committed – more than any teacher Bryant had ever met – to the education of his children, who were mostly the offspring of the askaris, Rhodesian Africans overseen by white officers and noncommissioned officers, and the labour brought in to construct the sprawling air base. But Ngwenya had confided to Bryant that he was also a member of the Southern Rhodesian African National Congress, a political group committed to improving the lot of the colony's black population, and other, loftier goals that went far beyond the bounds of reality, such as the right to vote and majority rule.

Bryant felt his heart beating faster as he approached the guardroom and the boom gate at the main entrance to the base. He wiped his hands on the side of his uniform trousers to dry them. At least he would have time to compose himself before he met the police.

'Stand fast!' Flight Sergeant Henderson barked as Bryant approached the gatehouse. Henderson ground his left boot into the pavement and snapped out a parade-ground salute. Two black African air askaris dressed in khaki uniforms, ankle boots, puttees and fezzes also came stiffly to attention. The askaris provided base security.

Bryant returned the courtesy with a casual brush of the peak of his cap. He thought he read a flash of contempt at his sloppy drill in the flight sergeant's slate grey eyes. He didn't care.

'Morning, *sah*!' Henderson boomed.

'Morning, Henderson. As you were, men,' Bryant drawled.

The flight sergeant relaxed his ramrod-straight body ever so slightly. 'Thank you, sir. A Sergeant Hayes and a Constable Lovejoy, a *female*, are waiting for you in the guardhouse, sir.'

'Thanks. Leave them with me.'

'Begging your pardon, sir?'

'Yes, what is it?' Bryant asked Henderson.

'That African, sir. Ngwenya. The schoolteacher.'

'What about him?'

'Well, he's a civilian, sir. Shouldn't be wandering about the base willy-nilly. I can have a word with him if you like, sir. Tell him to stop bothering you.'

Bryant looked at the smile and wondered if Henderson were actually being sincere, or if he were being baited. '*Mister* Ngwenya is welcome on the base anytime, Flight. Perhaps you'd like to volunteer for one of the work parties doing some construction work at the school?'

'Very busy man, I am, sir.'

Bryant opened the door of the guardroom. Henderson would keep. If the man had been operational, on a squadron serving as a wireless air gunner or a bomb aimer instead of a glorified gate guard, he would have seen plenty of black faces serving at the same rank as him. The Royal Air Force was happy enough to have Jamaicans and Nigerians flying and dying alongside Englishmen, even if Flight Sergeant Henderson had a problem with an educated Rhodesian walking around the base.

Bryant didn't consider himself a bleeding heart, but he did pride himself on judging a man by the way he acted, not by the colour of his skin. He'd grown up in

Dubbo in the far west of New South Wales, the son of a sheep shearer who roamed the plains from farm to farm. His mother had died during his birth and Bryant had been raised by an Aboriginal nanny and his father's sister and her husband. His childhood friend had been the nanny's boy, Alf. The pair had grown up as close as brothers. By the time his uncle, a wizened blacksmith his aunt said had been angry at the world since a horse had smashed his jaw, had sat him down at the age of ten and tried to tell him he should spend less time with Alf and more time with boys his own colour, it was too late. His uncle had knocked him to the ground when Paul had tried to object – confirmation, if it were needed, that the world consisted of only two types of people. Good blokes and bastards.

Pip Lovejoy loved her job. Unlike her other life on the dairy farm, being a policewoman was interesting, exciting, rewarding, and comparatively safe. But it could also be tiring. She'd been up all night. She put a hand over her mouth to conceal a yawn as she peered out the window of the Kumalo air base guardhouse, and thought back over the preceding hours.

'It's a murder. Grab your hat and jacket and put down that sandwich, Philippa. I don't want you throwing up when we get to the body. Sometimes they stink so much you swear you'll never get the stench off you,' Sergeant Hayes had said as he burst into the criminal investigation division office at Stops Camp, Bulawayo's main police station, a little after three that morning.

Sergeant Harold Hayes didn't like her – Pip was sure of it. Certainly he made it abundantly clear he hated the fact that women had been enlisted into the British South

Africa Police in the newly created Southern Rhodesian Women's Auxiliary Police Service to cover for the large number of young white men who had volunteered for service in the air force and army. Hayes was old enough to have served in the first war, but had joined the police instead. Pip thought her presence at Stops Camp, and the fact that many more women were joining the SRWAPS as the war dragged on, were constant reminders to Hayes of his lack of war service. He was arrogant and foul-mouthed and he hated blacks and women. But he couldn't stop her from loving the job.

'A murder?' she'd repeated, wide-eyed. Up until now the closest she'd come to death as a volunteer police-woman had been keeping onlookers away from a fatal car crash, and typing up scene-of-crime reports for the Criminal Investigation Division detectives. 'What about CID?'

'Suicide down at Esigodini, and a drunk driver's wrapped himself and his family around a tree. We're it, Lovejoy, and even though I've got to take you with me, I'm not letting them take this case away from me!'

Pip had ignored the insult – she, too, was excited about getting a murder case. She wolfed down the last of her boiled egg sandwich, put on her grey cap and jacket, and brushed the breadcrumbs from her uniform shirt and navy blue tie. The tie matched the cuffs and epaulettes of her uniform. She was a messy eater, always had been, but she made sure she looked her best when she was in public in her uniform.

'No, you don't have time to do your bloody lipstick, Lovejoy!' Hayes had barked at her as she glanced in the mirror behind the door.

She had pulled a face at his back and followed him outside to the car park. It was warm out. The rains would arrive in a month or so and the days were getting hotter, the nights balmier.

'Where are we going, Sergeant?' Pip had asked, unable to mask her excitement, as they climbed into the Dodge.

'You'll find out soon enough, young lady. Nowhere you've ever been before in your protected little upbringing, I'll wager.'

She'd let the condescension wash over her. The fat red-necked pig knew nothing of her life. At twenty-two years of age she did not consider herself young and neither had she been shielded from much during her life. Pip Lovejoy's parents had been farmers, and not very lucky ones at that. Her father had had an incredible knack for planting the wrong crops at the wrong time. He'd gone into cattle when the price of beef plummeted. Her mother was smart, smarter than her father, but too deferential to the old man to give advice. As things got worse, her father's drinking and gambling increased. Her mother had started to argue with her father, growing bolder as the old man slid deeper into a hole of his own digging. One day, Pip woke to find her with a purple bruise on one side of her face and a cut cheek. Shortly after, her father had wagered away the last savings they'd had and blown his brains out with a shotgun. That was when Pip was fourteen, at the height of the Depression. Her mother had started growing vegetables in the backyard of the rented property they'd moved to, in Fort Victoria, in the eastern part of the country, and managed to eke out a paltry living for herself, Pip and Pip's two younger sisters.

Pip was the smartest of the three girls and had won a scholarship to a good boarding school in Salisbury. She'd excelled and loved her time there. Surrounded by the wealthy daughters of Rhodesia's elite, she had been able to forget the traumas and privations of home. She'd won another scholarship, to university, where she had been accepted to study law.

'Keep a watch out, Lovejoy,' Hayes had said to her, breaking her train of thought as they drove through the darkened streets.

It was just as well. One, she certainly needed to be alert when they were out after dark, and two, she didn't need to rekindle any more memories of her time at varsity. 'Yes, Sarge.'

'It's sergeant, Lovejoy, not *sarge*. We're not in some second-rate American film.'

She stared out into the gloom of the resting town and felt her excitement mount as Hayes drove along the Sixth Avenue extension, out of downtown Bulawayo. It seemed they were heading into Mzilikazi, one of the African townships on the outskirts of the city. Hayes had been right about one thing – although she'd been born in Africa, she'd spent most of her life on farms or in school dorms, so she'd never really had a close look inside one of the chaotic, crowded communities in which much of Rhodesia's black population lived. It was one of the things she loved, though, discovering new places and seeing people through new eyes as a policewoman. She'd only lived on this side of the country, on the dairy farm, since her wedding a little over two years ago, so she didn't know Bulawayo or the region as well as her bellicose partner did.

The wide tree-lined stately streets of downtown Bulawayo narrowed to dusty dirt hemmed in by older, rundown masonry buildings, which, as the car lurched on, its wheels dipping in and out of potholes, turned to structures of tin, then asbestos sheet and then a mishmash of every building material available in the colony.

Even at this late hour there was light. Weak yellow beams from blackened paraffin lamps slicing out through cracks in shanty walls. And music. How incongruous, Pip thought, that a place that reeked of decay and human waste, and must look even worse in daylight, seemed to pulse with a chirpy, lively brand of music. Or was it so surprising? Was the lot of the people who lived here so bad that music was their only happiness? She hadn't ever given much thought to the plight of the blacks who worked on her farm. They always seemed genuinely happy to see her when they greeted her in the morning, when she had a *mombe* slaughtered for a special occasion, when they herded the milk cows past the house to the dairy. Who were the Africans who lived in the township of Mzilikazi? What were their lives like inside those crumbling asbestos homes with their bare earthen floors?

Unconsciously she started tapping her foot on the firewall of the police car, picking up the lilting rhythm of the penny whistle and the guitar. It reminded her a little of American jazz, or swing, perhaps a mix of both. *Kwela*, she had a feeling it was called. Township music. Black music. She had picked up enough Ndebele to know the word meant 'to lift' or 'to raise'. Maybe it raised their hopes, their hearts. Whatever its name, this was not the sort of music Charlie, her husband, would ever play at the farm on the gramophone – he preferred classical pieces. His choices reminded her of funerals. Pip strummed her fingers on the side of the police car's door,

29

out of sight of Hayes. She liked the rhythm and decided she would seek out some jazz records on her next shopping trip in town. She'd been reading the local newspaper, the *Bulawayo Chronicle*, during the night shift, and it was full of news about the fighting in Italy, and the Italian government's surrender. However, the Germans and Japs were still very much in the war, so there was no risk of Charlie coming home any time soon. She'd have plenty of time to destroy the records before his return.

Hayes stared across at her and even in the gloomy car she could see his disapproval. She stopped tapping her foot and strumming her fingers. She had a job to do.

People ducked down alleyways and closed doors at the sight of the police vehicle as it cruised along. It was getting less and less like the white part of town the deeper they pushed into Mzilikazi. The township was named after the warrior king of the local Matabele people, who had been defeated by the whites after an uprising at the end of the last century, but there was nothing proud or regal about where the blacks lived now.

Ahead she saw a crowd of fifty to a hundred people, mostly males, all Africans, thronging the entrance to a narrow alleyway.

'This'll be the spot,' Hayes said. 'Bloody Kaffirs can't resist congregating at the scene of a crime. One of them will have done it, Lovejoy, mark my words. Take note of their faces. Get the names of the ones closest to the body, the ones gawking at her.'

She swallowed the saliva that had suddenly filled her mouth, and wiped moist palms on her uniform skirt. Hayes had told her nothing of the victim. Now, at least, Pip knew the dead person was a woman. She wondered about the circumstances. The music was louder now, so they were probably near a shebeen. The bar was trading illegally, if it was open this late. He stopped the car.

Hayes smiled. 'Come on, Lovejoy. Let's get it done. Try not to faint on me. Remember, right or wrong, you're a member of the British South Africa Police, so try to act like one.'

'Yes, Sergeant.' She stepped out of the car, into a puddle. It hadn't rained for months. She shivered and recoiled at the smell of raw alcohol, vomit, cooking-fire smoke. She looked straight ahead and strode after Hayes. There were African women hovering on the fringe of the cluster of men. Garish floral-printed frocks. Empty eyes. She knew prostitutes were as much a part of a shebeen as the dark native beer, but she'd never seen one; at least, not that she knew of.

'Step aside,' Hayes ordered, and used his shoulder to push between two young African men in suits who blocked the footpath.

Pip slowed and watched the way the two men reacted to Hayes. The first touched his head, ducked to one side and began an apology that Hayes ignored. The second's eyes lingered resentfully on the policeman's broad back. The man was well-dressed, better than most in the crowd, in a dark blue suit, a wide tie of a matching hue, a white shirt and a black fedora. He picked his teeth with a toothpick. Pip felt the man had a learned or innate dislike of the police; that he knew his rights and resented the simple, yet arrogant act of being physically brushed aside, like an annoying branch of a tree on a walk in the bush. He looked like a spiv to her.

'What's your name?' Pip asked him, her voice little more than a croak at first. His eye line was about a foot above hers when he turned. The man smirked. She took a breath and bellowed: 'I said, what's your bloody name, man!'

He took a step back, the smile gone from his face as he removed the toothpick. 'Innocent. Innocent Nkomo, madam.'

'How long have you been here, Innocent?' Pip asked more softly, craning her head back and fishing in her tunic pocket for her notebook and pencil.

'For one hour, madam. Since they find her.'

The penny whistle played on in another building down a street littered with broken beer bottles. An old man

32

sat with his back against a tin wall. A dog sniffed him. Life carried on, even at a murder scene. 'What were you doing in the neighbourhood?'

'Drinking, madam. And dancing,' he said. She couldn't smell beer on his breath, though, and he seemed perfectly lucid. The whites of his eyes were clear and bright, not the hazy yellow that reflected a heavy night on the native beer. She wondered if he'd been up to something he didn't want her to know about.

'Was the victim in the pub, where you were drinking and dancing?'

The African smiled again and shook his head. 'She was not from around here.'

'Lovejoy!' Hayes barked.

Pip was annoyed that the man had smirked at her while she was interviewing him, and wondered what she had said to cause him to do so. 'Don't leave. I'll be back soon. I've got your name, Nkomo,' she said with as much menace as she could muster. Pip elbowed her way through the crowd of thirty or forty onlookers. Most were men, but here and there a woman with heavy make-up in a bright dress also barred her way. At only a shade over five foot three, she was aware that most of the Africans on the street towered over her.

'Here, Sarge, er, Sergeant,' she said to Hayes' back.

The policeman turned and, as he did so, his sombre

face was lit up by a blast of white light. 'The forensic photographer's here already, getting some shots of the body in situ. Take a look. She's about your age.'

Pip manoeuvred around Hayes' bulky body. She knew a few African women of her age, but none of them, not the young mothers on the farm, or the few shopgirls she encountered in town, would be out at night in an area like this.

'Oh my God,' Pip hissed, then drew her hand to her mouth. 'She's . . .'

'White. Surprised, Lovejoy?'

'Um . . .'

'Nothing surprises me after twenty-seven years in this job,' Hayes said. 'Control yourself, woman. Get a bloody grip. Well, go on, examine the body before the bloody coroner comes and carts her away.'

Pip was shocked. The woman was about her age, maybe a year or two older, and most definitely Caucasian. A sheet covered most of her prone body – the police photographer had left her face visible, though, to take his last close-up shot. Pip swallowed hard. There was a smell about the body she found hard to place. Maybe faeces. The girl's skin was a strange purplish colour, but there didn't appear to be any decomposition.

'Check her fingers, her joints, for signs of rigor mortis,' Hayes said.

She looked up, praying it was one of his tasteless jokes, but he stood impassively above her, arms folded. She took hold of the end of the white sheet and slowly drew it back. She caught her breath. 'She's virtually naked.'

Hayes bent forward at the waist, more interested now. 'Let me see.'

A shiver passed down Pip's back as she felt his breath on her neck. Creep. She did as ordered and lowered the sheet further.

Pip caught the smell again. She turned her face away, closed her eyes and almost gagged as she swallowed the rising bile. I will not lose control in front of him, she thought. I can do this. She opened her eyes and coughed to clear her throat.

'Get those bloody people back and out of sight!' Hayes bellowed at a young African policeman. The officer spread his arms wide and forced the onlookers back a few paces. 'Shield the view with your body, Lovejoy. We don't want these bloody perverts starting a riot so's they can get a look at a dead *murungu*,' he added, using the common African term for a white person.

'Her hands are tied, Sarge.' Pip wiped a bead of perspiration from her upper lip. She was glad she was kneeling, as she was sure her legs would have failed her if she stood.

'Let's have a look. What's that, silk?'

'Stocking, by the look of it. Her wrists have been bound with it. Her face looks familiar to me,' Pip said.

'You know her?'

'Not sure, Sarge. Hard to say when she's all dolled up like this.' Pip noted the heavy make-up, the ruby lipstick. 'It's almost like, well, like she was trying to look like a tart.'

'Watch your language, Lovejoy, and keep your voice down, for God's sake. Don't speak ill of the dead, either.'

Pip looked at him. Sweat was beading his forehead and he only glanced at the body for a second or two at a time. She noticed the way he stared at the woman's ample breasts and then averted his gaze, his cheeks reddened. She wondered if he had investigated many murders. As well as taking on women to fill the roles of men serving in the war, the BSAP had also promoted some male officers well beyond their capability to cover shortfalls in the senior ranks.

'We should check to see if she has been . . . if she has been assaulted . . . in a sexual way. See to it, Lovejoy.'

'You were told to get that bloody crowd back, man!' Pip shouted to the same constable Hayes had badgered. Unchecked, the young officer had allowed the crowd to close in on them again. 'Now, damn it!'

Perhaps surprised by the anger in the small woman's voice, the constable redoubled his efforts and, aided by a second officer, the onlookers were forced back to the corner of a burned-out shop. Pip had seen the charred remains of the hovel and wondered if it wouldn't be better for every house in the township to be made of life-saving asbestos. There probably wasn't even running water to fight a fire in this place.

Pip lifted the sheet. The woman wore no brassiere or pants, but had on a pair of stockings and a suspender belt. Pip took a breath to steady herself and looked closer at the body. Her pubic hair had been shaved off. Odd, thought Pip. There were dark bruises on her inner thighs, small blotches, like fingerprints. 'This really should be done by a doctor, don't you think, Sarge?'

Hayes coughed. 'Well, what about it? Do you think she was . . . abused?'

'I don't know. What do you class as abuse? She's tied up and she's dead in a laneway behind a shebeen.'

'Don't give me lip, Lovejoy. You're of the fair sex, but you're still only an auxiliary constable. I can see the bleeding obvious, can't I?'

'Sorry, Sarge,' Pip said, without feeling. She shuddered as she took the dead girl's cold right hand in hers and tried moving one of her fingers. The fingernail was painted a garish red. 'Her fingers are a bit stiff, but still pliable. The joints haven't seized up yet. I think that means she's been dead for between two and four hours.

I remember reading that muscles reach their stiffest between six and twelve. What do you think?'

'Hmm, sounds about right to me.'

Pip realised that neither of them had much of a clue about murder investigations. The woman was on her back. Pip eased a hand under her and gently rolled her halfway over. 'Bruising around her neck too.'

'Bloody Kaffirs.'

'You're sure an African did this?' Pip asked.

'Look at the neighbourhood. Don't see too many whites around here at any hour of the day.'

'Yes, of course, Sarge. But surely it's too obvious a place to leave a body. Why would an African killer dump her here in a laneway where she was bound to be discovered so quickly? Looks to me like someone was trying to make a statement, or maybe the murderer wanted it to look like an African did the deed.'

Hayes shook his head. 'Mark my words, it's the black peril. There's no controlling the African once the drink gets to him.'

Pip held her tongue. The black peril was the common name given to the whites' fear of black men sexually assaulting their women but, from what she knew, cases of this nature were actually very rare. However, there were laws against African men consorting with European women, even if it were consensual. In Pip's opinion the government would be better off enforcing the laws of assault against white men who hurt their wives, a crime not spoken of in the ordered society in which she lived.

'We'll talk to some of the bystanders. Find out if they saw anything unusual in the last few hours,' Hayes said.

Pip laid the woman back down in her original position and drew the sheet back up to her chin. She looked at the face again. The woman's hair was blonde, but cut short, in a bob. It was a fashion more suited to the twenties than the forties. Pip, like most women her age, had let her hair grow, although it was tied up in a bun now under the back of her police-issue hat. The hairstyle did remind her of something, though. 'I do think I've seen her somewhere before.'

'She could have been a film star with a face and a . . . well, a face like that,' Hayes said.

It was true, the girl had a beautiful face, even in death, and a body to match. 'It is like she's famous, like I've seen her in a magazine or . . . Wait, that's it. I've seen her in the newspaper, in the *Chronicle*!'

'So, who is she? She's obviously not carrying identification.'

'She's in the air force. She packs parachutes for the trainee pilots. She actually jumps out of aeroplanes to show how they work. She's stationed at the air base at Kumalo.'

'Ah, yes. Well done, Lovejoy. I read the same story. It's "Flying Felicity" we've got dead here in this shit hole.'

Pip and Hayes stood up from their uncomfortable metal chairs in the guardroom as the squadron leader walked in. She'd been staring up at a dozen photographs on the wall opposite her. Young, smiling men in air force khaki sitting and standing in front of military aircraft, shoulder to shoulder. She wondered where all the newly graduated pilots were now, and how many of them were still alive.

'Welcome to Number Twenty-One Service Flying Training School, Kumalo. I'm Squadron Leader Paul Bryant.' He shook hands with Hayes and nodded to Pip.

'Thank you for taking the time to meet with us, Squadron Leader,' Pip said. Rumpled was the word which first came to mind when she looked at him. His cap looked like someone had sat on it, and the wisps of hair that protruded out from under it needed trimming. The flight sergeant who had met them at the gate had so much starch in his uniform that Pip reckoned the fabric would snap if he bent over too far, but the squadron leader's uniform clearly hadn't seen an iron for a couple of days. Nevertheless, she thought the casual way he presented himself conveyed an air of relaxed, understated authority, as if he didn't need spit and polish to prove he was a military man. She didn't know what the medal ribbons below the embroidered pilot's wings on his chest were for, but she guessed by their number that he had already seen active service in the war, perhaps distinguishing himself in some way.

Hayes cleared his throat. 'Perhaps we could talk in private somewhere, Squadron Leader. Your office? What we have to discuss is quite a sensitive matter.'

'Of course, follow me,' Bryant said.

Pip stepped out her stride to keep pace with the men, and moved up beside Bryant as they walked along the footpath. They passed new-looking red-brick buildings with tin roofs, offices and barracks surrounded by manicured lawns edged with white-painted rocks. She wondered if news of the purpose of their visit would have preceded them. Bryant had avoided asking them any questions so far and his brisk, formal civility seemed contrived, as if he were nervously waiting for them to drop the bombshell about Felicity Langham.

'You're Australian,' she said to him.

'Not much gets past you coppers, does it? There are quite a few of us over here, instructors and trainees. There are also British, Canadians, South Africans, local Rhodesians, of course, and a smattering of trainees from other far-flung parts of the British Empire. We've even got a few Greeks from the Royal Hellenic Air Force.'

'I've met a few pilots and trainees in town, but never been onto one of the bases,' Pip said, eager to put the man at ease before they got down to business. Bulawayo was teeming with men in uniform these days.

'Well, I'll give you the gen – the information – on the Empire Air Training Scheme while we walk.' A twin-engine aircraft passed low overhead, on a final approach to landing. 'That's an Airspeed Oxford. The blokes learning to fly those will go on to bombers. The single-engine kites – aircraft – you'll see around here are American-designed AT-6 Harvards. The pilots on those will fly fighters, if they survive their training.'

'Survive?' Hayes interjected.

'Sergeant, here at Kumalo air base we've got a sewage farm at one end of the runway and a cemetery at the other. As some of the instructors like to say, and pardon my crudity, Constable, you've got a better than even chance of ending up in one of those places before your course is over.'

Hayes smiled and Pip grimaced. The man was adjutant of the camp. She'd expected something a bit more inspiring from him when addressing a couple of first-time visitors to the base. 'You were saying, Squadron Leader, about the air training scheme?'

'Call me Paul, if you like. The aim of the Empire Air Training Scheme is to produce about twenty thousand pilots and thirty thousand air gunners and observers a year, for service overseas.'

'Gosh,' Pip said, 'that's an awful lot of people.'

'You wouldn't know it from the newspapers and the cinemas, but we're losing an awful lot of people in this war,' Bryant said, deadpan.

Pip felt her cheeks colour. All she knew of the war was what she read in the newspapers and saw on the newsreels at the cinema. She was smart enough, though, to realise that the government censors made sure the reports put a brave face on things.

'Anyway,' Bryant continued, 'there are bases like Kumalo also operating in Australia and Canada. Here in Southern Rhodesia we've got airfields operational around Bulawayo, at Gwelo, and at Cranborne, Norton and Belvedere near Salisbury, to name just a few. Over here the scheme is implemented for the Royal Air Force by the Rhodesian Air Training Group. It goes by other names in Canada and Australia, but the aim is the same. As well as pilot training there are other schools where aircrew are trained as gunners, wireless operators and bomb aimers. All up, there are about seventeen thousand people serving in the training group, including five thousand Africans who work as askaris – providing base security – and in general duties roles, such as the cooks, cleaners, groundsmen and maintenance staff.'

'Seems a lot of effort, shipping people from as far away as England and Australia to do their training here,' Hayes said.

'I'll agree with you about shipping Australians here, Sergeant,' Bryant conceded. 'We could train our blokes just as easily back home. It's all about politics and the spirit of the Empire, I suppose. Above my level, anyway. But this is a good place to train Royal Air Force pilots and aircrew from Britain. For a start, you've got no shortage of sunshine and clear skies, and there are no German bombers to interrupt the training programme.'

'It must take quite a while, to get a pilot fully qualified,' Pip said.

'Twenty-eight weeks for a pilot, twenty-one for a gunner or bomb aimer. This has been a big year for us and the pressure is always on to train more and more people. We've got our biggest ever wings parade – pilot graduation – coming up in a few days' time.'

'How many people?' Hayes asked.

'A lot,' Bryant replied. 'We don't like to talk about exact numbers. Loose lips and all that. I'm sure you understand. If the Germans could find a way to sabotage the training here in Rhodesia or inflict mass casualties on the pilot trainees, the RAF might simply run out of aircrew to man its bombers.'

'Of course, but you said before, Southern Rhodesia was

picked as a base because it's safe,' Hayes countered.

'From what I read in the intelligence reports and the newspapers, there are more than a few people down in South Africa who wouldn't mind seeing Germany win this war,' Bryant said.

'You're talking about the Ossewa Brandwag?'

Bryant nodded. He'd read with interest the reports of the far right-wing movement, whose name, translated into English, meant the ox-wagon sentinels. The Ossewa Brandwag – OB, for short – were self-styled guardians of the ideals espoused by the original *voortrekkers*, the Cape Dutch Afrikaner pioneers who had set off into the wilderness of what was now South Africa to carve out a white homeland.

The OB had evolved in the years following the Boer War, a manifestation of lingering Afrikaner resentment at the British victory and their ongoing rule of South Africa. They were anti-British, anti-Jewish, and anti-black. The party's paramilitary wing – the *stormjaers* – bore a chilling resemblance to Hitler's prewar Nazi storm troopers, and had already been responsible for acts of sabotage in South Africa, such as blowing up power lines and robbing banks to raise funds for their activities. Even the group's symbol betrayed its Nazi sympathies. The OB eagle, beak turned to the right and clutching a circle containing an image of a covered wagon, bore a striking resemblance to the bird on the breasts of uniforms worn by German soldiers, sailors and airmen.

Hayes was dismissive. 'A few Afrikaner lunatics who want to refight the Boer War. Hardly representative of the whole community, and no real military threat – certainly not this side of the border, as they've no support in Rhodesia.'

'My office is in here, at the end of the orderly room,' Bryant said as they entered the brick building. Above the door's lintel was a casting of the RAF's flying eagle, beneath the Rhodesian lion, and the date, 1940, when the airfield had been commissioned. The orderly room was sparsely furnished, the walls painted a drab grey.

An airman stood to attention and Bryant motioned for him to resume his seat behind his typewriter. He led them into his office and sat down behind his desk, inviting them to sit on the two spare bare metal chairs.

Pip Lovejoy stayed standing, studying a panoramic black and white photo on the wall. It showed a large number of men sitting on the wings of a twin-engine bomber. 'You served in bomber command?'

'Yeah, I'm somewhere in that mob. You'd hardly recognise me, though. That was early in my first tour. Full of mustard and no grey hair. The kite's a Wellington. I went on to Lancasters on my second tour.'

'You must have quite a few stories to tell.'

'Look, Constable . . . Lovejoy, was it? I don't want to be rude, but I'm sure you didn't come here to talk about the Empire Air Training Scheme or my military career.'

'Of course. Quite right,' Hayes said, clearing his voice again. 'Constable Lovejoy will take notes during our discussions, if that's all right with you.'

'I hope I'm not going to be charged with anything. Whatever it was, I didn't do it,' Bryant said, hands up, smiling.

'It's a serious matter, Squadron Leader. One of the women serving here at Kumalo has been killed in, shall we say, suspicious circumstances.'

Bryant sat up straight in his chair. 'What? You mean murdered? Who . . . ?'

'A Rhodesian member of the Women's Auxiliary Air Service. One of your WAAFs, I believe you call them. Leading Aircraftswoman Felicity Langham, aged twenty-four.'

He closed his eyes. 'Oh, dear God. She is . . . was, well liked around here . . . It's a terrible loss to the base.' Bryant took his cigarettes from his pocket. He offered the pack to Hayes and the woman, but both waved him off. He lit his and inhaled.

'Well liked?' Pip asked, looking up from her notebook. 'What does that mean, exactly?'

Hayes shot her an annoyed glance and said, 'I was about to ask the same question.'

'Are you all right, Squadron Leader? You look very pale.'

'Fine,' Bryant coughed. He licked his lips, his mouth suddenly parched from the smoke. 'Um, we've had losses – deaths – here before, but never a woman. Flick was one of our parachute packers. They're mostly local girls. She also gave the trainees their initial instruction on how to use a chute if they got into trouble. She had a unique way of starting her lessons, and that made her a hit with the boys.'

'What do you mean, unique?' Hayes asked.

'She used to arrive at her lesson by jumping out of a Tiger Moth.'

'Yes, I read about that in the newspaper,' Pip said.

Hayes ignored her. 'She jumped out of a perfectly good aeroplane, one with no damage? I thought those things, parachutes, were only to be used in emergencies.'

'Flick, LACW Langham, had a rather different idea of excitement from most people. She jumped out of aeroplanes whenever she could, not just when giving her lessons. Parachuting's come a long way since the first war. Both sides are making widespread use of airborne forces and Flick reckoned one day people would pay to do it for fun.'

'Ludicrous,' Hayes said.

'I'm with you there,' Bryant agreed. 'I almost had to do it once, to save my life, but the prospect scared me shitless. Pardon the language, Constable.'

'No problem,' Pip said. 'Just then you referred to Miss Langham as "Flick". Were you two close?'

'What do you mean by that?' He tugged at the collar of his shirt. It felt hot inside the office, and he wanted to throw open the window, but he forced himself to sit still.

'You tell me.'

Hayes intervened. 'Constable, we're getting off our original tack and . . .'

'No, it's all right,' Bryant said. 'She was one of our instructors, and a damned good one. The permanent staff here socialise together sometimes and I knew her, as a casual acquaintance, as well as through her instructional duties. We'd chatted a few times, over drinks.'

'But she was a leading aircraftswoman – one stripe, if I'm not mistaken,' Pip said.

'Yes, she is – was – what we call a noncommissioned officer. And it's a single propeller in the air force, not a stripe.'

'But you're a commissioned officer, and a relatively senior one, I gather. I would have thought fraternisation between the ranks was not on,' Pip said.

Bryant noticed her eyes were following his cigarette

hand. He realised he was smoking very fast. Perhaps she was looking for signs he was nervous. He put the cigarette on the lip of the ashtray on his desk, carefully, so the tremor wouldn't be so noticeable. 'We didn't *fraternise* in terms of a relationship, if that's what you're hinting at, Constable. We have separate messes, on base, for officers, NCOs and trainees to drink at, but, sometimes, such as at the end of the course, a mob of us will go into town for a few drinks at one of the pubs. It's an all-ranks affair then. We don't stand too much on ceremony. We might be training people for the Royal Air Force, but it's certainly not all spit and polish over here.'

'We understand, Squadron Leader,' Hayes interjected. 'Did Miss Langham live on the base?'

'I'm really not sure. I'd have to check. I think she had a flat or a house in town. I'll get her file for you when we're done here,' Bryant said. He was relieved that the male officer had taken over the questioning.

'How would you describe her character?' Hayes asked.

'Good worker. Excellent instructor, if somewhat unorthodox. She seemed to enjoy life in uniform.' He looked across at the woman police constable and noticed she averted her eyes. Women, in his limited experience, usually fitted well into service life. They faced prejudice and sometimes outright abuse and intimidation from some of the men but, despite this, or maybe because of it, they often outshone men in similar ranks and positions. He'd seen it in England too. Women were filling jobs that they'd never dreamed of doing before the war.

'What do you know about her personal life?'

'Not much at all, Sergeant. As I said, we weren't what you would call close.' Bryant suddenly felt hot and he rubbed his finger around his collar. He saw the policewoman was still watching his every gesture, and that made him feel even less comfortable. He felt the sweat running down each side of his ribcage from his armpits and hoped it didn't show.

'Come now, Squadron Leader, we're all adults here. She was an attractive young woman surrounded by hundreds of men, most of them far from home. She must have enjoyed more than her fair share of attention,' Hayes said.

'That's none of my business. Tell me, how exactly did Miss Langham die?' Bryant asked.

'Her body was found in a part of Bulawayo which is, shall we say, unsavoury,' Hayes said. 'She was partially clad. Her body may have been dumped there, or she may have died there.'

'Was she assaulted?' Bryant asked. He wondered if his face betrayed his emotions.

'To tell you the truth, we don't know yet,' Pip interrupted.

'Do you think one of the men here on base might be responsible?' Bryant inquired, stubbing out his cigarette.

'It's too early to come to any conclusions,' Hayes said. 'In fact, Miss Langham was found in an area frequented mostly by Africans. There's a possibility she was abducted by someone and things went wrong.'

A bloody understatement if he'd ever heard one, Bryant thought. 'Poor Flick. Either way, whether it's a black man or a white man who's responsible, this could get nasty once word gets out.'

'Did she have many female friends that you knew of? Other WAAFs, perhaps?' Pip asked.

'I'd have to check that for you,' Bryant said, scratching his neck. 'I can ask around and get back to you, if you like.'

'What are your movements over the next few days?' Hayes asked.

'I've got to drive up to an area north of Wankie Game Reserve. One of our Canadian trainees, a chap called Cavendish, crashed his Harvard up there last week and I've got to conduct an investigation before the wreck is recovered. I'm leaving tomorrow morning. I'll possibly be away overnight. You can leave messages here for me with the orderly room corporal.' God knows where Smythe's Harvard would turn up, let alone if the Englishman were still alive.

'Sarge, we could save time by splitting up. I could stay

here and talk to some of the other airwomen, if that's all right with you, Squadron Leader,' Pip said.

'No worries here. You might as well start in the parachute hangar where Felicity worked,' Bryant said.

'We'll have a word outside, WPC Lovejoy. Squadron Leader Bryant, I think we're finished here for the moment, but we'll be back in touch in the next day or so, no doubt.'

'Anything I can do to help, just let me know,' Bryant said.

Bryant opened the door to his office and the orderly room NCO was standing just outside. 'Well, don't let me keep you, officers. Corporal Richards here can show you back to the gate if you're both leaving now, or I can take WPC Lovejoy to the parachute hangar, if you like,' he said to Hayes.

'Just give us a moment to confer, Squadron Leader.'

Hayes nodded and walked out of the orderly room.

The two police officers moved outside and Bryant heard raised voices. 'What were you doing hovering outside my door, Richards?' Bryant shot the pimple-faced young Londoner a withering look.

'I was just about to knock, sir. I just got a message for you, from the guardhouse. It was a phone call late last night, but the dozy buggers only just got around to calling it through.'

Richards handed him a sheet of message paper. 'Thanks,' Bryant said. He read it, then swallowed hard to maintain his composure. 'Were you listening in on that conversation, Richards?'

'No, sir, of course not.'

'If I catch you eavesdropping I'll have you posted to fucking Greenland. Do I make myself clear?'

Richards smiled sheepishly and said, 'Yes, sir. Can I ask, sir, are the coppers here about Felicity Langham's murder?'

'Who said anything about that?' Bryant replied.

'Word's getting around camp. A couple of the blacks in the kitchen were talking about it and some of the lads overheard, at breakfast.'

'Her body was found this morning. I don't know about murder, though. Do me a favour and let me know what the boys are saying about the news, will you?'

'If it's Kaffirs that raped her, sir, there'll be bleedin' hell to pay.'

One thing Bryant did not like about his young assistant was his attitude to Africans. It wasn't uncommon, of course, to hear people using derogatory terms for Africans, but in Bryant's book that didn't make it right. There had been a couple of black West Indian gunners in his old squadron, and a Sikh pilot from India. They'd all been good at their jobs, which was the only thing that mattered to him when he was on operations. A loud-mouthed Scot had made a point of taunting one of the Jamaicans in the mess, calling him a nigger. The man had laughed off the insult, but his crewmates had sorted out the troublemaker and afterwards the Scot had gone absent without leave and never been seen again.

'Keep your bloody opinions to yourself, Richards. And you know what I think about name-calling, so stow it. What I asked is for you to keep me informed about what people are saying. We don't want a riot on our hands.'

'Yes, sir.'

The orderly room door opened again and WPC Pip Lovejoy stepped in. 'I'm back,' she said.

'So I see. What about your sergeant? Sounded like a spirited discussion you were having with him.'

She failed to stop a little smile crossing her face. 'Some issues about who does what. He's going to check with the medical examiner.'

Bryant imagined it wasn't the first time the pretty young policewoman and her senior had clashed. 'Richards, escort Sergeant Hayes back to the front gate.'

'Yes, sir.' Richards put his forage cap on and excused himself, leaving Pip and Bryant alone.

4

Inside the cavernous metal-roofed hangar were a dozen long rows of trestle tables, laid end to end. On four of the rows were parachutes, in various states of being packed. The young women chatted as they methodically gathered in suspension lines and folded billowing panels of white silk.

Pip looked around her. She reckoned you could tell a great deal about someone from their home or workplace, by the things that were lying around, or objects that were missing. Glenn Miller's 'American Patrol' blared from a Bakelite radio on a table just inside the hangar door. The table was littered with dirty teacups, sugar, powdered milk and a scarred enamel teapot. An ashtray was overflowing with cigarette butts. She imagined it was forbidden to smoke over the precious silk of the parachute canopies.

Bryant turned the radio down then strode ahead,

towards the working women. Pip lingered by the entry for the moment. The tin wall behind the tea table was plastered with newspaper cuttings, photographs, torn pages from magazines. There were pictures of men in uniform – perhaps boyfriends or husbands – film stars and aeroplanes. There were articles from the *Bulawayo Chronicle* about the women's work at the base, and about visits by various dignitaries. She saw photos of half-a-dozen women in overalls and baggy khaki uniforms, but recognised none of them.

'Morning, sir,' called a red-haired woman from the head of one of the trestle-table rows.

'Morning, Susannah,' Bryant said.

Pip caught up with him. The woman he'd called Susannah was much taller than she was, with fair skin, green eyes and freckles. She was about Pip's age and wore overalls with the sleeves rolled up high above the bicep. Pip thought her arms looked very toned, almost muscled, from the constant work of packing and folding parachutes.

'Constable Lovejoy, this is Corporal Susannah Beattie. She's the NCO in charge of today's shift of parachute packers. Susannah, Miss Lovejoy . . .'

The woman's grip was firm, like a man's. 'It's missus, actually, but constable's just fine.'

'Sorry, *Constable* Lovejoy wants to ask you and the other

girls a few questions about Felicity Langham. I'm afraid it's not good news.'

'The rumour's true then?' She spoke with a trace of a Scottish accent.

Pip saw the woman look back at the other girls, who had stopped working to listen in to the conversation. 'I'm sorry, but Miss Langham has passed away,' Pip said. 'Squadron Leader, I wonder if you wouldn't mind giving us a bit of time by ourselves?'

'Of course,' Bryant said.

She sensed his reluctance to leave – he obviously wanted to listen in on the interview. He finally turned and walked outside the hangar and lit another cigarette. Pip led the red-haired corporal towards the tea table.

'Do you mind if I call you Susannah?' Pip asked, now that they were alone.

'Of course not. You're Pip, aren't you? Charlie Lovejoy's wife?'

Pip was taken aback. She'd got used to the fact that people were often a little nervous or off-balance when she asked them questions in her capacity as a volunteer policewoman. Now the shoe was suddenly on the other foot. She hadn't come out to the air force base to talk about her husband.

'That's right. You know him?'

'He went to school with my brother. Our Johnny practically worshipped the ground Charlie walked on. Top rugby player, head boy. And, if you don't mind me saying, very handsome. I remember hearing he got married. He's overseas, isn't he?'

Pip was uncomfortable talking about Charlie with this woman, though everything she had said was true. He was popular, successful and as good-looking as any of the male film stars on the wall behind them. 'Yes. He's in the army. He was in North Africa with the Long Range Desert Group. He's somewhere in Italy now,' Pip said. She pointed at the photographs on the wall and asked: 'Does one of these belong to you?'

Susannah pointed out a picture of a man – little more than a boy, really – with fair tousled hair, in RAF battledress with sergeant's chevrons on the sleeves. 'That's my boyfriend. He's RAF, a wireless air gunner. Dean Geary. He's in England.'

Pip looked at the young man's face, and at the others, all of a similar age, all smiling and keen. She wondered if it would ever end, the ceaseless flow of men from and through Rhodesia, if women would ever go back to being housewives.

'Now, what happened to Flick?'

Pip was annoyed that she had let herself lose track, and that it had been the other woman who had brought her back to the job at hand. She noticed that Susannah and the dead woman's other coworkers showed little if any emotion at the news about Felicity Langham. 'Her body was found in town last night, in an alleyway. Partially clothed.'

Susannah frowned and sipped her tea.

'Excuse me, but you don't seem overly sad at the loss of a comrade.'

'If it's false sorrow you want, Pip, I'm afraid you've come to the wrong place. Flick worked with us, but she was never one of us. It wasn't for lack of trying on our part, either, I might add. Me and the other girls went out of our way to make her part of the team, but Felicity Langham was only interested in one person in this life – Felicity Langham. She came from a good family, with plenty of money, and thought she was above us. The stupid thing is that we've got farm girls and million-aires' daughters working side by side on the rigging floor here. She could have fitted in if she'd wanted to.'

Pip cast her eyes over the press cuttings and photo-graphs behind the tea table. The first thing she'd noticed was the absence of anything to do with Felicity Langham, even though she knew the woman had appeared in the *Bulawayo Chronicle* on more than one occasion. She'd assumed there would have been some evidence of the parachute hangar's star performer. Susannah's words simply confirmed what Pip had initially deduced. 'What can you tell me about her personal life?'

'She liked a good time, did Flick. She was popular with the men, but never had a steady boyfriend, if you know what I mean. They weren't all from the base, either, from what I gathered.'

'What do you know about the men Felicity saw from town?' Pip asked.

'One of the lasses here went to school with Flick, before her parents sent her to finishing school in England. She reckons Felicity always had a thing for the wrong kind of men. Low-lifes, petty criminals. The kind of man who would treat her mean.'

'Are there any women on base who might have had cause to wish Miss Langham harm?'

Susannah raised her eyebrows. 'Forgive me, Pip, but maybe you should have been taking notes. Just about every woman on base would have wanted to scratch her eyes out at some time or another. But no, to answer your question, no one here would have wanted her dead. Out of the way, out of the newspapers and out of the lime-light, sure, but not dead.'

'Squadron Leader Bryant mentioned that the instructors and the other permanent staff sometimes get together on an all-ranks basis, for a drink. He said that's how he got to know Felicity.'

Susannah drained her tea and turned to put her tin mug down on a table. 'Hmm,' she said, pursing her lips, 'did he now?'

'From what you told me, Felicity didn't sound like the type to socialise with the other service people here.'

'Not with the girls, if you know what I mean. I personally don't recall ever seeing her at one of our nights out, but then again I can't recall seeing Squadron Leader Bryant out on the tiles, either.'

'You're saying he couldn't have got to know her at these social gatherings?' Pip asked. She had her police notebook out now and was jotting down salient points.

'I'm saying it's not my place to comment on what the second most senior man on this base may have told you. He knew Felicity, that's for sure, but where he got to know her, I haven't a clue.'

Pip pondered Susannah's emphasis on the words 'that's for sure'. 'Have you ever seen the two of them together, Felicity and Mr Bryant, I mean?'

Susannah said: 'You have to understand that Felicity was the type who would play up to men, especially men of senior rank, if she thought it would get her what she wanted.'

'What did she want, do you think?'

'I'd heard she fancied herself an actress, that she wanted to be in the films one day. Her parachuting stunts for the courses got her picture in the newspapers. Probably would have only been a matter of time before she ended up on a newsreel. Having the support of the base adjutant meant she could continue putting on her little two-woman shows for the troops.'

'So she would sometimes meet with Squadron Leader Bryant?'

'Aye, he came around here a couple of times in the last week or so, for a chat about something or other. But listen, Pip, don't get the wrong idea about Bryant. He might look like he just got thrown out of the pub at closing time, but he's a good man. Doesn't treat us like dirt, like some of the men, and seems to appreciate the work we women do. I'm not suggesting that there was anything going on between him and Flick, rather that it's not surprising that she was trying to keep in his favour.'

'I understand,' Pip said. 'Sorry,' she added, going back over her notes. 'You just said something about a "two-woman show"?'

Susannah explained that when Felicity did her parachute jumps it was always out of a civilian aircraft, a privately-owned Tiger Moth. Bryant, she said, was a stickler for the rules regarding aircraft flights. He wouldn't let Felicity jump out of an air force aircraft for her demonstrations, so she had to organise a civilian aeroplane.

'The pilot was one of Flick's snooty well-to-do set, a woman called Catherine De Beers. Lives in a big country house in the middle of nowhere on the border of Wankie Game Reserve.'

Pip wrote the name of the woman in her notebook. She'd heard of the family and had, in fact, met the woman's late husband. Hugo De Beers, a South African by birth, had been a professional hunter, a big name in the safari business up in Kenya and Tanganyika before the war. He'd also travelled the length and breadth of Rhodesia, hunting problem animals that threatened crops or humans. He'd shot a rogue lion on Pip's family's farm several years earlier. Trophy hunting hadn't caught on in Rhodesia, unlike other parts of Africa, although the area where Hugo De Beers had lived, on the border of the game reserve, would have been a good place for safaris – had Hugo lived to pursue that option. Pip looked up in the metal rafters of the hangar, where a couple of cape doves roosted and cooed, and tried to recall when De Beers had died. It must have been a year or two ago – killed in a shooting accident on his own property.

Pip could shoot, but she couldn't see the attraction of hunting for sport. She'd killed a couple of cobras around the garden with a double-barrelled shotgun, earning the ululating praise of her servants and their children, and she'd dispatched a rabid dog that had strayed into the staff compound. Charlie was different. Their home was decorated with his trophies – the skins of a lion, leopard and cheetah, and the mounted heads of various buck and a big old male buffalo that he'd shot either on or near their farm. The dead creatures gave her the creeps.

Susannah brought Pip back to the present. 'Anyway, Catherine would fly low and buzz the assembled students, climb to two thousand feet, and then 'Flying Felicity' would jump out and do her show for the boys. Afterwards, it would be drinks in the mess for Catherine and the officers.'

Pip's mind turned away from parachuting and back to Felicity's friend the pilot. Old Hugo De Beers must have been near sixty when he'd died. 'How old is Catherine De Beers, would you say?'

'All of about twenty-four, I'd guess. Quite a bit younger than her late husband.' Susannah raised an eyebrow as she sipped her tea. 'Look, I'm happy to help some more if you need it, Pip, but we've got a new course starting soon and a load of parachutes to pack. They have a pack life and even if they're not used we have to undo and rerig them.'

'No, that's fine, Susannah. You've been a big help. I shan't need to talk to the other girls, unless you think they might have anything different to say.'

'No, I doubt it.'

Pip said her goodbyes and walked out of the cool, gloomy hangar, back into the sunshine.

Paul Bryant stared out across the runway, but paid no attention to the three Airspeed Oxfords practising touch-and-go landings.

The walk to the parachute hangar had resurrected his memories of Flick Langham. He closed his eyes and let the sun's rays warm his face and bare arms. He had come here looking for her three days earlier. Susannah Beattie and some of the other girls had been chatting as their hands roamed expertly over billowing silk, folding the panels in a precise order, then stuffing the canopies into their canvas containers. Next came the suspension lines, gathered and folded and stowed. It must have been mind-numbing work, Paul thought, but the WAAFs always seemed to have something cheery to gossip about.

He'd asked for Flick, but been told by Susannah Beattie, in an annoyed tone of voice, that the woman was on a break. Bryant had already gotten the impression Flick spent the bare minimum of time actually packing parachutes.

He'd walked through the big cool building, parting a curtain of ghostly, suspended white canopies, and found his way to the back door. Flick was sitting on a stool outside, the back of her head resting against the corrugated-iron wall. A half-drunk cup of tea and a fashion magazine were beside her on the concrete footpath. Her eyes were closed.

'Hello, Paul,' she said.

'How did you know it was me?'

'I can smell you,' she said, opening her lids to reveal Mediterranean blue eyes. 'It's a nice smell. Tobacco, shaving soap, booze. A man's smell.'

He tried to be serious with her, but she had an incredible knack of putting him off-balance, of leaving him feeling almost short of breath when he was around her. She had a scent of her own, too. And it was hypnotic.

What had gone on between them had been complex, to say the least, and he'd visited the hangar to try to make sense of it all.

'Maybe I'm a bit old fashioned . . .' he tried.

'You're not the first, Paul.'

'I didn't imagine I was, but I'm not sure what's going on here, Flick.'

'It can be whatever you want it to be.'

He struggled with his words. 'It was . . .'

She smiled, for the first time. 'It was rather, wasn't it.'

How could he explain to her that, as much as he'd wanted her, there was the matter of their jobs, their difference in rank. But his confusion over what had happened and where things could possibly head from that point had less to do with the conventions of military life.

'God, you're so old-fashioned. I'd have thought after what you'd been through in Bomber Command, nothing would rattle you,' Flick taunted.

Too many things rattled him these days, too easily. The drink helped. The episode with Flick had helped at the time, but now it seemed to have complicated things.

She stopped being coy. Forced the issue. 'All right, Paul. What *did* you want to say? Do you want to pretend it didn't happen? Do you want things to go back to the way they were before? Do you want it again? Do you want me now, Paul, is that why you came snooping around here?'

'I don't know,' he said. And that was the truth. She was so incredibly beautiful. And that was the problem.

'Squadron Leader?'

Bryant opened his eyes and stubbed out his cigarette on the concrete. 'How did it go?' he asked Pip Lovejoy.

Pip gave him a brief rundown of what Susannah Beattie had told her. She wondered what he had been thinking about when she had disturbed him. He looked relaxed, leaning against the wall, but also like he was lost in some thought or other.

'You told me Felicity Langham was "well liked",' her tone accusatory.

'I know this is going to sound boorish of me, Constable, but the parachute hangar's an all-female show. Flick made a point of standing out and being different from the rest. It's probably no secret she fancied herself a cut above them. Don't tell me you're surprised she ruffled a few feathers in there.'

She wasn't but neither was she going to let him steer the conversation his way from now on. 'I've a few more questions for you, in fact, Squadron Leader. Tell me about Catherine De Beers.'

Bryant nodded as though he were expecting the question and Pip wondered why he hadn't told her about the other woman earlier. 'She was Flick's partner in crime, as it were, in the parachuting displays. Catherine's a widow, quite wealthy. I would have thought you'd have recognised the name, as a local.'

'I do.' They walked as they talked. Two air force women in baggy peaked caps and overalls grimy with grease approached them. One raised a blackened hand in a salute, which Bryant returned. Pip noticed the women's eyes lingering on her. The investigation would, no doubt, be the talk of the base by now. Pip was curious to know more about Catherine De Beers. If Felicity Langham had been as unpopular with the other women on base as

Susannah had suggested, then it seemed important she speak to the one other person who seemed to have been close to her. 'I want to know about her involvement here on the base.'

Bryant explained that as the other half of the parachute display team, Catherine flew her own aircraft, a Tiger Moth, and Flick would jump out of it. It was good for morale, he said, a great instructional technique, and good public relations for the WAAFs, the training group and the air force. 'I was happy for the show to go on, but only on the basis that Catherine used her own plane. The air force is a bit picky about civilians getting behind the controls of our aircraft.'

'When was she due to jump again?'

'She used to parachute once every couple of weeks. Sometimes they'd go to the other bases around the Bulawayo area to do the same display. However, it all ground to a halt the week before last.'

'Why?' Pip asked.

'Catherine pranged her Tiger Moth on a landing at her property. She ruined the undercarriage and snapped the prop. She'll be grounded for a while.'

'Mrs De Beers lives on a ranch near Wankie, doesn't she?' Pip asked, even though she knew the answer to the question.

'That's right. I'm going up there myself tomorrow.'

'Are you really? Why, may I ask?'

'You're the copper, Constable. I expect you can ask anything.'

As he walked, she noticed he exuded a relaxed air, and an indefinable, scruffy type of charm. She sensed a restlessness in him. Perhaps that was how pilots with desk jobs acted. He seemed more at ease when he was on the move. In his office, he had seemed cornered, like a scrub hare caught in a spotlight, confused and unsure which way to run.

'You're quite right there, Squadron Leader,' she smiled.

'I have to supervise an aircraft crash investigation and recovery, as I told Sergeant Hayes before he left.'

'Now I'm confused. Catherine De Beers' aircraft?'

'No, one of our trainees crashed his Harvard on her property a week ago – on her private airstrip.'

'An unlucky coincidence. What was one of your training aircraft doing trying to land at her place?'

'A bloody good question. The pilot was one of our Canadians. He claimed he had engine trouble, spotted the strip from the air and tried to put the kite down. He said one of his wheels must have gone into a hole dug by an ant bear or some other creature. It's been a bad couple of weeks for us. Catherine's crash has put a hold on the parachuting displays; the Canadian is facing disciplinary action; and this morning, as well as learning about Felicity, I received a report that another of our Harvards has failed to return from a navigation exercise.'

'Sounds like a dangerous business,' Pip said. She wondered if it were unusual to lose two military aircraft in the space of a couple of weeks. If so, the losses must be horrendous.

'I'll show you our cemetery some time, if you like.' He looked away from her, far out across the runway, where a twin-engine aircraft had just raised puffs of bluish smoke as its wheels bounced and burned the concrete.

'I'm going to recommend to Sergeant Hayes that we talk to Mrs De Beers as part of our investigation,' Pip said, wondering if the talk of cemeteries and aircraft losses had triggered some awful memory for the Australian. Another machine circled and flew low over their heads. Pip could feel the vibrations of its engine in her body and, after it had passed, could smell its oily exhaust. This was a foreign world to her, though for many women of her age it was a workplace – probably the first job any of them had ever held.

'Why Catherine? Don't you think Felicity's death could have just been a random attack? You seem to be starting with those closest to her.'

'I'll tell you the truth, Mr Bryant. I need to know how Felicity Langham ended up half-naked, tied up and dead in the wrong part of Bulawayo. If her death was the result of some sexual misadventure, it could very well have involved someone who was extremely close to her – intimately so – and that's why I'm looking at everyone who knew her, in any sense of the word.'

'Tied up?' Bryant asked.

Damn, Pip swore to herself. She'd given away information to someone she was questioning, without intending to. You're not a trained detective, Pip, she admonished herself. You've got to play this carefully. She had to regain control. 'Why did you lie to me, Squadron Leader?'

'What do you mean?' he asked.

'You told me you knew Felicity Langham through some social events, where the staff from the base got together after hours on an all-ranks basis.'

'Yes.'

'I've been told you're not exactly the most sociable officer on base, that you actually avoid such gatherings.'

'I think I'm the best person to recall how I met someone.'

A weak, vague response, Pip thought. She reckoned he was lying. 'When was the last all-ranks function you attended, Squadron Leader? I'll need a date, please.'

'I fail to see what difference it makes how I got to know LACW Langham.'

She noticed he looked away from her, unable to meet

her gaze. 'I thought it was "Flick"? How many times have you gone around to the parachute hangar in the last week expressly looking for Felicity Langham?'

Before Bryant could answer there was a thud of boots on the pavement behind them. Pip turned and saw a young uniformed officer running towards them, holding his hat on with one hand. He called out to Bryant to stop.

They waited for him to catch up. 'Excuse me,' Bryant said to Pip. 'What is it, Wilson?'

The young Rhodesian jogged to them and, still panting from the effort, said: 'They've found him.'

'Who?' Bryant asked. 'Take a breath.'

'Smythe. The Pommie, the one who went missing in the Harvard.'

'Dead or alive?'

'Dead, I'm afraid, sir. Murdered by natives, across the border in Bechuanaland, on the saltpans.'

'Bloody hell.' Bryant quickly explained to Pip that Smythe was the pilot of the aircraft that had gone missing on a navigation exercise, but was clearly way off course. The saltpans were in the neighbouring country and started more than a hundred and twenty miles west of Bulawayo.

If she had it right, Bryant was now dealing with three aircraft mishaps which had occurred on his watch – this latest one, the Canadian who had crashed his Harvard at Catherine De Beers' ranch, and the widow's damaged Tiger Moth, which, even though it was a civilian aircraft, had formed part of the Kumalo parachuting displays. Pip cursed silently. She'd been very close to finding something out about Bryant and Langham before the officer had interrupted them, though she could only guess what that something was.

The man scattered the last shovel full of salty white sand onto the distorted, leathery face of the bushman hunter. The other one was already buried.

He tied the spade to the top of his saddlebags and wiped his hands on his horse's flank. 'Steady, it's all right.' The horse was still spooked by the sound of the two shots that had echoed across the plains. 'There, there, don't worry, my boy.'

He spat on the ground. The bushmen had done as he had paid them to and had died as he had planned. They were good at what they did, like obedient, well-trained dogs, he thought. Unlike dogs, though, they could talk, probably would if the police caught them. Death was the only solution. Their passing meant nothing. There would be many others, come the change in power. In the new world, people like him would take their rightful place again. The enemies of the state, and those natives who did not fulfil a useful role, would be banished or removed, permanently. He had seen the light, abroad. It was time to illuminate the darkness in this corner of Africa.

He was tall and straight-backed. His fair features were protected by a broad-brimmed bush hat and he wore round sunglasses with metal rims to protect his blue eyes from the glare. He was no stranger to the saltpans of Bechuanaland and the deserts of the Kalahari, but he had been away from the African sun for too long. Snowy northern winters had leached the bronze from his skin.

He had hunted here, on the wide-open flats, with his father as a boy. He'd heard the stories of his people around the campfire, as the lions called to each other in the night. 'One day, my boy,' his father had said in their language, not English, 'we will take back our country from the *rooineks*. We will have vengeance for your mother and the countless other thousands of innocents who were slaughtered by the British. You will play your part, mark my words.'

Indeed he would. His father would have been proud of him. He was a soldier now, in a war against his people's enemies. He wore no uniform, though he had in Spain and Crete. He had studied and he had learned, about his chosen profession and, more importantly, about the vision for the new world order. It would work in Africa, as it was working in Europe. But it needed men of iron will to make it happen. Men who could endure hardship, and kill when necessary to protect an ideal.

He saw the vultures circling. Maybe they would find the body of the Englishman, maybe not. It didn't matter. He mounted his horse and headed east. Even riding, it would be two more days' travelling, at least, before he crossed the border. He eyed the Mauser rifle in the holster on the beast's flank. It was loaded and ready. Before he met his enemies there would be other dangers on this journey – lion, leopard, elephant wary of men who still hunted them for their ivory, black rhino who had a similar dislike of humans. He wasn't scared of the bush, but he was always wary and respectful of it. The other horse, tethered to his own mount, trailed behind. Strapped to its sides was the cargo, so precious, so important to his dream. He had nursed it halfway around the world.

The aircraft was long gone, much to his relief. He figured he would be off the pan and in amongst the mopani forests along the border of Bechuanaland and Southern Rhodesia by nightfall. If more aircraft came, to search for the Englishman, he would be hidden from view from the air. He relished the quiet emptiness of the saltpan and he rode on, towards the finalisation of his mission.

Bryant hated hospitals. The familiar odour of urine barely disguised by disinfectant sent a shiver up his back. He remembered the pain and the nightmares after the crash. He suppressed the memories as he followed Hayes and Lovejoy down a long corridor and turned left, following the sign to the morgue.

His mother had died because there was no doctor or hospital within fifty miles of the property on which his parents had lived. Rhodesia had surprised him in terms of the facilities that were available, even in this remote corner of Africa. The air training scheme had spurred development in some areas but, by and large, there was a pretty good level of services for both the blacks and the whites. Sometimes, if he squinted a little, to blur his vision, and let the heat and dust wash over his skin, and the buzz of the flies fill his ears, he could almost be back in Australia.

It wasn't even as though he saw that many black faces around Bulawayo – at least, not in the town centre. The men on his troopship, on the first trip over, had joked that they would be confronted by spear-wielding Zulus and bare-breasted African maidens, but he'd seen virtually nothing of traditional African culture or customs. What he'd learned of it had come from Kenneth Ngwenya. In town the shopkeepers and office workers and, here at the hospital, the doctors and nurses were all of British stock. Most of the African civilians he saw were uniformed messengers, maids, cleaners or, like the chap he could see through a window in the corner of the hospital grounds dressed in patched overalls, gardeners. He was watering a flowerbed in a corner of the hospital's front yard, desperately trying to coax some colour from the ruddy earth. The man reminded Bryant he was, in fact, a long way from home.

It was an odd place, he thought. Rhodesia. So very British in some ways, but, like Australia, a world away from Britain. Rhodesia was still a colony, whereas Australia had become a nation under federation. Odd, he mused, that a country whose population had descended from convicts now occupied a higher place in the pecking order than this one, whose white stock came from business people and gentleman farmers. Even the name came from a trader – Cecil John Rhodes.

Rhodesia had its own parliament and, since 1923, a prime minister; and while the people were fiercely loyal to Britain – about a fifth of the colony's twenty-five thousand whites were in uniform – he reckoned there would come a day soon when they wanted to set themselves up as a nation, as Australia had.

He'd felt confined in England, as though everywhere he'd looked there were people. No wide open spaces, like in Australia or Africa. The cold and the rain had been anathema to him. Even without the losses and the casualties, the weather had been enough to sap the blokes' morale. But even here, in this town of perfumed jacarandas, clear skies and sunny weather, he couldn't escape death. It was waiting for him.

'I hate these places,' Bryant said.

'I don't imagine anyone particularly enjoys a visit to a morgue,' Pip replied.

'No, hospitals, I mean. Sometimes it's harder confronting people who've been burned or maimed. I could have sent Wilson here, you know.'

'You would have had to come here anyway,' Hayes said, 'because we need someone to formally identify Miss Langham's body.'

Bryant was surprised, and a little uneasy at the prospect. 'I thought I was coming here to identify Flight Sergeant Smythe.' In truth, he wondered if he could identify the lost pilot. He barely remembered the man's face. To assist him he had brought the trainee flyer's personnel file, which included a small black and white portrait photograph. He most certainly did not want to see Flick's body.

'Miss Langham is an only child. Her mother is dead and her father is serving overseas. We're still trying to contact him. In the meantime, we need someone who knew her well enough to confirm her identity.'

'Very well,' he said, steeling himself. He'd lost count of the number of dead men he'd seen in the last two years, but a woman, and a woman he *knew*, might be different.

Pilot Officer Wilson's news of the discovery of Smythe's body on the saltpans west of Bulawayo, in Bechuanaland, had interrupted Pip Lovejoy's uncomfortable line of questioning, but Bryant knew he would have to face her again. He wondered what questions they would spring on him here, in the morgue, where they could probably tell he was less than fully composed.

Hayes knocked on a door and it was opened by a stooped, elderly white man with horn-rimmed glasses perched on the tip of his nose. 'Afternoon, Sergeant, Miss,' the man said.

'This is Doctor Lewis Strachan, our resident professor of pathology, who conducts postmortems for police investigations,' Hayes said, then introduced Bryant to the doctor.

'Welcome, if that's the right word,' the doctor said with a thin smile. 'Squadron Leader, I know this is a difficult task, but it's a necessary one. I've not commenced the full postmortem on either deceased person, although I have conducted cursory examinations of both. I have to warn you that the young man's corpse has been attacked somewhat, presumably by vultures.'

'I understand,' Bryant said. 'If you don't mind, perhaps we could get on with it.'

The doctor nodded. In front of them were two tables with bodies covered by white sheets. He pulled down the first.

Bryant had told himself he would show no emotion, but he drew a sharp breath when he saw Flick's ghostly white face. He really hadn't been prepared to see her like this. She was still beautiful, of course, and somehow, in death, looked more innocent than in life. But gone was the mischievous sparkle in her eyes; the insincere smile that she put on when talking to the Wingco; no tongue-poking behind Susannah Beattie's back. She had been no angel, of that he was sure, but he hoped she was somewhere peaceful now. 'It's her,' he said. He bit his lip at the sight of the angry ligature marks on the soft skin of her neck.

'For the record, this is Felicity Langham?' Hayes asked.
'Yes.'

Pip ignored Hayes, the doctor and the body. She looked across the table straight into Bryant's eyes. If he didn't love the dead woman, he had at least been with her, she thought. Those were not the eyes of a detached superior officer gazing on the body of an airwoman under his command. Bryant was reliving memories – of quite what, she could not know. If she'd had her way, she would have studied him for as long as he wanted to gaze at her and remember.

Instead, Hayes cut the moment short. 'Well, that's that then. On to the next, if you please, Doctor.'

Apart from being quietly appalled at Hayes' lack of sympathy, she was furious that he had given Bryant a chance to recompose himself and get back to business. She assumed his reaction to the viewing of the pilot's body would be markedly different.

Bryant opened the folder he was carrying. She noticed he didn't flinch as the doctor pulled back the sheet and revealed the gory mess that was Smythe's face. The eyes were gone, only empty sockets encrusted with dried black blood remained. The cheeks, too, had been torn in places by the scavengers' hooked beaks.

'Says in the file he's got a "distinguishing mark", a large brown birthmark on his back, on the upper right shoulderblade. Can you roll him over, Doc?' Bryant said.

'Of course,' the doctor replied.

Pip gagged and turned away. There had been a lingering smell of rotting meat in the room when they entered, and she could handle that, but the pulling back of the starched sheet and the movement of the body had intensified the smell incredibly. Apart from Felicity Langham, she had seen only one dead body so far in her six months as an auxiliary policewoman: a man who had been killed in a car crash. It had been a bloody affair but, as a farmer's wife, she was used to the sight of gore. The smell of this corpse, however, was unlike anything she had ever encountered. As the doctor moved the body, an audible whoosh of bodily gas escaped.

Pip felt the blood drain from her face. She clamped a hand over her mouth and nose to shut out the vile odours and hold back her bile, and mentally cursed her weakness when she noticed Hayes grinning at her.

'Try breathing through your mouth,' Bryant said to her. 'He's our man, Doc. Sergeant James Gerald Smythe, Royal Air Force, aged nineteen.'

'Thank you, Squadron Leader,' Hayes said, taking the details down in his notebook. 'Anything you can tell us at this stage, Doctor Strachan?'

Pip swallowed hard and glanced over at Bryant. She had been right about him, although it was cold comfort after the way she had very nearly embarrassed herself in front of the three men. She had wanted desperately to throw up, but managed to suppress it. Bryant was back to what she now regarded as his usual hard-bitten, melancholy demeanour. He was all business when it came to identifying the body of yet another one of his pilots. Hayes, again, was showing his stupidity by getting the doctor talking in front of someone who was proving to be of more interest by the hour in the investigation of Felicity Langham's death.

'Starting with the woman, Miss Langham, as we now know her, died of strangulation.'

'What did the killer use? Bare hands?' Hayes asked.

'There are ligature marks, as though something was wrapped around her neck – possibly a silk stocking, like those used to bind her hands and ankles. But judging by the bruising as well, I'd say the killer used his hands at some point.'

Pip watched Bryant closely, but said nothing.

The doctor spoke again. 'Another thing, and I presume it's all right to discuss this in front of the Squadron Leader, is that it appears Miss Langham had been sexually assaulted.'

Pip thought it was most certainly not all right to mention these details in front of Bryant. She looked at Hayes, expecting him to wrap things up, but he said, 'Really?'

'Yes. I discovered a certain amount of bruising around the genitalia and inner thighs. It also appears from other contusions on her body that she had been held tight, perhaps pinioned, by the wrists and ankles. It could very well be that she was assaulted, but that the man, or men, involved used, um . . . protection.'

'Don't worry, Doctor,' Pip said, seeing Strachan's embarrassment at discussing details in front of her, 'I know what you mean. I presume, Squadron Leader, that all of your trainees are lectured on the evils of venereal diseases.'

'When they arrive, and before their first leave,' Bryant said.

'And they're issued with condoms?' Pip asked.

Hayes gave a little cough.

'Yes,' Bryant answered.

'Unusual behaviour for a rapist, or rapists, to use one of those things, wouldn't you agree, Doctor?' Hayes weighed in.

'Perhaps. Perhaps not. I'm afraid I can't tell you much more at this stage. I may know more after the post-mortem. Now, as for the pilot . . .'

God, at last, Pip thought. She'd watched Bryant closely during the talk of rape, but detected nothing other than bewilderment in his face.

'He was killed by two poison arrows,' Doctor Strachan said.

'I heard he'd been attacked by natives,' Bryant said.

'The body was found with two of these in it,' the doctor said, holding up a short wooden shaft.

'Arrows?' Bryant asked.

'Yes. Of the type used by the San people. I've studied their culture. They're remarkable people, expert hunters and able to live on meagre amounts of food and water. They use a lightweight bow and arrow, with the wooden shafts dipped in poison made from the larvae of the *Diamphidia nigroornata* beetle. The poison's deadly, but it's relatively slow-acting. The bushmen don't usually aim for the heart or lungs, like a western hunter with a gun might. They rely on the poison working its way through the animal's body, which can take anywhere from a few hours, for a small animal such as an impala, to four or five days for a giraffe. They've patience a white man can only dream of.'

'So you think they followed Smythe through the desert for hours, until the poison worked?'

'No. I said he was killed by poison arrows but, in his case, not by the poison. One of the arrows pierced Flight Sergeant Smythe's heart. He bled to death very quickly. The depth of the wound indicates the arrow was fired from close range. The man, or men, who fired those arrows were aiming for his vital organs, and close enough to hit one of them.'

Bryant nodded. 'If you've studied these people, I wonder if you could explain to me why they'd kill an English flyer who was presumably wandering around the desert hopelessly lost? Hardly a threat to anyone.'

'Your flyers aren't armed, are they, with a pistol or other weapon?' Doctor Strachan asked.

'Not at all,' Bryant said. 'The guns on this bloke's Harvard weren't loaded. He was on a solo navigational flight, not even a gunnery practice, so he couldn't have been shooting up the local wildlife or population by mistake.'

'I'll admit, it seems very odd,' the doctor said. 'Although they've cause to hate some whites – not all that long ago they were hunted down and shot as vermin, like wild dogs – I've not heard of bushmen going out of their way to kill a stranded European. In fact, there have been tales of them rescuing people lost in the Kalahari and the saltpans, and leading them back to safety.'

'What worries me is the reaction of your boys once news of this gets out,' Hayes said to Bryant.

'If I have my way, news won't get out.'

Pip noticed that Hayes looked uncomfortable as he ran a hand through his thinning hair.

He said: 'Well, it seems, from what I've heard, that the local newspaper is already onto the story. It will run tomorrow. It's big news here, if a black man kills a white man. Something folk don't stand for.'

'What!' Bryant said. 'What bloody idiot told the press?'

Hayes's embarrassed silence told them all.

Bryant shook his head and looked back at the body. 'Is it true, Doc, that he was found like this, only wearing his undershorts?'

'That's how the body was clothed when I received it.'

Hayes nodded. 'He was found by a couple of big-game hunters. They said there was no sign of his clothes, or his aircraft, in the general area. Don't your trainees receive survival training?'

Bryant's annoyance with the policeman was clear. 'Of course they do. They're taught to stay with their aircraft. There are survival rations and a tin of water on board each Harvard, so it seems odd to me that Smythe took off into the desert so soon after crashing.'

'The heat and the endless white of the saltpan will do strange things to the mind in a short period of time,' the doctor said.

'Will you search for the aircraft?' Hayes asked.

'Yes. We'll divert some of the training flights that way, once I notify the authorities in Bechuanaland.'

'Wouldn't have thought your training flights were allowed to cross the border,' Hayes said.

'They're not. Smythe was way off course, there's no

doubt about that. He should have been heading north, not west. There'll be a full air force investigation, in addition to whatever you normally do.'

'The body was found in Bechuanaland – out of my country, out of my jurisdiction,' Hayes said. 'I'll make sure the doctor's report is passed to the police in Francistown, over the border, but it'll be up to them to investigate the killing.'

Probably a good thing, Pip thought. She reckoned Hayes was out of his depth investigating one murder, let alone two.

'If we're done, I've work to be going on with. I hope you all understand,' the doctor said. 'I'm sorry for the loss of two of your people, Squadron Leader.'

'Yeah, thanks, Doc. Me too. Now, if you'll excuse me, I need a cigarette.'

Pip said goodbye to Doctor Strachan and set off after Bryant. She found him outside. 'Squadron Leader Bryant, I've still got some more questions to ask you.'

'Look, Constable, I know you've got a job to do, but so have I. I've got a letter to write to Smythe's family and Flick's father, wherever he is. On top of that I've got to investigate the crash of our Harvard at Mrs De Beers' place near Wankie, and organise a search for Smythe's kite over several hundred square miles of desert in Bechuanaland. I'm going back to Kumalo now and I'll be back from up country in a couple of days. Make an appointment with the orderly room.'

She glared at him. 'I could arrest you now.'

He turned on his heel and tossed his cigarette into the gutter. 'What for?'

Pip fought to control her anger. She was fast realising that she had a lot to learn about masking her emotions during an investigation. 'Where were you last night?'

'In the mess, drinking, and then in bed, sleeping it off.'

'Liar.'

'What? I wouldn't have thought name-calling is recommended in the police manual. You're in over your head, Constable Lovejoy. Go back to directing traffic or filing. I've got work to do.' He turned away again.

'You don't drink in the mess, do you? You're a loner. I know the type. Susannah Beattie said you never socialise with the others. I can tell from your face you're a drinker. I'm betting it's a bottle in the desk drawer. If I go out to Kumalo now and interview every officer who was drinking in the mess last night, not one of them will say you were there, will they?'

He started walking away from her.

'It's time for you to start talking to me, properly, Squadron Leader. For you to start telling the truth about Felicity Langham.'

He stopped, turned and faced her. 'I want to find who killed Flick, probably more than you do,' he said quietly. 'That's the truth. But first I've got to tell someone else the awful bloody news.'

'Catherine De Beers?'

'Yes.'

'At least you won't have to do it alone.'

'What do you mean?' he asked.

'I'm coming with you.'

'You are?'

'Well, not physically with you. I'll be in a police vehicle. But I plan on interviewing Catherine De Beers tomorrow. I can break the news, if you don't want to.'

'It's a tempting offer, but it might be better if it comes from a friend.'

'Oh, I didn't realise you were friends with Mrs De Beers, too,' Pip said, trying to make it sound like an innocent observation. This was getting more interesting all the time.

Paul Bryant drove back out of Bulawayo on the Salisbury Road to Kumalo, his mind reeling from the events of the day. He passed only a few cars – due to the perennial fuel shortages most whites with business in town rode bicycles. The blacks walked. He was tempted to stop by a bottle store on the way – it didn't do to buy bottles from the mess – but willed himself to press on to the base.

A troop of baboons was crossing the road, its leaders barking and chivvying the others to hurry as Bryant's air force vehicle closed on them. They knew how to look after each other, he thought. He wondered if the deep emotions and petty jealousies that governed human life were apparent in the simple existence of these distant relatives of mankind. He hoped not, for their sake.

It was after five by the time he returned to his office. The molten gold light of the setting African sun had rendered the building hot as hell. Richards was gone and he had the orderly room and his office to himself. He slid open the second drawer of his desk, found the bottle of Santy's and filled his coffee cup to the three-quarter mark with gin. He drank as he sifted through the outstanding paperwork on his desk. The telephone rang.

He sighed and picked up the receiver. 'Adjutant, Squadron Leader Bryant.'

'Hello, it's Constable Lovejoy here. Sorry to bother you again.'

Not more questions, he prayed, instantly on his guard. 'No worries. What can I do for you?'

'It's about tomorrow. Your trip to Mrs De Beers' ranch.'

'What about it?'

'Um . . . we've got a shortage of vehicles at the police camp, big operation on tomorrow,' she said. 'My sergeant still wants me to interview Catherine De Beers and he's approved of me asking you for a lift.'

It sounded like a fib to him. 'You want *me*, that is, the Rhodesian Air Training Group, to transport you there?'

'I'll get up there eventually, one way or another, with or without you, Squadron Leader,' she said.

Damn her, Bryant thought. It would be better if he were around when she questioned Catherine, and better still if he could talk to the widow first. 'Very well, I was planning on taking an air force car. The others will be going by truck.'

'You're not flying?' she asked.

'No. And if I were, don't think I'd take you. We've strict rules forbidding the carriage of civilians, and that includes police officers.'

'You can pick me up at—' she began.

'I'll be leaving Kumalo at zero-five-hundred, Constable Lovejoy – that's five in the morning to you. Be at the front gate if you want a lift.' He hung up before she could best him again.

Kenneth Ngwenya saw the light on in Bryant's office. This late in the afternoon he knew his friend would be alone. The others in the office, including the clerk, an Englishman who treated all blacks like dirt, would have left for the evening meal or the bar in the mess by now.

He feared Paul's evening meal would be liquid.

The heat of the day was slowly ebbing. The sky was a deep pink as the sun slipped behind the curtain of dust that hung over the dry countryside. The askari fathers of his students would be on their way to the beer hall in the township off base by now, some chasing women other than their wives, but all the evening promised for Kenneth was a chat with the Australian and a few hours of correcting poor grammar by the light of a paraffin lamp. Somewhere a baboon barked, calling his family to their night-time tree to roost. The growing sprawl around the base had forced most of the animals that had lived in the bush to move further afield, but the baboons would stay as long as foreign airmen were stupid enough to keep throwing them their food scraps.

Kenneth did not resent the presence of the allied pilots and trainee aircrew, but he was surprised, from talking to some of them, how much more of their world he knew than they did of his. He was as patriotic as the next man – he had read enough in the newspapers to know that Hitler and Mussolini stood for nothing but evil – yet he and his political party quietly railed against the injustices that still beset their people, no matter how much the white Rhodesians liked to crow about the way they treated 'their' blacks, as compared with some other colonial powers on the continent.

What irked him most, though – and it had come as something of a shock to him – was that if he had been born in Nigeria or Barbados, he could have been training to be an air gunner or, if he were a Sikh or a Hindu, he could have been learning to be a pilot. All were subjects of the King, yet some nonwhites were still treated as inferior to others. How odd, he thought, to support a party that called for independence and majority rule, while at the same time lamenting he did not have the right to die for an ideology and a regime that treated him as a second-class person. He smiled as he knocked on the door to the operations room. One had to smile.

'Enter,' Bryant called.

Kenneth strode through the empty outer office and pushed open Paul's door, just in time to see the furtive disappearance of a bottle into the desk drawer. He feigned a cough. 'Sundowners already? You've still got an hour or so.'

'What are you, my conscience?' Bryant smiled.

Perhaps, Kenneth thought. He shrugged. 'It's not my business if you want to ruin your life, Paul.'

'Spare me the missionary zeal.'

Kenneth laughed. 'That doesn't come from my people. I was taught by the Jesuits, Paul. Fierce Irish drinkers. I saw what a religious man with a strap was capable of after a few drinks. That was enough to keep me away from alcohol. Besides, on my pay I can't afford it. How did it go with the police today?'

'I don't know. It was Felicity Langham who was found dead in town. They wanted to know who she kept company with, what she was like ... that sort of thing.'

Kenneth's eyes widened in surprise. 'Ah. And?'

'And what?'

Kenneth narrowed his eyes. 'Did you tell them about you and her?'

'There was little to tell,' Bryant said. Kenneth sensed he was being guarded. All he knew was that Bryant had mentioned her name a couple of times lately. He had not said anything specifically, but Kenneth had guessed there was something going on between the Australian and the parachute packer, whom he thought pretty, even if she was too skinny.

'Do they think it was an African who killed her, Paul?'

Bryant shrugged. 'If they do, they were spending a lot of time snooping around here for no reason. There were two of them – a man and woman. The bloke thinks it was a black. The woman's seeing conspiracies everywhere, I think.'

'Don't underestimate women, Paul. They don't think like us.'

Bryant laughed, and raised his coffee cup. 'Sure you don't want one – it's gin?'

'No, thank you. I am fine. Seriously, I am worried what will happen if the police find out an African did this terrible thing. I think there are some people on this base who are looking for an excuse for trouble.'

Bryant pursed his lips, then took another swig. 'There's more bad news coming in tomorrow's newspaper. It seems one of our student pilots was killed by bushmen after making a forced landing out on the saltpans. But don't worry, Kenneth, I'll keep the men in line, or they'll face the consequences.'

'I hope so. Paul, are you all right, my brother?'

'Yes, fine. Why do you ask?' He leaned back in his chair, seemingly surprised by the frankness of the question.

'Forgive me for intruding, but I got the impression you and Miss Langham may have been . . . *close.*'

Bryant paused. 'She was a Leading Aircraftswoman, Ken, an NCO. I'm . . . at least I was . . . her superior officer. Besides, you're hardly in a position to give me advice about women. Most men of your age would have a couple of wives and a herd of cattle by now.'

Kenneth smiled away the jibe. 'I have my career to think of first, Paul. And more study. That is my excuse. You, however, need to find a woman.' He believed Bryant's soul had suffered in the war, more than his body, and that only a woman's love could mend him.

He remembered the day they met – soon after Bryant had arrived at Kumalo to take over as adjutant. Kenneth had taken delivery of two precious planks of timber from the base carpentry store – a sly gift from the ageing white Rhodesian flight lieutenant in charge, who had worked as a woodwork teacher before the war. Bryant, still gaunt and pale from his stress-filled months in England, had stopped Kenneth as he was walking along the perimeter fence, the planks balanced on his head. Paul had questioned him gruffly, obviously thinking he had stolen the wood, and Kenneth had rounded on him, standing his ground and telling him that he was using the timber to build a classroom for the children of this new officer's men, whose welfare was being seriously neglected. He remembered how Bryant, unconvinced, had offered Kenneth a lift to the school in his air force car, the wood sticking out of the back window. On arriving, Bryant had shaken his head at the ramshackle collection of huts that passed for a school and the next day had organised a meeting with the base workshops, engineering detachment and a senior student from the trainee pilots' class. Bryant had known that the fledgling flyers all came from different walks of life and, within a week, had suggested strongly that a former surveyor, student architect and construction engineer all give up their next few precious weekends to design a new school. Volunteer work parties had been formed, and both Kenneth and Bryant had been pleasantly surprised at how the men, far from home and with little release from their gruelling training schedules except for boozy nights in the mess, had taken to the work. It had led to greater camaraderie between the blacks and whites on the base, and had, over time, cemented a growing friendship between Kenneth and Paul.

Bryant shook his head, though, at Kenneth's latest piece of advice. 'The odds are literally about a thousand to one of me finding a girlfriend on this base, mate. In case you hadn't noticed, men outnumber women around here. And you, you should spend less time with your head in the books and more time in the shebeens if you want to find a woman. Have you ever had a serious girl-friend?'

'No, not really.' There had been a woman, a few years ago, when he was studying in South Africa. He'd attended Fort Hare University, in the Eastern Cape. It was the first institute of higher learning for black Africans in the southern part of the continent, and had been established by Scottish missionaries just before the First World War. The woman was a member of the South African Communist Party, a firebrand who sided with others who whispered of force and armed revolution as the way to change the world. As much as he loved her mind and her body, Kenneth could never bring himself to agree with her on the value of bombs and bullets over words. She had left him for a young man of her own party. Factionalism had proven stronger than love, and Kenneth had been quietly devastated in his final year of study, before returning to his native Southern Rhodesia to take a job as a schoolteacher – the highest qualification his degree had qualified him to apply for. 'Once, maybe.'

'So, Ken, what is it today? More books? Building materials for the school?'

'There is a work party coming out to the school to help construct a new classroom tomorrow. It's term break, so a good time to get started. I wanted to see if you would come out some time and see the progress we are making. It's been a while since we've seen you at the school.'

'I'll try. Things have been a bit chaotic lately, and there's the big wings parade coming up as well.'

'I also thought you might have wanted to talk . . . about the woman who died.'

Bryant lifted a stack of manila envelopes from a corner of his desk. 'I've got a shed-load of paperwork to get through tonight, mate.'

Kenneth nodded. 'I understand.' He wondered what was going through Bryant's mind. It was getting darker outside, though, and it was a long walk to the single-room tin hut he called home. 'I'll come back in a couple of days after you get back from Wankie. We can talk then, if you like.'

'Sorry, mate. I didn't mean to fob you off, but work is work. How did you know I was going to Wankie?'

'I am the teacher, Paul. I am supposed to know everything.' Kenneth reached down and lifted his battered leather briefcase. It was second-hand and had cost the equivalent of almost all his first week's wages. He carried it everywhere. He pulled out a small parcel wrapped in brown paper. 'I have another request. This is some medicine for my father. He has pleurisy. He works as a security guard at the De Beers ranch. I told him I would buy it for him in Bulawayo and try to get it to him. It would mean a lot to me if you could . . .'

'Of course, Ken.' He took the parcel. 'I hope you don't think I'm trying to get rid of you, mate, but it's been a hell of a day, and that's the truth.'

Kenneth stood and buckled his bag. 'I understand. I'll ask you about the corrugated iron for the school roof next time.' They both forced a laugh, but Kenneth left the hut with the distinct feeling that his friend had got himself into some kind of trouble.

6

Bryant nearly drove straight past Pip Lovejoy in the dawn's half-light.

She stepped off the footpath outside the guardroom as the red-and-white-striped boom gate was raised by the African air askari on duty to let the convoy out. It was five after five in the morning and the sun was a hazy semicircle peeking over the horizon. She waved at the Humber sedan, which was followed by a Dodge lorry and a Bedford prime mover, towing a long, empty Queen Mary aircraft recovery trailer.

Bryant put on the brakes, and the still-dozy airman driving the Dodge very nearly rear-ended him. 'I didn't recognise you,' he said. It was the truth. He'd called the guardroom and asked if a female police officer was waiting for him. The duty NCO had replied in the negative.

'I left the uniform at home. I thought it might be easier for Mrs De Beers if I were a little less formal.'

It was an understatement. He'd fleetingly noticed the young woman standing beside a bicycle as the gate opened, but she had been half turned away from him. Even if he'd seen her face, he thought, he still wouldn't have recognised her. The loose, wavy blonde hair softened her face. He hadn't even been able to see what colour it was when she was wearing it tucked up under her police hat. Her outfit, too, showed off a body no longer constrained by mannish tailoring. She wore flared beige pants and a cropped red jacket that accentuated a bottom that was hard to ignore. He heard whispers and a wolf whistle behind him and looked up to see ten pairs of male eyes staring out of the cab and over the wooden side rails of the Dodge, eager to know who the attractive young woman chatting to the adjutant was. The top two buttons of the white blouse under her jacket were undone.

'You'd better get in the car before you cause an accident.'

'Thanks,' she smiled. 'I'll take that as a compliment.'

He wore an old blue uniform shirt, its collar frayed on the edge, and, as it was cool that morning, a blue airforce battledress jacket that came to the waist and normally buckled up with an attached belt. The belt, however, was undone and the jacket had clearly seen better days. It was stained with oil and dried blood –

some his, some not. The embroidered pilot's wings on the left breast were little more than a faded tangle of loose threads. He wore old khaki trousers and suede desert boots. He noticed her staring at his stained jacket. 'It can be a dirty business recovering a crashed aircraft.' He turned back to the rest of the convoy and called, 'Right-oh. Pull your heads in and let's get weaving.'

'That's quite a force you've got. Are you going to bring the aircraft back with you?'

'Once we've done an investigation the fitters will pull the wings off and partly disassemble her and lift her onto the Bedford. The askaris are along to provide some additional muscle.'

'I noticed a couple of them are armed.'

'I don't want any of my blokes being taken by a lion while trying to unbolt a pranged kite. Also, there might be something worth shooting for the pot.'

'I love the bush,' she said. 'It'll be nice to get out of town for a while.'

Bryant led the convoy through downtown Bulawayo. Only the city's earliest risers were stirring or working – black African street cleaners leaning into brooms, horse-drawn milk carts, a white policeman walking the beat, a straight-backed Matabele woman in a maid's pinafore gracefully walking down the road with a sack of maize meal perched on her head. The bag must have weighed twenty pounds at least. Few heads turned to watch the vehicles rumbling down the wide Jacaranda-lined street – the novelty of the colonial outpost's wartime role had long since worn off. Bryant turned right at the signpost that pointed north to Victoria Falls. The stately colonial buildings and white-kerbed avenues soon gave way to rough tar and the thirsty brown bush of stunted acacias and forests of mopani trees. This close to the end of the dry season, everything was in desperate need of water, a step away from death. The climbing sun warmed the right side of his face.

Once out of town the sealed road gave way to two parallel strips of tar, each about eighteen inches wide. Constructed between the wars, these 'strip' roads criss-crossed Rhodesia. The roads had provided work for soldiers returning from the First World War and had been laid for a fraction of the cost of a fully tarred highway.

'I take it Mrs De Beers knows we're coming,' Pip said.

'She knows about the aircraft crash investigation. I arranged this visit last week. If you want to know if I've called her and told her you're coming too, the answer is no. I did try phoning her last night, but I couldn't get through. She has a problem with elephants knocking down her phone lines.'

'All part of the fun of living in Africa.'

'There are worse places to sit out a war.'

'How did you end up here?'

Where to start? He was reluctant to talk about himself. 'You want the long or the short version?'

'It's a five-hour drive.'

'I joined up in October, 1939. Couldn't wait to get into the game.'

He remembered his naive mix of excitement and nerves as he'd fronted up to the recruiting office near Central Station in Sydney on a sunny spring morning. He'd done well at school and earned good enough marks to study mechanical engineering at the University of Sydney. Machines interested him, far more than a life on the land. His father was bent and bowed from a life-time shearing, and with precious little to show for his hard labour. The quiet home life on the farm where his uncle and aunt lived had started to bore him as he'd entered his late teenage years. He'd been a voracious reader and couldn't wait to get out and explore the world. University was hard at first – most of the other men in the course were from families far better off than his. But he was a good rugby league player and had made friends soon enough on the field and off. He had only recently graduated when, for the second time in half a century, Europe's problems became Australia's.

He shrugged. 'I was working as an assistant engineer in a factory making parts for tractors.'

'Sounds like a good job. Why give it up?'

'You're joking, right?' he smiled. 'I signed up for the air force. I'd been in the university air squadron and had been for a couple of flights in trainers. I fancied myself a fighter pilot.'

'Don't take this the wrong way, but you don't exactly strike me as the Errol Flynn type.'

He laughed. 'No offence taken, though you've got to work on your flattery. You can blame football for the nose.'

'I mean you've got a bit more character about you than those recruiting-poster types.'

He was silent for a moment. He glanced across at her and saw her cheeks had started to colour. He thought she had just complimented him, albeit in a backhanded manner. He wondered if she were trying to put him at ease before hitting him with more questions. Whatever she was up to, he reluctantly started talking – at least it would keep the conversation away from Flick's death.

'Anyway, the RAAF – Royal Australian Air Force – took me on and I cooled my heels for about a year after initial training. Finally – it seemed like it took forever – they put me on a boat to here, via Egypt, the Suez Canal and

Mombasa. That was early '41. I'd never been out of Australia – it was quite an eye-opener, that cruise.'

'What did you think of Africa?' she asked.

'I loved it, and that's the truth. I didn't exactly complain when they sent me back here. Anyway, I did initial training all over again, except in Bulawayo this time. Same boring stuff as back home – square bashing, saluting, polishing your kit. Eventually, I got to fly. We did elementary flight training on DH-82s – Tiger Moths – at Cranborne, near Salisbury.'

'It must be wonderful to fly. Did you enjoy it?'

'Back then I did. I thought I was going all right, but the instructors didn't recommend me for fighter training in the end. I went on to Ox Boxes – Oxfords – at Guinea Fowl air base, near Gwelo.' Like Bulawayo, the small town on the high plains of central Rhodesia had been transformed into a massive military encampment. 'I couldn't complain. I was getting paid to fly and it seemed at the time that Bomber Command was the only outfit giving Jerry any stick. We were taking a pasting in the Pacific, North Africa and Hitler had just invaded Russia. A lot of us training to fly bombers reckoned that fighters had had their day after the battle of Britain, and that it was us who would win the war.'

'Bomber Command *is* winning the war, if you believe

the newsreels at the cinema and the *Bulawayo Chronicle*,' she said.

He laughed. 'Sure. If you believe that, I've a bridge to sell you in Sydney.'

'It's not all going well, then, over there?'

He wondered how much to tell her. 'I don't talk about it a lot, back at base. The trainees'll learn the hard way, when they get to England. Even if you do tell blokes what it's really like, most of them either don't believe you or they think you're just trying to scare them.'

'I'd like to know.'

'You're good at asking questions.'

'I was studying to be an advocate – a lawyer – before I got married. But we're talking about you now.'

'A lawyer! Bloody hell. Well, since you ask, it's . . .' He couldn't think where to start.

She sat silently.

'From here, or Canada or Australia, where they also train flight crew, they send you to what's called an Operational Training Unit – an OTU. They give you a bomber – twin engine, usually – and you think you've hit the big-time. You're ready to go bomb the Führer, Goering, the lot of them, and win the war single-handed. Sometimes the OTUs get drafted into going on real raids, into Germany, when there's a big push on, but mostly it's just training missions, navigation exercises and practice bombing with smoke bombs. Occasionally, they'd send us on a nickel raid – that's dropping leaflets on occupied cities.'

'Sounds like a good way to get crews used to the real thing.'

'What they don't tell you, but you find out pretty soon the hard way, is that the loss rate in the training units is almost as bad as in the operational squadrons. About one in four aircraft, a quarter of all crews, are lost during training.'

'Twenty-five per cent casualties, before they even get to bomb Germany?' Her blue eyes were wide with surprise.

He nodded. 'Four kites – twenty-four blokes – didn't come back from training missions while I was converting to Wellingtons. That mightn't sound a lot, but this is happening every day. There were crashes on take-off or landing, and some got lost and never came back. I suppose they ditched in the North Sea.'

'Are things better in the operational squadrons, in terms of losses?'

'Worse. There are still accidents, but now you're flying into flak and night-fighters. The odds are against you from the start. During my first tour, on Wellingtons, we took a hundred per cent casualties. Obviously, not all of us died, but they kept replacing the crews that were lost and by the end of my tour we'd lost more men, in total, than were on the books when I'd started.'

'You survived,' she said. It was not a question as to how or why, or an accusation. Just a statement.

'Too bloody right, I did. Me and my crew, all of us. Thirty missions without a scratch.'

'Amazing, from what you're saying.'

He downshifted as the twin strips of tar that made up the road temporarily disappeared from under them as they moved through a dip. He guessed the sandy creek bed on either side of the road had been a raging torrent at some point during the last wet season and had washed the surface away.

'A bloody miracle,' he said in answer to her. 'And did we think we were hot? You bet your life we did. We drank for three days at the end of it. We all got gongs – medals – and six months leave. None of us took it, though.'

She was surprised. 'Why not? Surely you'd cheated death and earned your leave.'

'We knew we'd all have to do a second operational tour after our leave, but we decided, as a crew – even voted on it – to go straight on, as a team, and do the second thirty sorties without a break.'

She shook her head. '*Men.*'

'You have to understand, we were invincible, or so we thought. Also, the squadron converted to Lancasters. Four-engine bomber, an absolutely beautiful big brute of an aircraft. We thought we'd be safe in one of those.' He looked out the window at the endless African bush, stretching away for miles and miles in every direction. 'But we were wrong.'

'You don't have to go on, if you don't want to,' she said.

He stared straight out the windscreen as they drove, not looking at her, or the African children in ragged hand-me-downs waving at them as they passed through a rural village. This was more like what he had expected of Africa. Mud huts with roofs of thatched yellow grass. The tribal areas were out there still, if you scratched below the surface of white colonial Bulawayo. It wasn't until you flew over the country that you realised how much more existed beyond the stone buildings and tarred roads. It was like Pip's questioning. If people really wanted to ask, they had to be aware that the truth was bigger, meaner and less pretty than the facade. 'You asked,' he said.

'I know, but—'

'People should know the truth.'

'What do you mean?'

'That it's not like in the newsreels.'

'We do.'

'Right.' He slowed at the sight of dark-coloured animals on the road, near the crest of a hill. He thought they were more cattle, but as he got closer, he could see they were cape buffalo. 'I hear they're dangerous,' he said, pointing at the beasts.

'Very.' He said nothing more, even though she sensed that he had so much to tell and needed someone to tell it to. Clearly it wasn't going to be her.

'You're married,' he said after a while, as he glanced down at the simple gold band on her finger.

'Yes.'

'Where is he? Overseas?'

'Not sure, exactly. He's with the Long Range Desert Group. In Italy somewhere.'

He nodded. 'What did he do; before the war, I mean?'

She hated how people always asked about him first, as if the man were the keystone of marriage, and what happened to the woman before, during or after was inconsequential. 'We farm dairy cattle. Outside of Bulawayo, on the road to Plumtree.'

'Good country for it.'

'We try.'

'It must be hard for you, running the farm, working as a copper, fighting crime all by yourself.'

'I manage. I've got an excellent Matabele foreman who looks after the dairy.'

'You mentioned you were studying to be a lawyer.'

'Yes.'

'Jesus,' he groaned. 'This is like pulling teeth.'

'No one would accuse you of talking the legs off a table,' she smiled.

'Well, you should be proud of your old man. Those Long Range Desert Group blokes are the best.' He explained that one of the instructors at Kumalo had flown Kittyhawks in the RAF's Desert Air Force. He'd been full of praise for the way they were taking the fight to the Germans. The groups operated in small convoys, hundreds of miles behind enemy lines, moving fast and hitting hard. It was a job for tough men who were skilled at living in barren areas – Australians and Rhodesians. 'He must be quite a bloke.'

She chewed her bottom lip. 'Yes.'

'What's his name?'

'Charlie.'

He stayed silent, and she knew he was hoping she would fill the void with more talking. It was the same interview technique she had used on him earlier. He was a fast learner. But she wasn't going to fall for that.

'OK,' he said eventually. 'Enough about Charlie, then. I understand if you don't want to talk about him.'

'It's just . . . difficult. With him being away. You're not married?'

'Me? No way. I had a girl back in Sydney, but she sent me a letter halfway through my training over here telling me she'd met someone else. I'd expected to marry her.

It was only a couple of years ago, but it seems like a lifetime. I realise now I barely knew her at all.'

'You'll marry one day, though?' Pip asked.

'At the risk of sounding melodramatic, once I got to England I didn't think I'd survive the war. I still can't really picture myself in a bungalow with a backyard and fence and kids. Doesn't seem natural. You don't have children?'

'No.' Thank God, she thought.

'Time for that after the war, I suppose.'

'Yes. I expect so.'

He looked across at her, but she added nothing. 'So why didn't you become a lawyer?'

'I got married and became a farmer's wife instead.'

He nodded. 'You could be studying now, instead of being a copper, I expect.'

'I don't know about you, Squadron Leader —'

'Paul.'

'I think that, given the circumstances—'

'Paul, or you won't get another word out of me, and you ride in the back of the Dodge with the erks.'

She laughed. 'All right, Paul. I don't know about you, but I think I've had enough of life stories for the moment.'

'I agree . . .'

'Oh. Philippa. But nearly everyone calls me Pip.'

'I didn't kill her, Pip. You realise that, don't you.'

She saw he was still looking at the road, unwilling, or unable to meet her eyes. 'I don't know what to think, Paul. But I've no reason yet to suspect you.'

He looked at her now, and she thought she'd never seen eyes so heavy with sadness and loss and fatigue and bad memories.

'I don't have it in me,' he said.

She thought she believed him. 'How close were Felicity and Catherine De Beers?'

'You'll see when we give her the news. Rest stop ahead.'

Bryant stopped the convoy at a long whitewashed, thatch-roofed sandstone building on the side of the road.

'This place reminds me of holidays,' she said.

He got out of the car and stretched, raising his arms above his head. 'Twenty minutes, boys,' he called to the men in the Dodge. 'Let's get a cup of tea. So you've been here before?'

'Only a couple of times, as a kid. Then we went to Victoria Falls for our honeymoon and stayed in the big hotel there.'

'Happier times?' he said, instantly regretting the way it came out. 'Sorry. Not my business.'

She let the remark slide by, but was suddenly aware her short, moody answers to his questioning about her married life had betrayed her. Damn him. They were not on this trip to dissect her marital affairs. They took a seat at a white wrought-iron table outside, under the shade of a bougainvillea-choked gazebo, and ordered tea from the African waiter.

They sat at the table in silence, the sun on their faces, each lost in their memories.

They saw more game once they turned left off the strips of tar onto the dirt road that led to Matetsi, and Pandamatenga on the Bechuanaland border. According to the sign at the turnoff, they were about sixty miles from Victoria Falls, in the far north-western corner of the country. He'd flown over the mighty avalanche of water during his time in training in Rhodesia, on his first trip. He'd marvelled at the fine spray that looked like columns of smoke from the air. But here, the bush was parched from a lack of water.

'What are they?' he asked as they slowed to pass a herd of black and white antelope with magnificent curved horns.

'Sable. They're beautiful, aren't they? There must be some water nearby. The animals tend to congregate around the remaining natural water, or boreholes, at this time of year.'

'I wish I could get out here into the bush more often,' he replied.

'I know what you mean. I could live out here, I think, away from the city and all those people.'

'Me too. Catherine tells me there are huge herds of buffalo and elephant up here, as well as lion, leopard, cheetah, the works.'

'It's a great place. Almost makes you believe there's a God.'

Funny, he thought, but he was about to say the exact same thing. He'd seen nothing in England, or in the skies over Germany, to convince him there was a merciful supreme being or, if there were one, that he was on their side. He wondered where her apparent disillusionment with religion came from. Every now and then she looked like she, too, was harbouring painful memories, and they marred an otherwise angelic face.

The trucks juddered along the badly corrugated dirt road, through vast stands of mopani trees, intersected by parched riverbeds and flood plains covered in dry yellow grass. Dust filled the inside of the car and coated the airmen in the back of the Dodge. Bryant felt the grit cover his teeth. He hit the brakes as a huge bull elephant stepped out onto the road.

'Bloody hell!' he said. 'How am I going to reverse with this lot behind me?'

'Quiet,' Pip whispered. 'Your voice is more of a worry to him than the sound of the engines.'

A cloud of dust haloed the animal's big knobbly head as he shook it. His ears flapped like grey flags snapping in the wind. He raised his trunk and sniffed the air.

'Stay still,' Pip urged.

'I'm not going anywhere,' he hissed.

The elephant rocked back his massive circular left front foot and lowered his trunk.

'He's giving up,' Bryant whispered.

'Not quite.'

Without warning the trunk came up again and the bull's ears opened wide. He started running towards the Humber and, as he moved, let out a mighty trumpet blast from his trunk.

'Shit!'

'Wait,' Pip said. 'It's a mock charge. He's just trying to scare us.'

'Doing a bloody good job,' he said, his heart pounding.

The elephant stopped a few yards from the car, shook his head again, then turned and walked off into the grass.

'See?' Pip said. 'It's all about reading the signs,' she said. 'Knowing when someone is bluffing and when they really mean to hurt you.'

'You're good at reading signs, are you?'

'We'll see,' she said.

7

Catherine De Beers spurred her mount hard in the ribs and the horse galloped across the grassy vlei. The impala carcass bounced on the horse's rump behind her saddle.

'Here she comes,' Bryant said, pointing to the fast-moving dark spot on the yellow-brown landscape as he drove through the ornate thatch-crowned gate of the De Beers property, Isilwane Ranch, and up the half-mile driveway.

Catherine waved as she rode, long dark curls streaming in the breeze as she passed the modest mud and thatch staff housing, then returned both hands to the reins as the horse effortlessly cleared the stone wall surrounding the grounds of the main lodge. She leaned forward and patted the horse's neck as it slowed to a walk.

'Paul! How delightful to see you,' she called.

She dismounted with the fluid ease of a leopardess alighting from a branch, and strode, riding crop in hand, to the car. An African servant dressed in khaki shirt and shorts was waiting to take her mount. She tossed the reins to him imperiously, but otherwise did not acknowledge his presence. 'I see you've brought company. How wonderful. I've been cooped up here alone, starved of human contact, for an eternity!'

Pip Lovejoy looked Catherine De Beers up and down before she got out of the car. If Felicity Langham had a blonde Hollywood starlet's looks, Catherine had those of a classic beauty, as though she'd been brought to life from the glaze of a Greek urn or an Egyptian frieze. Lustrous black locks, eyes and lashes, and the full breasts, wide hips and nipped waist that American pin-up magazines were encouraging men around the world to consider the epitome of female beauty. The outfit helped too. Polished brown leather riding boots that came to her knees, skin-tight jodhpurs, and a simple but elegantly tailored blouse of sky blue. Pip had a slight gap between her two front teeth, which made her more than a little envious of the even, white smile that the other woman flashed at her.

'How do you do, I'm Catherine. We haven't met,' she said.

The accent was more British than Rhodesian, Pip thought. An affectation, perhaps. 'Hello, I'm Constable Philippa Lovejoy, Bulawayo Police. Pleased to meet you.'

'The police? Undercover, by the looks of it,' Catherine said, eyebrows raised.

'Pip's here on business, Catherine,' Bryant began.

Catherine looked puzzled, her eyes questioning the Australian. 'Do come in for some tea and you can tell me what all this is about, Paul.'

'Catherine, wait. This is serious. It's not good news. Something terrible has happened to Flick.'

Catherine looked away from him, into Pip's eyes. 'Tell me.'

Pip took a breath. 'Mrs De Beers, I'm sorry to inform you that Felicity Langham was found dead, in Bulawayo, the night before last. We suspect foul play.'

Catherine fainted.

Bloody hell, Pip thought to herself as Bryant called to the men in the Dodge to come and help him. Part of her job as a policewoman was to break the news of tragic deaths to relatives. She'd been on four such assignments with Hayes so far. Three of them were to tell parents and spouses about motor-vehicle accidents, and the fourth was to report a lost child had been found dead, at the bottom of an abandoned mine shaft. All were terrible in their own way and she had seen a variety of emotions from the grieving relatives. Some broke down in tears, some refused to believe the news, and some took it, at least in the first instance, with quiet stoicism.

This was the first faint she'd seen. It seemed somehow theatrical – and not completely out of step with the brief impression she had formed of the wealthy widow. The galloping across the veldt, the smooth dismount, the gushing way in which she had greeted Bryant, and now the collapse at his feet.

'Let's get you inside,' Bryant said. He had lifted Catherine by himself. 'Open the door,' he ordered a sergeant in overalls. 'The rest of you blokes wait by the trucks.'

'Paul . . . is that you?' she said, looking up into his eyes.

'It's me, Catherine. You've had a shock.'

'Tell me it's not true, about Flick.'

'I'm afraid it is.'

Pip followed them through the front door of the house. One of Catherine's servants, a plump woman in a starched pinafore, bustled into the kitchen and returned with a crystal jug of cold water.

'I think you should lie down,' Bryant said.

'Yes, thank you, Paul. Awfully embarrassed at this show,' she said.

Bryant walked unhesitatingly down a long corridor, his rubber soles squeaking on polished wooden floorboards. Pip watched him kick open a door with his right foot, then walk into the room. She moved to the doorway and peered inside. It seemed to be the master bedroom.

A four-poster bed sat in the middle of the room. A mosquito net hung from the tops of the posts to the floor. The furnishings looked plush and expensive. A mixture of English lace and ethnic African objets d'art. On top of the wide dressing table were two huge curved tusks, each with a procession of miniature elephants carved into them. The stool in front was made from an elephant's foot.

It was Catherine's bedroom, judging by the smell of perfume and collection of coloured fragrance bottles on the dressers, but the legacy of old Hugo De Beers was still there. As well as the tusks and stool there was a leopard-skin rug on the floor and an old rifle – a Martini Henry, she thought – mounted on the wall above an assegai, a Zulu stabbing spear. Incongruously, though, on the wall behind the head of the bed was an impressionistic oil painting of what appeared to be two naked women, their limbs intertwined.

Bryant elbowed the mosquito netting apart and laid Catherine on the bed. 'Patience will be here in a second with some water. Just take it easy for the moment.'

Pip looked at them. Like a couple, she thought to herself. Bryant had obviously spent time in the house. He knew the way to the bedroom without asking, and the maid's name. If she had to guess, assuming Bryant had been holding back parts of his story, she would have said that he had been romantically involved with Felicity Langham – and perhaps embarrassed by the fact that she was his subordinate, or worried that he would be incriminated somehow in her murder. Pip assumed that he had gotten to know Catherine De Beers through his relationship with Felicity. The fact that he obviously knew his way around the De Beers Manor – for that was how Pip already thought of the lodge – seemed to indicate that he may have been close to Catherine as well.

'Thank you, darling,' Catherine said.

Quite the dark horse, Pip thought to herself, raising her eyebrows behind Bryant's back.

Catherine De Beers looked up from her bed and saw Pip's surprise. 'Sorry, Constable. I might be raving a bit. I call everyone darling, by the way.'

'I've some questions to ask you, Mrs De Beers . . .'

'Catherine, please.'

'When you're up to it. Is now convenient?'

'I'm afraid my head is spinning a bit,' she said as the maid entered and laid a silver tray with a pitcher of water and a cut-crystal glass on a polished mahogany bedside table.

'Of course,' Pip said. 'Perhaps later?'

'I'm so dreadfully sorry about all this. Flick, Felicity, was such a dear friend. We were at school together and, well, I suppose Paul's told you of our aerial shows.'

'Yes. This must come as a terrible blow.'

Bryant interrupted. 'Let's leave it a bit, Pip, if that's all right with you. You can come down to the crash site with the boys and me, if you like. We can come back and see Catherine later.'

'Patience will make you some tea. Please show Constable . . .'

'Lovejoy,' Pip said, feeling like she was being expertly elbowed to one side by everyone in the room.

'Please make some tea for Constable Lovejoy, and show her to the sitting room, Patience,' Catherine said.

'Yes, madam,' the maid said. 'This way, please.'

'Won't be a sec,' Bryant said. 'I'll just make sure she's comfortable.'

Pip nodded and reluctantly followed the maid out of the bedroom.

'Oh God, Paul. Tell me it's not true,' Catherine said again.

He thought he saw tears welling in her eyes. 'They don't know how it happened. They found her, partially clothed, in a rough part of town.'

'I've warned her about some of the male company she keeps. Present company excepted.'

'About that . . .' Bryant began, a pained look of embarrassment crossing his face.

'You haven't told the police?'

He shook his head.

'Don't worry,' Catherine whispered. 'Mum's the word. I won't go spilling the beans to Constable Busybody. You hadn't had a falling out with Flick, had you?'

'What do you mean by that? Jesus, Cath, it's bad enough the cops think I'm hiding something.'

'No, Paul, of course I don't think you would hurt Flick. But I wonder who she got herself mixed up with.'

'You're almost saying her death was her own fault. It could have been a random attack.'

Catherine dabbed at her eyes. 'There were things you didn't know about her. You've known us for such a short time.'

'And I'm more confused than ever.'

'Did they tell you anything else, about the circumstances of her death?'

'The coppers let slip that Flick was tied up. The doctor who examined the body said she'd been raped and then strangled.'

Catherine turned her head away from him. 'Paul, I feel like a piece of me is dead. If I hadn't pranged my damn kite I would have been down in Bulawayo. I could have kept her safe.'

'Don't torture yourself, Cath.' He felt a measure of the same guilt. He couldn't bring himself to tell Catherine that Flick had called him the night she died. What made him feel even worse was the suspicion that if her message had reached him he wouldn't have left the base to meet her. It was confusing, what had happened between them, and his visits to the hangar to see her had not clarified matters.

'I hope you don't mind,' she said, a tear rolling down her cheek, 'but I really do think I need some time by myself.'

It's only just starting to hit her, he thought. 'Of course.' Bryant bent over her, kissed her cheek and brushed a strand of hair from her forehead.

'You're a dear. Tell the policewoman I'll talk to her when you get back from the crash site. I won't tell her anything that she wouldn't be able to understand. She looks more like a dowdy housewife than a detective, anyway.'

'Just rest for now,' he said. He walked out of the room. He thought Catherine's last remark was unnecessarily bitchy. He wondered if he should tell Pip Lovejoy the whole story, even if she wouldn't understand it. He had trouble understanding it himself. Still, if he told a version different from Catherine's, that would further complicate things. He shook his head and reached for a cigarette.

Pip thanked the maid for her cup of tea and said, 'Patience, does Mrs De Beers own a motor car?'

'Yes, madam.'

'Does she drive to Bulawayo often?'

The maid gave a little laugh. 'Oh, no. The madam *flies* to Bulawayo often.'

'Yes, I know that, but since her aeroplane crashed, has she taken the car to Bulawayo?'

'No, madam.'

'Where does she drive to?'

'Sometimes to Victoria Falls, madam, to shop or visit.'

'I see,' said Pip. 'Did you know Miss Felicity Langham, Patience?'

Patience looked about the room.

'It's all right,' Pip said, sensing the older woman's uncertainty. 'I mightn't look like it, but I'm a policewoman.'

The maid nodded. 'Miss Felicity stayed sometimes.'

'She and Mrs De Beers were good friends.'

'Oh, yes.'

'And Squadron Leader Bryant?'

'Is right behind you,' Bryant said. He smiled.

Patience seized her chance to escape and disappeared into the kitchen.

'The questions can wait,' he said. 'Catherine will talk to you in a little while. She's not taking it well. Don't pay too much attention to her amateur dramatics. She bungs it on a bit around strangers, but she really has been hit hard today.'

'I understand,' Pip said. She resented the way he was taking over the house, like he owned it, but held her tongue.

'Come with me and I'll show you what happens when you let a Canadian teenager play with an expensive aircraft.'

They climbed back into his car and the waiting mechanics and askaris extinguished their cigarettes and reboarded the two lorries. Isilwane Ranch's private airstrip was only about a half mile from the main house, but even on that short drive Bryant and Pip were treated to a mini-safari.

'They're roan antelope,' she said to him as a herd of twenty tan-coloured beasts with black and white faces and curved horns crossed the road, halting the convoy. The horse-sized antelopes trotted through waist-high golden grass, barely giving the humans a second glance.

'Never seen anything like them,' he said.

'That's lion spoor,' she said, sticking her head out of the passenger side window and inspecting a set of big pug marks in the dust.

'Glad we've got the blokes with the guns with us.'

She laughed. 'What happened to the big, brave bomber pilot?'

He ignored the jest as they motored down the road. 'What are they? More deer?'

'We don't have deer here. They're waterbuck. You can tell them by the white mark on their bottoms. It looks like they've sat on a toilet seat that someone's painted as a practical joke.'

'An old RAF prank. If there is a God, I'd hate to think he's a Pommie pilot officer.' They passed the shaggy grey animals and drove across a stone ford laid in a dry riverbed. 'Airstrip's up ahead.'

'You know your way around this place,' she said.

'I've been up here a few times in the past, but never really taken the time to look at the game,' he said, glancing away from her, out the driver's side window. 'It took a few meetings and a lot of paperwork to allow Catherine and Felicity to stage their parachuting display.'

'Forgive me for asking, but how did you know the way to Catherine's bedroom?'

'She gave me the grand tour when I first visited. What are you insinuating, Constable?'

'Oh, nothing. Look, there're some zebra grazing on the airstrip.'

Bryant drove along the grass strip, which had been cropped short by herds of zebra, wildebeest and impala. 'Catherine told me that one time she had to buzz the field four times, at low level, to scare off a pride of hungry lions who had killed a zebra in the middle of it.'

'This is wild country, that's for sure,' Pip said.

'There's our broken bird,' Bryant said, pointing to the crashed Harvard trainer.

'Doesn't look like it's going anywhere. What went wrong?' Pip asked as they got out of the car and walked towards the forlorn-looking aircraft. The sight of twisted metal and the cracked Perspex canopy made her shudder.

'The pilot, though I use the term loosely as he's probably never going to fly again, claims he had engine trouble and tried to make a forced landing here on the De Beers' strip. When he touched down, he said, the landing gear wheel went into a hole, possibly made by an ant bear, and snapped off.'

The lorries stopped behind them and the airmen and askaris all climbed out and headed towards the wreckage.

'I'd say the second part of the story is feasible, about hitting the hole, but I'll stake my wings that a test run of this engine would show nothing wrong with it.'

'Well, you've just lost another Harvard somewhere out on the saltpans in Bechuanaland. Perhaps when you find that one there'll turn out to be some engine fault that's common to all your aircraft. Why not give the pilot the benefit of the doubt until then?' Pip asked.

'We won't know what happened to Smythe's kite until we find it. But this guy, Cavendish, was supposed to be on a gunnery exercise on the day he crashed here.'

'And?'

'And the gunnery and bombing range at Miasi is about a hundred and fifty-odd miles from here as the crow flies.'

'So, you think he landed here deliberately? Why? To see Catherine, perhaps?'

'The thought had crossed my mind, but she reckons she never suggested Cavendish pay her a visit.'

'You're not convinced?' she prodded. She could see a hardness in his eyes. She wondered if it were jealousy. Had the young Canadian been making a play for a woman that Bryant had either a relationship with or designs on?

'Catherine was a regular visitor to the mess and got to know many of the trainee pilots. She's a flyer, as you know, and seemed absolutely fascinated by our aircraft, particularly the Harvards, which are the closest thing we have in Rhodesia to a fighter plane.'

'A poor man's Spitfire?'

'Yes, I suppose so. She's asked me countless times if she could fly one. Of course, I told her no.'

'So maybe she convinced Cavendish to give her a whirl?' Pip suggested.

'That's what I thought. He claims he never spoke to her, about landing his Harvard or taking her up. He's sticking to his story that he had to make a forced landing. And, as I said before, Catherine also denies he was coming to Isilwane to see her.'

Bryant surveyed the crash site. 'It looks like the Harvard went into a violent left-hand turn when the wheel went into the hole, assuming that part of the story's true. You can see the gouges in the grass where the propeller blades dug in and then bent around the cowling.'

Pip nodded, following his movements as he pointed out the evidence and made his deductions. It was the same as police work, and not unlike her murder investigation. They had a body – in this case, an aeroplane – some evidence of the crime, though in both cases there was a lack of obvious motive.

'The kite probably dug in, nose first,' he continued, 'and the force cracked the Perspex canopy. Then she slammed down on her tail again.' He put a hand on the warm metal skin and looked under the tail planes. 'The tail wheel's sheared off as well. Left-hand wingtip dug into the earth when the landing gear wheel snapped off.' He walked back to the front of the aircraft and looked in and around the engine cowling. 'No sign of oil or fuel leaks, or spray on the cockpit. OK, Flight,' he called to the senior mechanic, 'get the wings off her and start getting her ready for transport.'

'Yes, sir. Right, you lazy bastards, let's get cracking.'

Bryant walked along the airstrip, retracing the aircraft's final landing. Pip followed. 'Here's what's left of the landing gear,' he said.

She stood behind him, hands on hips. 'Looks like an ant bear hole to me. At least there was nothing he could do about that.'

'He could have stuck to his bloody flight plan,' Bryant shook his head. 'These stupid kids. As well as refusing to believe the odds against them on operations, they go and do their best to kill themselves here, with moronic stunts like this.'

'He *could* be telling the truth.'

'It's always engine trouble, or a broken compass. They can't even come up with original excuses for their bloody joy-flights.'

'Don't tell me you stuck to the book during training. Weren't you tempted to do a few unauthorised loop-the-loops or visit some pretty girl and show off your new aeroplane?' Pip asked with a smile.

Bryant turned away from her.

'Aha. A crack in the rigid facade, I see,' she persisted. He looked at her and smiled. She realised it was the first time she had seen such a smile cross his furrowed face. It was as though a different person had been uncovered, albeit briefly. In that instant, with his sheepish grin and the light catching his eyes, he also looked several years closer to his true age and, to her surprise, rather attractive.

'To tell you the truth, it was one of these stupid pranks that landed me in Bomber Command.'

'Come on, out with it. Or do I have to take you down to the police camp and put the thumbscrews on you?'

'You're right, Constable. Fair cop. A girl was involved.'

'I *knew* it! Was she pretty?'

'Very.'

'Good. You wouldn't have wanted to risk your career for any plain old farmer's daughter.'

'She wasn't on a farm. She lived in Salisbury. I was based near there, at Norton. I buzzed her house – flew over it at low level.'

'I wouldn't have thought that was a hanging offence.'

'Five times.'

'Oh dear,' she said, holding a hand to her mouth to hide her grin.

'And it turned out, there was an air commodore living four houses up. He had plenty of time to take down the registration letters on the side of my Harvard.'

'You're lucky you didn't end up spending the war cleaning toilets.'

'Maybe, maybe not,' he shrugged. 'The air commodore wanted me grounded, for good. Instead, the senior instructor told me I was too irresponsible to be put in charge of a fighter. I was switched to Oxfords and ended up flying bombers.'

'What happened to her?'

He shrugged. 'I offered to write, but she broke it off before I left.'

She suddenly felt sorry for him. 'That must have been hard.'

'She was smarter than me. I think she knew more than my friends and I did back then, about what it would be like in England. Wartime's not good for lasting relationships.'

She didn't want him to become maudlin. 'I don't suppose once you got overseas you could very well *buzz* attractive English girls in a Lancaster?'

'You'd be surprised!' He laughed out loud. A short, sharp burst of mirth that sounded so strange coming from him that she wondered if he'd laughed in a year.

'Don't you miss it? Flying, I mean,' she asked as they walked back to the main wreckage, side by side.

'I don't care if I never fly again,' he said quietly, almost to himself.

She looked up at him and saw the old face again, creased, sombre, tired. She said nothing. That face was not attractive, not within a decade of its true age. The war, his experiences, had robbed him of his youth, his humour and, as far as she could see, his reason to live. His passion, if it could be called that, now seemed to be doing everything he could to ensure that the young men who passed through Kumalo would at least get through their training alive. 'What's happening with your investigation of the other crashed Harvard?'

He shrugged again. 'I called the police post at the Bechuanaland border and they said they'd send out a recce party to investigate the spot where Smythe's body was found and have a look for his kite. We've diverted a couple of training flights over the saltpans to look for wreckage as well.'

'It's a big area to search,' she said.

'True, but we've got a fix on where Smythe's body was found. He can't have walked too far in a day, so that narrows the search area.'

They stopped at the wrecked aircraft again and Bryant said to the flight sergeant mechanic: 'How's it going?'

The big man's overalls were blotched with dark patches of sweat. Two younger mechanics stood by as he strained to undo a nut at the root of a partially severed wing. Clearly, he was a man who believed that when it came to some jobs he was the only one who could do the task properly. 'Bloody thing's twisted. It'll take longer than I thought to shift it.'

'Did you get the ammo out of the guns?' Bryant asked.

'*Yes*, sir. Fooking thing! Oh, sorry, ma'am,' he added when he noticed Pip. His tone betrayed his impatience with the stubborn wing and the implication that he might forget something.

'All right, Flight,' Bryant said. 'Don't burst a valve. We'll get out of your way.'

'Yes, sir. Get that bloody ammo stowed in the Dodge,' the man barked at a pimply-faced airman.

'We'll be up at the house when you're finished,' Bryant said.

'Very good, sir. Ma'am.'

Bryant and Pip started to walk back to the car, when the Flight Sergeant said, 'Oh, one thing, sir?'

'Yes,' Bryant said.

The mechanic wiped the back of a meaty pink forearm across his sweating brow. 'You asked about the ammo, and for us to keep an eye out for anything out of the ordinary.'

'Yes?'

'There's not a full load. Not nearly enough, and the guns are clean.'

Bryant walked over to where the Harvard's two .303 inch Browning machine guns were lying in the grass. One of the guns had come from the right wing, the other from a mounting on the top right-hand side of the aircraft's nose. He stuck his little finger inside the end of one of the barrels and rubbed it around. When he pulled it out it was clean, save for a smudge of oil. 'You're right. No cordite residue. They haven't been fired. But that tallies with what the pilot said. He reported engine trouble before attempting the gunnery exercise.'

'Long way from the gunnery range, sir,' the senior mechanic said.

'Yes, well, that's all part of the investigation. Now what about the ammo?'

'Like I said, sir, it's light. There's only fifty rounds with each of those guns.'

'I'd have thought he would have had a lot more than that on board,' Pip said.

'Aye, a lot more, ma'am,' the flight sergeant replied.

Bryant searched his memory, back to the brief time he'd spent flying Harvards, before being relegated to bomber training. 'That's six hundred rounds missing – three hundred per gun. I'll make a note of it in the report and check with the pilot.'

'No shortage of .303 rifles up here on a hunting estate, I'd wager.'

'Leave that line of questioning to me, Flight. Well done for noticing the loss – if that's what it is. The armourer could have been daydreaming on the job, I suppose.'

The flight sergeant frowned. 'I'll find out who was on that day and have a word, sir.'

Bryant and Pip left the men and got into the Humber. 'That's a bit of a worry, about the ammunition,' she said.

'Yeah. But this is an air force investigation. Remember

our deal – I won't cut in on your business if you leave me to mine.'

He was still part of her business, though, she reminded herself. The stroll around the crash site had been interesting, and it was nice to see the broken officer smile, if only once or twice, but she still had a very serious job to do. 'Well, whichever way you look at it, we've both got some questions for Catherine De Beers.'

Dust hung in the air as the dry season drew to an end, the tiny particles rising from the baked earth and parched grass and trees. Before the life-giving rains came there was always the risk, for plant and animal alike, that the water would come too late or too little.

It was the time of the predator. Lions called to each other at dusk, regrouping for the hunt; hyenas cackled in anticipation, beggars waiting for the scraps from the feast. Hungry herbivores used the cover of night to risk a sip from shrinking waterholes and drying rivers, while the leopard waited silently, unseen, in ambush.

And the sun, as if to mark this time of killing, came and went each morning and night in the form of a blood-red disc burning malevolently through the hanging dust.

'I still can't get over these sunsets,' Bryant said.

'I was born in Africa, and I never will. I love hearing the lions at dusk.'

'An odd lullaby,' he said.

'It's odd, but I find it comforting. My father, when we had the farm, used to say that if you can hear them then you know where they are, so they're not sitting outside the back door, waiting for you to take a pee in the middle of the night.'

He smiled. '*Braai* smells good,' he said, using the abbreviation of *braaivleis* – cooked meat – the Afrikaner term for a barbecue, which had carried north across the border from South Africa into Rhodesia.

'I'm still not happy about spending the night, Paul,' she said. 'There'll be hell to pay when I get back to work tomorrow. I hope Catherine makes an appearance soon.'

When they'd returned from the crash site in the afternoon, Bryant had knocked gently on the bedroom door and opened it. What he saw shocked him. Catherine was sitting naked on the floor, her knees drawn up to her breasts, a half-empty bottle of gin clutched in her right hand. Her eyes were puffy and red and her cheeks streaked with dried tears. She sobbed as he lifted her to the bed.

'I told Cook to spit-roast an impala,' she mumbled, as if in a daze.

'It's all right, Catherine. Get some sleep. We can talk later.'

He'd taken the remnants of the bottle from her and tucked her in. Mercifully, she had drifted off to sleep immediately.

It was dark outside now, though still warm enough for Pip and Paul to be in shirtsleeves. The mechanics stood around a fire pit full of hot coals as Catherine's African cook turned the carcass of the little antelope on the spit. The African askaris and the air force guards sat a little way off, talking among themselves.

Bryant had told Pip about Catherine's condition. 'It's put all of us behind schedule, but at least the erks seem to be enjoying themselves,' he said, as another chorus of laughter wafted over from the *braai*, along with the tantalising scent and sizzle of roasting venison.

Before taking to the bottle, Catherine had had the presence of mind to order her staff to fetch ice and two crates of beer, and make up some beds from spare mattresses in the lodge's workshop. The maid had shown Bryant and Pip to two newly made-up guestrooms, at opposite ends of the corridor from Catherine's central bedroom. In one respect, Bryant was glad of the delay. If he had been back at Kumalo, he would have been overseeing the arrangements for two funerals, not to mention being neck-deep in paperwork and administration over the current investigations. It would still be there waiting for him the next day. However, for the moment he found he was content to stand next to Pip Lovejoy and savour the familiar feeling of numbness spreading through his veins as his third bottle of Lion Lager took effect.

'Look, our hostess has risen,' Pip said, pointing with her glass of gin and tonic.

Bryant noticed Pip had been sitting on the drink since sundowners were served. Unlike him, she obviously wanted to keep a clear head for her meeting with Catherine. Once he had reported that Catherine was comatose, the two of them had spent a relaxing afternoon driving some more of the dirt roads around Isilwane Ranch. They had spotted giraffe, wildebeest and a trio of curly-horned male kudus, and had had a fleeting glimpse of a magnificent black-maned lion, not far at all from the house – possibly the same one who was now calling to the other members of his pride. They'd talked about wildlife and, as if a temporary truce were in place, nothing more about the investigations they were both involved in.

'Constable, Paul, can you ever forgive me?' Catherine asked as she strode from the house into the garden, a mug of steaming coffee cupped in both hands.

'There's nothing to forgive, Mrs De Beers,' Pip said.

'Thank you for being so understanding. Please call me Catherine and I shall call you Philippa, if that's not against police regulations.'

'Pip,' she said, smiling.

'How are you feeling, Cath?' Paul asked.

'I'm coping. Of course, I can't stop thinking about poor

Flick, but I suppose I'll have to accept it now.'

'I'm sorry for your loss. She must have been a dear friend,' Pip began.

Paul noticed that Catherine seemed to have pulled herself together. From the distraught mess he'd seen earlier in the day, a composed, svelte, immaculately groomed woman had emerged. Her eyes were a little puffy, but she had done her hair and made up her face. She wore a simple black dress belted at the waist, patent leather sandals and a string of tiny pearls. It was as if she had to dress to impress for every occasion, be it hunting in the bush or mourning.

'You really can't imagine,' Catherine said.

Pip wondered what that meant. 'You were at school together?'

'Yes, here and overseas. We were both sent to England for the last two years of our schooling, in the hope the Brits would make proper young ladies of us.'

'Must have been a bit of a culture shock,' Pip said.

'Oh, it was. I'd grown up on a farm and spent half my life hunting with my father. Flick's father was in trade – terribly wealthy, though – and her world had already been a whirl of parties. The two of us were plucked from very adult worlds and dropped into a boarding school full of prim and proper little girls who'd never said boo to a goose. It was the two of us against the world over there.'

'And you'd stayed friends ever since.'

'Yes. When the war started, Flick joined the WAAFs. She trained as a parachute packer and was absolutely desperate to try one of the silly things out. I took her up in my Tiger Moth one day and she just did it – jumped out. She was an incredible person,' Catherine said, tailing off as the memories cascaded through her mind.

'I need to ask you about the company Miss Langham was keeping, Catherine.'

'Of course,' Catherine said.

'I'm sorry to tell you this, but the way Miss Langham's body was found and certain other evidence at the scene indicate she may have been the subject of a sexual assault.'

Catherine closed her eyes and nodded. 'Paul told me. I still can't imagine why someone would do such a thing.'

'Sometimes these types of attacks are random, but in many cases the attacker is known to the victim. I need to know if Felicity was seeing someone, or if she had spoken of being pestered by a man, or men.'

'Hundreds.'

'Excuse me?' Pip said.

'Maybe thousands. She was *surrounded* by lovesick, homesick men, most still in or barely out of their teens. Hardly a day went by when Flick wasn't asked out to the cinema, to dinner or for something less seemly. I don't know if you noticed, but she was a beautiful young woman.'

147

Pip nodded. 'How did she take to these advances?'

'I could tell you she rejected them all, but that would be a lie. She was a vivacious girl with a zest for life. Wartime loosens some of the constraints of normal polite society, as I'm sure you've noticed yourself. She had a couple of affairs that I knew of, with trainee pilots. Both are overseas now; dead, for all I know. The last was two months ago.'

'There was no one recently?'

'No one from the base at Kumalo, not that I know of,' Catherine said, glancing at Bryant as if for confirmation.

Pip took a sip of her drink. 'Do you get down to Bulawayo often?'

'Not since just after I pranged my aeroplane. I was there recently for a function in the officers' mess. Since then I've been grounded, literally.'

'You don't have a motor car?'

'I do. Several, if you count the hunting trucks. I don't suppose the police are subject to petrol rationing, but we lesser mortals are, and it's damned hard to find someone who'll deliver way out here. Every now and then, when I have enough fuel saved up, I drive to Victoria Falls to visit friends and stock up on supplies.'

'When was the last time you saw Felicity?'

Catherine stroked her chin and gazed towards the star-filled sky. 'The morning of the day I crashed the aircraft.

We'd done a display at Kumalo, had morning tea in the mess with a few of the instructors, and then I flew home. That was the last time I saw her. Two weeks ago. Excuse me,' Catherine said, wiping a tear with the back of her finger, trying not to smudge her make-up.

'I'm so sorry. I know this must be hard for you,' Pip said.

'I hope you find the bastard who hurt her, Pip,' Catherine replied.

Pip nodded. 'So do I.' She changed the subject. 'You've a lovely home here.'

'I *had* a lovely home while Hugo was still alive. Now I've got a big, empty house full of nice things. It's not quite the same.'

'I met him once. He came to shoot a lion on our farm. He was larger than life.'

'In every way. He was a friend of my father's. I'd known him since I was a child.'

'Really?'

'Good Lord, nothing improper. Hugo was the essence of kindness and decency. I admired him as a child and, when I returned from England, realised I loved him as a man. You've no doubt heard I'm a shameless gold-digger who married a man thirty years my senior to get my hands on all this,' she said, waving a slender bare arm to take in the lodge and the ranch's vast grounds.

'I try not to listen to rumourmongers.'

'It's all right, Pip. You wouldn't be the first to think ill of me. But I tell you, honestly, I'd give all this up and live naked in the bush if I could have him back.'

'Hunting accident, wasn't it?' Pip asked. 'I remember there being something in the *Chronicle*.'

'A damn fool South African hunter. It was a terrible thing to witness.'

'You were there?'

'Yes. They were stalking a buffalo. The South African had shot but only wounded it, and Hugo was walking through some adrenaline grass trying to put the beast out of its misery.'

'Frightening,' Pip said.

'The South African was behind him and I was following. It all seemed rather exciting at first. I saw the whole thing. The Afrikaner tripped and his rifle discharged. It caught Hugo in the back, through the heart. At least he died quickly.'

'How horrible for you.'

'Yes and, no offence, Pip, but it was made worse by the rigmarole I went through with the police afterwards. Not unlike now.'

'I know it's difficult. One more question.'

'Go on,' Catherine said.

'Was Felicity seeing any men off the base – civilians?'

Catherine sighed. 'Pip, I understand you have to ask these questions, but I've a positive army to feed tonight, and this really is rather awful for me.'

'I'm sorry. But you've spoken of her admirers on base. What about other men?'

'I don't know, and that's the truth. There may have been others, but she never said a thing to me about them. Paul mentioned she was found in a black part of town.'

Pip looked across at Bryant. 'Yes, in Mzilikazi township.'

'Well,' Catherine said, 'I don't consider myself a racist person, but I would have thought that would give you some leads. I'd hardly think that one of the air force types would take her off base, to a seedy part of town, to have his way with her. She may have been abducted, at random, by an African.'

'We're pursuing a number of avenues of investigation,' Pip said.

'For a volunteer policewoman you certainly have the language down pat. I wish I could help you more, Pip, but I need to get this crowd sorted out and, I hope you understand, to work out how I shall cope with this news.'

'Thank you for your patience. I understand completely,' Pip said.

Bryant breathed a sigh of relief and wandered off to check on the *braai* and find another drink.

There was enough moonlight coming through the bedroom window for Pip to read the face of her wrist-watch. It was nearly midnight, about an hour since the last of the beers had been drunk. A creaking floorboard had woken her. The timber protested again.

Perhaps it was Catherine or Paul going to the bath-room. She needed to go too and she didn't fancy using the chamber pot she'd spied under the bed. Realising she would not get the chance to question the other two once the meal had started, she had relaxed and had another three gin and tonics. She regretted the last now. She swung her legs off the bed, slipped on her trousers and blouse, and tiptoed to the door. She opened it, then quickly pulled it almost closed again and peeked through the crack.

Catherine was dressed in a robe of white silk, her dark tresses streaming down her back. The fabric shimmered on her full hips as she walked down the hallway. She stopped and opened the door to Paul's bedroom, entered, then pulled it closed behind her.

Pip closed her door, then leaned against it with her back. She would have to hold her bladder for a little while.

*   *   *

152

Bryant had been dozing. He woke with a start and the touch of her finger. 'What are you doing here? Are you mad?' he whispered.

'I could never be mad at you, Paul, not even for bringing that nosy copper with you to my home.'

'We would have been gone hours ago . . .'

'Are you sorry that you had to stay?'

'Did you plan this?'

'Did I plan Flick's death? No. And, for the record, I don't think you did either. It hit me, Paul, harder than you can imagine. I can't believe she's not here.'

'Neither can I,' he said. He felt the coolness of the silk against his naked skin as she slid into the bed next to him. The springs creaked as it sagged with the extra weight. Bloody hell, he thought. They'd not only wake the policewoman, but also the airmen in the workshop if she started something here. Catherine, he knew, was not only unconventional in bed, but also extremely noisy.

'I just want you to hold me tonight, Paul. That's all.'

'Of course,' he said. As he closed his eyes he felt the wetness of her cheek against his.

8

'May I use your telephone, Catherine?' Pip asked. It was the first thing any of them had said in fifteen minutes, aside from good morning as they sat down to breakfast on the sunlit paved verandah at the front of the house. The cook was busy in the kitchen making up bacon sand-wiches for the airmen and askaris.

'Of course, Pip. But I can't promise the silly thing will work. It's out for days at a time.'

'I'd like to try to call the police camp and explain my absence.'

'You're welcome to try,' Catherine said. 'It's in the living room on the big sideboard.'

Pip excused herself, having already wolfed down her bacon and eggs. She was grateful to get away from the silence around the table. She sensed as soon as she greeted them that both Catherine and Paul knew she had caught them at it. She found the telephone and picked it up. She was in luck. There was a dial tone.

'Bulawayo Police,' the female switch operator said after two rings.

'Shirley, it's Pip . . .'

'Bleeding hell, where are you? Hayes is doing his nut this morning. You'll be lucky to have a job after this, girl. Hope you've got a good excuse for not showing up.'

Shirley was another volunteer policewoman who had recently joined the SRWAPs. She and her husband had only immigrated to Rhodesia a year before the war began, and Shirley had not lost the accent and bluntness bred into her in London's East End. Pip knew Shirley tended to overdramatise most things but, even so, she had not expected to be in so much trouble so soon. It was barely half an hour after the time she should have reported for duty.

'Put me through to him, please, Shirley.'

'Lovejoy! Where in the name of God are you? I should have you charged, so help me,' Hayes barked down the line.

'Steady on, Sarge . . .'

'Sergeant! And don't tell me to steady on, my girl. I've got a dozen witness statements to get typed up and charges to file. You should jolly well be here to help me. Sometimes I wonder if any of you bloody females are serious about this job or whether you only joined for the blessed uniform!'

Still confused, she ignored the insults and asked: 'What's happened?'

'Peace at last,' Catherine said, as Pip departed to find the phone.

'She wasn't much of a conversationalist this morning, was she,' said Paul, echoing Catherine's sarcasm.

'You're thinking about last night, aren't you, Paul?'

He looked across the table, trying to read her eyes. 'Guilty.' He shook his head and grimaced. He had woken, about an hour before dawn, feeling very aroused. She'd had her hand on him, encircling him.

'I can't sleep,' she'd whispered. 'You were snoring too loud. I feel lonely, Paul.'

He'd rolled onto his side and caressed her cheek. 'There's no easy way to get through grief, no matter how many times it happens.' That wasn't entirely true, he thought. He knew that if you did your best not to get to know someone, you barely noticed their passing. That was how he and the older hands in the squadron had coped, by virtually ignoring the newcomers.

'I'm glad you're here, that you brought the news,' she said in the darkness. 'I need you, now.'

'I'm here.'

'I need all of you.'

'We'll wake her.'

She slid from the bed and walked to the dressing table, lit a candle, returned to the bedside and stood, facing him, as he propped himself up on one elbow. She unfastened the robe and let it slide to the floor. The mix of fading moonlight and the candle's flickering flame painted her body a lustrous white-gold. His arousal was complete. The sight of her full breasts, the tangle of dark hair beneath her belly, the desire in her eyes, left him speechless. She dropped silently to her knees and unthreaded the silk tie from the loops on her robe. Holding it out to him she saw the hesitation in his eyes and said: 'Humour me. Nice and tight, Paul.'

He'd taken the tie, thrown back the covers and slid to the end of the bed. She'd held out her hands, wrists together, and he had bound her to the bedpost.

'Are you ... all right?' he asked, leaning across the breakfast table to refill the delicate china cup on the breakfast table.

'No, Paul, I'm not. Flick's dead, remember?'

'That's not what I was talking about.'

'I know. And yes, I'm sure I'm just fine.'

He couldn't read her moods. They hadn't been intimate for that long. It was hard to know what was going through her mind, what she wanted from him. He suddenly felt tired of trying.

'Do you still want to see me, now that Flick's gone?' she asked, breaking the awkward silence. 'The parachuting displays are over from now on – I'll never find anyone as brave or as silly as she was. Will I still be allowed on base?'

'You'll always be welcome as a guest,' he said. 'As for us, I don't know.'

'You're not giving me the brush-off, are you, Paul?'

'No. But it's been . . . well, confusing for me.'

'Confusing? Are you ashamed of what happened, of what you did last night?'

Yes and no, he thought. 'It's not something I've had experience with, Catherine. My previous times were . . .'

'Boring?'

'Let's just say different.'

'You're not looking for love, are you, Paul? Not searching for a wife, I hope.'

'No. Not while there's a war on, at least.'

'Good, because I'm not available. God knows I've had enough suitors. People in town had the gall to call me a gold-digger when I married Hugo, but you should see some of the oily scoundrels who've tried to get their grubby hands on this pile,' she said, waving imperiously at the vista of rolling bush-covered hills in front of them.

'You're cold this morning, Catherine.'

'Call it my way of dealing with grief. I've lost one friend. I don't particularly want to lose another. Neither do I need a *confused* man in my life.'

'The funeral is on Saturday,' he said, not wanting to talk about relationships. 'You're right for fuel now?'

'Yes, thank you for that. I'll be staying in the town house.'

Catherine owned the bungalow in Hillside where Felicity had lived. Another white lie he'd told Pip Lovejoy was that he wasn't sure if Flick had resided in town or on base. At the time his initial reaction had been to protect Catherine's name.

They stopped talking and Paul lit a cigarette as the maid arrived to clear the table. When the African woman had gone, Catherine said, 'Will you be at the wings parade on Monday?'

'Yes, why?'

'I was wondering, what with the investigation into Flick's death and the missing Harvard. I thought you might be tied up with other things.'

'No. I'll be there. As the adjutant I'm probably escorting some politician or senior officer. How did you know about the missing aircraft?'

She sipped her tea, then said: 'I overheard two of the airmen at the *braai* last night. Seems the kite went down over the border. Is that right?'

'It'll be all over the newspaper in Bulawayo today. No great secret. We haven't found the Harvard, but the body of the pilot was found by some big-game hunters.'

'Oh dear. Did he die of thirst?'

'It looks like he may have been killed by some bushmen.'

She shook her head. 'Nasty business. How's poor Andy Cavendish doing? Have you packed him off to the army or some such other awful fate?'

'I can't talk about an ongoing investigation, especially not with you, Cath.'

'Don't get all secretive with me, Paul. Look, as I told you last week, I was terribly flattered that he chose my airstrip to crash-land on, but I most certainly did not invite him to fly up here.'

'I know. You've made that quite clear, as has he. He's sticking to his story about engine trouble. But I've got another question for you, about Cavendish's kite.'

'Good Lord, I feel like I'm in the Spanish inquisition, what with snoopy Constable Half-Pint and now you grilling me. If you want answers from me, Squadron Leader, you'll have to torture me.'

He raised an eyebrow and smiled. 'That could be arranged.'

'Dirty swine. All right. Out with it, what did I do now?'

'How are you off for ammunition up here, Cath?'

'What? Bullets?'

'Three-o-three calibre, to be exact.'

'Paul, dear, as you very well know, Hugo was a hunter and this is, or at least was until the war got underway, a hunting ranch. I've got about a dozen .303s and enough ammunition to defeat the Wehrmacht. If the air force is running short of bullets I'd be happy to lend you some.'

He ignored the jibe. 'There are about six hundred rounds missing from the two Browning machine-guns that came out of that crashed Harvard,' he said, gesturing with a thumb at the disassembled aircraft sitting on the Queen Mary aircraft trailer.

'Come with me, Squadron Leader, and I'll show you my armoury right now. I've no need of your paltry bullets and, frankly, I'm a bit offended by the suggestion I'd nick anything from your silly aeroplane.' She folded her arms and sat back in her chair, a frown on her face.

'Sorry, but I had to ask. Any ideas?'

'Bloody Africans, I'd expect. I wouldn't suspect my staff, but there may be some scallywags from the neighbouring tribal lands who've been going over the wreck at night. If so, I'll probably wear the consequences through some increased poaching on the ranch.'

He stubbed his cigarette out in the ashtray. He believed Catherine, and had felt awkward asking. What still confused him was why someone would leave a single belt of ammunition in each gun. If a poacher were going to go to the trouble of opening up the Harvard's wing access panel to steal some bullets, why not take them all? His train of thought was broken by the sound of footsteps from inside the house.

Pip Lovejoy walked back out onto the verandah and said: 'Good news, of sorts, though I'm in deep trouble for not getting back last night.'

'What is it?' Catherine asked, sitting up straight.

'The police have charged an African man with Felicity Langham's murder.'

Catherine closed her eyes and shook her head. 'Bastard.'

'I really do have to get back to the station,' Pip said. 'Appears it's all hands on deck down there today.'

'Of course,' Bryant said, rising from his chair. 'Catherine, thanks again for your hospitality.'

Pip looked at the pair of them and smirked inwardly. Pretending nothing was going on between them; she wondered why they were going to such lengths to hide their feelings for each other. 'Catherine, again, my condolences for the loss of your friend. And thank you for your patience yesterday when we chatted.'

'I understand. You have a duty to pursue every avenue in an investigation. It was nice to meet you, anyway, and

I hope they hang the man who took my friend away from me,' Catherine said. She extended a hand to shake Pip's and, as she did, the long sleeve of her white blouse rode up her arm a little.

Pip took her hand and immediately noticed an angry red welt that encircled the other woman's slender wrist. 'Oh dear, that looks nasty.'

Catherine withdrew her hand from Pip's and dropped her arm down by her side. 'Nothing to worry about. I had the horse's reins wrapped around it yesterday and he got a bit frisky. Gave me a bit of a burn, that's all.'

Pip thought back to their first meeting. Catherine had been wearing a short-sleeved blue blouse and, when they'd shaken hands, she'd mentally noted how beautifully manicured the wealthy woman's hands were. She was sure she would have noticed the injury then. She smiled and said, 'Goodbye.' Paul Bryant, she noticed, had already left the table and was calling to the airmen to finish their sandwiches and climb aboard the trucks.

Bryant walked away from her and the men and stopped to chat with Catherine's stable groom, who was brushing a coal-black mare. The man pointed down the road towards the gate to Isilwane Lodge. She got into the car and Bryant joined her. When they stopped at the thatched gatehouse, he reached into the back of the car and pulled a brown-paper package from his canvas haversack. 'Enoch

Ngwenya?' he called to the grey-haired man standing by the timber gate.

The man came slowly to a semblance of attention and saluted. 'Yes, sir?' he coughed.

Bryant greeted the man and asked after his health – all in near-fluent Ndebele. Pip was impressed. The Australian handed the old man the package, and the gate guard softly clapped his hands together around it, twice, in the traditional gesture of thanks.

'What was that all about?' she asked him.

'His son is a friend of mine. He's the teacher at the Kumalo African school. The old man has pleurisy. That's his medicine.'

As the convoy drove south, across the Gwaai River, Pip was thinking about the silk stocking that bound Felicity Langham's wrists when Paul said, 'You didn't finish telling me your life story.'

'Right,' she said. She wanted to get back to the police camp as soon as possible and find out about the man who had been charged. She was confused about Paul Bryant, and not entirely sure she wanted to reveal more of herself to him. This morning she was surprised and unnerved to find she felt slightly jealous that he had slept with Catherine De Beers. She wanted to ask him about the marks on Catherine's wrists, but there didn't seem to be a tactful way of raising the subject. 'Not much to tell, really.'

'You said you were studying to be a lawyer.'

'I was. I met my husband at university in Salisbury. He was a few years older than me, in his last year of study. He graduated and we got married.'

'Do you regret it? Not finishing your study?'

She saw no reason why she should tell him the truth so, instead, said: 'Not at all. I've been very happy.'

He was frustrated, especially now that someone had been charged with Flick's murder, that he had been so guarded with her in the beginning. She had obviously doubted him and now, as a result, she was holding back information. There was no trust between them, he thought.

Not that it mattered – as attractive as Pip was, she was a married woman, and therefore off limits as far as he was concerned. He imagined she would be out of his life once he dropped her off at the police camp. They drove on in silence. She apparently had no desire to get him talking today, which made him think her friendly demeanour the day before was a well-rehearsed act that she used to put interviewees – suspects, perhaps – at ease.

As they reached the outskirts of Bulawayo, the sun's rays were slanting in through the side windows of the Humber, making the car's interior oppressively hot. 'Looks like a fire,' Bryant said as he veered off the road and stopped. He pointed to a pall of smoke rising straight as a dark column through the windless sky.

'Could be,' she said. 'It's to the west of town. Looks like it's near Mzilikazi township.'

He got out of the car and flagged down the Dodge, which pulled to a halt. 'Carry on to Kumalo, Flight,' he said to the senior mechanic. 'I'll take Constable Lovejoy back to the police camp. Dismiss the men when you get back. You can unload the kite tomorrow.'

'Yes, sir.' The trucks rumbled past them, and Paul got in and started the car again. He drove Pip into town.

'Well, this is it, I suppose,' Bryant said as he stopped the car at the front gate of the police compound. 'I imagine you'll contact me if you need any more information.'

There was the squeal of rubber on tar as the driver of a police car parked in the yard dropped the clutch and sped out of the gates, his siren blaring. Pip watched the car leave and said: 'Yes, I will. Thanks again for your help, and for the lift.'

'My pleasure.'

Pip closed the car door and walked through the gates into a gathering storm.

'What's the flap about, Henderson?' Bryant asked the air force police sergeant as he stopped the Humber at the entry gate to Kumalo air base.

'Riot in town, sir. Wingco expected you back yesterday. He's fuming.'

'What riot?' Bryant let the admonition from the flight sergeant slide by.

'Hurry up and get in that bloody truck,' Henderson barked at an airman carrying a rifle. He thrust a pistol into the white holster on his belt and said to Bryant: 'The local coppers arrested a black man for the murder of Felicity Langham.'

'Yes, so I heard. But what's that got to do with a riot, and why are you armed?'

'There was trouble during the arrest. The police went in a bit hard from what I gather. The chap they were after tried to make a run for it, and some of his mates got in the way of the law.'

'How does that involve us?'

'There were a bunch of our trainees and some erks sightseeing and shopping in town. They got wind of what was going on and tried to help the police out. There've been running street fights in town since this morning. Apparently, some of our men have been seeking revenge for the deaths of Langham and Smythe.'

'So, word's out already about the missing pilot?'

Henderson reached into the cab of the truck his men were clambering into. 'Only the bleedin' front page, *sir*.'

Bryant snatched the newspaper from Henderson. He

didn't need to read past the headline. *BLACKS INVOLVED IN MURDERS OF AIR FORCE MAN AND WOMAN.* 'Bloody hell.'

'That's what they say it's like in town. Wingco wants to see you. The police have called on us to reinforce them and to pick up our men.'

'I'm coming with you,' Bryant said. He knew Henderson's style. The man was a bully and Bryant was sure he was itching to join the fight rather than just arrest trouble-makers. He felt that he needed to be there to exercise some control. He was sure the Wingco would have ordered him out anyway. The explanations could come later.

'Jones,' Henderson barked. 'Fetch the squadron leader a pistol and ammunition from the armoury. Hop to it, man!'

The airman returned a few minutes later and handed Bryant a Webley revolver, a box of ammunition and a canvas holster and webbing belt. Bryant climbed into the open rear of the truck with eight askaris, three white noncommissioned officers and a couple of white airmen, mechanics who had been dragooned into service by Henderson as ad hoc riot troops. Bryant realised none of them had been trained for the mission they were setting out on. Reluctantly, he banged on the roof of the cab. 'Right, Flight S'arnt Henderson, let's get weaving!'

The vehicle lurched out the gate, throwing Bryant onto a wide-eyed African askari. He steadied himself against the side of the truck and loaded six bullets into the revolver. 'Listen to me,' he ordered the men around him as he snapped the pistol closed. 'No one, and I mean absolutely no one, fires his weapon without a direct order from *me* and me only. Understand?'

There were a few nods.

'Understand!' he bellowed in his best parade-ground voice.

'Yes, sir!' they yelled back in unison.

'Better. Now, if we go in there boots and all, we'll only inflame the situation further. Our mission is to pick up our fellow airmen – in handcuffs if they won't come quietly – then leave this mess to the police. Understood?'

'Yes, sir!'

The truck raced into town on the Salisbury Road, then weaved through city streets that were emptier than usual. Bryant guessed the smarter citizens of Bulawayo had locked themselves indoors. As they rounded a corner, onto the Sixth Avenue extension, and entered the outskirts of Mzilikazi, his worst fears were confirmed.

A line of BSAP officers stood blocking the road, shoulder to shoulder. Some carried small round riot shields. All had their batons drawn. Behind the twenty officers forming the cordon were another dozen carrying Lee-Enfield .303 rifles. The armed men held their weapons at the ready, butts in their shoulders.

Ahead of the police line a roughly equal number of young black and white men, a total of about sixty, Bryant guessed, were engaged in a series of melees. Some carried broken chair legs or other improvised weapons. Bryant saw a European wipe a bloody cheek with the back of his forearm. Two other white men were laying into a prone black youth with lumps of wood. Elsewhere, an African held an airman's arms behind his back while another punched him in the stomach.

A stray dog barked at the fighting men and an African woman wailed from the footpath, adding to the din of shouted curses and the thud of feet and fists on flesh. Another woman snatched up a small boy who had lingered to watch the fracas and ran off with him bouncing on her hip. The smoke Bryant had first seen was from a burning car. The road around the Studebaker was scorched black and the vehicle itself now was no more than a smoking, charred hulk.

Bryant saw that some of the policemen were also bleeding. It appeared they had regrouped and were about to charge into the crowd again. Henderson drew a loud-hailer from the front of the truck.

'Give that to me,' Bryant ordered. Henderson surrendered the instrument to him, and Bryant strode up to the police line.

'Who's in charge here?' he barked.

'I am, Squadron Leader.'

He turned and saw the rotund Harold Hayes standing behind him, truncheon in hand. 'You're a busy man. I heard you'd arrested a suspect,' Bryant said.

'I have. Get your men to form a line behind my armed officers. They'll be needed as back-up in case we have to open fire. I'll give the order when required.'

'Like hell, you will,' Bryant said. 'It's sixty-odd blokes having a punch-up. They'll settle eventually. We should just contain them and go in when they run out of steam.'

'You trying to tell me how to do my job now? It's your young fools who've caused this riot.'

'Way I heard it, Sergeant, was that some of our lads came to help yours after they ballsed up the arrest this morning.'

Hayes snorted. 'Well, they're the ones out of control now. Bloody foreigners acting like vigilantes on my patch. I'll arrest the lot of them.'

'A second ago you were considering shooting them.' Bryant looked up and down the police line and noticed, for the first time, two women standing just behind the front rank of men, between them and the constables armed with rifles. The women wore Red Cross armbands on their uniforms and carried bulky canvas first-aid satchels slung across their bodies. He saw one of them was Pip Lovejoy. He gave her a quick smile when he saw her looking at him, but she quickly turned away and stared resolutely back up the street towards the rioters.

The sound of shattering glass made them all look up the street. Two of the airmen had chased an African man into a barber shop and he had closed the door behind him. One of the whites had hurled a bin lid through the plate glass window. The black man appeared at the window, brandishing a cut-throat razor. The Europeans stayed outside, facing him down.

'This is about to turn nasty,' Hayes said. He lifted his own loudhailer and said into it, 'This is the police. You there, in the barber shop. Drop that razor or we will open fire!'

The whites looked at the policemen, but held their ground. 'Shoot the bastard!' one of them yelled in an Australian accent.

'Constable Grant, three paces forward!' Hayes shouted. A young uniformed policeman from the second line advanced to the cordon.

Pip Lovejoy made way for Grant, who elbowed his way through the front rank and brought his rifle up to the firing position. 'Oh, God,' she said.

'Load!' Hayes screamed. 'Drop that razor or we *will* fire.'

The African man looked over his shoulder, apparently searching for a way out. There was none. Bryant sensed the man's thoughts. If he dropped the razor the two white airmen would be on top of him before the police could arrive. If he did nothing, he would be shot.

'On my command, Grant, two rounds, rapid fire, at the man with the razor! Aim!'

'Shit,' Bryant said. He pushed past Hayes, stepped between two of the armed police officers, then, before Hayes saw what was going on, said to Pip Lovejoy: 'Excuse me, Constable.'

'Stop that man!' Hayes roared, red faced. Several members of the police line looked back at him as Bryant pushed his way through the front rank, which closed behind him. To move out to stop the air force officer would weaken the cordon and create an opening for the rioters. Also, the squadron leader was armed, having drawn his service revolver.

'Careful,' Pip called to him. 'Do you know what you're doing?'

He turned and gave her a smile and wink. 'No bloody idea.'

Bryant crossed the fifty yards of empty street that divided the police and fighting men. A few of them, those of both colour not immediately trading punches, turned and eyed him. He stopped, twenty feet from a white man who was standing over a prone black man, kicking him.

'Carmichael, isn't it?' he said quietly, just loudly enough for the man to hear.

The big Ulsterman, a trainee pilot, paused mid-kick and looked at him. His eyes were wide with the rage of the fight. 'These fookers killed our people.'

'Sir,' Bryant said quietly, but forcefully.

Carmichael turned away from the African, squared up for a second, but then looked into Bryant's eyes. 'Sir,' he said at last.

'That's better. The police have arrested one man for Langham's murder. Smythe's death remains the subject of an investigation. Get back behind that police rank now, or I swear you'll sit this war out as a shithouse cleaner in the hottest, driest part of Arabia I can think of – that's if you survive two tours over Germany as a rear gunner first.'

The Irishman looked down at the barely conscious youth and then back at his superior officer. For a moment defiance flashed in his eyes, as he stood there, fists clenched.

Then Bryant pulled the trigger. He fired two shots, into the air. The police line instinctively advanced a pace.

The individual fights halted, some in mid-punch, and several of the African men involved took their cue to run off down the street. The man who had brandished the razor, seeing his two white opponents staring at the madman with the pistol, hopped through the gap where the barber shop window had been, then ducked around the corner into an alleyway.

'Trainees and members of the Rhodesian Air Training Group, fall in behind the police. Now!' Bryant barked.

Enraged as they were, each of the airmen and trainee aircrew on the street knew that Paul Bryant could hurt them far more than any civvie policeman. At his word their worlds would change, for the worse. In spite of his orders, a few last blows were landed, but the remaining Africans took flight, one by one.

'Henderson!' Bryant called, not looking back but still staring the huge Irishman in the face.

'Sah!'

'Escort this fucking rabble back onto the truck.'

'Yes, sir. Right, escorts, move forward, at the double now! You heard the good squadron leader.' Henderson led the airmen through the police rank and each man paired off with one of the troublemakers.

Bryant turned and walked back towards the police cordon. He holstered his revolver and kept his hands by his side, hoping the shaking would not show.

'Well done,' Pip Lovejoy said as he walked past her again.

He paused and looked at her, noticing, for the first time, the bruise on her left cheek. 'Who did that to you?'

'One of your blokes. Funny way of seeking vengeance for the death of a woman, hitting another one.'

'Which one?' he asked.

'Don't know. All those Pommies look alike to me,' she said, forcing a painful smile.

'If you pick him out, let me know. He's history.'

'Don't go acting like a vigilante now because some hothead landed a blow on me. I've had worse and, besides, it's part of my job. It'll be up to us to lay charges, but I'd be more worried about some of those African lads who just got clapped for no other reason than their colour.' She paused, then added quietly: 'You just showed incredible leadership, Paul.'

He didn't know how to react to a compliment from her. 'They're airmen. They're used to following orders. It's why we put them through all that drill on the parade ground. You'll tell me if there are charges to be laid against any of them, won't you?'

'*No*, Squadron Leader, *I* will tell you if there are charges to be laid,' Hayes said as he strode towards Bryant. 'Get back in line, Lovejoy. We're going to sweep down the street to see if there are any other troublemakers to pick up.'

Bryant turned on his heel and walked towards the truck. When he looked over his shoulder, one last time to make sure all his men were accounted for, he saw Pip

Lovejoy turn away quickly. He wondered if she had been watching him go. He smiled to himself.

From his hiding place on the tin roof of an Indian tailor's shop, behind the masonry facade that bore the date of the building's construction, 1914, Kenneth Ngwenya watched his friend Paul Bryant elbow his way back through the police line and down the street to the air force lorry.

He and the others had initially thought that the police had been after them, but it soon became clear, from snatched reports, that the cops were looking for just one man – Innocent Nkomo – rather than the assembled members of the African National Congress and the Railway Workers' Union.

There had been no political trouble between the blacks and the whites in Bulawayo during the war years, and Kenneth had hoped things would stay that way. However, some of the far-left members of the union had mumbled about strikes and armed struggle, in virtually the same breath, at every monthly meeting. They were hungry for action and progress, and Kenneth could understand that, even if he disagreed with them. They argued that with so many white men away at the war, there had never been a better time for the workers to flex their collective muscles. Their reasoning, which Kenneth thought dangerously flawed, was that they could cripple the railways – and with that paralyse the whole country – with a general strike to gain better conditions for workers and to push for the vote for Rhodesian Africans. The unions thought they had the upper hand. Kenneth reasoned, passionately, that a country at war would not hesitate to use the police and the army to crush a strike by native workers.

A stocky itinerant Matabele carpenter, a member of Kenneth's own party, who taught woodworking classes at the Kumalo base school when he was in town, had been swayed by the unionists at today's meeting. The man, whose name was Joshua, had railed: 'If they turn guns on us, then we will turn guns on them. We have fought them before and we can fight them again. This time we will win!' Kenneth regularly cycled past the monument in Main Street to the two-hundred and fifty-nine white pioneers killed by his people nearly fifty years earlier during what had become known as the Matabele Rebellion. The old Gardner machine-gun atop the memorial's column was a stark reminder not only of the European blood spilt, by firebrand predecessors of Joshua's ilk, but also of the many more Africans killed by Rhodes' men and their guns. It would take a lot to convince Kenneth that death and destruction were a better alternative than education, passive resistance and, once the war was over, well-organised strikes.

Rhodes himself still looked down over Bulawayo, from his plinth on Main Street. The statue of the country's founder was, to Kenneth, a constant reminder of the oppression his people chafed under every day. However, much had changed since the pioneer column had entered the lands of the Shona and the Matabele a mere fifty years earlier. Rhodesia was part of the Commonwealth now, with an elected parliament – albeit all white – and not simply a money-making outpost of the British South Africa Company. The foundations of democracy had been established in this part of Africa. Kenneth was not opposed to the British system of government the colony had inherited – he just wanted to be part of it.

The screeching of police whistles brought his attention back to the streetscape in front of him. The bravado had vanished and base instincts of self-preservation had overtaken the firebrands. Big Joshua had lumbered into a back alley with two equally brawny railway stokers. God help any stray white who got in their way. Kenneth had used his mind rather than his heart to assess the situation. The police would probably have already positioned men behind the building. He'd followed Joshua out the back door, knocking over a tailor's dummy in the process, and leaped up onto a garbage can, then grabbed the guttering and hoisted himself up onto the roof, unseen.

The riot was over now. The police were marching down the empty street looking for stragglers, and Kenneth's heart was still pounding. While he and his comrades were not the law's quarry this day, the mere fact that they had met to discuss politics made them criminals. Innocent Nkomo, however, was somewhere in police custody. Kenneth had mixed feelings about that fact. The man was a criminal – his reputation was legendary in the townships – but he was surprised the sharply dressed scoundrel had been the target of a full-scale police manhunt, which had degenerated into a melee once the Kumalo airmen had joined in the fight. He could only presume, from the ferocity displayed by the white air force trainees and the police's heavy-handed methods, that Nkomo had been arrested for the white woman's murder.

Kenneth sighed and put his hand on his heart to still his fear. Innocent or guilty, yet another black man was probably going to hang.

9

Bryant sucked in a deep breath and knocked on the door just below the gold-embossed, engraved nameplate that said, *Wing Commander Rogers, DFC – Commanding Officer.*

'Come.'

'Morning, sir,' Bryant said.

'I'm glad you didn't preface that with, "good", Bryant.'

Bryant sighed inaudibly. This was going to be like his last trip to the base dentist. Long, painful and bloody. The Wingco always reminded him of a vulture – bald, hook-beaked, hunched and nasty. The man had a fierce and richly deserved reputation for intolerance of stuff-ups. The last two weeks had been full of them.

'Tell me about our latest casualty . . .' Rogers consulted a file on his desk. 'What's his name . . . ah, yes, Smythe. What's happening about catching the bushmen who killed him?'

'It's in the hands of the police in Bechuanaland.

They're sending out patrols to the known tribal areas.'

'They haven't a chance in hell of catching those bloody bushmen,' Rogers pronounced.

'We put up two flights of three aircraft yesterday to search the area where Smythe was found, but there was no sign of the downed kite. We've still no idea why he didn't stay with it.'

'It's a big, wide expanse of nothing out there on the saltpans. However, I'd have thought that if we had a location for where Smythe's body was found, the kite would have been relatively nearby.'

'I agree, sir. The game hunters who found him knew the area and were able to give us a pretty good fix.' Bryant checked the manila folder he'd carried in and found some notes made by the search party. 'Pilot Officer Wilson reported seeing tyre tracks made by the hunters' vehicle from the air, the only marks on the surface for miles, so they had the right spot.'

'Maybe he had a problem, got jumpy and bailed out. Perhaps his kite flew on and crashed further away?'

'I told the search party to look for chutes and clothing, but they found nothing.'

'Perhaps those bloody bushmen stole his clothes and parachute. I don't like having a kite missing, Bryant. Crashed is bad enough, but missing is, well, untidy.'

'Yes, sir.'

'Keep up the search.'

'Yes, sir.'

'Next.' The Wingco rested his elbows on the desk and steepled his fingertips together. 'Langham's murder investigation ... what's the gen from the police?'

'I phoned them this morning,' Bryant said, recounting his conversation with Pip Lovejoy. 'They arrested an African bloke yesterday, as you know. Apparently, they had an anonymous tip-off that he'd been seen with a white woman the night of Langham's death. They think he's also a major player in the black market in town – fuel, mostly. He tried to run for it when the coppers came for him. A police car went around the block to head him off and ran over an eleven-year-old black girl. She's alive, with a broken leg. A crowd gathered at the accident scene and a few hotheads started to get in the way of the arresting police – that's what sparked the fighting in the street, and our lads joined in. When the police searched the suspect man's car, they found some of Langham's personal papers and effects in the boot.'

'Pretty damning evidence.'

Bryant nodded. 'So it seems.'

'Now, tell me why you took nearly two days to investigate the crash up at Wankie and, of more relevance, why you chose to go there in person, given the events of the last couple of days.'

Bryant glanced at the row of medal ribbons on the Rhodesian-born, former fighter pilot's left breast. He was a veteran of the first war, with twelve kills to his credit. Bryant wondered at what point the presumably once dashing, rakish colonial airman had become an overbearing chair-bound bore. 'I'd arranged to conduct the investigation and pick up the kite several days ago, sir. Mrs De Beers was expecting us.'

'You could have telephoned her.'

'The line was out. Besides, as it turned out, she had to be informed about Felicity Langham's death. You're aware a police constable came with us?'

'Mmm. And not happy about it. The air force's schedules are not dictated by the whims of women, Bryant, not police constables nor attractive widows. Do I make myself clear?'

'Yes, sir,' Bryant said wearily.

'What's the upshot of your investigation into the crash at the De Beers place?'

'Cavendish – the Canadian pilot – said he hit a hole on landing, and that much is true.'

'What was he doing up there in the first place? Wasn't he supposed to be on a gunnery exercise?'

'Yes, sir. He claims he had engine trouble, lost his way and had to make a forced landing at the first strip he could find.'

'A catalogue of errors. More likely the widow De Beers flashed her smile – or something else – at him in the mess and invited him to drop around for tea, or something else, eh?'

Bryant had his own suspicions about Cavendish, very much along the same lines, but it annoyed him to hear the Wingco's innuendo-laden summation. 'He's sticking to his story and she says she never invited him to drop in.'

'I might have been tempted to show him some leniency if the silly bastard had told the truth. I hate liars, Bryant, even more than stupid love-struck pilots. Make that known to him and charge him.'

Bryant decided to hold off mentioning the ammunition missing from Cavendish's aircraft until he'd had a chance to question the soon-to-be-ex-pilot. 'There's the matter of yesterday's riot, too, sir.'

'How many of our chaps involved?'

'Twenty-four, sir. Eleven of them are sporting injuries of some sort from the fights they got themselves into. Bunch of idiots.'

'Understandable, though. Can't have the blacks rising up against the police, Bryant. Can't blame our fellows for siding with the law.'

'With respect, sir, our blokes kept the fight going long after the danger to the police had passed. They were pissed off about Smythe and Langham and wanted to take it out on the first black faces they saw. That's not siding with the law.'

'I'm not interested in your views on the law in *my* country, Bryant. Charge the lot of them with conduct to the prejudice of good order. I'll let them off with a severe reprimand when they come before me. I'll have a word with the police and make sure they don't go pursuing any criminal charges.'

'Yes, sir,' Bryant said. He thought it a pathetic punishment for the unchecked actions of the airmen. He, too, could understand their anger and frustration at the apparent murders of two colleagues, but he reckoned the riot was more about latent racism than any high-minded notions of justice.

'Now, I've something for you, Bryant.'

'Yes, sir?' He was relieved. The grilling had not been as bad as he had feared.

'Ossewa Brandwag. The OB are in the news again. HQ's sent us a signal telling us to be "vigilant". There's a possibility they may try to derail the Empire Air Training Scheme in some way.'

'I read in the newspaper the other day that the South Africans had arrested an Afrikaner OB agent who'd been trained by the Germans. I mentioned the possible threat to the policeman in charge of the Langham investigation.

He laughed it off, said they'd no support in Rhodesia.'

'We've got our fair share of Afrikaners living up here in Rhodesia. They're good people, the Boers, but they're good fighters, too. That fellow you read about in the newspapers, Willem Siewert, is facing the noose in South Africa. According to HQ, he's told the authorities down there that there was another man sent over with him.' Rogers read from an intelligence report on his desk. 'They were landed by U-boat on the Skeleton Coast, in South West Africa. One headed south, to Cape Town – that was Siewert, the one who was arrested. He says the other man headed north-east, into the Namib Desert, but claims he wasn't informed about his destination or mission.'

'I suppose that makes sense,' Bryant said, 'that they'd compartmentalise their information.'

'What we do have is a name, though, which is something to go on.' The wing commander pushed a piece of paper across the leather top of his mahogany desk.

Bryant did his best to ignore the giraffe's-tail fly whisk on the desktop – a colonial affectation of his commander's – and took up the paper.

'Hendrick Reitz. Born 1901, Barberton, Eastern Transvaal, South Africa, son of a prominent Boer commander. Mother was German apparently. Interesting. He studied at Stellenbosch University. Graduated with a degree in science – majoring in chemistry. Joined the

South African Department of Agriculture in 1927. Doesn't sound like a trained killer to me.'

'Read on,' Rogers said.

'Ah, completed postgraduate studies and a Masters degree in Berlin, 1934 to '35. Not heard of since then.'

'Only thing worse than a right-wing fanatic is an intelligent right-wing fanatic,' Rogers said.

Bryant had to agree with his superior on that count. 'If he was last seen heading "north-east" he could be coming our way.' Bryant continued reading the intelligence summary. 'This is interesting. Worked for a chemical farming supplies company in Salisbury, Rhodesia, in between leaving the agriculture department and his first trip to Germany.'

'He knows this country,' Rogers said, nodding. 'If he gets through South West Africa and across Bechuanaland, he could enter Rhodesia anywhere between Victoria Falls and Beitbridge.'

Bryant could see where Rogers was heading. He looked up at the map of Southern Rhodesia on the wing commander's wall, then stood and walked to it. 'Victoria Falls in the north, and Beitbridge in the south. Nothing of military value in either of those towns, but Bulawayo . . .' He traced his finger to the town, a key concentration of airfields and training facilities in the Empire Air Training Scheme. If Reitz were planning on attacking the scheme, he could hit one or more bases around Bulawayo and then easily melt back across the border into the vast emptiness of Bechuanaland.

'That's right. The OB have been getting cocky down south again, robbing banks, stealing firearms and explosives, disrupting the railways. We have to face the fact that we could be the next target. There's something else came through in the intelligence reports you should know about.' Rogers handed Bryant another piece of paper.

Bryant scanned the report. A Royal Air Force corporal based at Induna air base on the other side of Bulawayo had been robbed of his service uniform while on leave in Pretoria, South Africa. It seemed only the man's pride had been hurt. The thieves were white South Africans.

Rogers spoke up. 'I know our chaps on the gate do a good job, but it mightn't be hard for a white man in uniform to get past them with the proper identity card.'

'I'll brief the askari commanders and have the roving patrols doubled until further notice, sir,' Bryant said.

'Good man. Carry on.'

Pip Lovejoy sat in the corner of the whitewashed interview room at the police camp, taking notes and breathing through her mouth to avoid the strong smells of urine and sweat.

The man sitting across the table from Hayes was in

terrible shape. His left eye was so bruised and swollen she was sure he couldn't see out of it. His lip was split and crusted with dried blood. When he opened his mouth to speak she noticed a raw hole where one of his teeth had been knocked out. His open-necked white shirt was stained dark red and, when he'd walked in, wrists manacled, she'd seen the embarrassing stain on his trousers where he had wet himself. Pip hardly recognised the smartly dressed, somewhat cocky man she had interviewed at the crime scene where Felicity Langham's body was discovered. She was shocked at his condition, but reminded herself that given the evidence at hand, this man had brutally raped and murdered an innocent young woman.

'Look at me when you answer me, you lying black bastard,' Hayes said.

Pip winced as Hayes pounded the wooden table to emphasise his command.

'Now, I put it to you again that you abducted, raped and then murdered Miss Felicity Langham last Monday night or in the early hours of Tuesday morning.'

'No,' the man croaked.

'You're going to hang, you know. The way you do your time between now and then can be very much influenced by how much you cooperate with us. It can be easy . . . or it can be like last night,' Hayes said.

Pip had assumed the suspect, the ironically named

Innocent, had received his injuries during his arrest the day before. However, from Hayes' last comment, and other oblique references he had made during the interview, she now understood Nkomo had been beaten while in the cells. The thought sickened her. She supported the death penalty, and was certainly not in favour of going soft on rapists, but she believed in the due processes of the law: that people were innocent until proven guilty. Had she been Nkomo's lawyer, she would have seen Hayes charged for his violent bullying.

'I never saw this woman alive,' Nkomo protested.

'Liar! We know you were at the scene of the crime. Constable Lovejoy here spoke to you, remember?'

The prisoner cocked his head and squinted at Pip with his one good eye. 'Yes. I do not deny I was there.'

Pip looked away. She had told Hayes, on reading the accused man's name, and peering through the small hatch in his cell door, that she had spoken briefly to Nkomo on the night they had found Felicity's body.

'It's well known that an offender – a *sexual* offender – will sometimes loiter at the scene of the crime, continuing to gain some kind of sick thrill when the victim is discovered. That's you, isn't it, Nkomo? A sick . . . fucking . . . pervert.'

Pip shuddered. She was rapidly getting used to profanity, working in the police station, but Hayes seemed to be doing his best today not only to work over the suspect, but to shock her.

'Why didn't you ejaculate inside her, Nkomo? Not man enough?'

Pip took a deep breath and glanced down at her notebook. She wasn't sure how much of this was supposed to go into the official record of interview, but she also wasn't game to interrupt Hayes mid-interview. She looked across at Nkomo's face. He seemed, through the horrible mask of injuries on his face, genuinely to be confused by the last question. 'What?'

'You raped her, but you couldn't finish off, could you? You're weak, aren't you? I'm surprised you could even get it up.'

'I'm sorry,' Nkomo coughed, looking up with beseeching eyes. 'Please, Sergeant, *sah*, I don't know what this is about.'

'We found these in your car,' Hayes said, holding up two documents. 'Constable, let the record reflect that I am showing the accused the air force identity card and driver's licence of Miss Felicity Langham.'

Pip wrote that down, relieved she could note something remotely relevant and printable. No amount of confusion or protestation of innocence on the part of Innocent Nkomo could change the fact that he had Felicity's personal papers in the boot of his car. And something else. Something worse.

'And, Constable, let the record show I am holding a pair of female underpants up for identification. Who do these belong to, Nkomo?'

'I . . . have . . . no . . . idea.'

Hayes grasped the edge of the table, stood and, in one violent, ear-splitting movement, up-ended it into Nkomo's face, knocking him to the floor. The African sprawled on his back. A policeman who had been standing by the door moved towards the fallen man. 'Stay where you are, Constable,' Hayes barked. He stood over Nkomo and swung his foot hard into the black man's ribs. Nkomo groaned and coughed blood.

'Sergeant!' Pip stood, hands on hips. She realised Hayes' anger was blinding him. Nkomo was either a very good actor or he genuinely had no idea what the sergeant was talking about. If Hayes continued in this way the suspect might die under questioning.

He shot her a look of anger, mixed with contempt. 'If you haven't the stomach for this interview, Constable Lovejoy, we'll understand if you want to go powder your nose.'

That did it. She strode across to where Nkomo lay. He was a big man, tall, handsome and muscled, maybe thirty years old. She reached down and grabbed the chain linking the wrist cuffs. She leaned back and hauled him to his feet. Hayes stood to one side, mouth agape, apparently so surprised by her actions he was incapable of moving. 'How did Miss Langham's things get in your car, Mr Nkomo?' she asked.

'You heard me tell the sergeant before. I do not know how those things got in my car, and that is the truth. I swear to God. Someone has put them there. I did not kill this woman!'

'Can you possibly imagine what it's like to be raped, Mr Nkomo?' she asked in a quiet voice. Hayes opened his mouth to speak, but seemed to think better of it and remained silent as Pip righted the desk and chair and motioned Nkomo to sit. The African man sat and shook his head.

She stood behind and slightly to one side of the prisoner. 'The violation, the degradation, of having someone use your body without consent.'

'I did not . . .'

'The evidence speaks otherwise, Mr Nkomo. Do you know that a man can be raped?' He turned his head to the side and looked up at her. 'You've never been to gaol, have you?'

'No. I am innocent. Like my name.'

'Yes, very nice, I'm sure your mother was a good judge of character. You'll find out, you know, what it's like to be raped,' she said, matter-of-factly.

'I did not kill this woman!' Nkomo shouted.

Pip leaned down until her face was a few inches from his. 'Don't think you can raise your voice to me because I'm a woman. I'm capable of doing you as much harm as Sergeant Hayes, but in other ways.'

Hayes stood in the shadow, arms folded, beyond the circle of light cast by the single bare light bulb hanging in the interview room.

'I'm not talking about your guilt, or otherwise, of the rape or murder of Felicity Langham, Nkomo.'

He looked back over his shoulder. The angle was awkward, and he had to strain to see her face. 'What do you mean?'

'When you were arrested you had a hundred pounds, a fortune in cash, in your pocket. New suit, new shoes, a motor car. Most of us can barely afford to keep a motor car these days, and we can never find the petrol for one. Yet, according to my notes, Mr Nkomo, you had three forty-four gallon drums of petrol in a back room of the house where you live.'

'That was all bought legally—' he began.

'Shut up, Mr Nkomo. There's a war on, you know. Lots of things, like petrol, are rationed. Some people, some magistrates, for example, would put black marketeering during wartime up there with murder. You're going to gaol, Mr Nkomo, for possession of stolen goods.'

'You can't prove that.'

'Oh yes, I can. And you know it. How long do you think it would take me, if I asked a few questions in your neighbourhood, made a few well-placed threats, to get one of your neighbours to roll over on you? People are jealous of wealth, Mr Nkomo, whether ill-gotten or legally earned. Maybe we'll just sit in your house and wait for someone to come knocking at your door looking for petrol, or whatever else you've been peddling. And you, Mr Nkomo, will end up in gaol.'

He shrugged his shoulders. 'What has this got to do with the charges against me?'

'Everything. If we can't put you away for murder – though we've probably got enough evidence to convict you right here,' she said, pointing to the documents and undergarments, which she had arranged back on the table, 'we can lock you up for your other illegal activities, and that's a fact'.

'I am innocent. *Innocent* Nkomo!'

'So you say. After we've put you away for trading on the black market, after we pack you off to gaol, we can have a few quiet words in the ears of the prison warders.'

'What do you mean?'

'I'm sure your fellow inmates would be interested to learn how you cooperated with the police, how you sold out dozens of your contacts, how you've been working as a paid police informer for years.'

A look of horror passed over his face. 'But that is not true.'

'Men get lonely in gaol, so I've heard,' Pip said.

'Why are you doing this to me? I am innocent.' There was a sob in his deep voice now.

'Men have urges, needs, as I'm sure you're well aware. Rape can take many forms in a prison. Some men may decide to have sex with you for pleasure. More likely they will use it as a means to punish you, as a police informer.'

Behind Nkomo's back, Pip glanced across at Hayes, still standing in the gloom. She saw the whites of his teeth, bared in a leering smile, and his slight nod of encouragement. God, she thought, he's almost proud of me now. Is this how I have to act to be accepted as a police officer? She almost felt ashamed. She hated resorting to such disgusting tactics to make a man talk – even to threaten perjuring herself went completely against her own morals. However, it seemed the only other way of getting a confession out of a suspect, according to the Hayes interrogation manual, was with bare fists, or maybe more.

Nkomo coughed, clearing his throat. 'I am not an informer, but if I tell you what I was doing on the night it happened, what will happen to me? If I have done something illegal, you will still send me to gaol.'

'That very much depends on what you were doing,' she said.

'Will I go to gaol, really, for selling black-market petrol?'

'If that's all you were doing, there's a chance, a reasonable chance, you might get off with a fine.'

'The people who buy petrol from me, they are not only African people.'

'Not surprising. I don't see many Africans driving their own cars,' Pip said. 'What do you want to tell me, Mr Nkomo?'

'The sergeant asked what I was doing between midnight and two-thirty in the morning, the night the woman died.'

'Yes, that's right,' Pip said. Another pair of police officers had found the house where Felicity lived – it turned out it was owned by her friend, Catherine De Beers – and interviewed the neighbours on either side. One, an elderly woman, a busybody, Pip gathered, had noted that Felicity Langham had left her home at midnight. The woman had heard, but not seen a car drive away. Felicity's body had been found by a shebeen barman taking out the garbage to the alley behind his pub at two-thirty in the morning. It was a pretty narrow window for the murder to have been committed. 'You told Sergeant Hayes earlier that you were at your home between midnight and just before we saw you at the crime scene, but you hadn't adequately explained why you suddenly decided to go out drinking in the early hours of the morning. Are you changing your story now, Mr Nkomo?'

'I am innocent of attacking this woman. I was not at home, though, that night.'

'Bastard's been lying to us all night. Why should he tell the truth now?' Hayes said from the shadows.

Pip shot her superior an annoyed look and he shrugged, apparently allowing her to continue. 'The relevant information for us . . . for you, Mr Nkomo, is whether or not there are people who can corroborate your story.'

Nkomo lifted his manacled hands and put his elbows on the table. He lowered his forehead and wiped his sweating brow. 'There *are* people who saw me that night, but I do not know if they will speak for me.'

'You can leave that part to us. We want the names of *everyone* you spent time with that night; from dusk until dawn should do it,' Pip said.

Nkomo looked up at her, his swollen eyes wet with tears. 'Some of them I don't know their names.'

'What about for the time in question, midnight to two-thirty?'

Nkomo closed his eyes and thought for a moment. 'Yes, no problem. I have the names of the people I met at that time. There were three of them. I know because they are regular customers.'

'Customers, my arse! He'll just give us a list of his bloody mates, and they'll say whatever he wants them to say,' Hayes scoffed.

Nkomo looked up at him. 'I think you will be surprised, Sergeant, at who I do business with in the middle of the night.'

The RAF Kumalo pipe band played 'God Save the King' out on the parade ground, the pipers and drummers barely visible through the shimmering curtain of heat haze that rose from the baking Tarmac.

Poor bastards, Bryant thought as he stood at the window in his office. As well as the band's rehearsal, the three classes of trainee pilots who would soon graduate were practising marching on and off. The trainees' drill had to be as good as – or better than – their flying, given the bigwigs who would be attending their parade. They would be sweating like pigs, but not for the same reason as the man in front of him.

Bryant turned back from the window and looked him up and down. The young man's back was straight, his eyes staring straight ahead, but he was nervous.

'Relax, Cavendish, I'm not going to hit you. Cigarette?' He offered the Canadian his packet.

'Sure. I mean, yes, thank you, sir,' the younger man said, taking a cigarette.

Bryant lit it for him, then returned to his chair. He sat back as he smoked his own. 'I've read your statement, Andy.'

'Yes, sir.'

'And you know what?'

'No, sir, what?' There was a note of defiance in his voice.

'I think it's bullshit.'

'I had engine trouble, sir, and—'

'The erks pulled your kite apart this morning. Apart from a bent prop, they found absolutely nothing wrong with that engine. The flight sergeant in charge told me he'd be prepared to put it in another Harvard today and accompany the pilot on a flight test. What do you think about that?'

'I know what I saw.'

'Oh, yes,' Bryant said, looking down at the typed statement in front of him. 'Low oil pressure.'

'Maybe it was the gauge?'

'Nice try, Andy. The mechanics tested the gauges, all of them. No faults there. Why are you lying to me?'

'Sir, I am not.'

'Son – yes, you bloody well are. And I'll tell you the God's honest truth – and this is for your own benefit – the Wingco told me himself he hates liars worse than stupid pilots. His own words, Andy, not mine.'

'All I know is that I had signs of engine trouble . . .'

'*Signs*, Andy?' Bryant kept his voice calm, soft even. 'Don't kid a kidder, mate. I was back-squaded to bombers for a stunt almost as stupid as yours. At least I had the guts to admit that all I was trying to do was impress a popsy.'

'There was no woman involved, sir,' Cavendish said, looking straight ahead, unable to maintain eye contact with Bryant.

'Catherine De Beers is an attractive woman, Andy. Yes or no?'

'I'm a married man, sir. I married my high-school sweetheart just before I left Vancouver. I haven't looked at another woman since, and don't intend to.'

'Yeah, right, mate. Look, Andy, we're both men ...' Bryant began.

This time Cavendish stared at him, eyes ablaze: 'Believe one thing I say, *sir*. I would *never* be unfaithful to my wife. That is the God's honest truth.'

Bryant extinguished his cigarette and puffed out his cheeks. 'You're not helping me here, Andy.' He consulted the file in front of him and flicked through some pages until he found the one he was looking for. 'This is the charge form, filled out when you were first locked up.' Cavendish had been under detention for the past week and was dressed in plain but highly starched blue overalls and spit-polished boots.

Cavendish looked across the desk, trying to read upside down.

'Bootlaces, tie, belt, all that stuff they normally take off you when you're arrested. But here's the thing that caught my attention, Andy. Says here you had two hundred pounds in your wallet.'

Cavendish shrugged.

'Bloody hell. Two hundred quid? I haven't seen that much cash at one time in my life. Where did you get it? Not from air force pay. You haven't earned that much since you've been here.'

'My wife sent it to me.'

'Rhodesian pounds?'

'I changed the Canadian money she sent me into local currency.'

'And what were you going to buy? A car, a bloody house?'

'Sir, with respect, my financial affairs are my own business.'

'Like hell they are. Now you're in the air force, they're my business as well. You put up a black last month, didn't you? Had to front the Wingco while I was over at Salisbury for a conference. Think I wouldn't find out?' Bryant watched the Canadian's eyes roam across the ceiling. Putting up a black – committing a dangerous mistake during training, a breach of air force protocol, or any other misdemeanour on the ground or in the air, counted against a trainee and could affect his overall assessment.

'I'm not sure what you're talking about.'

'You were two months behind on your mess bill, weren't you?'

'I was a little short.'

'We feed you, we clothe you, we give you cheap grog on base. What did you do with your money, Andy? Why couldn't you even afford to pay your paltry mess bill?'

'I've been sending money home to my wife. I lost track and sent her too much. I didn't have enough to cover my mess bill. I apologised to the mess and to the Wingco.'

'Hang on, hasn't your wife just sent you the equivalent of two hundred pounds?'

Cavendish swallowed hard.

'Broke one month, rolling in loot the next. Since I left Australia at the start of the war and travelled to Africa via Egypt and then on to dear old England, I reckon I've seen every kind of vice known to man, and you know what, Andy?'

'What, sir?'

'I reckon you're a gambler.'

'There's no law against it, sir.'

'Oh, there is, if you do it on base. If you can't afford to pay your debts because of it. If you leave your wife in the poorhouse because you can't control your urges.'

'I've never gambled on base, sir.'

'I don't give a fuck where you do it, mate. All I want you to tell me is how you got that money.'

'I told you, sir, my wife—'

'Give that one up, mate. You're flogging a dead horse there. You sending her money . . . she sending you loot. That's all bullshit. How did you get the two hundred? You're a worse liar than you were a flyer.'

'All right, sir. You got me,' he said, leaning forward, eyes down. 'I won it in a card game in Bulawayo last week. If I've broken King's regulations on that count, then I'll face the music. You're probably going to kick me out of flight school anyway, so how bad can a gambling charge be?'

'That's better, Andy. As I said, the Wingco likes a man who tells the truth. You'll know your verdict soon enough. In the meantime, I'm going to do you a favour.'

'You are, sir?'

'Yes, Andy, I am. I'm going to talk to the Wingco and suggest that we confiscate a hundred and ninety of that two hundred and lock it in the safe here in the office for the next month. That'll leave you a tenner to get by with. It'll give you time to think about your gambling problem, and maybe change your ways. Assuming you're on top of your mess bill at the end of the month, I'll give you the rest of your ill-gotten gains back.'

'Sir . . . I appreciate the offer, but—'

'It's not an offer, Andy.' Bryant studied the Canadian's face. It was ashen. He looked like he'd just been told he was going to be hanged by the neck until dead. 'It's going to be part of your punishment.'

'Sir, you can't do this to me, I'll . . .'

'You'll what, Andy? The sooner you bloody well wake up to yourself and realise I can do anything I want to, the better off you'll be.'

'Sir, you don't understand . . .' He looked up at the ceiling and then at Bryant, who thought the kid might cry.

Bryant had read the pilot's service record. He was a farm boy who'd been shown too much of the big wide world too soon. He was a hopeless liar as well. He looked at the ceiling when he was telling an untruth, and straight into Bryant's eyes when he wanted to convey honesty. 'Do you owe other people money, Andy?'

Cavendish looked up and said, 'No, sir.'

'Look at me when I ask you a question.' His tone was hard, unforgiving now. 'Did you owe someone two hundred pounds?'

Cavendish looked up, his reddened eyes fixed on Bryant. 'Yes, sir.'

'Where did you get the two hundred?'

Cavendish looked at the floor and mumbled. 'What?' Bryant demanded.

'I can't say, sir.'

Bryant knew the answer anyway. If Cavendish wasn't smart enough to see he was offering him a break, then so be it. There was one other question he had to ask, though.

'Why was there ammunition missing from the guns in your kite, Cavendish?' He had dropped all pretensions of friendliness now.

'Sir? I don't know what you mean.' Cavendish fixed him again with his honest stare.

'There were several hundred rounds missing from the guns in your Harvard.'

'Sir, there was a full load for each gun when I picked up the kite. I personally checked them. I was supposed to be on a gunnery practice.'

'I know where you were *supposed* to be, Cavendish.'

'I wanted to make every round count, to get the best score I could.'

Bryant had read the instructors' assessments. Not only was Cavendish a good flyer, he was an excellent shot. He would have made a fine fighter pilot. 'Yes, and you wanted to clear your gambling debts. If you sold your ammunition to someone, I will personally put the last bullet we recover into your brain, right after the firing squad has filled you with holes.'

He could see Cavendish realised the threat was

anything but empty. 'Sir, I would shoot myself rather than sell air force property to someone. You might think me weak, sir, but I'm a patriot. All I want is a chance to fight in this war.'

'Well, you've fucked that up, royally, Andy.'

'I know, sir,' he said, his head in his hands. 'I know.'

10

Hendrick Reitz's journey had been a long one. Behind him, the setting sun was a red disc lingering in the dust as he crossed the rutted dirt track that told him he had finally entered Southern Rhodesia from Bechuanaland. To his left was the Deka River, more sand than water at this time of the year, though here and there springs and puddles along its course still drew game. He reined in his horse, stopping to watch a mixed herd of impala and kudu grazing. The kudu, the taller of the two antelope species, spotted him first, their big ears turning like antennae, straining to determine whether he was friend or foe. The little impala continued their grazing. He would have been tempted to shoot one or the other, but his saddlebag was still half full of biltong, enough dried gemsbok to keep him going for a few more days, which was all he needed. He'd found and shot the long-horned beast on the saltpan not long after he'd dispatched the two bushmen. It had been a good omen. God was looking after him and had seen him safely out of the desert.

His thighs ached after many days of riding. It had been too long since he'd been in a saddle. How his father, old Andries, would have laughed at his weakness. He smiled. He wished his father were still alive, to know of the strength Hendrick had shown in battle, of the blow he would deal to the hated Englishmen in a very short time.

A long trek. Nothing new for his people. They had been forced into the wilderness in the last century to carve out a new civilisation in the African bush. Hendrick, too, was at the vanguard of a new movement in Africa. The continent would be a better place to live once he and others like him were calling the shots again. This journey had taken him weeks, but it was merely the next-to-last step in the fulfilment of a destiny determined forty-two years earlier in that stinking, disease-ridden place of death.

'It was in the summer, when the rains came,' his father had told the story so many times he remembered it in the older man's voice. His father was fighting the British and their colonial allies in what they called the Boer War. Andries Reitz was serving in a Boer commando – one of the lightly armed mounted guerrilla groups that had proved a deep-lodged thorn in the British side for so long. He was what they called a bitter-ender, one of the diehards who refused to surrender.

'They could not beat us, Hennie,' Andries had told his son time and again. 'They could not defeat us like men, on the battlefield, because we were too good for them. We travelled light and we lived off the land. God provided for us, and the British, with their wagon trains and their heavy guns, could never catch us out on the veldt.'

'So why did we lose, Father?' Hendrick had once had the temerity to ask, at the age of seven.

'They beat us by destroying the one thing that was more precious to us than our cause, Hennie. It is time you learned exactly what happened to your mother.'

'She is with God, you told me,' he'd said, still innocent.

'She was murdered, Hennie, murdered by the *rooineks.*'

He'd been shocked, of course. He knew that there were some whites in his country who were of English descent, and others, like himself, who were Afrikaners – Dutchmen, the other boys called Hennie and his friends. The term *rooinek*, he had already learned, referred to the red uniforms and sunburned necks of the pasty Englishmen who had come to his country. 'They killed her?'

He'd learned the whole painful story. His father, a senior figure amongst the Boer forces even before his twenty-fifth birthday, had met his mother early on in the war. She was German. Ingrid Prochnow was a nurse, who had come to South Africa as a volunteer. There were many foreigners, his father had explained, who were sympathetic to the Boer cause, and who had cause to dislike the English and their allies. The Boers had the support of freedom-loving people from countries such as America, Ireland, Holland and Germany.

Ingrid Prochnow had ceased being a third-country noncombatant, though, when she married Andries Reitz, farmer, late of Nelspruit in the Eastern Transvaal. She became a farmer's wife and, in the process, an enemy of the British Empire.

'Lord Kitchener, Hennie, you know, the Englishman with the big moustache, like a walrus?'

Even now the sight of one of the old recruiting posters from the first war, a finger-pointing Kitchener telling Britons that the Empire needed 'you', turned his blood cold.

'It was Kitchener who knew how to beat us,' his father had scowled, mouth set, his eyes watery after a few drinks. 'They rounded up our wives and children – your mother was one of them – and put them into those filthy concentration camps, where they died by the thousands. Twenty-seven thousand Boer women and children, in two years, Hennie. Dead.'

The story had given him nightmares for years. But his

father had spared no detail, no matter how distressing, so that his suffering could be shared by the boy, so that his lifelong quest for revenge could be poured into his heir, like a transfusion of new blood, to make him harder, stronger.

'We had married and, soon after, she was carrying you in her tummy, Hennie, like a little lamb, you understand?'

He had nodded.

'She was weak, Hennie, because the English did not feed our women and children enough to survive. She was sick, Hennie, because the English made them go to the toilet in the open, like Kaffirs, and did not give them clean water to drink. She had the cholera, Hennie, when she gave birth to you.'

Reitz followed the Deka for another half-hour, until he found a reasonably open grassy area to make his camp for the night. He dismounted, tethered the horses and started a small fire. As he unrolled his bedding he remembered the tears in his father's eyes every time the old man told the story. Andries was a giant of a man, with a foul temper when his son disobeyed him. He could ride all day and drink all night. Hennie had seen him knock another man out cold with his bare fists. But when he spoke of his wife, he always ended up in tears.

'It wasn't you, Hennie. It was the cholera, the sickness,

that made her weak. She gave birth to you, saw you, kissed you, then she died. My sister, Henriette, your aunty, saw it all, told me all about it. They murdered her, Hennie, as sure as if they had put a bullet in her heart.'

Reitz chewed on a slice of biltong, savouring the saltiness of the dried beef, then took a swig from a metal flask of brandy. He lay back, his head on his saddle, his rifle by his side, and looked at the stars. As a child he had believed what his father had said, that each of those stars was a loving mother, or a tiny baby killed by the English, and that one day, when God saw fit, they would all be together, in heaven.

He took another swig of brandy and thought about the war. As a soldier he could understand the strategy that Kitchener had employed and, if he thought about it rationally, coldly, even admire the thinking behind it. Isolate the rebels from their kinfolk, their source of food, news, moral support, and they would, inevitably, wither on the vine. Containment of noncombatants sympathetic to partisans and denial of the bandits' succour and shelter made perfect sense. What galled Hendrick Reitz most of all, what steeled his nerve even at the age of forty-two, what had driven him into the arms of his mother's people, were two things.

The first was the fact that the English had not been content merely to contain the Boer women and children.

Through a deliberate policy of neglect they had created the unsanitary conditions that allowed diseases such as cholera to thrive. They had exacerbated the problems of disease through overcrowding and underrationing in the camps. When the Afrikaner women and children had become sick they had been too weak to fight off the illness. It was a slow way to kill off a race. There was an unmistakable cruelty in Kitchener's methods, and that sickened him.

The other thing that undermined Kitchener, and the English, in Hendrick Reitz's opinion, was that they had done this to people of the same race.

The Führer was waging a war against communism, and against racial pollution in Europe. For some races, such as the Jews, the gypsies, and the Slavs, it was time to pay. The Aryan race was superior to others, there was no doubt in his mind about it. Hitler had even tried to bring the stubborn, stupid English into the Aryan fold, but they had rejected him. So typically intolerant and narrow-minded of the *rooineks*.

It had been natural for Hennie to enter the Ossewa Brandwag when he came of age. It was during the First World War, in 1917, that he had joined the brotherhood. His father was serving a prison sentence for his part in the aborted Boer Rebellion of 1914, when troops in the north-west of the country had aligned themselves with the Germans across the border in South West Africa and tried to seize government. Hendrick had been cared for by his Aunt Henriette and she had done nothing to stop him pledging allegiance to the cause.

On a rainy night on a farm outside Barberton, near the concentration camp where he had been born, he met with a group of six men from the OB and told them he was ready to swear his allegiance. In accordance with the movement's traditions, he stood before them, with his hand on the Holy Bible. Two *Stormjaers* also stood with him, one in front, the other behind him, each with a loaded revolver pointed at his heart.

In the candle-lit room, he read aloud from a sheet of paper. 'I promise solemnly before Almighty God, of my own free will, that I will implicitly subject myself to the demands which my people's God-given calling requires of me. A higher-placed authority will find me obediently faithful. All commands which I receive will be carried out promptly, and kept secret. May the Almighty grant that I shall be prepared to sacrifice my life for the freedom of my people. May the thought of treason never occur to me, realising that I will voluntarily become a prey to the vengeance of a *Stormjaer*. May God grant that I will be able to exclaim with my comrades: If I advance, follow me! If I retreat, shoot me! If I die, avenge me! So help me God.'

Hendrick had inherited his father's height and build

– which made him an ideal choice as a rugby forward – and, thankfully, his mother's brains, fair hair and blue eyes. His father had told him that Ingrid had been planning on studying to be a doctor when the war in South Africa had broken out. Already qualified as a nurse, she had abandoned thoughts of further study to help the outnumbered Boers in their cause. This simple fact, when he thought about it, was almost enough to bring Hendrick Reitz to tears.

He had excelled at university and, at his father's insistence, had not publicly advertised his hatred of the English or his ties to the OB. 'You must gain their trust, Hennie. The English run our country now, whether we like it or not. You will have an opportunity to hurt them one day, but you cannot do that from a gaol cell at the age of eighteen.'

During university terms he had immersed himself in books of chemistry and biology and, in the holidays, after his father was released from gaol, he rode into the bushveld with him and hunted lion, buffalo, elephant and buck. His professors said he had the naturally analytical brain of a scientist, and his father took great pride in telling his old comrades from the war – those who had survived – that his boy had the eyes of an eagle, the stealth of a leopard, the strength of a buffalo and the courage of a lion.

The lowly assistant researcher's job in the agriculture department had been a fairly natural first step for a newly graduated chemist, but to Hendrick it had opened up a new and exciting world. He worked on the development of new pesticides to kill crop-eating bugs and cattle-crippling parasites. Soon outshining his career civil-servant colleagues, he was offered, before his thirtieth birthday, a position as senior research scientist with the South African arm of a German chemical company, which was putting the government's research work into commercial practice.

Hendrick Reitz had become, in the space of a few years, an expert on killing. As a farm boy at heart he wanted to find new ways to poison the insect and mammalian pests that had made his father's life, and the lives of other farmers, so hard. As a scientist, he wanted to make sure the business of killing was quick, economical and painless.

In 1934 he had been offered a position with the chemical firm's head office, in Berlin, and the opportunity to complete postgraduate studies in Germany while he worked. A senior German executive from the parent company, on a business trip to South Africa, had learned of Reitz's intelligence, ability and background.

Hendrick had been awestruck by the majesty of Berlin

under Adolf Hitler and the National Socialist Party. At the urging of the partner who had recruited him, Hendrick had attended a couple of party meetings and then joined the Nazis. The move had been good for his career, too, as most of the senior people in the firm proudly wore the striking red, white and black swastika badge on their suit lapels. He soon became engrossed in the ground-breaking work German scientists were conducting in the development of new types of poisons.

By now well established, both socially and in the company, Reitz seemed to have everything a young man could want. He had a nice apartment in a good Berlin neighbourhood, money to spend on a beautiful blonde-haired secretary and party member named Ursula Schultz, and a secure job with a promising career path.

That was enough for Hendrick Reitz, the intelligent, handsome young scientist – all the things a long-dead mother would have wanted for her only son – but it did not satisfy his other needs. He was his father's son – a man who gained as much satisfaction from hours of stalking through the bushveld, the kick of a rifle in the shoulder, and a well-placed shot that took the prey down clean. The novelty of winter snows, expensive cigars and tawdry nightclubs was slowly wearing off. He took some solace in the arms and bed of Ursula, but he was handsome and vain enough to realise he could find a woman virtually wherever and whenever he needed one. He wanted more, so he enlisted in a Wehrmacht militia battalion. He was selected for officer training by virtue of his education. His unusual background, Afrikaner accent, outstanding marksmanship and his party connections earned him the attention of senior commanders on more than one occasion.

Keen to advance his standing in the military and to seek new challenges, he volunteered for a course in radio communications early in his commission. As a result of his new skills he was transferred from the infantry to a posting as a ground liaison officer stationed at a Luftwaffe aerodrome close to the research laboratory where he worked on weekdays. He was a link man between the army and air force, and worked with officers more senior than he from both services on improving ground-to-air communications and in the development of new doctrines for the tactical support of land forces by aircraft.

When Spain erupted into civil war, Reitz immediately volunteered to serve with the German Condor Legion, dispatched by Hitler to assist General Franco's nationalist forces against the left-wing republican government. The legion comprised artillery and aircraft, but it did need officers who could serve with nationalist units and provide radio communications between the Spaniards on the ground and the Luftwaffe aircraft supporting them. Reitz fit the bill on all counts.

He had, as he had always expected, enjoyed the job of soldiering as much as the challenges of science, Reitz reflected as the fire beside his bushveld bed died to glowing coals.

War, of course, was vastly different from hunting in the African bush, but the skills his father had taught him served him well. He was able to suffer the hardships of life in the field better than many of the men he fought alongside.

He held his nerve under enemy fire, and time and again was able to save his comrades from defeat in battle and wreak havoc on their communist-backed enemies by calling in Luftwaffe airstrikes with pinpoint accuracy.

Though he would never dare voice his concerns aloud, one thing that did unsettle him during his time in Spain was the deliberate aerial bombing of towns full of civilians. It seemed to Reitz that rather than cowering a civilian population, aerial bombing often seemed to increase their resolve and conviction in their cause.

The exception came on 26 April 1937, when Reitz was serving with nationalist forces in the Basque region of northern Spain. Ten miles behind the republican lines was the small town of Guernica, crammed with retreating soldiers and refugees. Reitz spent the afternoon on his radio relaying the changing position of his Spanish unit to the Condor Legion's command and passing on information about weather conditions and enemy positions as streams of German Heinkel He-111 and Junkers Ju-52 bombers roared overhead. Two days later, when the nationalists entered the town, Reitz saw the full effects of fifty tons of high explosive and incendiary bombs. More than sixteen hundred people had been killed and fires still raged in the town. It was not as big as raids he would later witness directed against Germany, but he was awed by the terrible, decisive might of massed air power against a civilian target. A little less than two years later the last of the republican resistance crumbled, and Franco's *Nacionales* entered Madrid in triumph.

After Spain he dealt with the boredom of service in a peacetime army by applying for more military courses that would challenge and interest him, and by throwing himself back into his civilian work. His firm had made impressive progress during his time away in the development of a new, extremely deadly family of pesticides called organophosphates.

Reitz, like most of his comrades in and out of uniform, sensed a larger war was coming. Germany was about to reclaim its place in the world, and they all wanted to be part of the machine that would make that happen.

In September 1939, when Germany invaded Poland,

Reitz was mobilised back into full-time duty. Many of the regular air force and army officers he had served with in Spain were now in positions of greater power and he pulled enough strings to be transferred to the elite Luftwaffe *Fallschimjager*, the paratroopers. His wish to return to action was granted in 1940, when German airborne forces spearheaded the invasion of Holland. The following year, Reitz and the company of veteran soldiers he now commanded as a *Hauptman* jumped onto the Greek island of Crete, where they faced tenacious resistance from the British, Greek and Australian defenders.

He smoked a final cigarette as the African night closed in around him, savouring the memory of the fierce fighting on the Mediterranean island. Some of his men had been shot and killed while still under their parachute canopies in the sky. Those who survived the landing took a bloody revenge on the Englishmen and their colonial lackeys. Reitz remembered the first Briton he had killed, a machine-gunner, at long range. Although as an officer he was entitled to a sub machine-gun or pistol, he chose instead to carry a Mauser rifle with telescopic sights. His men called their African-German leader *der Jager*, the hunter, in homage to his big-game hunting days. In the hours and days that followed his landing on the island his personal tally of dead enemy soldiers climbed steadily to twenty-one, while at the same time he commanded his company brilliantly.

Shrapnel from a British mortar shell, just a day before the enemy's surrender, took him out of the fight. He spent time in a field hospital in occupied Greece, where the worst of the metal fragments, dirt and scraps of his own uniform were removed from his left calf and thigh. Afterwards he was transferred back to Germany for convalescence leave.

The Germans won the battle of Crete, but the fighting bled the cream of Hitler's elite airborne units dry. Grimly, Reitz wondered what his future would hold as he hobbled around the verdant grounds of a Bavarian rehabilitation hospital. One thing the invasion had rekindled in him was a remembrance of a part of the world that was never really cold; at least, not as cold as Bavaria – Africa.

Salvation came in the form of the silver-haired Doktor Strauss, the man who had recruited him to his firm from its South African outpost. The doctor visited him in hospital, having tracked him down through pretty Ursula, who still wrote letters to Reitz once a week, without fail.

'You mightn't think it to look at me, but I'm not without connections and, as a result, influence,' the doctor told him after they had exchanged pleasantries.

Reitz was exercising harder and harder each day. He had given up his walking stick, and the elderly doctor was breathing hard keeping up with him as they walked the perimeter of the hospital grounds. 'I have a distant cousin, you know, who is quite high up in military intelligence. His name is Canaris.'

'Not Admiral Wilhelm Canaris – the head of the Abwehr?' Reitz asked, awestruck. Strauss' relative was not just high up, he was the supremo.

'The very same. We had dinner recently. He asked about how the war was affecting our business. I let slip that we'd suffered a steady drain of good people, starting with one of my best scientists, a South African who had fought in Spain, then left us again to become a paratrooper, and was currently recovering from wounds he had received in Crete. Well, you should have seen the old fox's eyes light up. 'South *African*, you say,' he says to me.

'I can't imagine why, but he wants to meet you,' Strauss said.

The summons came a week later. Reitz was ready to leave the hospital anyway. He reported in full uniform to the headquarters of German military intelligence, the Abwehr, a dark maze of offices known as the *Fuchsbau*, or fox's lair, on Berlin's Tirpitzufer.

Canaris was a legendary figure. The distinguished naval officer had overseen intelligence officers in Spain during the Great War. With his shock of white hair he was referred to by some as 'old white head'. His big antique desk was cluttered with stacks of books. A dachshund sat on a bed in a corner of the office and whined. The short, elderly man turned and made a clucking noise to soothe the dog.

He looked up from his desk at Reitz, standing stiffly to attention, and motioned for him to sit. 'I'm a busy man, Hauptman, so I'll come to the point. The Führer himself is interested in Africa – southern Africa, to be precise. Rommel is rolling back the allies in the Western Desert and it is felt that creating dissent in the south of the continent would prove a helpful distraction.' That first conversation, of course, had been before the Afrika Korps had been stopped at El Alamein, in 1942. 'They think they're safe there in South Africa and Rhodesia, away from the action, and I want them to think otherwise. You were in the Ossewa Brandwag, I understand.'

'*Jahwohl*, Herr Admiral.'

'How viable is this OB, Reitz? Will they take up arms against their government?'

Reitz thought briefly about the question and how best to answer it. For every ten loudmouth drunkards in the organisation there might be one like him, a man who had the courage to fight for his beliefs, and not just rant around the *braai*. 'The OB's leader, Hans Van Rensburg, is a doctor of law, sir. Some, including myself, think he is too soft, as he does not sanction sabotage, but many of our *Stormjaers* are ready to take up arms.'

'Yes, yes, I'm sure, Reitz,' Canaris said dismissively. He scanned the captain's file again, then looked up at him, and said: 'Spare me the rhetoric. Would you kill your countrymen, those who are opposed to Germany and our ideals?'

'The OB wants Germany to win the war. They see a victory by Germany and Italy as a prerequisite for the establishment of a racially pure Afrikaner nation, independent of England. There are enough of them who will fight – who will kill – starting with me.'

'You'll be medically discharged from the paratroopers – honourably, of course – and you will return to my cousin's chemical firm. He, too, has need of your service.'

'But, with respect, Herr Admiral, I thought that . . .' Reitz panicked, fearing that he had said the wrong thing and would sit out the war in a laboratory in Berlin.

'You don't think from now on, Reitz. My people do your thinking for you, make your decisions for you. There are some things even I am not privy to. My cousin is working on something of great importance to the Reich. We have reached a gentleman's agreement over your future. He will use your mind in the laboratory for the next few months, and when I am good and ready I will use your less cerebral talents, and your contacts, in South Africa.'

Chemical warfare. That's what his old firm was up to. How, when or where the fruits of their labours were to be used was never mentioned, and not speculated on in the corridors or laboratories. But the company Reitz had left experimenting with new ways to poison cockroaches, crop diseases and mice, had now set its sights on bigger prey – man.

'Our aim,' Doktor Strauss had told him on his first day back at work, 'is to develop toxins that attack the central nervous system, quickly, cleanly and efficiently. We are not so inhumane as to wish a return to the primitive days of the last war, where men were burned and blinded by the fumes from chlorine gas. We want something that does a better job, quicker – a substitute for a bullet, if you will.'

It felt odd, being back in a suit and a white lab coat, but Reitz still felt himself at the cutting edge of Germany's war effort. The idea of chemical warfare did not worry him. As the doctor had alluded to, both sides had used poison gas in the first war. What he hoped, however, was that a new form of toxin, if it could be developed, would be employed at the strategic level somehow, in order to shorten the war with fewer German casualties. The doctor had progressed a fair way. 'It was some of your early work, Hendrick, that set us in the right direction. I recalled your papers on the poisons that the bushmen of southern Africa's deserts use to immobilise and kill their prey. We are on the road to developing our own version of a nerve agent that will work along similar lines, but we still have work to do on methods of delivery.'

As the firm's labours intensified and they came closer to development of a final, lethal product, Admiral Canaris intervened. Reitz left Ursula and his expensive suits and lab coats, and vanished into the shadowy world of military intelligence. At a secret school at Quentzsee in Brandenburg he learned the arts of espionage and sabotage, and refreshed his already finely-honed skills in radio communications and killing.

Canaris' first assignment for him was intelligence gathering. He wanted a man who could infiltrate the white population of South Africa and quietly make contact with the senior figures and supporters of the Ossewa Brandwag. Reitz was not being tasked to assassinate anyone, nor blow up railway lines or power stations, but his mission was no less risky. If any of the men and women he were to contact had had a change of heart since the start of the war, or had been compromised by South African intelligence officers, then Reitz could be betrayed, captured and hanged as a spy.

His heart had soared as he'd rowed himself ashore from the U-boat north of Cape Town, knowing he was home and, not only that, back to help make a better

South Africa. He'd travelled the breadth of the country and even beyond its borders, in search of the leading lights, both overt and covert, of the OB. Some of them he knew, either personally or as people his father had met. All except one still hated the British but, disappointingly, only a handful gave a decisive and positive answer to the question of their willingness to engage in covert military action against the British Empire.

The one who had made his peace with the British, who had mellowed in his old age, was a very real threat to Reitz, now that he had shown his hand as a Nazi sympathiser. He had to end the mission prematurely and flee South Africa via neutral Portuguese Mozambique, crossing on foot through the wilds of the Kruger National Park in the country's north-east.

Back in Germany, Reitz returned to his civilian job and was pleased to see great progress had been made. A fast-acting, lethal nerve agent had been developed for tactical use. 'It is called sarin,' Doktor Strauss told him over coffee on his first day back. 'It was actually patented back in 1938. It's named after the initials of the surnames of its founders – S-A-R from Schrader, Ambros, Rudriger, and I-N from Von der Linde. A tiny drop or a mist of vapour will kill a man.'

Reitz nodded. He knew three of his former rivals on a first-name basis. 'So what's new about it?'

Strauss smiled. 'Sarin's problem was that it wouldn't keep more than a few weeks. We've worked on that, refined it. Our latest version of the agent will keep for up to a year. It can be transported anywhere in the world and kept stable and safe until it is time for its use. The weapons people at the army proving grounds at Raubkammer have conducted successful tests in launching sarin in artillery shells. They're working on other means of delivery as we speak.'

Canaris, meanwhile, was disappointed at the lukewarm reception Reitz reported from many of the former stalwarts of the OB. However, he was still wedded to the idea of causing mayhem in some form in southern Africa, in order to hurt the allies and siphon troops away from elsewhere on the continent. Hendrick Reitz had already formulated the germ of an idea, and he briefed the admiral on it, shortly after his return to work at the laboratory.

Reitz convinced Canaris that there was enough support in Africa for someone from outside – a man such as himself – to return and deliver a hammer blow against the British and their South African allies, which would hurt their war effort and inspire other Afrikaners to take up arms.

Which was why he was back.

11

Pip straightened her police uniform cap and squared her shoulders. They stood at the tall, imposing mahogany door of a sprawling whitewashed house in Hillside, between decorative pillars fronting a long, shady verandah. Cape doves cooed in the trees overhanging the home and a big sandy-coloured Rhodesian Ridgeback snuffled curiously at the hem of Pip's skirt. The home and its stone-walled garden provided a tranquil oasis in the midst of the dusty outer suburb. The house spoke of money – a different Africa from the one Pip had grown up in. She swatted the dog gently on the nose.

'I don't have to tell you that this could go bad for both of us if *you're* wrong,' Hayes grumbled, his words very nearly puncturing what little resolve she had mustered.

She wiped her sweaty palms on her skirt. She noticed Hayes used a finger to wipe beads of sweat from his top lip. She knocked.

An elderly African male in a cropped red jacket and black trousers opened the door. 'Sir, madam. May I help you?'

'We're here to see . . .' Hayes coughed, as if he would choke on the words, 'Mr Justice Green.'

'Whom may I say is calling, please?' the grey-haired African asked, eyebrows slightly raised.

'Sergeant Hayes and WPC Lovejoy. Bulawayo Police.'

'Very good, sir. Please wait here.' The man closed the door.

'Bloody hell, who does he think he is?' Hayes fumed.

'I suppose he's smart enough to know the judge wouldn't want to front a couple of uniformed coppers without some notice,' Pip said.

'The law is the law, Lovejoy. No one, not even a judge, is above it,' Hayes said.

Pip thought that Hayes, as usual, was blustering to cover his own inadequacies or, in this case, fear. She felt her heart beat faster. She was terrified. She checked her watch. They had been waiting five minutes since the butler disappeared. The door swung open again.

'Mr Justice Green will see you now. This way, please, sir, madam.'

The butler's shoes clicked on the terracotta tiled hallway floor as the police officers followed him into the cool, dim interior of the home. Pip noticed the oil paintings on the wall were mostly of idyllic pastoral scenes. England, by the looks of them, although she had never been there herself. They passed an ornate carved wooden sideboard stacked with fine hand-painted china. The servant knocked on a door halfway down the corridor and a voice said, 'Come.'

'Good morning,' Justice Cecil Green said, standing from a dark leather chair set behind an antique roll-top desk.

Pip looked around as she greeted the judge and shook his cold, bony hand. The walls of what appeared to be the judge's study were covered with books – legal texts, by the look of it. His desk was clear, which made her wonder what he had been doing there, and why he couldn't have met them at the door. Perhaps, she thought, he wanted them off-balance and had deliberately kept them waiting in order to give him time to compose himself in a place where he felt master of his surroundings.

'I'd ask what I can do to help you, officers, but, to be quite frank, my first question is why you didn't see fit to telephone me first. What's this all about? Not bad news, I hope?'

Pip had asked around the police camp and found out that Justice Green was a widower, with no children, so they were hardly likely to be calling to tell him about the death of a close relative.

'No, your Honour,' Hayes began, eyes downcast, struggling to find a way to broach the subject. 'I'm sorry for the unannounced visit, and to impinge, as it were, on your valuable time. I know that you're a very busy man and . . . it's just that . . .'

'What, Sergeant? I do hope this is not about a case I'm hearing at the moment. You know that would be most improper. Now, please, how can I be of assistance to you?'

'Well, sir, you see, we've come into possession of some information which would seem to, well, that is, there's an allegation that—'

'An allegation?' the judge spat, as if offended by the word. 'I do hope you haven't come here to accuse *me* of something.' He finished the sentence with a hearty laugh.

Pip looked into his grey eyes and saw a flash of fear. She'd thought the laugh was too loud, forced. It echoed off the walls of the office and only silence remained. The judge, she noticed, was looking at Hayes, as if daring him to ask his question, and had pointedly ignored her since limply shaking her hand. She realised that Hayes, never at a loss for words when it came to bullying an inferior, had gone to water. If she didn't say something fast, the judge would have his manservant usher them out in no time flat.

'How much petrol's in your Daimler, your Honour?' Pip blurted.

He was tall, bald and thin, and stooped from a working lifetime of poring over evidence and transcripts. He stared down at her, shoulders hunched and neck extended, looking, Pip thought, like one of the ugly Marabou storks that hung around the town garbage dump. 'I beg your pardon?'

'How much petrol's in your car?' she asked again. 'Simple question.' She glanced across at Hayes, whose normally ruddy face had drained of colour. He looked away from her. She was on her own.

'Why on earth would you want to know that?'

'Why on earth wouldn't you want to tell us?' Pip retorted. Hayes, she saw from the corner of her eye, was mouthing something to her. 'Enough' she thought he was trying to say. The man was a coward – the realisation made Pip feel even more determined to press on.

The judge looked at her, eyes narrowed, and said: 'I could give you twenty legal reasons why I don't have to tell you anything, right here and now. What's this about, *Constable*.'

She hated the mocking tone in his voice as if he, like so many men in the police and elsewhere, didn't think she had the right to wear the uniform. 'Your Honour, perhaps you'd like to call an advocate. Do judges have lawyers?'

'I don't mind telling you, I do not like your tone, young

lady, and I do not like you barging in here, asking meaningless questions. Sergeant?' He looked angrily at Hayes.

Hayes, still dumbstruck, shrugged and looked pointedly back at Pip.

'Why on earth would I need the services of a lawyer?' the judge demanded.

'How much petrol's in your car, your Honour?' Pip asked again.

The judge ran a hand over his bald pate. 'Sergeant, I demand that you explain right now what this is all about. Or am I to suffer this woman's riddles all morning? If I *do* make a call to anyone in the next few minutes, believe me when I say that it will be to the chief constable.'

Hayes coughed. 'Well, sir, it's like this . . . we, that is, Constable Lovejoy has some information, and—'

'I could arrest you, your Honour,' Pip said, interrupting Hayes.

'You wouldn't dare,' said the judge.

Now, Pip thought, he looked more like a bird of prey than a scavenger. Those eyes frightened her. She knew he could end her police career – if that's what it was – with a single call. 'I'm investigating a case of black market petrol dealing. I could arrest you, on suspicion of buying petrol illegally, take you to the station, and then get one of your colleagues to sign a search warrant so I can measure how much fuel you've got in your car and garage, and see how that tallies against your ration coupons. We'll get statements from court clerks, garage attendants, your servants and enough other people to ascertain how often you drive, and how far. After that, it's just some fairly simple mathematics to see if you can do the number of miles I *know* you travel, with the amount of fuel you should be able to buy legally.'

'Enough!'

'Mr Justice Green, you are under—'

'Wait, wait!' said the judge, holding up a hand. 'Before you do anything *rash*, my dear—'

'Constable, your Honour.'

'Very well, *Constable*, perhaps you wouldn't mind by starting with a little background information as to why you might possibly even start to believe that I might be guilty of this petty crime.'

'Buying and selling fuel on the black market when there are people fighting and dying in a war doesn't seem too *petty* to me, your Honour. I would have thought you'd agree.'

The judge coughed. 'All right, out with it. Charge me – and we'll *see* how much luck you have getting someone to sign a search warrant – or ask me what you came here to ask me.'

Pip swallowed hard. She had bluffed her way this far but she knew, and the judge had just told her in so many words, that even if she took the game to the next level, he could – and would – defeat her. However, the fact that he wanted to talk indicated he probably did have something to hide.

'We didn't come here to charge you with buying petrol on the black market, your Honour,' she confessed.

'Very wise,' the judge said. 'Go on.'

'We arrested a man for the murder of Felicity Langham yesterday . . .'

'So I heard. A Mr Nkomo, I believe. What of it, and what's that got to do with me? You've not come to charge me with conspiracy to murder as well, I hope!'

'No, sir. But the accused, Mr Nkomo, says he has an alibi – a series of alibis, in fact – during the hours when she was most probably murdered.'

'It's not my position, as a member of the judiciary, to comment on or be privy to details of a case before it reaches court, but I have heard, through sources, that the man in question was caught in possession of certain items belonging to Miss Langham. Is that not correct?'

'It is, your Honour, but the man's alibi still needs to be checked.' She thought for a moment about how best to ask the next question, then said: 'Innocent says he was with you between the hours of midnight and one in the morning on the night in question. Is that true, sir?'

The judge scratched his chin, as if either trying to remember or deciding whether or not to answer the question. 'You're taking the word of a common criminal, against a judge, that I was somehow, for some reason, consorting with him in the middle of the night. I must say, this is quite absurd.'

'I'm merely asking you a question. Were you or were you not with this man at that time?' Pip persisted.

'What's the window of time in which you think the young woman was killed?'

'That's not information we need to share with you, sir,' Pip said.

The judge bridled. 'I presume, young lady, you wouldn't have had the gumption to confront me like this if you didn't think the time this man *allegedly* met with me fell into that window?'

Pip gave a little smile. 'You're a very perceptive man, your Honour.'

'For what it's worth, sir, I think the man's guilty,' Hayes chirped up, as though he now thought it was safe to enter the conversation. 'There are three hours in which we think the killing took place.'

Pip shot him a dark look. The last thing she needed was for the obsequious toad to give the judge an easy out.

The judge stayed silent a few seconds, staring at Hayes.

Eventually, he said: 'Sergeant, I've made it clear that I resent the impertinent way in which you and Constable Lovejoy have intruded into my home, and I resent the allegations of impropriety you are inferring.'

'Yes, sir, my apologies, sir. This wasn't my idea, by the way.'

Pip closed her eyes in frustration. She had blown it. They would never hear the end of it, and Hayes would make what little time she had left in the police service a misery.

'However,' the judge continued, now looking down at Pip, 'Constable Lovejoy, I can confirm, and will do so, if required, under oath, that Mr Innocent Nkomo was in my presence, in the garage of this property, from the hours of midnight to one in the morning on the night Miss Langham's body was found.'

Hayes was wide-eyed with surprise.

'Beyond that, Constable, I will say nothing more.'

'I don't need you to, your Honour.'

'I know you don't.' The judge gave the merest hint of a smile, then turned to Hayes and said: 'Sergeant, if it was not your idea to confront me, then, in my humble opinion, it *should* have been. Murder – particularly a killing of this nature – is a very serious offence indeed. Constable Lovejoy has shown great conviction by confronting me to confirm Mr Nkomo's whereabouts. I'd have thought the police could do with a few more like her. Now, if you've no further questions, I'll bid good-day to you both.'

'Oh, sorry, one more question, your Honour,' Pip said.

'As much as I admire your zeal, Constable, I'd have thought I made it clear I've nothing more to say.'

'I understand, sir, but I need to ask you if you have ever passed on Innocent Nkomo's telephone number to anyone else.'

The judge answered immediately. 'No, I have not, and I will not tell you how I got in contact with him in the first place. Now, I have things to attend to.'

They thanked him and walked outside. Pip resisted the urge to say anything to Hayes as she walked down the judge's driveway in front of him.

'Bloody hell,' Hayes said. 'What do we do now?'

Pip turned and saw the sergeant really didn't have a clue. At that moment she felt sorry for him, and shared his same sense of emptiness. This was a murder investigation, she reminded herself, it was not a competition between her and Hayes to see who was the smartest – or the bravest.

'Well, it seems Innocent Nkomo has a rock-solid alibi not only from midnight to three – when the doc thinks Felicity was murdered – but also for a good three hours beforehand. With travelling time between his various appointments it seems impossible for him to have picked up Felicity somewhere and raped and murdered her.'

The judge was the fourth person they had spoken to. They'd saved the most difficult interview until last. Innocent Nkomo had a diverse client base, all of whom, apart from buying illegal petrol on the black market, seemed pillars of the white community. His other customers had included a seventy-five-year-old retired headmistress, a bank manager and a doctor. All had shown the same nervousness as the judge about incriminating themselves, and the same red-faced shame at being caught out, but Pip had managed to convince them all that she was not interested so much in *what* they were doing, as whether or not they were doing it with Innocent Nkomo.

They had all confessed to being with him. She thought it a credit to them. Even though they had engaged in criminal activity, none of them would lie if it meant the death of an innocent man – even one not so innocent as, well, Innocent.

'I can't see the judge, the headmistress, the banker or the doctor as being involved in Felicity's death. They all live in far-flung parts of town, and there's nothing to connect her to any of them,' Pip said as they got back into their car.

'So that means if Nkomo's telling the truth, and

someone planted Felicity Langham's stuff in the boot of his car, it must have been one of the two mystery clients we can't account for.'

'Exactly,' Pip said. 'So we're almost back to square one.'

Innocent Nkomo had told them that in addition to his regular customers, the only people who had been anywhere near his car on the morning after Felicity had been murdered were two new, unannounced customers. They were both white – one male and one female. He had given a rough description of both of them, and told the police where he had met them, but it wasn't much to go on.

As Hayes skirted the southern part of Bulawayo, Pip reviewed the notes she had taken during Nkomo's interrogation, and the man's own statement. 'So, we're looking for a blonde woman aged in her mid-twenties to early thirties, and a dark-haired man in his early thirties. He said he'd stopped to see what the fuss was about in Mzilikazi, when we found him at the crime scene, after picking up some more cans of fuel for his next delivery. Nkomo met the woman in town, at five in the morning in a lane near the Empire Club. He sold our mystery man four gallons behind the Catholic Church at seven o'clock. Nkomo said both customers telephoned him at home, asking if he had some timber for sale.' It was a primitive code, but told the black marketeer that the new clients had both been referred to him by someone who had used his services before.

'We'll get some officers to ask around both neighbourhoods to see if there were any witnesses to the meetings. Might get better descriptions, or maybe someone will have recognised the customers,' Hayes said as he turned right onto the Salisbury Road.

'A church early on a weekday morning and a lane behind a closed club? Not much chance there'd be too many people walking past. Nkomo's not dumb – that's why he does his work either at night, at his regular customers' homes, or in places where no one's milling about. A black man selling stuff out of the back of a car in the neighbourhoods where his customers live would draw too much attention during the day.'

'What choice have we got?' Hayes asked.

She was stumped. 'We've got to concentrate on the mystery man.'

'I agree with you there,' Hayes said.

'Yes. We should get out the photo files of men with prior convictions for sexual assault and show them to Nkomo. He might recognise one of them as his mystery customer.'

'It's a long shot,' Hayes said. 'And we've still got Nkomo's full list of clients to go through. There might be a cross-match somewhere.'

Pip nodded. Nkomo, at their instruction, had been left

in his cell to write down the names of all of his petrol clients. The man had admitted to them that he sold to dozens of people, and that he did not know them all by name.

'If we resurrect your theory that Felicity was killed by someone who knew her, we could have another look at the men she's been with.'

'Her neighbours and the girls she worked with at the air force base haven't been able to come up with any names,' Pip said, though there was one man she still had her suspicions about.

'Perhaps we've got to look at that again.'

'Yes, perhaps. But now we've got a funeral to attend. Two funerals, in fact.'

Pied crows, fat from the food scraps generated by a thousand airmen and women, wheeled over the base rubbish tip. A lone vulture circled in search of death. Other birds were sometimes struck by aircraft on take-off or landing and, every now and then, the cooks shot a baboon or monkey which had grown too bold. The spoil from two freshly dug graves insulted the neat, manicured lines of the military cemetery. Two African gravediggers, their blue overalls black with sweat, leaned on their shovels a discreet distance away from the air force plot, where only whites were buried.

In the base chapel, a uniformed Rhodesian WAAF played 'Nearer My God To Thee' on the organ and the two hundred mourners sang or mouthed the words as best they could.

'Squadron Leader Paul Bryant, our base adjutant, will now say a few words,' the ageing air force chaplain said as the organ sighed to silence.

There was only seating for half the crowd. The rest stood outside, watching through open doors. A public-address system had been rigged up so that those outside could hear the service.

Bryant heard a faint echo outside from the speakers, washing over the still runway. Unusually for Kumalo, the hum of aero engines was missing today, all training having been suspended for the double funeral. His amplified scratchy voice rang out through the Tannoy. 'We come together today to say goodbye to two members of our family,' he began.

Pip Lovejoy, standing at the back of the crowded chapel, looked at him and fancied she caught him searching the crowd for her. Most of the women were in air force uniforms, but Pip noticed a woman wearing a broad-brimmed black hat, trimmed with lace, sitting in one of the front pews. She couldn't see the face, but imagined it would be Catherine De Beers – ostentatiously dressed for the occasion.

'Sadly, many of us in this chapel, on this base, are not strangers to death. These will not be the last members of our family – our air force family – to whom we have to say farewell. The presence of so many of you here and outside is a testimony to the high regard in which both Leading Aircraftswoman Felicity Langham and Flight Sergeant James Smythe were held by all of you.'

Pip looked around at the capacity crowd of mostly young men – little more than boys. She wondered how many of them had come to this noncompulsory church parade on a Saturday morning because of Felicity Langham and the morbidly fascinating circumstances of her death, as opposed to because of the hapless Sergeant Smythe.

'Both were taken from us in their prime. This is the nature of war, ladies and gentleman, but the crime – for that's what we're talking about here – was that Felicity and James were killed not by an enemy bullet or shell, or even by an accident in training. They were killed by other people, for reasons still unknown.'

There were murmurs from the congregation. Pip sensed they were still angry, and that it might not take much to stir them into misplaced action again. The last thing anyone needed at the moment was another race riot. She'd been toying with the idea of doing as Hayes had and leaking some information to the local newspaper, stating that they were still investigating Felicity's murder and that the police were looking for a mystery white man. However, she had eventually thought better of the idea. Better the real killer – if the unknown man were now the prime suspect – thought he had got away with his crime. She looked back at the pulpit and noticed that Paul Bryant was staring directly at her.

She lowered her eyes a fraction to avoid his gaze. In front of the pulpit hung a tapestry of the badge of the Rhodesian Air Training Group. In the centre of the crest was the famous stone eagle of Great Zimbabwe, discovered in the rock-walled ancient city near Fort Victoria, not far from where she'd grown up. The proud, erect bird of prey stared resolutely ahead, majestic, unshakeable. She looked up at Bryant again. His gaze mirrored that of the eagle in front of him.

'As much as we might feel compelled to take action, or to help others find the killers of our brother and sister,' Bryant continued, surveying the room before returning his stare to Pip Lovejoy, 'we must put our faith in the local police. We can be secure in the knowledge that the perpetrators of these terrible crimes will be brought to justice.'

She thought he was trying to emulate the sanctimonious tone and words of the chaplain. It was very unlike Bryant, from what she knew of him. He had obviously made an extra effort, dress-wise, for the funeral. The knife-edge creases in his tunic and trousers, the perfectly knotted tie and his newly trimmed hair were also very un-Bryant.

'But I'll tell you this, people,' he said, leaning forward on his elbows to get closer into the audience, 'nothing the coppers do, or the courts, will take away the bloody pain. Excuse me, Father,' he added, turning to the chaplain, who replied with a little frown.

Pip looked around and saw most of the uniformed people were sitting up straighter, on the edge of their pews. There was that commanding presence again – a quality he used sparingly, but effectively.

'And you just have to learn to live with it.'

There were a few murmurs and some head-shaking at the harshness of his stone-hearted comment.

'That's right, that's what I said. You'll see more death and injustice in the years to come than any of you had ever thought possible. Be angry about these deaths, but ask yourselves something, every hour of every day from here on in. Ask yourself, here at Kumalo, and overseas if you're going to an operational squadron, if you have done everything, and I *mean* bloody everything, in your power, to ensure that each and every one of the men and women you serve with will still be alive at the end of that hour, that day.'

There was silence in the chapel and outside now.

'Was there something one of us could have done to make sure Felicity Langham did not end up in the clutches of a murderer, that she wasn't alone, maybe friendless on the night she died?'

Pip looked across at a pew near the front dominated by WAAFs and saw Corporal Susannah Beattie, the senior parachute packer and Felicity's superior, hang her head.

'I probably could have. I'm the adjutant. It's my job to keep tabs on morale and make sure we all work together, as a team, as a family.' He looked across at the two flag-draped coffins and said: 'Forgive me, Felicity, if I could have.'

Pip looked at him and saw him swallow hard, as if fighting back his surfacing emotions. It was a small mercy, she thought, that Felicity, an only child, had no family in Rhodesia to attend the funeral. They would have been confused by the veiled admonitions in Bryant's eulogy – and perhaps their absence gave him a free rein. The girl's mother had died in a riding accident several years earlier, while her father, a veteran of the first war, was serving in Italy as a major in the pioneer corps, a collection of ageing veterans who performed civil engineering works for the army. Pip had drafted the cable to send news of his daughter's death to him, and she'd found it one of the saddest duties of her life.

'To those of you who knew James Smythe, to those of you who instructed him, ask yourselves what you knew of him, if you can understand how he ended up miles off course, in another country, for Christ's sake. Sorry for that one, too, Father. Forgive us, James, if we failed you.'

He paused. 'If we don't look out for each other, if we don't work with each other, despite our differences, our jealousies and our prejudices, more of us will die than survive this war.'

'Volleys, load!' barked Flight Sergeant Henderson. At his command the ten askaris worked the bolts of their .303 rifles, each chambering a blank cartridge. The funeral party's drill was good, ebony hands moving perfectly in unison. Their dress was immaculate – starched high-collared tunics, shorts, puttees and spit-polished ankle boots. The brass buckles on their First World War pattern webbing glinted in the morning sun. It was not the first, and would not be the last, burial they attended, though the cause of death was usually an aircraft crash rather than murder.

Pip thought it a terrible irony that probably the only time these proud Ndebele warriors would fire their weapons during the war would be to mark the death of airmen and women who would never see action.

'Present!' The rifles were pointed across the two open

graves and heavenwards into the cloudless African sky. 'Fire!'

Pip flinched as the first volley shattered the peace of the cemetery and sent half-a-dozen glossy starlings winging into the azure sky. Henderson gave the same commands twice more, then ordered the firing party to unload.

The sun warmed her back but couldn't stop the chill running down her spine as the two trumpeters sounded the mournful strains of the Last Post. She glanced across at Paul Bryant, standing smartly to attention and, like the other officers present, saluting. At the conclusion of the refrain, the trumpeters paused for a few seconds, then blew reveille. Catherine De Beers, she noticed, was dabbing at her eyes with a white handkerchief. Susannah Beattie had an arm around a crying WAAF. Pip wondered if the tears were for Felicity Langham, perhaps out of guilt, or if the young woman cried for the dead English pilot.

Pip ran her eyes along the other wooden grave markers in the cemetery. There were at least a score of them and the names came from nearly every corner of the British Empire – Canadians, Australians, Britons and Rhodesians. There were even a couple of Greeks. Pip pondered the waste of it all. To survive the invasion of Greece, to escape to England and then be shipped to Africa, only to die in training. She'd learned, early on in the war, that men were buried in the country where they died, as it was impractical to ship so many bodies home. She wondered where Charlie was right now.

Henderson ordered the firing party to fix bayonets and then slope arms. They turned and marched away from the graves, hobnailed boots crunching the gravel in perfect synchronisation. A procession of more than a hundred mourners fell in behind the Askaris and the Kumalo pipes and drums band. The bagpipes were from half a world away, but their keening lament seemed to fit the landscape, in an odd way, as naturally as the whine of a yellow-billed kite that climbed and dived like a fighter plane above the column.

Pip mingled her way through the trailing crowd until she was beside Bryant. It wasn't hard to get to him. For all the strength of his performance in the chapel, it was clear that in day-to-day life he was something of a loner. While other instructors and trainees huddled in preordained cliques, smoking cigarettes and chatting, Bryant remained at the edge of Felicity's grave, staring down at the coffin.

'That was a moving speech,' Pip said as she came up beside him.

He didn't look around. 'It's an old one. I used to give it to my crew, and the others in my flight.'

'It had an effect,' she said.

He laughed, short and sharp, finally turning to look at her. 'Well, that'll be the first time then. These stupid bastards will still fly off into the blue yonder chasing herds of bloody wildebeest and zebras across the veldt until they realise, too late, they're lost, or they'll fly too low trying to impress some pretty girl, or they'll bloody crash-land on a farm where they're hoping to bed the farmer's daughter. Nothing I say sinks in.'

'You're too hard on yourself. That's your problem,' she said. 'Fancy a drink?'

'Too bloody right I do.'

They followed the crowd, walking down the edge of the concrete runway away from the cemetery until they came to an open hangar. In front of a parked Harvard, trestle tables had been laid out and white-jacketed African mess stewards were having trouble flicking the caps off bottles of Lion lager fast enough to fill the outstretched hands of officers and airmen.

'Any excuse for a piss-up,' Bryant said.

'A wake's as good a way as any to say goodbye to a loved one,' Pip said.

'If I'd been to a wake for every bloke I've known who died in the last couple of years, I'd be dead of alcohol poisoning by now,' he said.

She smiled. She knew that black humour was a way

of coping with tragedy. Policemen, she'd noticed, were the same. The worse the accident or murder, the more coarse and inappropriate the jokes. 'Did you mean that, about Felicity, I mean?'

'What, that I wonder if I could have done more?'

'Yes.'

'Of course I did. I knew she was being ostracised by Susannah and the other girls, that she was getting too big for her breeches and antagonising them with her fame. I could have reined her in a bit – maybe put an end to her circus antics with the parachute displays. Maybe then she would have decided to live on base, instead of off it, been one of the girls, so to speak.'

She nodded, then casually said: 'Funny, when I first asked you, you weren't sure whether she lived on or off base.'

He looked at her, then closed his eyes.

She sensed he was fighting back other emotions this time.

'Two beers,' he said to the steward as they finally reached the tables, whose white draping was already stained with spilt beer and beginning to fill with empties. He took the bottles and a glass for her. 'Come with me, away from this lot.'

She followed in silence, looking over her shoulder, searching for Hayes. She couldn't see him anywhere.

'You want the truth?' he said. They were outside the hangar now, the hot sun stinging the tops of their heads and shoulders. There were still airmen in sight, hanging around, smoking and drinking, though out of earshot.

'Of course,' she replied.

'I suppose it's all right, since you've caught the bloke who killed her.'

She had said nothing to him about Nkomo's alibi, or her growing suspicion that the evidence had been planted in the petrol-seller's car, probably by the real killer. She felt her pulse quicken with excitement.

'We were ... intimate, Felicity and I.'

She *knew* it. She had so many more questions for him now, and her mind reeled with them. 'Why didn't you tell me?' was all she could put into words, immediately regretting the tone she had used. It was as if she were offended, personally insulted that he had not trusted her enough to tell the truth. Damn, that had come out all wrong.

'Why do you reckon? I could tell from your questioning that you thought whoever killed Flick must have known her. Why put myself in the box seat and end up being dragged down to the station by you and Sergeant No-Neck?'

Despite herself, she smiled briefly at his succinct char-acterisation of her colleague. 'You've been trying to cover up those first few lies ever since you told them.'

'Guilty,' he said.

'And you had no alibi for the night Felicity was killed – none we could check, anyway.'

'Right again. I got drunk, as I do most nights, in my own room, on base, reading a book, then fell asleep, fully clothed, until I woke at dawn the next morning.'

'Tell me about you and Felicity.'

He took a long pull on his beer, then reached down and lifted his right trouser leg. Pip stepped back in alarm.

'Don't worry, it's not a knife or a gun.' He pulled a crumpled packet of cigarettes from the inside of his khaki sock. 'When you're in parade dress you're not supposed to have anything that shows through your pockets and ruins the line of the uniform. Bloody uncomfortable walking around with a pack of cigarettes on your ankle, though.' He offered a cigarette, but she wrinkled her nose and shook her head. He lit his. 'Things are going on in this war that are so unlike anything that's ever happened before, you start to wonder whether they're true or if they were a dream.'

'It's a different world today, that's for sure,' she agreed, wondering where he was heading.

'That's how it was with me and Felicity.'

'Different?'

'Unlike anything I've experienced. Look, despite being

Australian, I actually used to be something of a gentleman – before the war, at least. I'm not one to brag about my private life, if you know what I mean.'

'Nothing you can say will shock me, Paul,' she said. She silently cursed herself again, this time for using his Christian name. It had been a slip. Despite her assertion about being unshockable, she suddenly thought that she did not want to hear what had gone on between him and another woman. Perhaps she should have involved Hayes.

'It's not my aim to shock you, but it's complicated, what there was between me and Flick. It was . . . it wasn't like a normal relationship.'

'Complicated?'

'Paul, dear Paul! There you are!' gushed Catherine De Beers as she barged between Pip and Bryant and kissed him on the cheek.

Pip took a step back. She noticed Bryant looking around, as though uncomfortable at the thought someone might think he and Catherine De Beers were anything other than professional acquaintances.

'Hello,' Catherine said. 'Patricia, isn't it?'

'Philippa. Pip. How are you holding up, Mrs De Beers?'

'Catherine, please. What can I say? My best friend in the whole world is now lying under six feet of dirt at the end of an airstrip. Would you like a drink? They've nothing but beer at the bar.'

Pip smelled alcohol on the other woman's breath. Catherine reached into a black shoulder bag and extracted a pewter hipflask. 'Brandy,' she said. 'All that's kept me going the last couple of days.'

'No thanks,' Pip said.

'Paul, join me in a drink?'

'I'll stick with beer, thanks. You're not driving home this evening?'

'Not to the ranch, no. I'll stay in town at—'

'At the place where Felicity was living?' Pip asked. 'During our investigation we discovered that you own the house Miss Langham lived in.'

'*Discovered?* All anyone had to do was ask. It was no great secret Flick and I were friends. Well, after tonight I won't be needing that house at all. I'll probably sell it.'

Pip noticed that Catherine was slurring her words a little. She stayed standing close to Bryant, almost but not quite touching him, as if she needed his close physical presence to support her.

'You won't be coming into town any more?' Bryant asked.

'I won't be coming to this part of the country any more. I'm leaving the ranch and getting rid of the town house. I've decided to move back to Salisbury.'

The surprise showed on his face. 'What? When?'

'I'm driving back to the ranch tomorrow, and then

leaving for good on Monday, as a matter of fact,' she said to him.

'Why the rush?'

She looked him in the eyes and said: 'I think you know. There's nothing here for me now, Paul.'

'But your things, surely you can't pack that quickly. Give yourself time to—'

'My staff are packing as we speak. I'm going to stay in an hotel in Salisbury – Meikles – and then with friends until my things arrive.'

'Catherine, I hate to interrupt, but I was hoping to have a chat with Paul before I leave.'

'Don't mind me,' Catherine said, her voice thick with sarcasm.

Bryant got between the two women, and said to Pip: 'Actually, I also need to talk to you about the search for our missing kite – poor old Smythe's Harvard. We've heard nothing from the coppers across the border, and our aerial searches haven't found a thing. I wouldn't mind going out to the place, just to see if there's something the locals have missed.'

'I'll make some calls this afternoon,' she said. 'You'll want to drive across the border?' She realised her gaffe as soon as she'd said the words. She didn't mean to dredge up his reluctance to fly, not in front of Catherine.

'Yes,' he said. The brief flash of embarrassment was

plain for her to see. 'The drive will take a couple of days, which means I won't be able to go until later next week, after all of the flap over Jan Smuts' visit is over.'

'The Prime Minister of South Africa's coming to the parade?' Pip asked.

'You hadn't heard?' Catherine interjected. 'It's the worst-kept secret in Bulawayo. Smuts and Huggy are both coming.' Sir Godfrey Martin Huggins – Huggy, as he was known to his supporters – had been the prime minister of Southern Rhodesia for the past ten years, and showed no signs of flagging in that office. 'Poor Paul and his men have been painting rocks and marching to and fro in preparation for weeks. I'm only sorry I won't be there to see it.' Pip noted another heavy dose of sarcasm.

It was the first Pip had heard about the dignitaries' visit. She imagined, though, that others at the police camp were involved in the planning for it. It irked her a little she had found out this way. She wondered if Hayes had been trusted with the information. Smuts had fought the British during the Boer War, but had made his peace with his foes at the cessation of hostilities and gone on to serve as a general in command of South African forces during the First World War. Under his leadership, South Africa was ostensibly a strong supporter of England's war and the Empire, although Pip knew there were many Afrikaners who would rather have aligned themselves with the Swastika than the Union Jack. Having said that, there were thousands of South Africans of all backgrounds fighting the Germans and their allies.

'It's a big deal,' Bryant said. 'This is our biggest course so far, so the politicians are clamouring to be a part of it.'

'I'll be in Salisbury by then,' Catherine said, 'so you can give my invitation to someone else.' She looked across pointedly at Pip.

Pip realised Catherine wanted time alone with Bryant. They had, after all, just buried a mutual friend. The questions would have to wait. 'I'll leave you to it. Again, I'm sorry for your loss, Catherine. I'm working Sunday, Paul. Give me a call tomorrow and we'll see about your trip out to the wastelands.'

'Will do,' he said, and watched her walk away.

It was probably not Pip's responsibility to organise cross-border investigations, but Bryant suddenly felt as though he wanted to spend some more time with her. He'd felt oddly calm after telling her about his experiences in Bomber Command, and he wondered if he might exorcise some of his thoughts about Felicity by talking with her.

Catherine interrupted his thoughts. 'God, I'm hardly gone and you're already looking for a replacement. Stop leering at her bum, Paul.'

'What? Oh! No, not her. Don't be silly, Cath,' he said, hoping he sounded convincing.

'I've seen the way she looks at you. She's got more on her mind than police business. I wonder if she has her own handcuffs?'

'Stop that,' he said. 'Now, what's this rubbish about you leaving? This is the first I've heard of it.'

'It's not rubbish. Don't take offence, Paul, but I meant what I said, there's nothing here for me now.'

'No offence taken. I know you weren't expecting me to propose to you.'

'You'll be gone soon enough anyway,' Catherine said.

'Who says?'

'It's the war. People come and people go. If the air force doesn't send you back on operations they'll probably find some other godforsaken training base to park you.'

He shrugged. She was most likely right. 'What do I say now? Thanks for the memories?'

'That's a nice start. Flick meant more to me than you'll ever know, Paul.'

'I've a fair idea,' he said.

'No, it was more than just that. We were like . . . it's hard to describe. Almost like a couple.'

'I understand.'

'No, I don't think you really can. There's no way to say it that doesn't sound perverse or tawdry. I wanted so much for her to stay at the ranch, to give up her silly air force job, but she wouldn't hear of it.'

'She loved the parachuting – even if she didn't get on with the other girls here.'

'Those bitches.' There was no hiding her disgust. 'They were jealous of her beauty, her spirit and her fame. Your eulogy touched a chord in me, Paul. I've also been wondering if there was something I could have done to prevent her death. I hope that black they've arrested goes to the gallows.'

'It's a pretty safe bet,' he said, offering her a cigarette and drawing one for himself out of the pack with his lips. She accepted and he lit both of them. 'I'll miss you, Cath,' he said.

'Will you? I think I confused you, Paul. I don't think you were ready for either Flick or me to complicate your life.'

'I haven't known a woman like you before. You're so . . . so . . .'

She smiled, finishing the sentence for him. 'So much like a man, is that what you're trying to say?'

'I don't think that's quite what I meant.' He grinned.

'I like sex. I like it whenever and with whomever I please. In that respect, I'm very much like a man. I wanted you, and I had you, and I enjoyed you. I'd like to think the feeling was mutual.'

He laughed. 'Direct was the word I was looking for.'

'There's no time for coquettishness in war, Paul. You of all people should know that. Do you have to go to this silly wings parade on Tuesday?'

'You know I do.'

'Why not come to Salisbury, meet me at Meikles.'

'I can't take a day off when two heads of state are coming to the base! Besides, I couldn't afford to stay at that hotel,' he said.

'I'd pay. Two days, two nights. Just you and me. Call it a farewell celebration.'

He smiled. 'You know I have to be at the parade. I could visit you in Salisbury once you get set up?'

'I'm not your popsy, Paul. I'm not going to be waiting breathlessly for you every time you get a weekend off. It's a one-time offer, Squadron Leader.'

'Then a handshake will have to do,' he said, raising his beer bottle in a friendly toast.

'I really wish you'd reconsider.'

'I've got a job to do, Catherine. As you pointed out, we're in the middle of a war.'

'Well, you've made your choice. If you'd rather have the air force than me, I understand completely.'

'Don't be churlish.'

'Churlish? That's a word for little girls. I'm treating you like a man would treat a woman. If we do it, we do it on my terms. I've had my fun with you, and now I'm leaving you to your policewoman.'

'Don't be angry. Maybe you should give it a few days. You're still in shock over Flick's death.'

'I'll be in shock over Flick's death until the day I die.'

'Do you want me to come to your place in town later?' he asked her.

She shook her head. 'I've just buried the love of my life, Paul. I'm not so much like a man that I'd be thinking about sex tonight.'

Pip stared at the list of names without reading it. It was stuffy in the police interview room and she was perspiring in her shirt sleeves.

She was annoyed at the way Catherine De Beers had interrupted her conversation with Paul, just when he was on the verge of telling her about Felicity Langham. Paul had slept with Felicity Langham – been intimate, as he had put it. She had so many more questions to ask him. How long ago? How many times? Did Catherine De Beers know he had slept with her best friend? It was an effort, but she forced herself to concentrate on the case. She looked across the table at Nkomo and said, 'You've nice handwriting, Innocent.'

'You still haven't told me, Constable. Did my alibi hold up? Did the people I told you I was with confirm it?'

'You're a smart man, Innocent.'

'Would you believe I was studying to be a schoolteacher, before the war started?'

'I'd probably believe you if you told me you were the illegitimate son of Winston Churchill,' she scoffed. 'It's your stock-in-trade, fast talking. You're still charged with murder, until we see fit to release you.'

'You haven't answered my question,' he said.

'And I don't have to, so shut it.'

The list was long. The fifty or so names would take ages to track down. She would have to find out which of Innocent's regular customers had recently passed on his code word and phone number to a man aged around thirty, with dark hair. The description of the man was as vague as that of the unknown woman to whom he had sold fuel before the man. He'd said she was tall and blonde and good-looking. Nothing more.

'Are you sure there is nothing else you can tell us about the man you sold petrol to on the morning after Miss Langham's death?'

He shrugged. 'If I could, I would. I've told you what I remember about him.'

'Yes, yes, I know.' She stared at the list and then at the ceiling. Something clicked in her mind. *What he looked like.* 'I asked you what he looked like, but I didn't ask you what he sounded like, did I?'

Innocent pursed his lips, then closed his eyes as he tried to remember the brief conversation they'd had.

'What did he say to you, Innocent?'

'I am trying to remember. It was not very much. We said good morning. I introduced myself and asked him his name. He was a rude man. He said: 'None of your bloody business, just hand over the petrol.' He gave me the money and I took the first can from my car and put it where he wanted, around the corner, in the alleyway.'

'You said before you didn't see his car.'

Innocent exhaled. He'd told the story so many times. 'That's right. He told me to take the can around the corner. Then, when I came back, he was lifting the second can out of the boot. If he is the killer of this woman, then that must have been when he put her things in my car.'

'Yes, yes. I know that's what you think. But let's stick to the facts for now. What about his accent? Was he Rhodesian? Was he British? Think, Innocent, think.'

'I am not sure. White people all sound the same to me.'

She shook her head. 'Very funny. Your life's on the line, Innocent. Face up to the fact that I'm about the only person in this police camp who believes you.'

'I know,' he said, his face serious again. 'I worked in a filling station, while I was studying, you know.'

'So?'

'So, that is where I learned about fuel. How to find it, who runs the local market.'

'Go on.'

'You know, in all the years I worked in a filling station, I never once saw a white Rhodesian man so much as lift a petrol can or fill his tank or wash a windscreen. It wasn't the customer's job to do such things. It was mine.'

Pip sat back in her chair and folded her arms. She thought about all the men she knew. Rhodesian men were a breed unto themselves. They would gladly burn meat on a *braai*, but wouldn't cook in a kitchen or wash or dry a plate. In poorer households, those without servants, the wife did all the housework. A Rhodesian man would light a fire and boil a kettle in the bush for tea, but would expect it to be prepared and served for him in the home. A white tradesman might own his own business, and do his fair share of hard physical work to get the job done, but if he went to someone else's shop or business, he would not lift a finger. She couldn't imagine Charlie, her husband, dirtying his hands or moving anything more than a wagging finger when there was a black man about to do it for him. In fact, she detested the way he would call one of the herd boys from the bottom paddock to lift a single bag of grain onto the back of the truck, rather than do it himself. 'So what is your point?'

'I am not sure. I am not being rude when I say this, Constable,' Innocent said, 'but I thought it was odd that this man would be helping me shift cans of fuel.'

'Think again what he said to you.'

'I just can't remember. It was so quick, the meeting.' Innocent laid his head in his palms.

She stood from the table and walked around to him on her way out. She put a hand on his shoulder and said: 'Think harder, Innocent. Alibi or no, you'll go to the gallows if some of the people around here have their way.'

'That is not fair,' he said.

'Life rarely is, Innocent.'

12

Church bells echoed down Bulawayo's broad, empty boulevards.

Parts of the town, especially today when they weren't thronged by people, reminded Bryant of country towns he'd visited in New South Wales. As in those bush towns, Bulawayo's streets were wide enough to turn a bullock dray. The roadsides were decorated with purple-flowered jacaranda trees, another reminder of home. He eased off on the throttle of his Triumph motorcycle and caught the blossoms' scent. It reminded him of perfumed English girls at squadron dances. He gunned the bike again and roared up the deserted street towards the police camp.

He'd risen early and gone to his office just after dawn, where he attended to a score of signals relating to the big parade. In Rhodesia, the war effort slowed at weekends, but it never really stopped. He had the final timings for the scheduled arrival of Smuts' DC-3 Dakota aircraft at Kumalo on Tuesday and, as per the plan he'd drawn up, the South African prime minister would arrive on time, half an hour after his Rhodesian counterpart's motorcade got in from Salisbury. There had been yet another parade rehearsal, postponed to Sunday because of the double funeral the day before, and this one had ended in fits of laughter when Isaac, a burly, well-liked Matabele cook dressed in his best Sunday suit, had been escorted out in front of the massed ranks and introduced over the Tannoy as The Honourable Jan Smuts, Prime Minister of South Africa. A scowling Flight Sergeant Henderson had stood in for the Prime Minister of Southern Rhodesia, Huggy Huggins, and while he and Isaac had taken the airmen's grinning salute side by side, Henderson had been clearly unimpressed at Bryant's use of the black man to represent such an important politician. The men had liked it, though, which was the important thing as far as Bryant was concerned. They'd had to endure more square-bashing than any previous course and, after the deaths of Langham and Smythe, he wanted to give them something to smile about. Before dismissing them, Bryant had warned the soon-to-graduate flyers to keep their noses clean on their final weekend, and to save their urge to overindulge in alcohol until after the VIPs had departed on Tuesday afternoon. His work day was not over yet, though.

Even the police camp had a lazy, weekend feel to it as he passed through the gates. There was no one visible in the grounds and he parked the bike next to the one police car in the lot. He strode into the office and a lanky white police officer looked up reluctantly from the newspaper he was reading.

'Can I help?'

'I'm looking for Constable Philippa Lovejoy. She's expecting me.'

The man straightened and grimaced, as if he had just swallowed something rotten. 'Er, can I ask the nature of your business, sir?'

'Police business,' he laughed. 'I've been assisting her with the investigation into Felicity Langham's murder, and the disappearance of one of our aeroplanes.'

'Oh, you're air force?'

After the parade, Paul had changed into mufti, an old pair of khaki trousers, an open-necked white cotton shirt and a pair of locally bought *veldskoen* desert boots. 'Squadron Leader Paul Bryant,' he said, finding his air force identification card in his shirt pocket and laying it on the desk.

'Ah, yes. Very good, sir. She said you'd call.'

'That's right. Look, mate, is she here or not?'

'It's not good news, what's happened, sir,' the constable began.

'What? Has something happened to her?' He was suddenly alarmed. He'd awoken that morning feeling strangely refreshed and positive. He hadn't had any night-mares and he'd felt relieved rather than sad that Catherine De Beers was leaving for the other side of the country. He realised, too, that he was genuinely looking forward to spending the morning chatting to Pip Lovejoy, and to the possibility of getting her involved in the search for the missing Harvard. Now, he felt dread.

'Not to her. To her husband,' the policeman said.

'Oh, Christ,' Paul said, shaking his head. 'Don't tell me . . .'

'Afraid so. She telephoned this morning. She'd just found out. Charlie, that's her husband, has been killed in action.'

'Poor girl. When you see her, tell her I dropped in and I'll follow up my request with Sergeant Hayes.'

'No, sir . . .'

'What do you mean, no?' he asked, puzzled.

'It's a bit odd, but when she called in this morning to say she wasn't coming in, she said that when you dropped by, to tell you that she still wanted to see you and, if you wouldn't mind, perhaps you'd call around to her place.'

'Really?'

The constable looked at the airman in a new light,

and wondered if there were something going on between Pip and the Australian.

Paul caught the look and said: 'I'm a bit surprised, frankly. I'd have thought she'd want friends or people close to her to be with her today.'

'My thoughts exactly,' the constable said.

'Well,' he said, genuinely bemused, 'you'd better tell me how to find her place.'

He followed the signs out of town towards Plumtree, a small farming settlement near the Bechuanaland border, to the west of Bulawayo.

He gave the bike full throttle on the open road, sticking to the narrow strip of tar on the left-hand side, and following the course of the railway line, which darted in and out of sight amidst small granite kopjes and stands of long, straw-like grass on his right. The speed helped clear his mind. His body became part of the machine, leaning into the corners, hunching low as he hit a downhill stretch and pushed her to maximum speed. He couldn't decide how to feel about being invited to Pip's place.

He still couldn't read her, although he knew she was passionately dedicated to her job, and to seeking the truth. She seemed far more intelligent, committed and diligent than the bag of wind she worked with.

Given the investigation into Flick's death seemed pretty well over now they had a man in custody, that only left his request for help with the cross-border search for them to discuss. He couldn't accept that she would call him out to her home on the day she'd learned of her husband's death to talk about a missing aeroplane.

Bulawayo was set on a huge plateau and on a day like this it seemed he could see for miles in every direction. A baboon ran across the road in front of him. He followed its path and saw it was part of a large troop of thirty or forty. Several of the females had tiny, big-eared babies, either suckling or hitching a lift, riding jockey-style on their mothers' backs.

He thought about how close he had come to telling Pip everything about his relationship with Felicity and Catherine until, with superbly ironic timing, the wealthy widow had intruded.

Catherine. Around her he was like a child watching a burning firework. He was drawn by her beauty, by her fire, by her danger. Touching her, trying to hold her, he had realised from the start, was a dangerous business. Impossible, as it had turned out. She'd been an experience, he decided. Like first-time fumbling sex. Exciting, new, unknown. Something he'd never forget, but not something he needed every day. He smiled at the crude analogy, but didn't feel bad, as he sometimes had when he'd said his last goodbye to some young English girl he'd met on leave in a pub or dance hall. This time he had been cut loose, by her. He respected her honesty. Whatever judgement one could make of Catherine De Beers, she could never be called a liar. She was honest, to the point of brutality, about her emotions, or lack of them.

Was Pip calling him to her so she could ask him more about Flick and Catherine? That, too, seemed unlikely, no matter how curious she was about the web that had been woven around him and the two women. It was still so utterly amazing that he wondered whether it had actually happened, or whether it had all been a dream.

And Flick. Of the two of them, she and Catherine, she was the one he would have liked to have known better. He wondered if he'd been like every other man on base, if he had simply wanted her because she had that movie-star unattainability. She was the closest thing to a celebrity at Kumalo, probably in all of Bulawayo, but he had been invited into her world. She wore her worldliness like a new designer dress, something Catherine might have bought for her, or handed down. But even when she tried to shock him he had detected an innocence beneath her words, the gestures, the acts, as if she were indeed a film star playing a role designed to tease him, to please Catherine.

He threw back his head and screamed into the rushing wind. 'Aaaaaah!' There was only one thing he was certain of right now. He was alive.

A trio of big, curly-horned Kudu bulls that had been grazing on the side of the road took flight at the sound of his cry and the growl of the bike's engine. The graceful antelope bounded high as they ran from him and he envied their freedom and the simplicity of their life. A Rhodesian farmer had told him there were plenty of leopard still stalking the rocky bushland around Bulawayo, and he wondered if there were still lion in the area. He loved Africa's simple, natural rhythms of life. There were dangers everywhere in the bush, but nature had equipped both predator and prey with the skills they needed either to kill or to have some chance of survival. Nature had given the retreating antelope speed, agility, good hearing and horns to stab back at a cat.

Paul Bryant, by contrast, was out of his element, in a foreign country, dealing with emotions and situations neither training nor nature could prepare him for. He felt utterly defenceless.

The ranch was called *Lala Panzi* – a place to lie down. Under the words were the names of its owners, Charles and Philippa Lovejoy.

Bryant turned off the strip road at the carved wooden sign swinging from a mopane pole on rusted chain links, onto a corrugated dirt road. On a low ridge to his left was what he took to be the staff compound, where the farm workers lived. A cluster of red-earthen huts with reed thatch roofs, garden-size plots of straggly maize, whippet-like yapping dogs, cooking fires. An Ndebele woman in a flowered smock looked up from her outdoor washing tub. A line of sheets hung limp in the air, the drying time slower by the day as the promise of summer wetted the air. A man sat in the shade of a *kiah*, his home, smoking. Four children, in ragged hand-me-downs, started running down the hill towards the track at the sight of the man on the motorcycle – rare excitement, indeed. Bryant waved at them. The children shrieked with joy. The woman lowered her head to the washing; the man closed his eyes.

Fat cattle grazed on golden grass in an open paddock on his right. Tick birds rode shotgun on their spines and white egrets shadowed their movements on long, skinny legs. A teenage herd boy in patched overalls raised his stick in a wave. Bryant felt an odd contentment as he bounced along the half-mile track, taking in the simple, timeless rural scenes on either side of him. He'd chafed in the countryside back in Australia, eager to get away from his aunt and uncle and into the thick of city living.

Out here, though, he soaked up an innocent peace and quiet that was missing from the constant drone of aero engines and barking warrant officers at Kumalo. He screwed his eyes tight for a couple of seconds, driving by instinct alone, as he tried to force the image of a burning Lancaster out of his mind.

When he opened his eyes he was still in Africa, in front of a modest though well-kept whitewashed single-storey farmhouse with a steeply pitched thatched roof. The grass in the fenced yard in front of the dwelling was as green and clipped as any he'd seen in England's home counties, the flowers bright and cheery. Africa was all around, but inside the chicken wire fence was an ideal. A pretty good knock-off of a little piece of England, re-engineered and built from memory.

Pip pulled back the curtain at the rumbling sound of the motorcycle in her driveway. She'd imagined he would be in an air force car, if he came. The priest had been in a car. She'd only just got rid of him, after two inter-minable hours.

She drained her gin and tonic. It was her third. Unusual for her, to be drinking before midday. Charlie would have approved. Would have told her she'd finally *loosened up*. When the priest was around she'd had to quaff the second one fast – in one gulp in the kitchen, in fact – just to get through the second hour of patronising condolences and talk of what a good man her husband had been, and how he was now enjoying a better life.

A better life. Was that an impossible concept to grasp? Maybe not. She'd ask Squadron Leader Paul Bryant his thoughts on that one. There was a knock on the door. Too soft, too tentative. He was scared, she thought, or reluctant.

He looked at her when he opened the door, and couldn't hide the surprise on his face.

'Well, say something, Squadron Leader,' she said.

What he wanted to say was certainly not appropriate. He'd taken in every detail in a single, brief glance, and captured the image of her in his mind, like a photograph. She stood in front of him wearing shorts hemmed at barely a third of the way down her thighs, which showed off a deliciously slender pair of legs, and a yellow short-sleeved summer shirt that was tied, rather than tucked in, at her waist. The narrowest sliver of pale skin was visible above the waistband of her pants. She'd made up her face and her blonde hair framed it perfectly. Her fingernails, like her toenails and lips, were painted blood red. 'I'm sorry for your loss, Pip.'

'Thank you, Paul, and thanks for coming out to see me. Do come in, please.' She smiled, turned and led him into the house.

He tried hard not to look at her bum, but failed. Why, he wondered, had she dressed like this?

'Would you like a drink?' she asked, looking back over her shoulder.

He checked his watch.

'Don't worry,' she said, 'I'm three gins ahead of you already.'

'Hate to see a lady drinking alone.'

'A lady wouldn't. Scotch or gin?'

'Scotch. Plenty of ice and water, please.'

'Let's sit outside. The sun's glorious today.'

'Lovely morning,' he agreed. 'Believe me, Pip, I know how hard it is. I've been through the loss of people close to me.'

She handed him his drink and led him onto a sunny flagstoned verandah, which looked out over a neatly manicured garden.

Bryant looked around. 'Nice place. Lots of antiques inside, I noticed.'

'All his stuff. It's like living in a museum. Too many ghosts of long-dead Lovejoys. Too much England, not enough Rhodesia. Not enough . . . reality.'

He sipped his Scotch. It was nice taking a drink with someone else for a change, even if the circumstances were rotten. 'People have different ways of coping with death, Pip. I reckon I've seen most of them.'

'So, you're not surprised that I'm not wearing black or gone into purdah?'

He shook his head. 'Do you want to talk about him?'

'No.'

'OK.'

'Well, maybe later.'

'Why am I here, Pip? Don't you have . . . friends?'

'I told you before that I'm fairly new to this side of the country. Being stuck out here on a farm doesn't improve your social life much. You do meet a lot of other lonely farm wives, though.'

Lonely? There was more to it than that, he thought. He remembered the way she'd clammed up when he'd asked her about her husband in the car. 'Friends usually try to say what they think you want to hear.'

'Aha,' she said. She leaned back in her chair and took a long sip of her drink. 'I hoped you were as smart as I thought you were. For a while there you had me thinking you were just another fly-boy trying to break the squadron record for how many women you could bed per country.'

He frowned. He'd seen people drink too much when someone died. It usually ended in tears or a fight, frequently both.

'Sorry,' she said. She put a hand to her eyes to shield them from the sun. 'That must have been the gin talking.'

'I can listen, if you want to talk,' he said.

'I think that might be the answer to your question.'

Now he was confused, losing track, and he hadn't even finished his first drink. Then he saw the pleading in her eyes, the innocence belied by the tough talk. The same look he'd seen from Flick. 'Oh, of course. That's why I'm here, to listen.'

'Maybe. You're not a friend, Paul. Don't take that the wrong way.'

He put his hands up in a gesture of peace. 'No offence taken.'

'You've seen things, done things, I know.'

He shrugged.

'You don't pretend, Paul, do you? Not when it comes to life and death.'

'No,' he said instantly. 'Never. The truth hurts, as they say, but you can't escape that kind of pain.'

'Look at my eyes.'

'What about them?' he asked. He'd been tempted to say, 'very pretty', but not even he would flirt with a woman in mourning.

'Not red-rimmed? Not puffy? Not tear-filled?'

'Sometimes it takes a while. Sometimes it takes a very long while.'

'It's not going to happen.'

'Why?' he asked.

'I'm not drinking to drown my sorrows, Paul. This is a celebration.'

He let the word hang there. He'd never celebrated a death. No, that wasn't true. His crew had got plastered during their second tour after Nigel, one of the gunners, had downed his first enemy night-fighter, not long before he was decapitated by a cannon shell. 'What are you celebrating?'

'Freedom.'

He looked hard into her eyes and saw no trace of irony. Her mouth was set, awaiting his reaction, but her eyes were smiling. They were, indeed, free. 'Did he hurt you, Pip?'

She nodded.

'People knew him, here, in Bulawayo? He was a local boy?'

She nodded again.

'So they're going to be crying for him, singing his praises. Expecting you to be the grieving widow.'

'He's everywhere, all around me, Paul. The boys at the police camp played rugby with him, his mother pops around to visit at the worst possible times, even that bloody Susannah Beattie in your parachute hangar knew him.'

'No ringing endorsement there,' he smiled. 'But you knew the real Charlie, right?'

'Yes. The real Charlie.'

'People don't become heroes, don't become good people, simply by donning a uniform and going off to war, Pip. But a lot of civvies, a lot of family and friends don't see it that way.'

She returned his stare. 'That's the hardest thing,' she said, her voice a little croaky now.

He thought he saw her eyes soften, moisten. Not from a sudden remorse for the loss of her husband, or guilt at her feelings. 'You're worried that now you'll be denied justice, that no one will know what he was really like.'

'Yes.'

'I've seen cowards, thieves, bullies, thoroughgoing bastards each and every one of them, saved by the bullet.'

'By death?' she asked.

'Blokes who should have been charged and sent to the cells, who probably would have ended up there, are now mourned as the "valiant dead" because a piece of shrapnel or a night-fighter's tracer carved them up before they got their just desserts.'

'Better for their families, that they think their sons and husbands died heroes, than have them returned in hand-cuffs, I suppose,' she said, turning her gaze to the garden.

'Do you want to talk about him? About what he was really like?'

She turned back and took a deep breath. 'I'm sorry, Paul. I've no reason to lump this all on you. I don't even know why I left the message for you to come here.'

'Yes you do. You know, don't you?'

'What?'

'That it can help. Talking about what you went through.'

'That's rich coming from Mr Strong Silent Type.'

'You were investigating a murder. I didn't think my life story was part of that.'

'He hit me.'

He drained his drink but said nothing.

'Let me get you another,' she said.

He put his hand over the tumbler. 'No, thanks. I'm fine for the moment.' He stayed silent, waiting for her to resume.

'We were very much in love, you understand, at university,' she said. 'I was so blinded by that love, I gave up my studies – my future.'

'He never hurt you then?'

'Never. Of course we weren't living together. We weren't . . .'

'But he was a different person when he drank?' Bryant asked. He knew the type. He had an uncle like that, and a bruised aunty who was proof of the man's darker side.

'Yes. Whenever I saw him drinking it was at a university party, or around friends. He was funny, the life of the party. But as soon as we were married – on our honeymoon, in fact – I saw the other side of him. I saw him after he'd had a few too many, before he passed out.'

'He hit you on your honeymoon?'

Pip looked out over the garden. She nodded.

'Bastard,' he muttered, shaking his head.

'Yes, he was. On the first night at the Falls Hotel we flattened two bottles of champagne over dinner, and he'd already had a few beers. He had a couple of brandies afterwards. When we went to bed, he was impotent. He became angry, blamed me.'

He looked down at his shoes.

'He hit me, several times. After that, whether it was the exercise, or a rush of some sort, he . . . well, he was ready again. I didn't want him to touch me by that stage, so he forced me. From then on that was pretty much the script for our lovemaking, if you could call it that.'

'Why did you stay with him?' he asked.

'God, I've asked myself the same thing over and over again. I don't know. I was close to reporting him on a couple of occasions, but I've since learned that the easiest thing for policemen to do in these situations is to turn a blind eye. I suppose I kept hoping that he'd come around, that he'd go back to being the person I married. I cried with joy the day he went away to the army, and in pain the night before.'

'Is it part of the reason why you volunteered for the police?'

'Despite your crude Australian way of putting things, you're quite perceptive, you know.'

'Were you going to arrest him when he came home?' he asked, trying not to sound flippant.

'Right again. A small fantasy of mine, to see him in court, before a judge. However, I've also learned as a police volunteer that first-time offenders are often given lenient sentences – an admonishment or a fine. If I'd reported him – or even arrested him myself – and he hadn't gone to gaol, I'm sure he would have killed me.'

'Really?'

'He held a gun to my head once, when he was very drunk. He made me do things . . . But I don't want to talk about that.'

'I understand.'

'Do you, Paul?'

'The evil that men are capable of? Yes. The way some men can't control their emotions, and how drink brings out the very worst in them? Yes. Do I understand that power and the abuse of it can be part of sex? Yes.'

'Have you ever hit a woman, Paul?'

'No.'

'I believe you. Did you hurt Catherine De Beers the other night, at her ranch, when she crept into your room?'

'I wouldn't say no to that second drink, Pip. A beer would be fine, though. I don't need hard spirits right now. And, for the record, no, I did not hit Catherine De Beers the other night, or on any other occasion.'

She didn't move from the garden table. Instead, she looked hard at him, her gaze boring into him, searching for his soul. 'I didn't ask you if you hit her. I asked you if you hurt her.'

'No, I did not hurt her.'

Pip rose and walked back inside, taking his empty glass with her. He looked up into the cloudless African sky. Such perfect weather for flying. Such a clear, uncluttered, perfect blue. If only things on earth were as transparent, as simple, as liberating as flying.

'What are you thinking now?' she asked as she sat a dewy bottle of Lion Lager down in front of him.

'Thanks,' he said. 'Oddly enough, I was thinking about flying. Something I haven't done for a long time. You asked about Catherine.'

'Yes.'

'It's a longish story.'

'I've told you mine and you, as I recall, were going to tell me yours before the Widow De Beers interrupted us yesterday.'

'A promise is a promise. Am I talking to Pip Lovejoy here, or Constable Lovejoy?'

'We're one and the same.'

'Fair enough,' he shrugged. He raised the bottle to his lips and took a long swig. 'Hard to imagine it all only started a couple of weeks ago.'

Pip had fetched herself a glass of iced water. 'I got the impression you two had, what's the word, *known* each other for longer?'

'No. Not long at all. It was just after she'd crashed her plane, on the airstrip at Isilwane. She drove down to Bulawayo and came to an officers' mess dance at Kumalo. I only went because it was expected of me, as adjutant.'

'She couldn't keep doing her aerial displays with Felicity, after her crash?'

'That's right. She cornered me at the dance and asked me to let her fly a Harvard, and for Felicity to jump out of it. I said absolutely no way on earth was I going to sign over a valuable trainer for her to joyride in. She was sulky, but she stayed with me for an hour or so. We danced, and we had a couple of drinks together, and, well, one thing led to another.' He looked at the floor.

Catherine had worn the blue dress, the silky one that slid over every curve the way the ocean caresses a golden sandy shore. When another pilot had twirled her on the floor, in a jitterbug, nearly every man at the dance had seen tantalising glimpses of bare flesh above the tops of her nylon stockings. She'd danced and flirted with several other men, he didn't recall them all, but she'd come to him for the last dance of the evening, to 'Moonlight Serenade'.

'I'd do anything to fly in one of your aircraft, Paul,' she whispered in his ears as he guided her across the concrete floor. The small of her back was damp with perspiration.

'I can't change the rules, Catherine,' he replied.

'I said, "anything", Paul.'

He saw the look in her eyes and knew she meant it. He felt his body start to stir just as the dance ended and he shepherded her to a quieter corner of the hangar, behind the parked aircraft, grabbing fresh drinks on the way from a steward carrying a tray.

'What would it take, Paul?' she pressed, sipping her brandy and dry, her free hand brushing a strand of hair from his forehead.

'An act of parliament that allowed women to fly, and your enlistment in the air force, I suppose.'

She said, straight-faced: 'I can't wait. You know there are women flying military aircraft in England and the United States. There was a picture of Pauline Gower, the commandant of the British Air Transport Auxiliary, in last Friday's *Chronicle*. The ATA fly bombers and fighters from factories to operational squadrons.'

'True, but we don't have a branch of the ATA here

in Rhodesia, and we don't have any aircraft factories.'

'Flying excites me,' she said, moving closer to him.

He felt the touch of thigh against his leg. He looked around to make sure no one else saw. 'I used to like it too,' he said.

'It excites me a great deal. I do what I have to in order to fulfil my pleasures, Paul.'

'How's your drink?' he asked.

'Finished.' She crouched and placed her empty glass on the floor. She looked up, her dark eyes fixed on him. As she stood she ran a fingernail along the crease in the front of one leg of his uniform trousers. Her finger stopped at the belt of his tunic. The arc lights in the hangar roof were all on, illuminating the drunken party-goers, some of whom were in mid-kiss. 'What are you going to do now?' she asked.

'Right now? Go to bed, I expect,' he said, checking his watch. It was after eleven.

'If you're not going to let me fly one of your aero-planes, will you at least let me use your telephone?'

'Of course,' he said. 'We can go back to the orderly room. It'll be empty.'

'Can you direct me to the ladies' room first, please?' she asked.

When she'd finished they walked together to the orderly room, close, but not holding hands. Had he guessed, he wondered later, what would happen next?

He sat behind his desk, switched on a small lamp and pushed the phone across to her. He riffled through some papers, inwardly groaning at the mountain of administrative work waiting for him the next day. She sat on the desk, opposite him, and picked up the receiver. Instead of dialling, though, she slowly, casually, brought her left leg up until her foot was resting next to his in-tray.

He stared at the expanse of bare skin as the blue silk slid down her thigh. She adjusted the suspender and looked at him. 'You can touch it, if you like.' She held the telephone by its cord, the handpiece dangling in front of his eyes like a swinging hypnotist's watch. She moved her foot in an arc across the desk, sweeping aside some paperwork. She was seated there now, in front of him, her other foot on the table, knees raised near her chin, her hands behind her, supporting her.

He looked at her face, then down, over her breasts.

She said: 'I took my knickers off in the ladies' room. I do hope you don't mind?'

He stood and she reached for the fly buttons on his uniform trousers. He grasped her hips and pulled her to him, sliding her bottom across what remained of his day's work. She lay back, arms flung wide as he entered her in one fluid movement.

* * *

'It was just one of those things,' he said to Pip.

'Like buzzing a young lady four times in your aircraft?'

'Five.'

'It sounds like she was trading sex for a ride in a Harvard,' Pip said, unable to conceal an equal measure of surprise and disgust.

'She persisted, but I told her I still couldn't let her fly an airforce aircraft.'

'It all seems rather businesslike to me,' Pip said. 'The woman was practically prostituting herself.'

'Well, I've never paid for it, and I wasn't about to,' he said. 'She told me that whether or not I relented she still wanted to see me again. She invited me over to dinner, for the following night.'

'And you went, of course,' Pip said, rolling her eyes skyward.

'I *am* a man, Pip.'

Pip laughed at his candour. She hadn't thought about Charlie for a few moments, which was nice. What was not so nice, and more than a little embarrassing, was the way she'd felt a warm tingle deep in her belly, the first sign of her own arousal, as she'd imagined Paul and Catherine De Beers making love. Perhaps that wasn't the most appropriate term. One word would describe it better. She felt her cheeks start to colour.

'Anyway,' he said, setting his beer bottle down on the

wrought-iron table, 'I went around the next night, bouquet of roses in hand . . .'

'Ever the gentleman.'

'Don't know about that. I thought gentlemen weren't supposed to tell.'

'I'm a police officer, remember. I'm soliciting a confession out of you.'

'As long as that's all you're soliciting,' he said, smiling.

'I've never flown in an aeroplane before and, much as I'd like to, I'm not prepared to go *that* far.' She was glad she'd stopped at three gin and tonics. One more and she might really have started flirting with him. It felt so nice, she thought, to be alone with a man and not be afraid.

'So we have dinner at her place. All above board, you understand, until we get to dessert,' he said.

'Go on.'

'After dinner, we . . . well, we weren't alone.'

'Felicity lived in Catherine's Bulawayo town house, didn't she?'

'Yes.'

'And she came home? Nothing unusual about that.'

He looked at the ground. It seemed he was unwilling, or unable, to meet her eyes. 'I told you at the funeral that Flick and I had been close.'

'Yes, but . . .' It suddenly dawned on her. She saw his

embarrassment and suddenly understood – at last, she thought she was beginning to understand.

'You and Felicity made love in Catherine's house that night?' She couldn't hide her shock, or her disapproval. 'But they were best friends, Paul.'

He took a deep breath. 'No, it wasn't like that. It wasn't behind Catherine's back. This is coming out all wrong, but there doesn't seem to be a right way to explain it to a stranger, let alone to myself.'

Pip put her hand over her mouth. 'You don't mean that she ... that you ... that Felicity ...' It was her turn to feel embarrassed when he looked at her and nodded his head.

The whole thing had been so unreal as to be like a dream. He and Catherine were in the bedroom, undressing each other, when Felicity walked in on them. Not a knock, not a word. At the time he was dumbfounded, had reached for his clothes, then been speechless himself when Flick and Catherine kissed.

The young woman whom he'd seen time and again at Kumalo, had spoken to during her preparations for her parachute jumps, had admonished once for being late for duty, was now naked, in bed with him and her closest friend.

Catherine was the only one to speak. Not words of

love, not even of lust. Commands. She instructed and Felicity obeyed. When he and Catherine had been together, at the ranch, she had wanted him to take the lead in their lovemaking. With Felicity, it was Catherine who was very much in charge.

Images reeled in Pip's mind, like the dirty postcards Charlie had kept hidden in his bedside drawer. There was one of two women together, one pretending to strike the other, whose hands were tied in front of her, on the buttocks with a cane. It had been taken in Egypt during the last war, handed down to him by some filthy old uncle. She'd never felt attracted to other women, but had known girls at school who had kissed and held hands more often than polite friendship might dictate necessary.

'So,' Pip asked, 'did you . . . I mean . . . with *both* of them? Did they?'

'Gentlemen don't go into that level of detail, Pip. I can tell you, though, that there was something incredibly strong between Flick and Catherine. Maybe even love, in a strange sort of fashion. Cath misses her like hell. It's why she's leaving town.'

'What about you? Doesn't she care for you, too?' Pip asked him, trying yet failing hopelessly to comprehend the strange tangle of relationships.

'She wanted to fly that aircraft a great deal. I like to think we had fun, and that we each enjoyed our time together – Catherine and I, that is – but in the end I think she was just using me.'

'Well, now you know how most of the world's women have felt at one time or another,' Pip said.

'I know. Catherine explained that to me yesterday, as well.'

'Did you see either of them separately?'

'I spoke to Felicity at the base a couple of times, as Susannah Beattie probably told you. I was trying to make sense of what had gone on, and to decide for myself why she'd become involved with Catherine and me. But no, Flick and I were never together again in that way.'

'Why did you lie about that, out of interest, about not knowing her?' Pip asked.

'I was shocked by Flick's murder and, to tell you the truth, a little bit guilty about what had gone on. In a sense, it was true, I didn't really *know* Flick, and we hadn't had a relationship. I was ashamed, too, that Catherine might have been using her bond with Flick to help get her own way. I think the unspoken promise was that Catherine would let me into the world she shared with Flick, if I caved in to her request. How could I explain all that to a copper the day after Flick had died?'

'Why would Felicity have just "let you in" to her relationship with Catherine, anyway?' Pip asked.

He nodded, as though he had been expecting the question and had given it much thought. 'The way I saw it, Catherine made the decisions. It seemed that Felicity would do anything Catherine told her to, and let Catherine do anything to her, no matter how bizarre. It seemed like they both enjoyed their respective roles.'

'Catherine got you to tie her up when you made love at the ranch, didn't she?'

'Look, can we change the subject? This is getting a bit *too* embarrassing now.'

'Tell me. I saw the marks on her wrists when we left,' Pip said.

'Tell you what,' he said. 'I've had enough truth for one day. How about a little escapism?'

'What did you have in mind?'

'I'll show you how I escape my bad memories these days. Come outside.'

'I am *not* getting on that death trap with you!' she said when he straddled the Triumph.

He kick-started the bike and revved it hard. 'Get on!' he yelled over the noise.

'No!'

'Yes!'

She looked at him, and then at the farmhouse. She

turned and walked back towards the front door. She heard the note of the engine drop and looked over her shoulder. She saw the look of disappointment, then smiled cheekily. 'I'll just fetch us something for the road!'

He gave a whoop, gunned the bike again and did a spin around her circular driveway, kicking up sand. He finished outside her front door just as she emerged with two cold quart bottles of Lion and a calico bag. 'Put them in the panniers,' he said.

She stowed the food and drink, having no idea where they were going or for how long. The important thing was that she was leaving the farmhouse that had become a prison, the life that had, until this morning, seemed more like a sentence. She was free. She climbed onto the bike and, unsure where to hold on, tried to grasp the seat under her.

Bryant let out the clutch, and the bike leaped forward like a thoroughbred leaving its gate.

Pip squealed, a shriek of pure joy, mixed with a little real panic as the force threw her backwards.She wrapped her arms around his waist in order to stay on.

He knew the trick would work. It always did. Now he felt her pressed against him, her breasts brushing his back, her chin almost touching his shoulder as she yelled into his ear, 'Where are we going?'

'Away,' he said.

She closed her eyes and savoured the feel of the sun on her face as they sped back towards Bulawayo. For a moment she worried that someone from the police camp, either on duty or off, might see them, might say something. She was supposed to be a widow in mourning. The hell with them all, she thought. She hadn't done anything this wild since university.

The bush, the shanties, the houses, shops, people out for a Sunday stroll were all lost in a blur as he took her back towards town. He slowed momentarily to turn right onto the Matopos Road, the bike tipping so low she could have reached down and brushed the Tarmac with her fingertips.

He gave the machine its head, making conversation impossible on the miles of undulating hills between Bulawayo and the Matopos reserve.

She thought it an almost eerie place, full of precarious, naturally balanced granite boulders, prehistoric rock paintings, and the bones of Rhodesia's founder, Cecil John Rhodes. She'd visited the place a couple of times with Charlie and friends of his, for picnics. A semblance of domestic normality. A lie. The Matopos held no fond memories for her, but no one who visited the reserve could doubt its raw natural beauty.

He looked back over his shoulder at her. 'Let's find a quiet rock.'

They motored, slower now, through the reserve, past a family who had stopped for a picnic, until they found a broad, flat-topped boulder, with a mix of shade and sun. Paul stopped the bike and held out his hand to help her dismount. She took it and held onto it for a second after she'd regained her balance. 'Thank you for this,' she said.

'You're the one providing the food and booze, so thank you.'

He took the beer bottles from the pannier and held them in one arm. He leaped up onto the boulder and extended his free hand to her again.

'I can manage, thanks,' she said.

'Suit yourself. You can see for miles from up here.'

She scrambled up onto the warm, smooth lookout and set down the calico bag of rolls and cold chicken. When she stood again she surveyed the brown scrubby bush. There was a waterhole a couple of hundred yards in the distance. 'Look. Eland.'

His eyes followed where she was pointing and he saw a massive antelope, with a sagging dewlap and humped back. 'Magnificent,' he said.

'There are rock paintings of rhinos around here, but they were hunted out years ago. It's a terrible shame. These hills are crawling with leopard, you know.'

'Stop it, you're scaring me,' he joked as he upended

one of the beer bottles and used the lip of its cap to open the other. Froth spilled from the mouth and he licked it from his hands.

'So, how are you going to open the other bottle?' she chided him.

'With my teeth?'

'You'll do no such thing,' she said. She took the bottle from him and fished a steel bread and butter knife from the food bag. She held the beer in her left hand, with her index finger crooked around the neck. Using her other hand she placed the end of the knife's handle under the rim of the cap and, with one sharp, deft movement, accompanied by a loud pop, levered it off. The metal cap sailed high into the air.

'Don't know many girls in Australia who could manage that,' he said.

'We're raised as true ladies out here in Africa. Equal to any task. Cheers.'

'What will you do now?' he asked her. 'Stay in Bulawayo?'

'I want to go back to university, but I also like my job here.'

'Can't imagine there'll be too many places for women in the police once the war's over.'

He was right, unfortunately, but she believed that the inroads women had made into male-dominated professions could not be turned back completely. 'Do you think the war will ever end?'

'Has to, some time. The Yanks are pouring thousands of men and millions of dollars' worth of machinery into England. There was talk of an invasion, of Europe, even when I was still over there. Has to come soon. The Eyeties have folded and the Russians have started to push the Jerries back, but they've still got plenty of fight left in them, so it won't be finished this Christmas.'

'I'm so glad it hasn't touched us here, not in terms of the fighting, at least.'

'It's funny, though,' he said. 'The way it's provided an opportunity for people like you to do something, well, different with your life. Something positive.'

'You learned to fly. That's a skill you can use when it's all over.'

He shrugged. 'I haven't wanted to get into an aeroplane for a long time, not since England.'

'You never did finish telling me your story, did you?'

'I thought we'd had enough truth for one day,' he said.

She opened the food bag and then laid the chicken and bread out on the calico. 'Can I make you a roll?'

'Please.'

'You don't have to talk about it, Paul. But, God, it felt so good to tell someone today how I really feel.'

'When I'm on the bike, like today, it almost feels like

flying,' he said, accepting the food from her and adding his thanks.

'You should try it again sometime.'

'I dunno,' he said. 'Too many memories.'

'Are you scared?' she asked, taking a mouthful and washing it down with beer.

He snapped his head around, turning his gaze from the African bush back to her eyes. 'Yes.'

'What happened during your two tours?'

'That was part of the problem. I didn't finish my second tour. I was wounded,' he said, looking down at his food. A slender lizard, about as long his hand, and painted the colours of the rainbow, inched towards a crumb.

They both watched in silence as the lizard fought to overcome its natural fear of humans, balancing the risks between a safe exit and a feast.

'Were you hurt badly?' she asked. From the corner of her eye she saw the little reptile dart away with its mouth stuffed full of crumbs.

'Probably not badly enough to keep me from flying.'

'Did you ask to be grounded?'

'No, I did not, and that's the truth. Not that it mattered.'

'Well, then it's not like you shirked your duty or anything like that. Why do you feel so bad about it?'

'If I tell you, will you stop asking me questions?'

'No,' she said.

He sighed. 'Will was a good friend. No, more than that. We were like brothers.'

Paul Bryant shook the rain from his uniform cap as he and Will Freeman entered the briefing hut.

'Fucking rain,' Will said.

Paul laughed. If he'd had a quid for every time his English flight engineer, his mate, had said that during the year they'd flown together, he would have had enough to buy Buckingham Palace and Big Ben. 'Cheer up, could be snowing.'

'Give it a month. Christ, Paul, why couldn't they have sent us to the bloody South Pacific or somewhere warm to get killed?'

Paul passed a cigarette to Will, then lit it and one for himself as they took their seats in the crowded room. Will never had his own smokes and Paul usually saved him the effort of asking for one. Their unspoken agreement was that he supplied Will with cigarettes and Will always bought the first three beers. 'Three to go, mate,' he said.

'Please, God, make it a nickel and I'll become a priest,' Will whispered as the wing commander walked up onto the wooden stage.

Paul had also been hoping – he never prayed – for a nickel, the codename for a leaflet-dropping mission over occupied

France, but he already knew better. 'Fat chance,' he muttered as a hundred pilots, engineers and navigators from half-a-dozen different English-speaking countries scraped their chairs back and got to their feet. 'I cycled out to the flight line this arvo and took a squiz at the weight and balance sheets. They put 2154 gallons of fuel in her, Will.'

'Aw, fuck,' Will said. 'A full load. That means—'

'Be seated, gentlemen.' The Wingco said, his New Zealand accent softened by several months in England. 'The target for tonight is the Ruhr.' He pulled a curtain drawstring theatrically and a large-scale map of Germany was revealed.

Around them there were other muttered curses, shaking heads and closed eyes. 'Happy Bloody Valley,' Will muttered.

There was nothing happy about the Ruhr Valley, Germany's industrial centre, and the most heavily defended piece of real estate in the Reich. The target, within that seething, smoky, deadly conglomeration of iron and steel, was a ball-bearing factory.

'I don't have to tell you how important ball bearings are to the German war effort,' the Wingco said.

'Not as important as my balls are to me,' Will muttered.

Paul took down the details of the route, weather conditions, code words, the colours of the day – flares that could be fired off by one aircraft to alert another it was a friendly – all the details that had become part and parcel of his life. When he checked the page of notes he saw the tip of the pencil tapping the paper and realised his hand was shaking.

'Good luck, chaps,' the wing commander said at the conclusion of the briefing.

The rain cleared as they rode to their kite in the back of a truck. 'Who's for P-Popsy?' called the cheery English WAAF driver.

'Still on for tomorrow night, Brenda?' Will called back, to the accompaniment of wolf whistles and jeers.

'Cheeky sod, you know I wouldn't be seen in public with a rogue like you, Will Freeman,' she said.

'Who said anything about public? We can leave the lights off if you like.'

'Out!' she screamed.

Paul smiled, but there was no mirth in it. He knew Will's incessant joking was just a means of hiding his fear. They knew each other too well.

'Three to go, Paul,' Will said to him. It was their ritual. Paul spoke the number of missions they had to complete in order to finish their current tour at the start of every briefing, and Will said it at the door of the aircraft. They shook hands and then hoisted themselves inside awkwardly, their bodies bundled in sheepskin-lined boots and flying jackets, helmets and yellow Mae West life preservers.

Sweat, leather, hydraulic fluid, fuel and dried blood. The smells of their Lancaster, P-Popsy. She was more fish-wife than popsy. Loud and lumbering and creaking with age, but Paul loved her all the same. He took his seat in the cockpit and began the litany of checks as Will settled in behind him.

His first tour, in Wellingtons, had been a comparative doddle. While other kites in the squadron had fallen to enemy fire, or been involved in midair collisions, or simply got lost, he and his five crew members had survived unscathed. A bloody miracle. Will had joined the crew for their second tour, as the Lancaster carried an extra man, a flight engineer, to monitor the engines and the myriad other working parts on the big aircraft. It was a measure of the man that Will had not only integrated easily into the tight-knit band of survivors, but also become the pilot's best friend.

Will liked to joke that he had bought the affection of Paul and his crewmates. A successful London car dealer prior to the war, he had produced a crate of vintage champagne – a rare luxury in England – after his first sortie over Germany.

In the air, however, it was skill and nerve that counted more than money, and Will had impressed Paul with his thorough knowledge of their aircraft and his cool head under fire. Between their deadly trips over the Channel,

Will had concentrated on an even more difficult mission – to get his increasingly withdrawn skipper out of his shell and keep him abreast of the earthly delights available to aircrew on leave.

'All right, mate?' Paul asked, looking over his shoulder.

Will gave him a thumbs-up and Paul punched the booster coils. He followed a sequence so familiar he could have done it drunk with his eyes closed. Port inner first, curls of bluish smoke escaping from each exhaust stub as the Rolls Royce Merlin engine roared into life. Next was the starboard inner, followed by the port and starboard outer engines. As always, there was the familiar but peculiar mix of satisfaction and disappointment. Satisfaction that Popsy was humming, all engines fine as he waved to the airman on the ground to haul away the chocks from the wheels; and disappointment that there was no mechanical reason to scrub the mission. Their destiny awaited in the encroaching gloom of the English twilight.

He gave a thumbs-up to the ground crew and taxied out onto the perimeter track. Popsy trundled slowly, one of a queue of Lancasters heading for the takeoff runway. The kite in front of him was away.

He swallowed his fear, for the fifty-eighth time on operations. Will was on his twenty-seventh mission, the four remaining members of his original crew on their fifty-seventh. As the pilot, Bryant had completed an additional mission, his first, as a passenger on another aircraft, before taking his own men up for their first time. The crew's luck had changed during this second tour. They had lost two members of the originals – Nigel, their mid-upper gunner had lost his head to a piece of flying shrapnel from a flak burst. Harry, a fellow Australian manning the front gun turret, had been spitted by a cannon shell from a vertical-firing gun on a Junkers 88 night-fighter, which had snuck up underneath Popsy on the eighth mission of their second tour. The wind gushing through the holed turret had blown Harry's blood back on to Paul's face, so that he'd needed to keep cleaning his goggles.

Paul tried not to think of the dead men, but it was getting harder, not easier, with each sortie. He turned onto the strip, applied full brakes and ran up all four engines again. Popsy shuddered and groaned, rattled and hummed. He looked across at the yellow and black chequered control caravan. A green light flashed in the Perspex dome on top. Bryant released the brakes and the Lancaster thundered down the airstrip. He pulled back on the control column and lifted Popsy, her seven crew and ten thousand pounds of killer cargo into the sky. In the bomb bay was a four thousand pound 'cookie' – a high explosive bomb that looked more like a huge steel barrel – and fourteen clusters of bundled incendiaries.

It took them half an hour to climb to their operational height of ten thousand feet, the airspeed indicator showing three hundred knots. Once over open water, Paul held the oxygen mask containing his intercom to his mouth and said: 'Gunners, test fire now. Try not to shoot down any of our own blokes, though.'

All three turrets, nose, mid-upper and the arse-end charlie opened up, firing short bursts, and reported their guns were fine. Unlike a propaganda newsreel he'd had to endure before a film at the local cinema, no one on board said, 'Enemy coast ahead'. That would have been stating the bloody obvious. Searchlights knifed the sky and long, arching trails of glowing red tracer from anti-aircraft machine-guns told them they were on the other side of the water, crossing the Dutch coast. 'Keep your eyes open, boys, for theirs and ours,' he said. Completely unnecessary, he knew, but the acknowledgments he received back told him that at least everyone was still awake. Around them they glimpsed the hulking shadows of the Lancasters and, way off to port, a squadron of Halifax four-engine bombers. It was a big raid. A crowded sky. Collisions between friendly aircraft were not unusual.

Nearly three hours after taking off, a light show ahead told Paul they were in Germany – a glowing orange carpet of fire, spotted with the reds and greens of marker flares dropped by the pathfinders that flew ahead of the bomber stream. By the time P-Popsy and her crew were over the target, the searchlights and eighty-eight millimetre cannons would be warmed up and ranged, thanks to the advance aircraft.

'Happy Valley, in all its glory,' the front gunner announced.

'Shut it,' Paul ordered, too terse. His nerves were showing more and more on every mission. 'Just concentrate on bagging us a fighter or at least a searchlight, mate,' he added, hoping to soften the rebuke to the overeager teenage gunner.

The Lancaster lurched, the port wing dropping so rapidly that men were thrown against the Perspex of their turrets and the cold metal fuselage walls.

'All right, skip?' Will asked over the intercom.

Paul wrestled with the control column and dragged the bomber back into a level attitude. 'Someone's fucking slipstream,' he muttered. In a black sky filled with as many as a thousand other bombers it was not uncommon to hit the invisible trail of an aircraft in front. It was always a shock, but not nearly as dangerous as hitting another kite.

'Corkscrew port! Corkscrew port!' yelled the rear gunner, the tinniness of the intercom heightening the fear in the man's shrill call.

Bryant threw the mighty bomber into a sickeningly steep diving turn that made every panel and rivet vibrate in protest. His actions were instinctive, born of training and the real thing. The call from the gunner had only one meaning. He heard the four browning machine-guns open up from the rear turret.

'I see him,' said the mid-upper gunner, calmer, more experienced. 'FW 190. Mad bastard. He's still on us, skip.' His twin guns joined the chorus coming from the tail turret.

It was a new tactic the Luftwaffe had introduced, called 'wild boar', and it was plain crazy. Unlike other night-fighters, who stealthily sought out bombers on their way to or from Germany over quiet skies, the volunteer *wilde sau* flew small single-engine fighters over heavily defended targets. They waded into the bomber streams while the British aircraft were on their final bomb runs, in a bid to disrupt their aim and catch them unprepared. The result was as unnerving and dangerous for the bomber crews as it was for the German pilots, who risked collision and being hit by their own antiaircraft fire, as well as bullets from the bombers' gun turrets.

Paul pulled back on the control column, levelling for a second, and saw a flash of glowing tracer stream past his cockpit. Will was half standing behind him. He pushed the Lancaster into a right turn this time, and caught a glimpse of the single-engine fighter as it flashed past them. As the enemy aircraft moved ahead of them the front turret opened up.

'Think I hit him!' cried the exultant gunner.

Their luck was in. Probably an inexperienced pilot. Paul was low now, down to three thousand feet, and while his evasive tactics had helped them lose the night-fighter for the moment, four hungry searchlights, their operators surely having seen the aerial gunfight, now hunted him.

'Nearly over the target. Shit, they've got us, skip,' the bomb aimer swore, his gloved hand over his eyes to shield them from the piercing glare.

Bursts of smoke and shrapnel erupted around them as the antiaircraft gunners below followed the searchlight's guiding beam. A second, then third, beam found them, locking them, painting the black belly of the bomber brilliant white. The flak batteries found their range.

'Steady,' the bomb aimer said, his voice quaking.

This was the worst time of any mission, Paul thought. On the final run-in, coned by searchlights, just waiting for the flak to hit them. If he threw the Lancaster into a tight turn now they might miss the target by a mile, and the trip would have been for nothing. As always, it was still a tempting thought.

'Left, left,' cooed the bomb aimer, correcting their course. 'Steady.'

White-hot chunks of shrapnel from a nearby burst peppered the aircraft, making a sound like hail on a tin roof. Cannon shells sailed around them as more and more German guns took advantage of the searchlight operators' skill and luck.

'Fuck!' Will cried behind him as the Lancaster was rocked by a nearby explosion.

Paul wrestled with the control column. It had felt like a giant had swotted them and sent them sliding sideways.

Acrid, chemical-smelling smoke filled the fuselage.

'Bombs gone!' yelled the bomb aimer.

The Lancaster rose of its own accord, suddenly relieved of its deadly cargo. The leap caught the searchlight operators unawares and, for a moment, they were in blissful but confused darkness. Paul dove hard to starboard and took them down so low that the bomber was buffeted by the hot air rising from the fires below. He turned west, towards England, and didn't level out until they were little more than church-steeple height over the German countryside.

'Bomb bay doors aren't closing, skip,' Will said into his intercom. On terra firma they were mates, equals; in the air, Paul was always the boss. Will's job, as flight engineer, was to monitor continually all the working parts of the Lancaster – engines, hydraulics and other moving parts, to ensure all was performing as it should. 'Shit. Hydraulics are gone. Try the flaps, skip.'

'No good,' Paul replied. 'Must have been bleeding out since the flak burst. It's been all right up until now. Bomb aimer, check the bomb bay and make sure we at least got rid of everything.'

'Roger, skip.'

The smoke had cleared inside now, blown out through the scores of holes drilled by the shrapnel and, while he waited for the bomb aimer's report, he said: 'Let's hear it. Everybody all right?'

One by one all the crew reported in. Thank God, Paul mouthed, the crew were all alive as well. All he had to do was get them back in one piece.

'Um, skip, bad news,' the bomb aimer said.

'How bad?' Bryant asked into his intercom.

'Could be better. We've got a cluster of incendiaries still on board.'

'Shit,' Bryant said. 'We'll try to drop them over the water.'

'Roger, skip.'

The crew stayed silent as they crossed into occupied Holland, still searching the starlit skies for black night-fighters. Bryant skirted some light flak and soon they were over the coast. They weren't out of trouble yet, though, not by a long shot.

Once over the water, Bryant told the bomb aimer to try to drop the incendiaries.

'No go, skip,' Mac said.

'I don't like the idea of landing with a cluster of bloody fire bombs on board, but there's nothing else we can do,' Paul said.

Unable to operate the flaps because of the lack of hydraulic pressure, he kept the Lancaster at the same altitude until, at last, they crossed the English coast.

'All right, Will, give me some air.'

In front and to the left of Will's panel was a knob that operated an emergency supply of compressed air, contained in two bottles. If the hydraulics were inoperable, as was the case now, the bottled air was blasted through lines in order to perform the same operations. This would automatically force the landing gear down, and supply enough pressure through the lines to operate the flaps. Will pulled the knob, and they felt the Lancaster's speed drop. 'Done, skip.'

'Check the landing gear, Will,' Bryant said.

'Shit, it's not our night, skip. One down, one half down – not locked. The flak must have damaged the struts as well as the hydraulics.'

Paul heard the note of fear in his friend's voice, and felt his heart pound in his chest. He took a moment to consider the situation. The landing gear was inoperable, and they had a cluster of fire bombs stuck on board. He gave his orders. 'All right, here's the drill. We're going to Woodbridge.'

They all knew the place, as did every crew in bomber command. Woodbridge was a three-mile-long strip of cleared ground on the Sussex coast, lit by a continuous line of parallel petrol-fuelled burners, designed to provide an all-weather emergency landing ground which, through the heat its burners gave off, would also dissipate heavy fog. The system was named after the group that set it up, the Fog Investigation Dispersal Organisation, or FIDO.

Woodbridge was a graveyard of bombers. Because of its length, aircraft too shot-up to land safely were also diverted there to take their chances. There was silence on board P-Popsy.

Paul continued his orders. 'I'll radio Woodbridge on approach and take us to two thousand feet. When I give the order, every man will bail out. And that's an order. Once you're all accounted for, I'll bring the kite down. We'll meet on the ground and then it's my shout at the first pub we can find.'

Again, there was silence as each of the six crewmen contemplated his fate. While none of them relished the thought of a night parachute jump, they all knew that the skipper was giving them the best chance they had at survival, and that the odds were not good that Bryant would survive a crash landing.

'Point her at the sea and jump out as well, skip,' Will suggested.

'I thought about that, Will,' he said over the intercom, for all of them to hear. 'I'd have to put her in a steep dive, otherwise the old girl might carry on until she ran dry or, worse still, maybe hit one of our ships. I don't want to bail out in a dive – I'd end up getting caught on the tail plane.' His fear was valid. It was a fault with the otherwise well-designed bomber that the only quick way out of the cockpit was through a removable Perspex panel over the pilot's head. Too many pilots had thought they were jumping to safety, only to be killed by a collision with the vertical tail fins when they bailed out. 'I'm taking her down.'

Bryant radioed Woodbridge as they closed on the field. He overflew the twin lines of flaming markers below and put the Lancaster into a slow turn. 'All right, fellas. Places, everyone. Sound off!'

One by one they confirmed their readiness to jump. Mac, the bomb aimer, said, 'Skip, why don't you think again about bailing out and—'

'Enough, Mac. I couldn't live with myself if old Popsy took out a fishing boat or veered off and landed on a farmhouse. I'll see you in the pub, mate.'

Paul turned and glanced at Will. Something was wrong.

He held his oxygen mask aside, so the others wouldn't hear, and yelled, above the engine noise, 'Where the fuck is your parachute?'

'I'm staying with you,' Will called, grinning wildly.

'No, you bloody well are not. Get your parachute on. Now!'

'No!'

Bryant shook his head. 'I don't need you here in the cockpit.'

'I know, Paul,' Will yelled, laying a hand on the pilot's shoulder. 'Truth is I'm pissing myself at the thought of jumping. I'd rather take my chances on a pancake landing, with you.'

Bryant looked into Will's face and saw that it was deathly white. He hadn't expected the depth of his friend's fear of parachuting. 'Jump, Will. That's an order!'

'With respect, stick your order up your arse, sir.'

He brought the Lancaster out of its turn and headed straight and level at two thousand feet towards the start of Woodbridge's seemingly endless runway. 'Right-o, everyone . . . ten seconds. Now! Bail out! Bail out.'

'There they go,' Will said. 'I count three, four; no, five chutes, Paul, they're all away safe.'

Paul radioed Woodbridge and told him all of his crew, minus the flight engineer and himself, had exited the aircraft.

'Roger P-Peter,' an anonymous English female voice replied, using the Lancaster's proper designation, rather than the crew's unofficial name for their Lancaster. 'Crash wagons will pick them up and once they're all accounted for we'll give clearance to land.'

'Roger,' he said.

A short while later the WAAF radioed him, confirming all five members of the crew were safe and on board a truck. 'They'll see you on the ground. Good luck, P-Peter, and God speed.'

Despite his fear and the adrenaline that now coursed through his veins at the thought of the dangerous landing, the simple blessing touched him. 'Maybe I'll see you, too,' he said.

There was a pause, and she replied: 'Please stick with official wireless procedure, P-Peter. But in answer to your last . . . yes, that would be nice.'

Will punched him on the arm and gave him a thumbs-up. 'Two to go after this one, Paul,' he yelled into his ear.

Paul knew his chances of walking away from a belly landing in a Lancaster were not good. Coming in with incendiaries on board reduced the odds to something in the vicinity of a million to one, he reckoned. 'When we land, you go out first, Will, through the cockpit roof.'

'Don't be ridiculous. I'd have to climb over you and

put my foot in your lap to get out. The hatch is above your head. You get out and I'll be on your tail so close you'll think I've turned queer,' Will replied over the intercom.

Will was right. 'All right, but remember, we'll only have a few seconds if those incendiaries decide to cook off.'

'You don't need to tell me.'

'Strap in and brace yourself. Here goes nothing.'

Will clapped him on the shoulder then returned to his seat, behind Bryant.

Bryant mentally went through the checks for an emergency landing. He tugged on the restraint straps holding him into his seat until they were so tight it was hard for him to breathe.

He brought the kite down and pulled back on the throttle levers, cutting the power and airspeed to a hundred and thirty miles per hour. The gas burners that illuminated the emergency runway gave off enough heat to create an artificial thermal and the Lancaster, as heavy as she was, rode the hot air for a while, as if reluctant to come back to earth.

When he was about twenty feet off the runway, Paul pulled back on the stick, bringing the nose up. The airspeed dropped and the big aircraft started to stall, just as the tail wheel touched. The Lancaster settled and, for a heartbeat, rested on her one locked undercarriage wheel. However, once the massive weight settled on the damaged right wheel, Paul felt the wing sink towards the concrete.

He held his breath and prepared for impact. A shower of sparks fantailed up as the wingtip touched the runway. 'Brace!' he yelled. As the forces of friction started to take hold, the Lancaster began swinging to the right. The forward speed increased the severity of the turn, and Paul and Will were flung violently in the opposite direction as the Lancaster slewed to the right, off the wide runway.

The sparks and sickening sound of tearing metal gave way to the thuds of propeller blades tearing into mud and turf as the big aeroplane bounced and skidded on and on.

Paul pulled the fire extinguisher switches as the aircraft finally half rolled, half skidded to a halt. They should, hopefully, control any blaze in the engine bays, but the real danger was from the incendiaries in the belly of the stricken aircraft. He was vaguely aware of a flashing light beside him as the crash wagons chased him along the edge of the runway.

And then it was over. The silence came as a shock to him, and he shook his head to try to clear the fog of fear, relief, confusion and adrenaline.

'Paul! Paul! Get up, man. Get going,' Will called from behind him.

Paul tried to move, then remembered his restraint straps. He released the buckle and opened the emergency hatch above him. He smelled smoke and fuel somewhere, and heard the ping-pinging of tortured hot metal contracting.

'All right, mate?' he asked, turning to check on Will. Will's face looked even whiter than before.

'I'm fine, now get the bloody hell out of here. I'm right behind you.'

Bryant grabbed the metal frame of the cockpit and heaved himself out. The damp English air had never smelled better. He slid down the side of the cockpit and onto the wing. He looked over his shoulder and saw Will, kneeling in the pilot's seat, and waving. 'Run! Run, Paul, I'm coming!'

He needed no further urging, now that he was sure Will was all right. He slid off the wing and ran towards the flashing red lights. He covered about seventy yards and then slowed and glanced back, fully expecting to see Will Freeman gaining on him.

An ambulance pulled up beside him. 'Where's the other man?' an airman yelled at him.

'I don't—'

His words were obliterated by a boom that shook the boggy ground beneath him and a shock wave that knocked Bryant and the medical orderly to the ground.

He rolled painfully over onto his side. Radiant heat and the blinding brightness of burning incendiaries from the flames engulfing the rear half of the Lancaster seared his cheek, and his leg was afire with pain. Above the fire and the blare of an ambulance klaxon, he heard screaming.

Two airmen in bulky fire-retardant suits were running towards the cockpit. Paul dragged himself to his knees, but fell when he tried to stand. Blood oozed from several holes in his trousers, made by pieces of flying metal blasted loose from Popsy's skin.

The firefighters raised arms to the hoods protecting their faces. The blaze had spread quickly to the nose of the Lancaster. Bryant heard a final scream and saw something moving and burning inside the cockpit. The noise finally died.

He heard voices and looked up to see the other members of the crew standing around him.

'Well done, skip,' one of them said. He thought he heard irony, even bitterness, in the empty compliment.

'Shame about old Will, though.'

Pip rolled onto one elbow on the rock and looked into his eyes. She saw the raw pain still there, the self-loathing, the emptiness where the dogged fighting spirit of a bomber pilot had once been.

'Funny thing is, they gave me a gong for that. A medal. Distinguished Flying Cross.'

'It wasn't your fault that Will died, Paul,' she said.

Deep down, he knew she was right. He'd replayed the scene a thousand times in his mind and his nightmares, sober and drunk, and usually came to the same conclusion. But that didn't make it any easier to deal with. 'That's not the point, though, is it?'

'Why?'

'He died and I lived. Where's the fairness in that? I was the pilot, the skipper. I should have forced him to jump, should have pushed him out of the plane before me, but I didn't. I found blood on the shoulder of my flying jacket later. Not mine – I'd been wounded in the leg. I realised then that it was Will's. His face had been so white, but I thought he was just scared, like I was. He must have been too badly hit to make it to his jump station. It probably happened when the flak hit us. I suppose he thought that the medics would get to him eventually.'

'Look at me,' she ordered him as he turned his face away. She grabbed his chin between two fingers, realising as she did that it was the first time they had touched, and that some invisible line had been crossed. She brought his face back around to hers and fixed him with her gaze. 'Will would have known that you would have

329

stayed with him if you knew he was wounded. That's why he didn't say anything.'

He shrugged.

'It's true, you know it. He said nothing so that you'd have a chance at living.'

'I've thought about that many times.'

'You saved the lives of five other men, too, Paul. Don't forget that. You deserved your medal.'

'Bullshit. I deserved what I got. A chit from the medical officer that kept me off flying duties, even when my leg healed up, and a posting to the middle of fucking nowhere to see out the war. They wanted me out of sight where I wouldn't be bad for morale and the butt of conversations about the cowardly pilot who left a wounded man to die in a burning kite.'

'They – whoever *they* are – probably realised that you'd done your bit and needed a break.'

'It doesn't work that way, Pip. You see, the MO knew that I didn't want to go back, that I couldn't finish my tour. I was spent. He did me a favour by not stamping LMF on my file and kicking me out.'

'LMF?' she asked.

He shook his head as he spoke. 'Lack of Moral Fibre. Jesus, how I despised the men who went absent without leave, who just disappeared because they couldn't take it any more. I thought them weak, disgusting, and there was I, in the end no better.'

'I saw the way you put down that riot the other day, Paul. I saw you stand up to those men, and I saw the way they respected you. There was nothing lacking out there in the street. That took courage, and it required the respect of a bunch of men who had turned into an unruly mob. You probably saved some lives that day too.'

'It's getting late,' he said, gesturing to the waning African sun, the long shadows on the plain below them. 'I should get you home.'

'Have you ever talked to anyone about your last mission?' she asked as she gathered up the food bag and the empty beer bottles.

'No. You're the first.'

'Then we've both shared our deepest secrets. I can't forget my husband, Paul, for all the wrong reasons. He was a part of my life, but I'm free now. As terrible as it sounds, his death has given me a second chance. Will Freeman is gone, and you must remember him, for the right reasons.'

'I do,' he said. 'Every day of my life.'

'And he gave you a second chance, Paul. It's up to us what we do with the rest of our time from now on,' she said as she turned away from him and walked down the face of the granite rock, which glowed a soft, warm pink in the sun's late rays.

It was nearly dark by the time they got back to her farm.

'Now, how about that cup of tea,' she said as she climbed stiffly off the Triumph's pillion seat.

'I should be getting back to the base,' he said, still straddling the bike.

She thought he'd come so far that day, opening up to her as she had to him. She remembered the feel of his bristly jawline in her fingers, the hard muscles of his stomach as she'd clung to him through the twists and turns of the road there and back. She thought again of the erotic trysts he'd been involved in. She wondered what it would be like to be Catherine De Beers – to make love to whomever she wanted, whenever she wanted. The drink had worn off and her head was clearer, and she felt that to say goodbye to this handsome stranger, for that was still what he really was, would leave an emptiness, a hunger in her. 'Nonsense, come in for a cup. We don't want you falling asleep on the way back to base.'

'All right then.' He put the bike on its stand and followed her in.

She stood in the doorway of the kitchen, arms folded, looking at him. Not smiling, not frowning. A little confused, as if she had forgotten what it was that she had to do.

It was dark and warm inside the farmhouse, like a cocoon. 'Tea?' he said, standing, facing her, not more than two feet away.

'Maybe . . .' she began.

'Later . . .'

He stepped to her, crossing the barrier and pulled her to him. She fancied she could feel the heat from her cheeks reflected off his face. They kissed, greedy for each other. He put his hands under her bottom and lifted her off the ground.

She lost herself in the taste of his mouth, the grip of his muscled forearms, and she let him lift her. 'Down the hallway,' she whispered. 'Second door on the right.'

'No, here,' he said. He laid her on a big, velvet-upholstered wingback chair and knelt in front of her.

'What are you doing?' She was unsure of exactly what he wanted. Why was he kneeling?

He put a finger to her lips, then unbuttoned her shorts. She raised her hips to let him slide them down. He hooked two fingers in the elastic waistband of her pants, and she accommodated him again.

She glanced down and saw he was fully aroused. 'Paul . . .'

'Shush,' he said as he placed a hand on each of her

bare knees and parted her legs. He lowered his head and opened her with the tip of his tongue.

She squirmed, amazed and a little shocked at what he was doing down there. 'It *tickles!*' she said. Then, as his hot tongue found the spot where she sometimes touched herself, alone in her bed at night – the place that Charlie had never bothered to find – she closed her eyes and felt herself melt into the chair. 'Oh my.'

He could read her body. It felt to her as though he knew her intimately already, her body's signs, its messages to him. She was breathing faster, heavier, and starting to chew rapidly on her bottom lip. He stopped. She opened her eyes and mouth, silently beseeching him.

'Second door on the right?' he said.

'You're a fast learner,' she breathed.

He stood and picked her up, carrying her in his arms. They kissed hungrily all the way to the bedroom. He kicked open the door and laid her on the cover. She sat up, reaching for him, hurriedly undoing his belt and fly buttons as he pulled her half-undone blouse over her head. She couldn't see, but felt he was doing something down there, to himself.

He stayed standing and she wrapped her legs around his waist, as though they'd planned it this way, and gasped as he entered her, slowly, and with a mixture of tenderness and strength that she'd not thought possible in a man. He felt different from Charlie. Bigger, for sure, but she could accommodate him. But the texture was different. It suddenly dawned on her. He was wearing something.

'Don't hurt me,' she said, looking up into his eyes.

'Never,' he said. 'That's a promise.'

He leaned forward to kiss her hot cheeks at the end of each long stroke.

Pip started breathing rapidly again. He'd brought her so close with his tongue and now it was as if he had never stopped. She felt her body starting to grip him harder, involuntarily. She dug her nails into his back and lifted herself off the bed to meet him, crushing her breasts to the wiry hair on his chest. Suddenly, too soon, her body shuddered. She felt his climax, saw it in his eyes, but there was no wetness inside her.

He looked down at her and she felt the tears start to well in her eyes. Still inside her, he reached down and wiped her cheek with a thumb. 'Are you all right?'

She smiled. 'God, yes.' It was the first time she had experienced an orgasm with a man. Charlie had been her first and only lover, and he'd needed to hit her to get an erection. He'd cared nothing for her pleasure. How could she tell this handsome, troubled, scruffy stranger that he'd changed her life, sexually?

'Stay there,' she said, and started to move again under him.

13

Fortunately, Pip had left a curtain open in the bedroom. The dawn light woke them. 'I've got to go,' Bryant said as he pulled on his trousers.

She lay back, one arm crooked behind her head, and watched him. 'I wish we could stay here all day – never leave the bed,' she said, surprised at her own lasciviousness.

'I'd pass out, I think. I want to get across the border and check out the area where Smythe went down. Also, there are still a few things to do to get ready for tomorrow's wings parade.'

'You'll never do all that in one day. Besides, I thought you weren't going to drive across into Bechuanaland until after the parade was all over.'

'I'm a pilot, aren't I?'

She beamed at him. 'You're going to *fly*!'

'Yep. I'll take a Harvard.'

'Good for you, Paul!'

He sat back down on the bed next to her and took her hand in his. 'I woke up feeling like I'd just come out of a terrible fever, or a nightmare. I can't ever change what happened to Will, but it was strange just how much it seemed to help talking to someone about it all.'

'I know just how you feel. It helped me to talk as well.'

He leaned forward and kissed her. 'I've got to face up to the rest of my life, Pip. The medical officer back in England suggested I talk to a trick-cyclist, but I fobbed him off. I wonder now if that would have helped.'

'I'm better therapy than any psychiatrist,' she grinned.

'Mmm, you are.' He brushed a strand of golden hair from above her eye. 'I think I have to start flying again, just to make sure. I just hope I remember how.'

'Oh, Paul, you'll be fine.'

His eyes widened as a thought entered his head. 'Want to come?'

'Surely that's against regulations?' He hadn't let Catherine De Beers go up in military aircraft, and that made Pip feel special, though she didn't let on.

'I could say it was part of our new air force–police liaison programme.'

She laughed. 'That would be the programme we began last night.'

'Exactly. How about it?'

'It's tempting, and I might take you up on the offer some other time, but I've still got some work to do on the murder investigation.'

He stopped buttoning his shirt. 'I thought that was all sewn up. You've charged that African bloke, haven't you?'

She saw the puzzlement in his face. 'True, but there are still some . . . loose ends we have to tie up.'

'I'd have thought they'd have given you a few days leave at least, after getting the news about your husband.'

'No one put a limit on it. Besides, if you're not going to stick around and liaise with me any more, I may as well be at work. I shall try very hard to play the grieving widow, devoted to her job.'

'I'm sure you'll give an admirable performance. When can I see you again?'

'You mean you want to?'

'Of course . . . if you do.'

She hadn't thought that far ahead. She'd been drunk yesterday, unsure of whether or not she would sleep with him, right up to the moment where he'd taken her in his arms. 'I want you to know, Paul, that there haven't been other men, since Charlie went away.'

'It wouldn't worry me either way.'

'No, but all the same, Charlie was my first and you, um, were my second. Don't think I'm not . . . God, what's the word?'

'Grateful?' he suggested as he tied his shoelaces.

'Yes, I suppose so. I'm very grateful . . .' she started to laugh, '*very* grateful for last night, but things have moved rather quickly between us, don't you think?'

'Are you giving me the brush-off?' he asked. She thought she saw the sadness creep back into the eyes that had seemed so bright a moment before.

'No, no! Please don't get the wrong idea. Yes, I do, very much, want to see you again.'

'Let's not rush it, then,' he said, businesslike. 'Come to the wings parade tomorrow. I'll arrange an official invitation for you and introduce you to Jan Smuts. After that we can get some dinner in town.'

'That would be lovely. I've never met a prime minister. Don't you have to stay for some sort of celebration afterwards, though?'

He gave a derisive snort. 'The last celebration ended with a WAAF's knickers being run up the parade ground flagpole. I'll let the graduating pilots have their fun by themselves and then deal with the aftermath on Wednesday.'

'Dinner would be lovely,' she said.

He leaned over and kissed her again. Neither of them wanted it to stop, but she knew he had to go if he were going to get back to the base and changed into uniform before eight. 'I'll see you tomorrow, at the parade,' he said.

'What should I wear?' she asked.

'Don't wear your police uniform. I want to ravage you when I see you in it.'

She laughed and threw a pillow at him. 'Get out!'

Bryant whistled as he piloted the bike at full speed back to Bulawayo, and waved a cheery, sloppy salute at the stony-faced Henderson as an askari raised the boom gate for him.

Before heading for his office and the flight line he turned off on a back road that led to the askaris' barracks and, beyond that, the growing cluster of mud and thatch huts where the African men's wives and children lived. It was here that Kenneth Ngwenya's school was continually being expanded to keep pace with the influx of labour to feed the base's ceaseless growth.

The four classrooms and administration building were a mix of the ancient and modern. The walls were mud brick painted with air force whitewash, the floors a traditional hard-wearing mix of cow dung and water which dried to a smooth, concrete-like hardness. The roofs were corrugated iron – a donation from the air force.

Ngwenya was not teaching, but he still wore his customary dark suit pants and white shirt. He stood, hands on hips, talking to a white Rhodesian Air Force engineer.

The men exchanged greetings as Bryant stopped the

bike beside them. 'Looks like you're making headway,' he said.

'Sheesh, man, if I could get my workers to pull their weight like this we'd have the new hangar up in half the time,' the engineer said, wiping his brow with the back of his uniform shirt sleeve.

Bryant watched a mixed gang of black askaris and white trainee pilots and base staff pulling on a rope to raise a long wooden post into a foundation hole. The Africans sang a deep, rhythmic cadence, which the whites did their best to emulate. It had the desired effect – after a few seconds of trying, all the men started pulling together. Bryant noticed that one of the air force men was Carmichael, the Ulsterman who had been in the thick of the riot in Bulawayo a few days earlier. He laughed and clapped an askari on the back in a friendly gesture as the pole slid home. Bryant had made service on the next school work party a condition of Carmichael's return to duty. The man had tried to protest, but Bryant had reminded him of the consequences of disobeying another order. A gaggle of African children in torn hand-me-downs danced around the workers, shouting encouragement.

'Squadron Leader Bryant, can I speak with you for a moment?' Kenneth asked, adopting a formal tone in front of the engineering officer.

'Don't mind me, I've my work cut out for me keeping these Pommie *skellums* on the job,' the Rhodesian said, then walked off, clipboard in hand.

'Hello, Kenneth, how's it?' Bryant asked.

'Did you notice anything unusual about Mrs De Beers when you went to her ranch the other day?'

Bryant was surprised by the way his friend came straight out with this question, ignoring the pleasantries that usually preceded any conversation with an African. He was also concerned by the sombre look in Kenneth's eyes. He explained how Catherine had broken down at the news of Felicity Langham's death, but said nothing about anything else that had gone on during the visit. 'It was a normal reaction, I suppose.'

'No, I meant her demeanour towards her servants. I spoke to my father again this morning by telephone. He said Mrs De Beers is leaving, but he was very distressed. He said someone had beaten him.'

'Who, Catherine?' Bryant was shocked. He'd noticed that she was abrupt to the point of rudeness with her African staff, but he could never imagine her physically abusing them.

'No. My father was almost incoherent. He said it was a man who had hit him, but I couldn't get a name out of him. Most whites I know, whatever their feeling about Africans, are at least civil towards their staff, Paul. I want

342

to involve the police if this is a criminal assault on my father.'

Bryant understood, but didn't know of another man in Catherine's life. Kenneth's story intrigued him as much as it concerned him. 'As you know, she's planning on moving to Salisbury, Kenneth. We might be too late to contact her.'

'Nevertheless, I am going to catch the bus up there to see my father. I still have a few days before classes resume. I wanted you to know where I was going and, if it comes to it, I would like to think you would stand by my father if this becomes a police matter.'

It would be the old man's word against that of another – presumably a white man if he were a friend of Catherine's. He didn't fancy the old man's chances but he wanted to help Kenneth if he could. 'If I hear from her again, I'll find a way to raise it with her. I promise I'll let you know what she tells me.'

'How the bloody hell are you today, Corporal Richards?' Bryant said to the orderly-room NCO as he swung open the door.

Richards had never had such a hearty greeting from the adjutant, and his confusion showed plainly as he said, 'Err, fine, sir, and you?'

'Fit as a fiddle. Get on to dispersal and organise me an aircraft. A Harvard.'

This was odd. Very odd. Richards had never seen the adjutant fly. Some of the old sweats reckoned he'd lost his bottle in England. 'An aircraft, sir?'

'Big things with wings and propellers. While you're at it, pull the files on the investigation into the loss of Smythe's Harvard. I want the map showing the site where those hunters found the body. Don't stand there looking like I ordered you to have sex with a zebra, Richards!'

'Yes, sir. Or, no, sir.'

'Get on with it!' he barked good-naturedly.

Richards picked up the phone and dialled dispersal. After telling the equally surprised duty officer that the adjutant was going flying, he found the file Bryant wanted.

'Ah, good. Thanks, Richards.' He looked up. The corporal was still standing there with the same bemused look on his face. 'That'll be all, Corp.'

He checked the map and reread the reports prepared by the pilots who had overflown the place where Smythe's body was found. The site was easily located thanks to the presence of tyre tracks left by the vehicle the white hunters had been driving. Bryant had overflown the saltpan once, during his initial training, and remembered being told that footprints or tyre marks stayed clear for years. He shouldn't have any trouble finding the place.

He rolled the map, put on his cap and headed out into

the morning sunshine. He thought about Pip Lovejoy as he strode across to the dispersal hut, absent-mindedly saluting airmen and trainees along the way. The way she smiled, the firmness of her lithe, petite body.

'Morning, sir,' said Johnson, a Canadian flight lieutenant. Johnson was one of the instructors on Harvards at Kumalo, and duty officer for the day.

Bryant returned the other man's salute and greeting.

'Your kite's ready, sir,' Johnson said. 'Gassed up and good to go. Perhaps you'd like me to run you through the cockpit layout?'

'Phil, I trained on these things – even though it was a thousand years ago, when Pontius was a pilot.'

The tall Canadian smiled and said, 'Didn't mean no offence, sir.'

'None taken. Now, which end is the propeller on?'

'What's got into him?' an English sergeant fitter in grimy overalls asked Flight Lieutenant Johnson quietly as Bryant left the hangar and walked to his waiting aircraft.

Johnson scratched his head. 'Whatever it is, I want some of it. Haven't seen him this cheery since I got here.'

An airman passed the restraint straps over Bryant's shoulders as he settled himself into the front seat of the

Harvard trainer. He had already done a walk around the aircraft and he buckled himself into his parachute harness. The packed silk canopy was beneath him, doubling by design as a seat cushion.

He scanned the instrument panel. His bravado in front of the Canadian had been as false as the smile and thumbs-up he gave to the young airman, who now jumped off the wing, leaving him all alone in the cockpit. The smells brought back a thousand memories, a thousand nightmares. Leather, fuel, oil, sweat, fear. He swallowed hard and forced himself to concentrate.

In front of him, the erk began turning the two-bladed propeller. He remembered the lessons now. Oil sank to the bottom of the big radial engine. By turning the prop through five full rotations the airman was redistributing the oil through all of the nine cylinders. His brain needed similar priming. A member of the ground crew had thankfully left a typed checklist in the cockpit.

He made sure the brakes were on and looked at the fuel gauges on the cockpit floor on either side of him. The tanks were full. The oil temperature needed to rise to forty degrees after start-up, so he pulled a lever shutting off the air intake, which kept the engine cool in flight. Radio, off. Generator battery switch, on. Magnetos, off.

He checked the flaps and the rudder and then set the throttle half an inch forward and the fuel mixture to rich. Next, he grabbed the handle of the manual Ki-gas primer in the lower centre of the instrument panel, turned it and pulled it out, using his right hand. With his left he worked the fuel pump handle, between the aileron and rudder trim wheels. When the fuel pressure was up around three or four pounds per square inch he pushed the Ki-gas primer handle in, which squirted fuel into the engine's lower cylinders. As the engine was cold he repeated the procedure eight times, then locked the priming handle back in place by pushing it in and turning it to the right.

'Right-o. Here goes nothing,' he said to himself as he depressed the inertia starting pedal on the floor between the rudder controls.

The starter whined and the engine caught, coughing white smoke from the exhaust. He switched the magnetos to 'both'. The smell, the noise, the vibrations were almost too much and, for a brief instant, he thought he might lose courage, panic and shut it all down. He licked his lips and wiped his hands on his shirt. Outside the cockpit he saw the erk grinning up at him. He forced a smile and gave a thumbs-up. He reopened the oil cooler shutter and released the brakes. The Harvard lurched forward.

Bryant turned on his radio and requested clearance for take-off as he taxied, S-turning away from the hangar. His heart was racing and his mouth was dry as he stopped at the end of the runway and reapplied the brakes. He ran the engine up to seventeen-hundred RPM and the whole airframe shook in protest. He checked its running in coarse and fine pitch a couple of times, then took it back up to two thousand RPM. Gyroscope, compass, altimeter and temperature gauges were all fine. The WAAF in the tower radioed his clearance. There were no excuses for not doing this.

He'd been so used to the lumbering Lancaster that the Harvard felt like a racing car by comparison as he released the brakes. At thirty-five knots he sensed the tail coming up, and at seventy he was off the ground.

'You beauty!' he said aloud. Off the ground, gear up at a hundred knots, he felt the past two years slip away from him, along with the paperwork and square-bashing bullshit of Kumalo, and the heat and dust of sleepy Bulawayo. He was back in Africa flying for the first time all over again.

He banked to the west and saw the orderly grid of Bulawayo's wide streets stretched out below him. He resisted the urge to buzz the police camp – but only just. He might feel like a nineteen year old after his night with Pip Lovejoy, but he was still the base adjutant. Carrying out some silly prank to impress a girl would undermine his authority the next time he chastised a trainee for doing the same thing.

Following the main road west, towards Plumtree, he soon picked out Pip's farmhouse. Lala Panzi's cattle showed as tiny black dots against the parched, golden grasslands. He slid open the cockpit canopy and revelled in the sun's warmth and the sky's breath.

Near the border he saw more spots on the landscape and decided to investigate. He pushed the Harvard into a dive and dropped to eight hundred feet over the open veldt. They were wildebeest, a herd of sixty at least, and they started to panic and run at the sound of his engine. He followed them for a while but, not wanting to torment the poor confused creatures, climbed back up to three thousand. From the sky, Africa was breathtaking. A boundless wilderness, teeming with the most extraordinary creatures in the universe, dotted here and there with farms and mines promising wealth and peaceful prosperity. Here in Rhodesia, it was very easy to forget there was a war on.

There was another side to Africa, of course, and his mission reminded him of that. Coming from Australia he was not stupid enough to think he could easily understand the relationship between Africa's blacks and whites. It was true a small minority of whites held absolute power over a much larger number of black Africans, but there was nothing he'd seen or heard in his time on the continent that would indicate a willingness or burning need for bushmen living in the remote corners of the interior to kill a stranded white man – in this case, Smythe.

Had the Englishman provoked them in some way? Had the bushmen sought to save the downed pilot? Had the pale-skinned Englishman, his brain half fried by the sun, perceived them as a threat rather than saviours and tried to fight them?

The dried grasses and stunted acacias gave way to drier ground now, hard, flat, waterless terrain which eventually became the vast saltpan. The glare from the midmorning sun was almost blinding, and Bryant pulled a pair of sunglasses from his pocket and put them on. He checked the map strapped to a board on his right thigh, and the compass on his instrument panel, and saw that he was on course. He took the Harvard down lower and searched for the small kopje the hunters had referred to. He soon saw it, as plain and incongruous as an angry pimple on other-wise alabaster skin, and steered towards it. Smythe had been found a half mile due west of the rocks.

He saw the faint shadows of tyre marks on the salt. The hunters and the pilots who had searched for Smythe's kite were right – they were easily visible. He decided to take a look at the pattern of the tyre tracks from higher up, and circled in order to gain altitude.

From three thousand feet he could see the long line of twin ruts heading in from the east, and a nearly parallel set of tyre marks going back the same way. However, now that he could take in a wider view, he saw another set of treads, some distance away from the others but not connected. Odd, he thought. Perhaps the marks were made by another vehicle some time before. However, from what he'd been told of the surface of the saltpan, the other vehicle could have been through two days or twenty years ago.

The more he looked at the other set of tyre marks, the more confused he became. There was something else wrong with them. The only way he would be able to check what type of vehicle made those marks – and possibly how old they were – was to take a closer look at them. On foot. He reckoned that if the saltpan could take the weight of the hunters' truck laden with food and dead beasts, then it could take his Harvard. He circled around again and pushed the Harvard into a dive

'Constable Lovejoy,' Sergeant Hayes said stiffly, 'on behalf of everyone here, we'd like to express our deepest sympathy at the loss of your husband, and offer these flowers as a token of our . . .'

Pip waited, straight-faced, as Hayes fought to find the right word.

'Err . . . regret,' he said finally, and handed her a bouquet of lilies.

He couldn't even pay his condolences in a sensitive manner. She wanted so much to tell him that she despised him almost as much as she had her husband, but it didn't seem the right moment. 'Thank you, Sarge,' she said instead.

Hayes grimaced at the abbreviation of his rank, but held his tongue. 'We didn't expect you back so soon.'

What did they think of her, she wondered? What did it matter? 'I felt the best thing for me to do would be to immerse myself in my work, help me forget my grief, if you know what I mean.'

'Of course,' Hayes said.

He meant no such thing. They all thought Charlie was a good man. Always the first to buy a round at the pub, and a good rugger and cricket player. They probably thought she was a snooty cow, incapable of grieving for her own husband. Better that than hanging around here taking men's jobs from them.

Hayes cleared his throat. 'I've been talking to our man Nkomo.'

'What did he say?'

'Reckons the last man to buy fuel from him that night was a foreigner.'

'Any more?' she asked.

'I think it may be an Australian we're looking for. Or maybe a New Zealander. Who says "mate" quite a lot?'

'Australians, I suppose. They're very casual.'

'Well, that's what Nkomo recalled, that the man had called him "mate". He thought it quite odd, and I must say I agree. Fancy someone calling a Kaffir "mate"?'

She found Hayes' tone, and his guffaw after he'd spoken, offensive. 'Well, I believe there are quite a few Australians and New Zealanders here at the moment,' she said.

'The logbook from yesterday said one popped by the station, and that he was given your home address,' Hayes said. 'Bryant.'

The implicit accusation caught Pip completely off guard. She felt her cheeks start to redden and looked down, pretending to adjust a button. 'I asked that Squadron Leader Bryant be given my address. I've been helping with his investigation into a missing aircraft.'

'Hmmm,' Hayes said, rubbing his chin. 'Didn't know we were in the missing-aircraft business, Lovejoy.'

'No, Sarge. Just helping him get in touch with the police across the border, that's all.'

She saw the raised eyebrows, the suspicion in his eyes. She wondered if he had guessed what had gone on between her and Paul. She felt a moment's shame and hoped her cheeks weren't betraying her.

The CID office phone saved her from further probing.

'Yes,' said Hayes into the mouthpiece. He listened to

the caller then said: 'All right. I'll send her out. You've got a visitor, Philippa. Mrs Catherine De Beers.'

'I thought she'd left town,' Pip said.

'She's at the charge desk, waiting for you.'

Pip excused herself and walked down the corridor to the front office, where the long wooden counter was located. Catherine De Beers stood at one end, as far as she could from two uniformed male police officers who held a handcuffed skinny young African man between them.

'Eyes forward,' one of the officers barked, and clipped the prisoner on the back of the head with an open palm.

Pip shook her head and noticed that both the officers were sneaking glances at Catherine themselves. She seemed to be a born head-turner, Pip thought, but today she literally outshone everyone in the drab police camp. She wore a yellow sleeveless summer dress with bold white polka dots, a wide-brimmed white hat and matching gloves that came halfway up her forearms, and yellow open-toed high heels. She ignored the men in the room and her stern look brightened a little when she saw Pip.

'Catherine, what a surprise. I thought you'd be well and truly on your way to Salisbury.'

'Hello, Philippa. I should have called, I know. I'm on my way, but I didn't want to leave this side of the country without seeing you again.'

'Really? Come through,' said Pip, lifting a hinged section of the counter, 'and we'll find somewhere private.'

Catherine's high heels clicked on the polished concrete floor. As they passed various offices, Pip was aware of more men craning their necks, and it wasn't for a glimpse of her in her police uniform. Pip smelled perfume as well. Catherine would be the talk of the station for the rest of the morning.

'We've got an interview room free. Sorry, it's not very salubrious, but it's private. Can I organise some tea for you?'

'No, thanks. I can't stay long.'

'Very well. Take a seat and tell me what's on your mind.'

'It's hard to know where to start. It's all a bit . . . delicate.'

Pip looked at the glamorous widow. She'd gathered from their brief meetings that the woman had a flair for the dramatic. This could go on all morning. 'You can speak freely, Catherine, and anything you say in here is in the strictest confidence.'

'I see. It's about Squadron Leader Bryant . . . Paul.'

Pip stayed silent and hoped her face didn't betray a single emotion. 'Yes?'

'Yes. Look, I know this is terribly forward of me, but you're a smart woman, Pip, I can tell.'

355

Get on with it, Pip said to herself.

Catherine continued: 'Paul and I have been very close recently. Very good friends.'

'I could see that. I'm sure he's disappointed you're leaving.'

'I don't know about that. One thing I do know, however, is the way Paul looks at a girl when he's, well, interested in her. I saw him looking at you that way at the funeral on Saturday, Pip.'

Pip leaned back in her chair and folded her arms. 'I'm sure you're mistaken, Catherine.' She suddenly felt terribly guilty, as though she were being accused of taking another woman's man away. But that was silly, she told herself. Catherine was leaving, with no thought for Paul's feelings at all.

'No, no. I've been there, I've seen it and please let me point out that if he *is* interested in pursuing something more than a professional relationship with you, I don't mind a single bit.'

Pip didn't know quite how to take that. The woman seemed to be giving her *permission* to see Paul. Quite bizarre. 'Look, I hate to sound rude, Catherine, but I've got a busy day ahead of me and . . .'

'Quite. I don't want to waste your time. Came here to help you, if you've got five minutes,' she said, sounding miffed.

'Sorry, please go on.'

'Say for argument's sake Paul *is* interested in you, and you feel the same way, all I'm saying is that you should be very careful.'

'Careful?'

'I would have ended my relationship with Paul whether I were leaving town or not. In fact, I'm sure he's part of the reason I *am* leaving.'

'It's probably none of my business, but why is that? Why don't you want to see him any more?'

Catherine put her gloved hands on the metal table and leaned forward, to emphasise her words, and said: 'Oh, it *is* your business, Pip. I'm doing this as one woman to another, trying to stop you from making a mistake. Paul comes across initially as very vulnerable, very caring, like a lost little boy who needs someone to take care of him. But once he's wooed you with that brooding, tortured hero routine, a different man appears.'

Pip swallowed hard. Unfortunately, she knew only too well how men could change their colours. 'What do you mean, different?'

'It's especially bad when he's had too much to drink.'

Oh, dear God, Pip thought. Paul had held off the booze yesterday, even though she had started early.

Catherine said: 'He gets violent.'

Pip fidgeted with her hands, under the table where

Catherine couldn't see them. She felt perspiration starting to form under her arms. It was a familiar feeling that swept over her, but one she hadn't experienced since Charlie went off to war. Fear. 'Does he . . . did he . . . hit you?'

'Remember the comment you made about my wrists the other day, when you said goodbye at my place?'

'Yes.'

'I told you I'd wrapped my hands in my horse's reins, but you knew I was fibbing, didn't you?'

'How did it happen?'

'He tied me up, Pip. He enjoys doing that. He did it to Felicity once, as well.'

Pip's eyes widened. 'Felicity?'

'It's complicated. The three of us were all very good friends.'

Pip was aware of just how close the three of them had been, but said nothing.

'Recently, however, I discovered that Paul had been seeing Felicity without me.'

That was different from Bryant's story. She couldn't imagine, though, what Catherine had to gain by lying. 'Again, Catherine, I appreciate you telling me this, but I just don't see what it has to do with me,' Pip said.

'I know, I know. Look, Pip, I'm a very broad-minded person. I like men, and I liked Paul, very much, but I didn't want to marry him, or possess him. If he wanted to see Flick as well, that was fine by me. But then she told me that he had hurt her, as he had hurt me. That upset me greatly.'

'He tied her up?' Pip asked, a mounting sense of dread pumping through her veins.

'As he did with me. At first I played along with it, as I suspect Felicity did. Stranger things have happened to me in the bedroom, I assure you!' she said, forcing a little laugh.

Pip nodded for her to continue. She thought of Charlie's postcard of the two women and the cane.

'But once I'd surrendered to him, as it were, once my hands were tied, literally, he became very aggressive.'

'Aggressive?'

'He hit me. Not on the face or arms, where it would show. But elsewhere. Flick said he did the same to her. The way he made love to me, to us, I should say, was not tender as it should be.'

'Did he rape you, Catherine?'

'A strong word. Perhaps too strong. I did try to ask him to, well, take things a bit slower, that night you stayed at my place, but he ignored me. He seemed to think my protests were some sort of an act, all part of the fun as it were.'

Pip shook her head. 'You were very friendly to him at the funeral,' she said.

'It's complicated. I can't help but feel that I led him on somewhat, although I certainly didn't want him to touch me in that way after that last night. I think that he could be a dangerous man, Pip, that unchecked he might manifest all that pent-up rage inside him in some other way. I don't expect you have the foggiest idea of what I'm going on about, or of how someone could keep up pleasant appearances with a man after he'd hurt her . . .'

Pip looked down at the table. Catherine's words sliced through her heart like a scalpel. How many times had she wondered if *she* had somehow been responsible for Charlie's rage? Why had she, like Catherine, felt she had to 'keep up appearances' instead of calling the police? 'How violent do you think Paul could get? Do you think he could have killed Felicity?'

'Of course not!' Catherine said, shaking her head. 'Definitely not and, please understand, I did *not* come here to infer any such thing. Besides, you've already caught the low-life who killed Flick.'

'Felicity's wrists had been bound with a silk stocking,' Pip said.

'Yes, well, I don't know about that. A coincidence, I suppose. I am *not* saying Paul Bryant is a killer. All I came here to do was to try to warn you that if you *were* contemplating seeing Paul socially, to get off on the right foot and to let him know you won't stand for any perverse acts of violence.'

Pip leaned back in her chair and thought about how best to phrase her next line of questioning. A terrible idea was forming. 'You mentioned the other day, when I was at your ranch, that it was hard for you to get petrol. I think you said that even if you *could* get it on the black market, there was no one who would deliver it to you, out in the bush.'

'Correct,' she said.

'I'm curious as to how you've found enough to make the trip across the country.'

'I had some hoarded away that I was going to use to drive down to the wings parade and then back home with. It's just enough to go one way to Salisbury instead. I decided not to come to Paul's little parade, or to have anything more to do with him or Kumalo.'

'I see. But you said, if I recall correctly, that the fuel you were going to use had come from your crashed Tiger Moth.'

Catherine looked down at her lap and said, 'Um . . . yes, that's right.'

'Catherine, please look at me. Did you get some fuel from anywhere else?'

She looked up at Pip, but couldn't hold her eye. 'Why are you asking me this? I came here to help you, Pip.

361

Are you accusing me of committing a crime, of buying black market fuel?'

'I'm not accusing you of anything, Catherine, and, believe me, if you did get hold of some illegal petrol, I don't care a fig about it. What I want to know is *how* you got it. You wouldn't have had enough fuel to get down to Bulawayo to buy more, would you?'

Catherine shook her head, still looking down.

'Did you buy it at Victoria Falls? Your maid told me you'd driven there sometime last week.'

'Cheeky little bitch,' Catherine muttered. 'No, in answer to your question, I did not buy petrol at Victoria Falls. Although I tried to! How's that for honesty?'

'Very admirable. So, how did you get the extra fuel?'

Catherine looked up at her, licked her lips and said, 'Someone brought me some.'

'A friend?'

She looked away, pouting. 'Not any more.'

'Was it Paul Bryant? Did he bring you some fuel, Catherine?'

'I didn't come here to get anyone arrested for black marketeering, Philippa.'

'I give you my word, no one is going to be arrested for buying or selling fuel. Where did he get it from, did he tell you? Was it from air force stocks?'

'Good God, no! He'd die before breaking one of his

precious air force regulations. He's such a stickler for that. Wouldn't even take Flick and me up for a joy-ride in a Harvard. No, he didn't get it from the air force, I'm sure of that.'

'Ah, so it *was* Paul.'

'Damn,' Catherine said. 'Caught me with my guard down. Oh, all right, damn it! Yes, it was Paul, he brought me some black market fuel, from some spiv in town. There, I've said it. Why is this so important? Am I to be hanged for receiving illegal fuel?'

'No,' said Pip. Her heart started to race. 'Do you know when he bought it by any chance?'

'He brought it to me the day you and he came to my place to ... to tell me about Flick,' Catherine closed her eyes at the painful memory.

'But when did he *buy* it?'

Catherine opened her eyes and said: 'The day before, I believe. I imagine these black marketeers work at night, so it must have been ... um, the night Flick was killed, I suppose. Is something the matter, Pip?'

Pip put her hands on the desk to stop them from shaking. She felt like she needed to be sick.

14

Hendrick Reitz had followed the Deka River into the northern part of Wankie Game Reserve for as long as he dared. When he'd finally seen the dirt road running through the protected area, which crossed the river at a low-level drift, he had turned left, towards the safari lands beyond the northern border of the protected area. He'd kept the road in sight, but had not used it in case a game ranger stumbled across his tracks.

A pride of lions had circled his encampment the previous night. They'd spooked his horses but not him. He'd kept a fire burning through the night and, with his Mauser beside his sleeping bag for company, had listened to the low growls of lionesses on the hunt. A tawny shadow had darted through the flickering light cast by the flames. Reitz had sat up, sleepily, and grabbed the cool end of a burning log and waved it in an arc around his sleeping bag. He'd smiled as the lioness retreated into the darkness, then gone back to sleep.

The next day he had seen vultures circling in the clear blue sky and diverted a little north-west of his intended route to investigate. Lions, probably the ones who had invaded his camp, had taken down a zebra. He watched them, through binoculars, as they fed, their greedy faces dark and sticky with blood. He was pleased they had found an easier kill, probably a lame animal, than his mount or packhorse. With their bellies full they would not be following him.

Reitz was in the Matetsi safari area now, and he was starting to recognise familiar kopjes and dry riverbeds. He had enjoyed good hunting in the concession when he worked in Rhodesia before the war. He stopped the horses at the confluence of two almost dry streams, dismounted and let the beasts drink from a small pool. He took the compass from the breast pocket of his khaki bush shirt and flipped open its leather pouch. He double-checked his bearing, but he knew he was heading in the right direction.

For the tenth time that day he checked the straps holding the canvas-wrapped cylinders to the saddle of the packhorse. Each tube was four feet in length, and about a foot in diameter. All was still in order. To have come this far, from Germany, under the seas, to South West Africa and across the deserts of Bechuanaland to

Rhodesia, only to lose his cargo in the bush because of a faulty buckle would be an unpardonable failure. He would not have cared if the lions had taken his mount the night before, but he would have shot each and every one of the cats if they'd tried to drag away the packhorse and its precious cargo. Countless thousands of hours worth of effort by some of Germany's top chemists – he was vain enough to count himself in their ranks – and weapons-development scientists had gone into the construction and filling of those cylinders. A new weapon for a new phase of the war. Lightweight, effective and economical. He would take many lives with the contents of those cylinders and, in the process, he would save the lives of many more innocent German civilians.

On his return from his first spying mission in Africa he had begun seeing more of the attractive Ursula. She was not as adventurous in the bedroom as some women he had bedded, but he had, in time, educated her about his likes and dislikes. She'd been a willing student. While his heart would forever be in Africa, Ursula satisfied his physical needs and helped ward off the cold northern winter. Had he loved her? Probably not. However, he had become very attached to her. Certainly he had enjoyed her company, as well as her creamy-skinned, athletic body, and her cooking. She would have made an excellent wife, he thought, if he had intended on staying in Germany and making a home there.

He mounted his horse and tugged on the other's reins, setting them on the final leg of their long trek. He crested a low hill and took in a breathtaking view. Spread out before him, dotting a grassy vlei that stretched to the horizon, were a breeding herd of thirty or more elephant and scores of antelope, a half-dozen different species at least. God's bounty, a gift to his people and those worthy of sharing it with them. Many times he'd tried to describe such scenes to Ursula.

'You will take me one day, won't you, Hennie,' she'd asked him as they'd shared a deep, steaming bath in his Berlin apartment. The room was lit by candles, not for romantic reasons but because a daylight bombing raid by American B-17 Flying Fortresses had knocked out their electricity.

He remembered the night well. His body was still tanned and lean from his time in Africa, and she held her arm against his, teasing him about his colour. 'You don't look very Aryan now,' she laughed.

'So why are you sharing your bath with a black man? What would the other girls in the party say about that?' he asked, enjoying the weight of her body pressing down on his. Her back rested on his chest. He reached around her and soaped a breast the colour of snow, teasing the dark nipple to life with his slippery fingers.

'They'd probably ask me if you had a brother.'

'I don't,' he said, feeling suddenly morose at the thought of his German mother dying as she brought him into the world.

'I'm sorry, Hennie. I didn't mean anything by that,' she said, reading his mind. He'd told her his family's tragic story.

'It's all right,' he said.

'What's to become of us, Hennie?'

He really had no answer to that question, none that would please the girl, anyway. 'I don't know, but I would love to show you Africa one day, when this is all over. When we've won.'

'So you will take me.'

'Yes, I suppose I will. I'll take you right now, in fact,' he added playfully, feeling the effect her slick flesh was having on his.

'You cheeky sod,' she chided, splashing water backwards into his face. 'Oh no!'

He cocked his head: both of them were silent now as they listened to the all-too-familiar drone of an air-raid siren winding up to full pitch. 'The flak has started. I hope they nail some of the bastards tonight.'

Ursula stood in the tub, soapy water cascading down over her body onto his. He reached for her. 'Stay.'

'The RAF has a terrible sense of timing. I can see they haven't knocked the wind out of your sails, though,' she added, looking down at him, 'but don't expect me to be able to concentrate on lovemaking while there are bombs going off around us. I'm going to the shelter.'

'I'm staying,' he said. 'No bloody Englishman is going to stop me from enjoying a hot bath.'

She shimmied into her dress and fetched a bulky overcoat, headscarf, muffler and hiking boots from the closet. 'I can hear them now,' she said.

'Lancasters, by the sound of them,' he said, soaping under his arms.

'Come with me, *please*, Hennie. You know I hate how you stay here just for the hell of it. What are you trying to prove?'

He smiled at her. 'Prove? Nothing. I'm not going to be killed by a bomb in a bathtub, Ursula. If I am going to meet my maker in this war, it will be in battle, or serving my country in some other way.'

'How can you be so sure?'

'God's put me on this earth for a purpose.'

She laughed as she wrapped the muffler around her neck, then looked down and saw he wasn't smiling. 'You seriously believe that?'

'I do.'

'I've seen the bodies of tiny children killed by British

bombs, Hennie. While you were away, the little twins who lived in my block were blown apart. Why didn't God have something in mind for them?'

He shrugged. 'I just know that my life has been a journey and that it will not end here, in a Berlin bathtub. Perhaps my purpose is to avenge the deaths of those two little girls.'

'Revenge,' she said, shaking her head. 'I'm as committed as you are, to the Führer, to the party, to the firm, Hennie, but revenge solves nothing. Now, get your clothes on and come and cuddle with me in the air-raid shelter.'

'Be careful,' he simply said to her, dismissing her with a wave. In any case, he no longer felt aroused, just disappointed she didn't share his confidence.

'Bye, lover. Ask your God to watch over me and the hausfraus in the shelter,' she said. With a wave, she was gone.

He closed his eyes and slid down deep in the bath, letting the water wash over his face. He needed someone whose will was as strong as his, someone who would not doubt him, who would stand side by side with him as his journey continued. After the war he would need the support of a good woman, someone to raise their children in a free, independent Afrikaner nation.

The last thing he remembered before the blast was finishing washing himself and putting his hands on the side of the tub, preparing to push himself up. When he awoke he was lying cold and naked on the tiled floor, the heavy cast-iron bath on its side. Plaster dust and grit coated him, sticking to his wet skin. His ears rang but, after running his hands quickly over his skin, he realised he had suffered no injury. 'Thank God,' he croaked, his throat and nose full of dust.

Staggering to his feet he walked through the bathroom doorway and, in a moment that might have been comical if viewed through someone else's eyes, nearly fell two storeys. Half of the building had simply vanished. He stood there, on a precipice, nude and freezing. He crawled back inside, wary of the creaking floor beneath him. He found his clothes and pulled them on, then felt his way blindly through the remains of his apartment block. Fortunately, the main stairwell was intact and he, along with four other survivors who had not left for the shelters, made his way out into the street. Just in time, too, as another long slice of the building collapsed in a cloud of dust. Fire-engine bells clanged nearby and the street was lit by a hissing flame from a broken gas pipe. People staggered like drunkards in the roadway, shocked or injured, others either insane or numbed with grief. The shelter! He ran along the buckled footpath and turned the corner. The air-raid shelter was little more than the basement of the block three down from his. The cellar of his building had been flooded for some time and, as such, was no use as a refuge. It took him a couple of seconds to realise that he had, in fact, taken the correct turn.

The apartment block beneath which Ursula and dozens of other civilians had sought sanctuary no longer existed. In its place was a mound of broken bricks, burning timbers and shattered furniture. A nearby woman wailed. An air-raid warden swore and stared skywards. Flak batteries still boomed up the street, their empty brass shell casings tolling like bells on the sidewalk.

'Come on! Let's get this cleared!' Reitz yelled at no one in particular.

An old man climbed over the rubble and joined him. Soon others rallied to them and Reitz organised a chain of people to shift the debris in order to reach the cellar below. Brick by brick, timber by timber, they slowly started clearing the rubble. Every few minutes, Reitz ordered them to stand still and shut their mouths so he could listen.

'Quiet, I said! Listen.' He'd heard the sound of a child crying, and of someone banging metal on metal – perhaps two pieces of broken water pipe. 'There are people alive down there! Quickly now, put your backs into it!'

Urged on by the noises made by survivors, and by Reitz's continual chivvying, the volunteers redoubled their efforts. After an hour's toil that left him sweating despite the night's chill, Reitz was finally able to reach between two clumps of fallen masonry and feel hope.

It was a hand. A woman's, he thought. Slender and smooth, though sticky with blood. 'Can you move?'

'My leg,' she sobbed. 'I think it may be broken.'

The voice was not Ursula's. He'd not allowed himself the luxury of emotion – of hope or fear or worry. He'd been too busy organising the rescue. Now he started to imagine the worst. 'Hold on, stay still. We'll get you out.'

The woman was the first. She might have been pretty, but her face was now a mask of blood and the bone shone white through her thigh. Fortunately for her she had passed out and no longer cried from the pain. There were more. Two little girls, not more than nine years old, he guessed; a wailing baby, followed by its mother. 'Praise God,' an elderly man in shabby clothes said as Reitz handed him the infant. 'My grandson.'

When there were no more survivors emerging from the hole, it was time to start looking for those who had died. Most of the people who had accounted for lost loved ones drifted away, but a small force of volunteers and firemen stayed around to continue the grim job of disinterring the dead – or what was left of them. Reitz's hands were slick with blood and his shirt and trousers stained a deep red. He was no stranger to death, but the grim work reminded him again of the bombed villages of Spain.

'Here's another woman, Hendrick,' cried old Hans. The man, sixty if he was a day, whom he'd never met but was now on first-name terms with as a result of their shared labours, had climbed into the remains of the shelter with a flashlight. Reitz was close behind him.

Hans shone the light on her face. Reitz sat back on a pile of bricks, oblivious to water running down his face from a broken pipe above him. He ran a hand through his wet fair hair. He said nothing.

'Hendrick? Give me a hand, please.'

He sat, motionless, staring at that beautiful, pure, young German woman. A little more than an hour ago her body had been pressed against his, the two of them melding into one warm form in the deep steaming bath. He'd been able to feel her heart beat as she'd lain on him. She'd smiled and joked with him and, before the bath, he'd been as close to her as two people could be. Now Ursula was dead.

'Hendrick? My God. You know her?'

He'd nodded. 'Yes. She was . . . she and I were . . .'

'Those bastards,' Hans said, rolling his eyes skywards as he clapped a bony hand on the South African's shoulder. 'I'll get one of the other firemen to help me.'

'No, thank you, Hans. I will do it.'

They removed the heavy timber beam that had fallen

across her belly and nearly cut her in two in the process. He hoped she'd died immediately. Her face seemed peaceful.

He lifted her in his arms and shuffled to the access hole he had created. They had saved some of the civilians, but there was nothing he could have done sooner to rescue Ursula. As he emerged he smelled the smoke of a hundred fires, the fading scent of cordite drifting down the street from the now-silent eighty-eights. He didn't know where to take her, so he simply laid her in the street, sat down in the gutter next to her and lit a cigarette. A child cried nearby. An old man retched dust from his lungs.

She'd mocked him before she'd left for the shelter. 'Revenge solves nothing,' she'd told him. As he smoked he wondered if she would feel the same now, say the same words if it were she staring down at his broken body.

Revenge. He might have learned to love Ursula, if they'd had the time. She might have borne him children in a new South Africa, ruled by his people. The British had taken his past – his mother – and now part of his future.

He'd been brazen enough to tell Canaris what he thought could be done in Africa, how a mighty blow could be struck against the RAF if the high command had the guts to take the fight to a new, unconventional front – to go around the normal rules of war.

'I'm not convinced, Reitz,' the old Admiral had confessed when Hendrick had first floated the idea. 'I don't want another failure like Operation Weissdorn. We put our faith in another one of you Afrikaners, but Leibbrandt was a disaster!'

Operation Weissdorn was the German code name for a botched plan in 1941 to assassinate the South African Prime Minister, Field Marshal Jan Smuts, and seize power in an OB-led coup d'état. Its leader, the former South African heavyweight boxing champion Robey Leibbrandt, was betrayed to the police and arrested. Leibbrandt was languishing in gaol, his death sentence having been commuted to life in prison.

The main reason Canaris had initially been wary of the type of attack Reitz favoured was that it would take the war against the allies to a new level. He'd half suspected the admiral was too scared to take such a bold step.

Ironically, the deciding factor in giving the go-ahead for Reitz's bold scheme was Jan Smuts. Reitz had been summoned to a second meeting by Canaris, and the wily old admiral's eyes glowed with barely concealed enthusiasm.

'You are not the only Afrikaner working for us,' he began.

'Of course not, sir,' Reitz said.

'A source in the South African bureaucracy has delivered us some interesting news, Reitz. It seems that Herr Smuts is going to be visiting Rhodesia soon as the reviewing officer for a graduation parade of RAF pilots at a base near the town of Bulawayo.'

Reitz licked his lips: the admiral's barely disguised enthusiasm was infectious. It was an effort for him to hold his tongue.

The admiral leaned forward, his elbows on the desk, and lowered his voice, as if fearful a hidden microphone might pick up his words. 'The Reich has suffered setbacks in recent months. Our momentum in Russia has slowed and the Italians have let us down.'

Reitz nodded, imperceptibly. He shared the older man's paranoia. To voice the obvious publicly could earn one a bullet in Berlin.

'The Ossewa Brandwag has a membership of more than three hundred thousand – you confirmed this for me yourself – but its support will wane, Reitz, unless it sees proof that Germany is far from beaten, that we will win this war.'

To this, Reitz nodded vigorously. He couldn't resist pre-empting Germany's top spy: 'Sir, if we could assassinate Smuts and—'

'And eliminate scores, perhaps hundreds, of newly qualified RAF terror flyers, think of the message that would send to your Afrikaner brothers and sisters in South Africa.'

'The new National Party does not advocate armed violence against Britain or the South African government, but with Smuts out of the way, the Afrikaners would rise up. No politician could hold them back.'

'Your country is at a turning point, Reitz. We will not have another chance to convince your people to take up arms, as they should have four years ago. Just think Reitz – U-boat bases at the Cape; German bombers operating out of Johannesburg or Pretoria, within striking range of the undefended training bases in Rhodesia; perhaps ten or twelve divisions of Afrikaner soldiers to fight for Germany. We would turn back the tide in Russia, and perhaps even reclaim Italy.'

Reitz thought about the possible repercussions of South Africa changing sides. 'The South Africans fighting for Britain would want to return home. There may be civil war.'

Canaris shrugged. 'If the South African division leaves Italy, all the better for us. I think, however, by the time the English-speaking soldiers returned home they would find their country ruled by the Afrikaners. Our intelligence suggests that the vast majority of able-bodied men who support England have already enlisted and are serving outside of Africa. There would be little resistance to a coup d'état. You told me yourself that the OB still has men inside the police force and the army within South Africa.'

Reitz nodded. Despite Jan Smuts banning membership of the OB by anyone serving in the military or civil service, there were many covert supporters still in place.

'Our source also says that high-level talks are planned between Smuts and the Rhodesian Prime Minister, Huggins, during the field marshal's visit to Bulawayo. This man Huggins, we know, supports the concept of all of the British colonies in southern and central Africa merging to form one entity. If that happens, your people will no longer have the numbers amongst the whites.'

'It would be a nightmare, Herr Admiral, if we were part of a bigger country with white English-speakers in the majority,' Reitz agreed.

'It would be an even stronger display of Germany's continued might if we could eliminate two leaders in one attack.'

'A fifth of Rhodesia's population are all away at war – virtually all of its able-bodied white men and many of its blacks. Militarily the country is poorly defended, despite the large number of Commonwealth airmen in the country,' Reitz said.

'I like the way you are thinking. And so will the Führer once we present our plan to him. I'm going to see that you get your chance to kill some English flyers, Reitz, but I'm also going to make sure that we deliver a blow far more serious to the allied war effort than the loss of some pilots. We missed Smuts in 1941, Reitz. We will not miss him again.'

'No, Herr Admiral!'

Reitz pushed these memories of Berlin aside and dismounted as he approached the top of a hill crowned with rounded granite boulders. He tethered the horses and walked, bent at the waist, to just below the crest, then lay down on his stomach. He did not want to be silhouetted against the skyline on the peak in case anyone saw him. He lifted the binoculars slung around his neck and peered through them.

In the shallow valley below him the bush gave way to a long rectangle of dried yellow grass. At the end of the clearing he saw a large wooden hut – a hangar, he presumed. Two thirds down the length of the open strip he saw the wreckage of a biplane. He swung the glasses off to the right. Beyond a kilometre or so of mopani the native vegetation surrendered to manicured green lawns surrounding a cluster of thatch-roofed buildings. He could just make out the lettering on the carved wooden sign hanging over the gate.

Isilwane Lodge. He crept back to the horses.

* * *

Paul Bryant pulled back on the stick and the Harvard climbed away from the baking white ground. The clear blue sky and the cool air blowing in through the open cockpit were a pleasant relief from the sweltering stillness and painful glare of the saltpans. He felt the sweat under his arms chill then dry.

His investigation of the tyre treads on the pan had yielded more questions than answers, but he had a pretty good idea where to start asking them.

He checked the fuel gauge and did some quick mental calculations. Kumalo and Bulawayo were virtually due east of where he was now, circling one last time over the place where Smythe's body was discovered. Catherine's ranch, Isilwane, was north-east, maybe a couple of hundred miles. Fuel shouldn't be a problem. He checked his map. There was a dirt road along most of the border between Southern Rhodesia and Bechuanaland. All he had to do was follow that road.

He didn't expect to find her at home, as she had told him at the funeral that she was leaving for Salisbury today. To make the capital she would have had to leave early in the morning, and it was getting close to noon now. He wasn't exactly sure what he was looking for, but he thought that if some of her servants were still there, packing or cleaning up, he might ask them some questions about comings and goings at the ranch. He was starting to see the crash of Cavendish's Harvard at Isilwane Ranch and the disappearance of Smythe's aircraft as more than just a run of bad luck.

The bush was a uniform khaki. The rivers he overflew were all dry, just sandy thoroughfares. He spotted a large herd of elephants marching in search of water and dropped a few hundred feet to take a look. A big matriarch lifted her trunk and raised her ears wide at the drone of the oncoming aeroplane. She looked skyward. At this altitude he couldn't hear what noise the elephant made, but some signal had been passed to the others. The herd closed up and started generating a dust cloud as their leader urged them to hurry. He banked to starboard and gave them a wide berth.

The border road ran straighter than any river and was easy to pick up. He turned to port and followed it northwards. He knew Catherine's place was just beyond a fairly substantial river. He glanced at the map on his thigh again and followed the road with a finger, to where it intercepted the watercourse. There it was. The Deka.

An hour later, staring ahead through the Perspex, he saw a winding sandy serpent and then cross-checked its shape with the map. That was it.

Below him, Catherine's ranch came into view as he overflew a granite-studded hill crest. He put the Harvard into a shallow dive and, by the time he was over the main homestead, was so low the tops of the tallest trees in the garden were bending in his prop wash. He looked over his shoulder as he pulled back the stick and climbed again, but saw no one come out of the house to look.

He banked the aircraft lazily and circled around for another low-level beat-up, this time down the airstrip, in order to scare off any wild animals that might obstruct his landing. He looked left and right out of the cockpit and thought he saw movement amidst the mopani trees. Something dark was galloping, but he didn't have time to make it out. A wildebeest or one of the many antelope species that flourished in the reserve, he thought.

The strip was clear, except for the wreckage of the Tiger Moth, so he circled again and readied the Harvard for landing. The drills his instructors had drummed in at his initial service flying training in Rhodesia came back to him. On take-off, the checks a pilot had to complete were summarised by the memory jogger TMPF, which stood for trim, mixture, pitch and fuel. Now, as he readied for landing, he said aloud, 'UMPFF.' Undercarriage, mixture, pitch, fuel and flaps. He bounced once, still not completely at home in the Harvard, which was a fraction of the weight of a Lancaster, and then settled her onto the grass. He swung the nose to the left and taxied down the extreme edge of the airstrip before turning back to the wooden hangar at the other end. He didn't want his tyre marks to be confused with any others on the field. He applied the brakes, stopped by the building and cut the engine.

It was hot again back on terra firma, and he felt himself start to perspire as he pulled off his leather flying helmet, unstrapped himself and climbed out of the cockpit.

Before checking the hangar he decided to walk the length of the airstrip. Despite the heat he welcomed the exercise, and the solitude of the bush. The only sounds around him were the calling of various birds, none of which he recognised. He was well aware that the property was also home to all the major predator species – lion, leopard, cheetah and painted hunting dogs, so he kept his eyes peeled and, as an added precaution, unbuckled the flap on the canvas holster at his waist. A Webley revolver might not take down an elephant, but he figured it might be enough to dissuade a curious cat. Since Smythe's death he had ordered that all pilots on solo flights go armed, in case they had to make a forced landing and encountered a threat on the ground.

Catherine's wrecked Tiger Moth was still out on the edge of the airfield. That was odd, he thought. Although it might be a long time before the aircraft could be repaired, he was sure there was enough of it worth salvaging and storing. Out in the elements, the metalwork would rust and the timber framework and fabric skin would eventually rot away.

He scanned the grass as he walked. He saw again the deep furrows ploughed by Cavendish's Harvard after its wheel had found the ant bear hole. Also, he could see the faint indentations left by Catherine's biplane on its last landing. The grass was almost knee-high in places, and it appeared as though it sprang back fairly quickly, otherwise there would have been many more tracks from Catherine's other landings, before her crash. He couldn't tell for sure, but it didn't look to him as though the strip had been used recently by anyone other than himself, Cavendish and Catherine. He turned and walked back to the hangar.

It was a substantial structure. Most of the farm airstrips he had visited barely had more than an open-sided lean-to to protect the owner's aircraft. This was a fully enclosed building with a tin sliding door. It was big enough to house Catherine's Tiger Moth and a workshop. The white-painted metal was hot to touch. He grasped the handle and started to slide it.

A noise from inside made him start in fright and take a step back. He drew his pistol and thumbed back the hammer. He felt his heart pounding. His mouth was dry. He put a foot on the edge of the sliding door and kicked it along its tracks. At the same time he held up the pistol.

It was dark inside and he blinked, his eyes momentarily unable to adjust from the brightness to the gloom. A shadow ran along the wall. He raised the pistol but held his fire. A growing wedge of light knifed the darkness as the door rattled on its way. There was a crash to his left and he swung. A figure ran towards him, and Bryant dropped to one knee and took aim. As his finger started to squeeze the trigger, he heard a grunting then a wild cry of 'Wah-hoo!'

He lowered his pistol and laughed as a large baboon scuttled out of the darkness and sprinted past him into the light. He holstered the weapon and took a look around.

The hangar was empty. At least, it did not contain an aircraft. There was a workbench and a cupboard along one wall, presumably full of tools. There were three forty-four gallon petrol drums on the floor, but when he kicked each of them they echoed emptily. Catherine had told him the truth about her desperate fuel shortage. There were no fresh oil stains on the concrete floor, nothing to indicate an aircraft had been parked there for some time. At the rear of the building he found a hole where the baboon had presumably entered. The lower sections of a few timber planks had succumbed to termites, and the primate had been able to snap off sections of wood. There was nothing more for him to see here.

386

Bryant holstered his pistol and walked back out into the sunshine. He lit a cigarette and thought about what he should do next.

Reitz had been surprised and alarmed to see the aeroplane circling the ranch. Pleased with himself that he had decided to take the long route, around the airstrip, rather than crossing it, he had nonetheless had a few anxious moments when the noise of the low-level pass over the landing ground had startled his horses.

Now he lay at the base of a stout marula tree and watched the aviator through the Mauser's telescopic sight. He could kill the man easily from this range. No more than two hundred metres, and the fool was standing still, in the open. So easy, but that seemingly simple solution would create many more problems than it would solve. He would have to dispose of the body and he was unsure how soon it would be before the man's colleagues mounted a search. He couldn't fly, and the aircraft was too heavy for one man to push into the hangar in order to hide it. As much as he longed to shoot this flyer – who represented everything Reitz hated about the British in this war – he would not pull the trigger.

The man looked thoughtful as he smoked his cigarette. Reitz hoped he would get in his aircraft and fly away. He wondered what the pilot had been searching for in the hangar.

Reitz tracked the uniformed man with the barrel of the Mauser. He was not walking to his aircraft. Instead, he turned and walked purposefully away from the hangar and onto the dirt road that led from the airstrip back to the main house. Reitz had seen the road from his earlier vantage point. From his own careful study of the lodge and its servants' quarters from the hilltop, he had deduced that all of the buildings were empty. He wondered why the pilot was heading that way. Perhaps he was lost, or short of fuel, and was looking for help, or to telephone his base. It didn't matter. What was important was that disaster had been averted and now, again with a little luck and God's grace, he might be able to take one more Englishman out of the war.

He guessed it was about a kilometre from the landing ground to the homestead. It would take the man at least twenty minutes to walk there and back. It would also take some time for the pilot to realise that there was no one home, so Reitz figured he had maybe a half-hour all up. Plenty of time. The pilot was out of sight now.

Reitz checked the horses' tethers and then darted across the grassy runway. He stopped at the aircraft and crouched in the shade of a wing. He scanned the bush around him and satisfied himself again he was alone.

Putting a bullet in the pilot's brain would have been the quickest way to take him out of the war, but what Reitz had in mind was to put an end to both man and machine. He walked around the Harvard. He climbed up on a wing and looked into the cockpit. He noticed that the pilot's seat was actually an open-topped squarish metal box. Instead of a cushion, the man flying it sat on his parachute, which he presumably buckled to himself once he took his position. Reitz wondered if he shouldn't also doctor the man's chute, just to make sure he killed himself. As a paratrooper, parachutes were no mystery to him. However, if the man did manage to land his aircraft safely, and survive, such tampering might be discovered. He did not want to arouse the suspicion of the air force on the eve of the completion of his mission.

He considered puncturing the fuel tanks, which he guessed would be in the wings, but this would take time, and there was the problem of finding a container big enough to drain the gas into. Besides, the pilot would presumably check his fuel gauges before take-off.

He stepped down off the wing and started another circuit around the aircraft, stopping at the engine. He looked up at it. How to stop the engine in such a way that the man would crash soon after flight? A breeze behind him chilled the sweat on his back and that gave him an idea. Beneath the engine cowling was a large oval-shaped vent. He reached up and put his hand inside, and felt around. The intake turned upwards, at ninety degrees, towards the lower cylinders. He knew enough about engines to know they got hot and therefore needed to be cooled. If he could find something to block this air inlet, he could push it up the vertical shaft and out of sight to anyone standing on the ground.

Reitz jogged into the hangar and fetched a wooden box and an old rag spattered with paint. He stood on the box, to give himself extra height, and reached inside the air vent again, stuffing the rag as deep inside as he could reach. The aircraft's power plant would get very hot soon after take-off. How soon, though, he had no way of knowing.

There were no smoky lunchtime cooking fires outside the basic whitewashed mud and thatch staff huts behind the big house. No half-naked African children played in the fenced dirt compound, no dogs yapped at him. The house looked similarly bereft of life.

The front door was unlocked. 'Hello!' Bryant called. 'Anyone home?' His voice echoed through the empty homestead. The heels of his boots squeaked on the polished floorboards in the hallway.

In the dining room the long table was covered in a white sheet, likewise the chairs. It was the same in the drawing room. The cream walls were checked with rectangles of bright white here and there where oil paintings and family photographs had been removed. Dust particles danced in a stray ray of sunlight that stabbed the gloom through a gap in the drawn curtains.

In the kitchen and bedroom he found half-packed teachests and the floors littered with strands of dry straw. Evidently there was still some more packing to be done, or perhaps Catherine had simply abandoned some things to the mothballed home. In the bedroom he stooped and looked inside one of the boxes, brushing aside some straw with his hand.

There was a gleaming copper chamber pot. He smiled. Very rustic, but probably not at home in a swanky town house in Salisbury. Under the vessel was a stack of old newspapers and magazines. He moved the pot and pulled out a handful of newsprint. One of the pages of a yellowing copy of the *Chronicle* newspaper, dated 8 July 1938, was dog-eared at a top corner. He flicked it open. It was an article about Catherine's late husband, the wealthy professional hunter Hugo De Beers. A slightly blurry photograph showed the thin, silver-maned man standing beside a dead elephant. Hugo had one foot resting on a massive tusk, almost as long as the hunter was tall. The headline read: 'LOCAL HUNTER SLAYS CROP RAIDER'. Bryant tossed the paper back in the box. The other newspaper editions and journals were similarly flagged and all had stories about De Beers.

He was going to put them back, but then he came across a story not from the news or finance pages – there seemed to be almost as much coverage about De Beers' business investments as there was about his hunts. This page showed a collection of wedding photographs from the social pages. The picture, taken in early 1940, showed a radiant, smiling Catherine clinging to the arm of the old man. She looked the picture of virginal innocence. Bryant smiled again and shook his head.

He lifted the chamber pot to replace it and the newspapers, but another clipping, now on the top of the stack, caught his eye.

'BIG GAME HUNTER SHOT DEAD!' screamed the bold headline. He picked it up and replaced the others in the box. He heard a cough behind him and turned in surprise.

'Ah, good morning, sah,' an elderly African man in blue overalls said.

'Oh, hello, how are you?' Bryant asked. He held the newspaper by his side and slightly behind him.

'I am fine, sah. Can I help you?'

Bryant had met the man before. 'You're Kenneth's father.'

'Yes, Enoch, sah. Enoch Ngwenya. I am the head of security for Isilwane.'

It was a lofty title for the nightwatchman. 'Ah, right. Enoch. How is your sickness, Enoch?'

'The medicine is helping, sah. The madam has left-i,' Enoch said, waving his hand around the empty room.

'Ah, right. Yes, so I see. She told me she was going to Salisbury, but I thought I might catch her at home today. I landed my aeroplane at the airstrip.'

'Yes, sah,' Enoch said, narrowing his eyes.

Bryant noticed the man had a black eye and a long scabby cut above his right eye. The skin around the gash and his cheek was puffy and swollen. 'Kenneth told me you had been hurt, Enoch. How did that happen?'

'Sah?'

'Your eye.'

'Oh,' the man said, looking at the floor for a moment. 'I was kicked by one of the horses, sah. It was an accident.'

'Kenneth told me that another man had done this to you. Was he a friend of Mrs De Beers?'

'The madam has left-i, sah,' Enoch said again.

Bryant wasn't sure whether the old man's grasp of English was lacking, or whether he was too embarrassed – or scared – to answer the question. 'I'm a friend of Kenneth's, Enoch. If someone has hurt you, we can tell the police.'

The old man's eyes widened. 'No, sah. It is fine. I just-i bumped my head.' He rubbed his temple and forced a smile.

'Was there a man here, with Mrs De Beers?'

'The madam has left-i, sah,' Enoch said.

Bryant gave up. It was up to Kenneth now to see how he could help his father. 'Where are the rest of the staff, Enoch?'

'Mrs De Beers has dismissed them, sah. I am the only one left here. It is my job now to protect the empty lodge, but the madam has told me to take two weeks' leave first.'

Bryant saw the mix of regret and relief in the man's eyes. He still had a job, albeit a boring one. 'Were the other staff disappointed?'

The old man shrugged. 'Everyone needs to work, sah.'

Bryant had little to gauge Catherine's behaviour by, but he had been surprised at just how rude and condescending she had often been to her domestic workers. She had a variety of distasteful terms for Africans, and tried to use as many different ones as possible in his presence. As an outsider, a foreigner, he was a little shocked, but he'd said nothing.

'When did she leave, Enoch?'

'Very early this morning, sah. I was told to burn those newspapers, sah,' he said, gesturing to the box. 'The madam gave me the pot-i as a gift, sah,' he added proudly.

'Good for you, mate.' Bryant could imagine Catherine laughing at the back-handed compliment paid to the security guard by such a gift.

'I am sure the madam would not mind if you wanted to take a newspaper to read, sah,' Enoch said, nodding down at Bryant's half-concealed hand.

He suddenly felt guilty, like a thief caught red-handed. He wanted to be out of the house quickly now. He'd have to try to contact her by telephone. She'd told him she was staying at the Meikles Hotel in Salisbury while her new house was being sorted out. 'Thanks, mate,' he said to Enoch, and stuffed the newspaper into his trouser pocket as he walked out.

He trudged back down the dirt road towards the airstrip. 'Bugger,' he said aloud to himself. He looked at his watch. It was after midday now. There would be a stack of minor but nonetheless necessary tasks for him to attend to, in preparation for tomorrow's big parade. He'd end up working late into the night. What he really wanted now was a cold beer.

He began his pre-flight inspection of the Harvard. The kite had handled beautifully over Bechuanaland and there was no evidence of any oil leaks around the engine. He looked along the fuselage, checked the tail wheel and ran his hands over the elevators, rudder and trim tabs.

He checked the wings, then the landing gear underneath, for hydraulic leaks. As he'd been away from the aircraft for a while he turned the propeller, as the mechanic at Kumalo had done before he left, in order to redistribute the engine oil.

He climbed quickly into the cockpit and ran through the remaining checks rapidly. The sooner he started up, the sooner he could get up amongst some cool air. The engine coughed to life. The oil temperature had climbed to forty degrees, so he opened the air intake again. Everything looked fine.

He brought the undercarriage up as soon as the wheels had cleared the grass. Ahead of him was a clear sky and typically perfect flying weather.

'Christ, I could do this for a living,' he said to himself. The irony made him smile.

'Constable Lovejoy,' Flight Sergeant Henderson said as he leaned into the window of the police car which was stopped at the red-and-white-striped boom gate at the front of Kumalo air base, 'to what do we owe the inestimable pleasure of your company this time?'

Pip tried her hardest to smile. Something she did not feel like doing. She recognised the air force policeman from the riot in town, and detested the way he was staring at her breasts. 'I need to talk to you and whoever was on guard duty on the night of Felicity Langham's death.'

'Me?'

Henderson's smarmy self-confidence evaporated and a look of panic crossed his face. Despite the turmoil that raged within her she was able to crack a genuine smile now. The job did have its perks. 'Don't worry, Flight Sergeant. I'm not here to arrest *you*.'

Henderson snorted and nodded to the askari to lift the boom. 'Park over there,' he ordered.

Pip drove while Hayes fidgeted with his belt buckle in the seat next to her. 'Is there something going on between you and Bryant? You need to tell me now, you know, if there is,' he said.

'No,' she said, then switched off the ignition and got out of the car.

'Now, what's this all about?' Henderson asked as Lovejoy and Hayes entered the guardroom and removed their hats. 'And when's that black bastard going to swing for killing Langham?'

Pip pursed her lips. Henderson sat in a reclining wooden office chair behind a metal desk. He leaned back and put his hands behind his head.

'Do you mind if we sit?' Pip asked.

'Suit yourself,' said Henderson. 'We're a bit short on tea and biscuits, though.'

She ignored his sarcasm. 'I need to see your record

of people coming and going at Kumalo for the night of Miss Langham's death and the morning after.'

'Not as easy as it sounds,' Henderson said. 'We only record vehicle movements, not personnel, and then we only take note of vehicles coming onto the base. When people leave, even by vehicle, is their business. We're more concerned with making sure the wrong people don't get on base. Anyway, what's it matter? You've got a suspect. Been charged, too.'

'Our investigations are continuing,' Pip said flatly. 'Now, if you'd be kind enough to fetch your register . . .'

'You think the Kaffir had an accomplice? Not one of our lads?'

'The register, please, Flight Sergeant.'

Henderson frowned. 'Sixpence!' he roared.

Hobnailed boots clattered on concrete and a uniformed askari trotted into the room and snapped to attention. 'Sergeant!'

'Fetch the vehicle register for last week, Sixpence,' Henderson ordered.

'Do you check vehicles coming onto the base – search them, I mean?' Pip asked while they waited for the man to return with the log.

'Not if we know the person driving, if he's got a valid ID.'

'What do you know about the trade in black market

petrol?' Hayes asked Henderson, speaking for the first time.

'Cripes. Is that what this is about? You think Langham was mixed up with the black market?'

'Just a question,' Hayes said.

'I know it goes on, same here as in England, I'd expect. I know, too, that the powers that be keep a close check on the fuel that's used on this base. No air force petrol ends up on the street on the black market – and that's a fact. Old Bryant would hang, draw and quarter anyone who tried.'

'But that doesn't stop airmen ... officers, from purchasing fuel outside?' Pip probed.

Henderson thought about the question, and his answer. 'Some of the staff have got private vehicles over here. Cars, motorcycles. They've got to get fuel somewhere. Big country you've got here. Can't get far on the fuel ration.'

'But you don't check vehicles coming onto the base for illegal fuel?' Hayes asked.

'No,' Henderson said, shaking his head. 'Why should I? That's your job, I would have thought. Ah, here we are. Good man, Sixpence.' Henderson took the ledger from the askari and dismissed him. He flicked through the pages, looking for the date in question.

Pip looked at the page Henderson was studying, although it was upside down from where she sat. She saw that as well as lists of vehicles and personnel entering the base, there were notes taken of messages phoned through, and actions taken. 'You get telephone calls here after hours?'

Henderson nodded as he read. 'Yes. The main telephone switchboard is only manned from eight in the morning to five in the afternoon. At other times the telephone rings here in the guardroom. Don't know that you'll find much of interest. Quiet night, by the look of it. Perhaps we should wait until the adjutant gets back before I hand over official air force documents.'

'He's still flying?' Pip asked.

'Haven't seen him land.'

'I could get a court order, a search warrant,' Pip said.

Henderson eyed her coldly. He looked again at the entries. 'Nothing untoward that I can see.' He shrugged and slid the book across the desk.

Pip ran her fingers down the inked entries for the night Felicity died. There were various deliveries noted, and the midnight bus that brought airmen home from a night on the town. She felt a shiver down her back. 'What's this? Telephone message for Squadron Leader Bryant, received 22:25 hours?'

'What it says. Someone called at 10:25 at night for him,' Henderson said casually.

'How do we find out what that message was?' Pip asked.

'Why do you want to know about the adjutant's phone messages?'

'As I said, Flight Sergeant Henderson,' Pip's voice lacked any trace of courtesy, 'I can come back with a search warrant.'

A slow smile of understanding dawned on Henderson's face. 'Well, I suppose I could get whoever was on duty that night to join us.'

'That would be greatly appreciated,' Sergeant Hayes said.

'Who's the duty NCO listed at the top of that page?' Henderson asked Pip.

She checked and said, 'Corporal Evans.'

'Ah yes, one of the armourers. Sixpence!' The African trotted back into the room and snapped to attention. 'Be so good as to dash across to the armoury and find Corporal Evans, please.'

'Sah!' the askari said, and doubled outside.

Pip studied the remaining entries. Her heart beat faster. 'It says here that Squadron Leader Bryant entered the base at 07:45 hours on the morning that we found Miss Langham's body.' Bryant had told her that he'd been drinking in his room the night Felicity was killed and had fallen asleep after reading a book. He'd said nothing about leaving the base for any reason.

'You're very interested in the adjutant all of a sudden, aren't you?' Henderson said.

'What time does the adjutant start work?' Pip asked.

'Same as most of them, eight in the morning. Odd, though.'

'What's odd?' said Pip.

'It's him and Langham, isn't it? Were they an item?'

'That's really none of your business, Flight Sergeant,' Pip said.

'You want me to cooperate with you, waste half my day, but you won't tell me, not even as one police professional to another, what you're up to.'

'The details of civilian police investigations are always kept private,' she said.

'Then you'd better go fetch your search warrant. I've got work to do in the meantime,' Henderson said, and pushed back his chair as though he were about to stand.

Bastard, thought Pip. The man just wanted some titillating gossip that he could spread around the base. Getting a warrant would be a pain, but she would have the satisfaction of seeing Henderson having to kowtow to the power of the law. All the same, she wished there were some way she could make him change his mind. She, too, pushed her chair back, happy to call Henderson's bluff.

Hayes stayed seated. 'I suppose the air force frowns on fraternisation between the ranks,' he said.

Pip looked at him, surprised. Henderson stayed seated. 'Right you are. Not on for officers to be getting too close to their subordinates. Bad for discipline. Undermines morale, it does.'

'Mightn't look good on a service record. Might affect promotion,' Hayes said.

Henderson smiled. 'If we're talking about who I think we are, then that wouldn't be much of a threat to him. He's reached his terminal rank, as we say. Not the most distinguished of service records.'

'Nothing to lose by lording it over a pretty WAAF then, I suppose. Probably talked up his part in the war to ease the way, so to speak.'

Henderson chuckled. 'If he did, it would have been lies. Word is the bloke ran out on one of his mates. Left him to burn in a crippled kite.'

Pip frowned. She hated the way this was heading. Still, lying might still prove to be one of the Australian's greatest talents. It was unethical and morally reprehensible, the way Hayes was feeding Henderson titbits of innuendo to get him talking. But, she realised, it was working. She kept silent.

'She was a pretty girl, Felicity Langham,' Hayes said.

'You're right again there,' Henderson said. 'But tell me, on the quiet, are you having second thoughts about the Kaffir you arrested?'

'Well,' Hayes said, scratching his chin, 'as my colleague Constable Lovejoy here pointed out, it would be improper to go into details, but, as one professional to another, I'm sure you'd agree we're duty-bound to continue our investigations if, say, a suspect turns out to have a pretty strong alibi.'

'Ah,' said Henderson.

Pip thought the man was about to salivate.

'Raped, I heard,' Henderson said.

'No great secret,' Hayes said.

'Dealt with a nasty rape case myself a year back, on a base in England, at Biggin Hill. Pilot officer and a WAAF NCO. Turned out they'd been seeing each other, in the Biblical sense, and had broken up. He'd gone after her and hurt her. Often, they say, the perpetrator knows the victim.'

'Often,' Hayes confirmed.

'So what was odd,' Pip interjected, 'about Squadron Leader Bryant arriving fifteen minutes early for work on the morning after Miss Langham was killed?'

The two men exchanged a brief glance, as though they resented her interrupting their veiled conversation. Henderson looked at Hayes and raised his eyebrows. Hayes nodded, as though telling his new confidant that it was all right to answer the question, that he would reveal more details if they liked his response. Pip held her tongue.

'Well,' Henderson said, pausing, smiling, 'thing is, Mr Bryant lives on base.'

'So he'd spent the night out on the town, or, perhaps, with someone?' Hayes said.

'It would seem so,' Henderson said, leaning back in his chair and making a steeple with his two fingers.

'But you've no way of knowing what time he left the base?' Pip asked.

Henderson shrugged. 'Duty NCO might know.' He craned his neck and looked out the window behind him. Sixpence, the African askari, and a white man in blue overalls were marching down the sidewalk side by side.

'Flight,' the corporal said by way of greeting to Henderson as Sixpence presented him to the door. He was in his early twenties, with fair tousled hair. His face and bare arms were sunburned and his overalls dark under the armpits with sweat. He looked at the police officers and said in a thick Welsh accent, 'Whatever it was, I didn't do it.'

Pip smiled. 'We just want to ask you a few questions.'

'Go ahead, Taffy,' Henderson ordered. 'Grab a pew from next door and join us.'

Evans returned and dragged a metal chair into the room. He placed it closer to Henderson's side of the desk than where the police sat, as if seeking protection from the senior airman.

'They won't bite, Evans,' Henderson said.

'We'd like to ask you some questions about a night

and morning during which you were the duty NCO, Corporal Evans. Do you remember the night Felicity Langham was found dead?'

'Yes, miss. I hope they hang the bastard who did that. Sorry, miss.'

'No need. I hear a lot worse at the police camp,' she said, smiling again to put him at ease. 'I've got the log here, which includes entries you made. Would you like to see it?'

He shook his head. 'Got a good memory, I have. Especially of that night.'

'You took a phone message for Squadron Leader Bryant, at 10:25 that night. Do you remember it?'

He frowned as he concentrated. 'Ah yes, from a woman, it was.' The corners of his mouth turned up. 'Not the only bloke who's had a call from some local girl in the middle of the night, like. But, all the same, I remember being surprised that the adj was getting called by a woman.'

'Surprised?'

'No disrespect, but he doesn't strike me as the kind who gets out much, who has much of a social life.' He glanced at Henderson, who nodded and smiled in agreement.

'Who was the woman who called?'

'Now that, I'm afraid, I don't know. I was busy at the

gate at the time, checking a truck full of aircraft parts that had come up from South Africa, as I recall.'

Pip checked the ledger and saw the note. The lorry had arrived two minutes before the call was taken. 'So how did you answer the phone as well?'

'I got one of the askaris to answer it. He called out the window to me, while I was at the truck, see, and said it was a woman looking for the squadron leader. I was busy so I told him to take her name and phone number and we'd pass it on.'

Pip tried to hide her annoyance. 'Can we talk to that askari?'

'It was Wilfred, Sarge,' Evans said to Henderson.

'Bad luck there,' Henderson said. 'His mother died last week. I've sent him on leave halfway across the country to Gwelo. He'll be gone two weeks at least.'

'Could ask the squadron leader himself, I suppose,' Evans suggested.

'He's not here at the moment. Off flying around,' Henderson said.

'How are messages usually passed on?' Pip asked.

'I do remember that Wilfred said the woman sounded very agitated, like, and so I told him to take it to the officers' mess and leave it there for him. They might have woken him to tell him. I'm not sure. Wouldn't have a clue who the steward was on duty that night, though.'

Another brick wall. Pip looked at Henderson.

'We could check,' said the flight sergeant, 'but it'll take some time.'

'Corporal Richards in the orderly room might remember,' Evans suggested. 'I told Wilfred to make a copy of the message and drop it off at the orderly room the next morning, as well.'

'That's very thorough of you, Corporal,' Pip said.

'Got my arse kicked, beg your pardon, got told off good and proper once when a message didn't get through to the wing commander, so I always try to cover myself these days, when it comes to senior officers, like.'

Pip nodded. So, Paul may or may not have got a message that night from an unknown woman.

'I'll call Richards,' Henderson said, reading Pip's mind as he picked up the telephone.

While the air force policeman dialled and waited for Richards to answer, Pip said to Evans, 'Do you recall Squadron Leader Bryant leaving the base during that evening?'

Evans shrugged. 'We don't make a record of people leaving the base, miss.'

'Yes, I know that. But, please, think about it. Do you recall seeing him?'

Evans stared at the ceiling and frowned again. 'I really can't say one way or another. Quite a few people went

408

out on the town that night – you'll see that from the logs of people coming back in the small hours. Also, we had three more lorries to check in. Then when word came about Felicity Langham, there was a lot of coming and going in the morning. Yourselves included, if I remember correctly.'

Pip nodded once more. She glanced in the log again and saw that their arrival at the base had been recorded.

'Hang on,' Evans said. 'Can I see the logbook, please? I think I remember the adjutant coming *on* to the base that morning.'

'You're absolutely correct,' Pip said, and passed over the book, pointing to the entry.

'That's right. I remember thinking . . . let's say I remember thinking that the old man might have had, well, a bit of a pleasant evening for a change.'

Pip smiled to encourage the young armourer.

'Yes, that's right,' he said, remembering. 'He drove into the base that morning – not long before we all heard about Felicity. So, I suppose that answers your earlier question. He must have got the message Wilfred took to the mess and gone out to . . . er . . . see the lady in question.'

'Quite possibly,' Pip said. The earlier feeling of nausea started to return.

'Richards? It's Flight Sergeant Henderson here.' The

air force policeman's telephone conversation now silenced the rest of them in the guardroom office. 'You remember the morning after Langham was killed? Yes, we all do. I've got some police officers here and they want to know if you received a copy of a message for Squadron Leader Bryant that morning.'

Pip, Hayes and even Evans all watched Henderson intently.

'You didn't think to mention that to anyone?' Henderson asked after a few moments. 'No, I suppose you're right.' Another pause. 'No, you *don't* need to know what this is all about. Any sign of the adjutant yet?'

They waited while the man on the other end of the line answered.

'Very well. Do me a favour and call me when he lands.' Henderson hung up. He leaned back in his chair and said, 'Evans, with the permission of our police friends here, I think you can leave us.'

Evans looked vaguely disappointed when Pip said: 'Thank you, Corporal, there's nothing else we need from you. You've been a great help.'

After the corporal left, Hayes said to Henderson, 'Well?'

Henderson couldn't hold back a smile. 'The message,' he paused, savouring the hunger in their eyes, 'was from Felicity Langham.'

'Bingo!' Hayes said. 'We'll need to talk to him.'

'You heard me ask Richards to call when the adjutant lands. Do you want to wait here, or should I call you?' Henderson asked.

Pip knew there was one more thing they had to do before they confronted Paul Bryant in person. 'We've got to go back to the police camp for a while,' she said.

'We do?' Hayes asked.

'Yes.' To Henderson she said, 'There is one other thing you can do to help us, though.'

'Anything,' he said quickly, meaning it.

'I need a photograph of Squadron Leader Bryant.'

Pip and Hayes walked back into the police camp. She clutched three pages torn from past editions of the *Bulawayo Chronicle*. They walked down the corridor to where the holding cells were and Hayes told the constable on guard duty to open Innocent Nkomo's cell.

The first cutting Pip held was one of many stories the *Chronicle* had run on the activities at Kumalo air base. This one, which Henderson had pulled from a notice-board in the guardroom, was about a visit by a class of local schoolchildren. Squadron Leader Paul Bryant, evidently as one of his duties as adjutant, had escorted the students on a tour. There was a photo with the article that showed Bryant standing on the wing of a Harvard, leaning over a young boy who was seated in the cockpit.

411

Bryant wore a smile, but his eyes revealed his obvious lack of interest in the task he had been set. She had also taken two other clippings from the board, which each featured a different pilot or airman from the base. All had dark hair and all looked to be aged between twenty and thirty.

The constable turned the key in the cell door and it creaked open. 'On your feet, sunshine,' he said to Nkomo, then left Hayes and Lovejoy to do whatever they wanted with him.

They walked into the cell. 'Sit down, Innocent,' Pip said to him. The black man obeyed and sat on his bed.

'Have you come to hang me?' he asked.

'Watch your bloody mouth. You're not a free man *yet*,' Hayes said.

Innocent looked up at the burly sergeant, then at Pip. She saw the renewed flash of hope in his wide eyes as he registered Hayes' last word. 'I am sorry. What else can I do to prove to you I did not kill that woman?'

Pip stepped forward and laid the three newspaper clippings down on the bed next to the prisoner. She had folded each of them around the border of the main picture relating to the article, so that Innocent could not recognise a name from the caption or accompanying article. 'Look at the three photographs on these pages. I want you to tell me if you recognise any of these men and, if so, where you last saw them.'

'The man was not wearing a uniform,' Innocent said, studying each of the three images.

'Air force officers don't have to wear uniforms when they are off base,' Pip said. It was something else that narrowed the field of suspects, assuming the last man Innocent had sold fuel to was a foreign serviceman. All enlisted airmen and noncommissioned officers wore their uniforms when in town.

'It is this one. He is the one,' Innocent said, stabbing one of the articles.

Pip did not want to look. She turned to Hayes, who, standing behind Innocent out of sight, gave the slightest nod of his head. Pip tasted bile and swallowed hard. 'Where do you recognise the man from?' she asked. She looked down and swore to herself.

'He was the last man who bought fuel from me, on the morning after the woman died. He was the man who helped carry the petrol cans for me. I left him alone at the back of my automobile. He must be the one who put that woman's things in my car!'

'Leave the deductions up to us, boy,' Hayes said.

'Are you sure this is the man?' Pip asked.

'Sure,' Innocent said.

Hayes looked over the prisoner's shoulder. 'It's him, all right. We've got the bastard.'

Pip turned and started to walk out of the cell.

As soon as she was out of sight of the constable on duty in the corridor between the holding cells, she ran for the ladies' toilet. She slammed the door of the stall closed behind her and threw up into the bowl. Involuntary tears streamed as she knelt on the cold concrete floor.

Shirley, the police receptionist, opened the door of the restroom and called out: 'Pip? Are you in here?'

Pip wiped her mouth with toilet paper and flushed. 'Yes,' she croaked. She opened the door.

'Blimey, you look a mess.'

'Thanks,' Pip said.

'I saw you run down the hallway. Thought you might need some help. Are you ill? Or is it about your Charlie?'

'No,' Pip said.

'Not pregnant?' Shirley raised her eyebrows.

'No.' She thought of the way Bryant had used a condom when they had sex – and of the lack of semen in Felicity Langham's battered body. She shuddered and felt like retching again.

'What's wrong, love? Is it a man?' Shirley asked.

'Yes. Unfortunately, it is.'

Harold Hayes said nothing as they drove through Bulawayo and out of town on the Salisbury Road, but

Pip noticed his grin as he glanced away from her, out of the driver's window.

She assumed he thought she was a stupid bloody woman. She just felt empty. When they pulled up at the Kumalo gate, the air force duty NCO leaned into the cab and greeted them.

'We're here to see Squadron Leader Bryant,' Hayes said.

'Not around, I'm afraid. Still off flying, isn't he,' the man said in a cockney accent.

'All right. Tell the base commander we want to see him,' the policeman countered.

'Hang on a mo'. I'll call the wing commander's office. I'll need some names, though.'

'Sergeant Hayes and Constable Lovejoy. It's a matter of the utmost urgency.'

'I'm sure it is, guv,' the air force corporal said.

'Let me handle this once we see the base commander,' Hayes said as they waited for the corporal to return.

Pip nodded. She was having a hard time thinking straight. Her mood altered from sadness to the point of near tears, to a white-hot anger at the betrayal and lies she'd endured. She had trouble comprehending the enormity of what she had discovered about Paul, and about what that deduction said about her. She couldn't congratulate herself on solving the murder – and Hayes never would – and if she were right about Bryant, it meant she had fallen for a man even worse than Charlie. God, she wished Paul were there, so she could confront him; at the same time, part of her wanted him gone forever, so that she would never have her suspicions confirmed.

The corporal returned a few minutes later and said: 'Wingco'll see you now. You know where to go?'

'Yes,' said Hayes.

An askari raised the boom gate and Hayes drove past the guardroom to base headquarters on a newly swept road flanked by white-painted rocks. Here and there black workers and uniformed airmen were raking leaves, polishing standpipes and cleaning vehicles. A red-faced corporal screamed orders at a ten-man section of askaris marching up the road. The men's hobnailed boots slammed into the Tarmac as one when they halted, then they about-faced and marched back towards the gate. Pip guessed the burst of activity was in preparation for tomorrow's graduation parade and the arrival of Smuts and Huggins. Hayes stopped the car outside the main administrative building.

Pip's legs felt leaden as she trudged up the stairs and followed Hayes into the wing commander's office. A uniformed Rhodesian WAAF offered them tea, but Hayes declined for both of them.

The door in front of them opened and a gaunt, bald-headed officer said: 'Wing Commander Stephen Rogers. How do you do?'

Hayes shook hands with the man and introduced Pip.

'Have a seat,' Rogers said. He folded his hands on the table and said, 'What's all this about then?'

'You're aware of the investigation into Felicity Langham's murder?' Hayes asked.

'Of course.'

Stupid bloody question, Pip thought. She had forced herself, on the drive out to the base, to suppress her feelings of betrayal and misery and to view this latest development coldly and professionally. It wasn't easy. She steeled herself with a deep breath and said, 'We've come into possession of new evidence, which implicates one of your officers in the crime.'

Both men looked at her as if surprised she had a voice. Hayes said, 'We believe one of your men may have killed Miss Langham.'

'What?' Rogers said. 'I don't understand. I thought you'd arrested the culprit. An African?'

'Were you aware Squadron Leader Bryant was involved in a sexual relationship with Miss Langham?' Pip asked the wing commander.

'No, I most certainly was not!' Rogers replied. 'Are you saying . . . ?'

Pip let the question hang for a moment. She studied his face and reckoned Rogers was telling the truth. 'I'm saying that we have evidence that Squadron Leader Bryant was contacted by Miss Langham on the evening of her death and that the pair met.'

'Bryant?' Rogers said, the incredulity clear in his reply.

'Yes. On another occasion Paul Bryant voluntarily admitted to me that he had been involved in an intimate relationship with Miss Langham.' Even though the evidence against Paul was damning, Pip felt a pang of guilt at betraying his confidence.

'News to me. And against King's regulations to boot,' Rogers said. 'But why would he kill her?'

'That's what we want to ask him. We believe that Squadron Leader Bryant raped and killed Miss Langham and then planted certain items in a vehicle belonging to the original suspect in the killing. We won't know his motive until after we've questioned him. But first we have to arrest him,' Hayes said.

'That will be hard,' Rogers said, scratching his bare pate.

'Why's that?' Hayes asked.

'He's missing.'

'What? Has he done a bunk?' Hayes asked.

Rogers consulted a piece of flimsy message paper on his desk. 'This just came in. Bryant flew to Bechuanaland this morning to investigate the loss of one of our aircraft. About two hours ago he radioed a distress call, saying his aircraft's engine was overheating. An Oxford from

418

Induna air base was in the area, some way north of the flight plan Bryant was supposed to be following, and picked up the call. The aircraft headed for the rough position Bryant had transmitted and, when it got there, found burning wreckage in thick bush near Gwaai River. The Oxford circled the crash site for as long as it could, but the pilots saw no sign of a survivor or a parachute. I've organised a search party by road and air, but it'll be hours before anyone can get there. Couldn't have come at a worse time. The whole base is tied up in preparations for the arrival of Prime Ministers Huggins and Smuts tomorrow for the big wings parade. I don't know what evidence you've got on Bryant, but it was damn foolish of him to go off flying on a day like today in the first place.'

'So when you say he's missing...' Pip began.

'What we really mean is missing, presumed dead,' Rogers said.

15

Bryant opened his eyes and groaned. He blinked, but even that small movement hurt. He tasted blood in his mouth and spat. His eyes wouldn't focus. He saw a blur of copper-coloured dots. Leaves, he thought, then passed out.

The sun was low on the horizon when he came to again. The bush around him was bathed in a golden yellow light, so pleasing to the eye, so relaxing, so ethereal, he wondered for an instant if he were dead. He felt nauseated and his armpits and thighs ached. He coughed and looked around him. He was hanging in a tree, but still alive.

He remembered radioing a distress call from the Harvard when he'd realised the awful truth, that the engine was cooking, and that it wasn't just a faulty temperature gauge. How had it happened?

He'd been flying low – stupidly, he now realised. He'd

caught sight of movement in the bush below and dropped from ten thousand feet to two thousand to watch a herd of zebra running across an open vlei. Idiot, he said to himself. How often had he reminded the instructors to ram home to their student pilots the foolishness of low flying for fun?

He had been too low to turn back to the grassy flood plain, or to glide to the north–south road, which would have made a good emergency landing field. He'd glimpsed the twin strips of Tarmac as he called for help, so he knew he wasn't far from the main route between Bulawayo and Victoria Falls.

He'd had to make the decision in an instant. His heart pounded now, as he hung from the branches of a mopani tree and remembered it. Ahead of him and past each wingtip were acres and acres of bush. There was nowhere for him to make a forced landing with a dead engine. There'd been an eerie silence after the engine finally died, the incongruous sight of the still propeller, the rush of wind on his face as he'd slid open the cockpit. At fifteen hundred feet he'd climbed out and jumped. He saw again, in his mind's eye, the Harvard gliding, pilot-less, into the bush below. He'd not even had time to tighten the parachute straps, and the ache in his armpits and crutch was from the violent tug of the harness as the white silk canopy blossomed above him.

The ride to earth – well, almost to earth – had taken no more than forty seconds. Not enough time to look for landmarks, barely enough to get himself into a landing position. He'd crashed through the dry canopy of the trees and prayed he would make it to the dusty ground below. No such luck.

He looked down. About twenty feet, he reckoned. 'Shit,' he said aloud.

Bryant checked himself out. Apart from the bruising from the opening shock of the parachute, his hands and arms had been shredded by bark and branches. His right shirt sleeve was ripped and blood stained the khaki material. He made a fist and flexed his arm muscles. No serious damage. He ran his fingertips over his cheek and forehead and felt wetness. There was fresh blood and he winced as he touched the cut by his left eye again. Lucky not to lose half his sight, he thought. He felt groggy as well as nauseated, and wondered if he had suffered a concussion. His head throbbed with a dull ache, as it did when he was hungover. His tongue felt swollen and sore and he realised he must have bitten it during his landing. His left trouser leg was torn and the skin felt badly scratched.

The tree creaked and he looked up. The branch his parachute canopy had snagged on was bent at an alarming angle. The drying winter sun had turned the once green leaves of the mopani, and those all around him, the colour of dull copper.

Birds chattered around him and, in the distance, he heard the mournful *whoop* of a spotted hyena. He felt for the pistol at his belt and was reassured when he touched the handgrip. Behind and to the right of him, he heard a rustling of leaves. He looked over his shoulder and flinched.

The leopard lay on a thick branch of a neighbouring tree, one front paw tucked under its chin, the other dangling lazily on the other side of the bough. It fixed him with cold yellow eyes and slowly raised itself until it was crouching on all fours. Its curled, white-tipped tail flicked once.

Bryant looked away from the cat again and fought to steady his breathing. It was no more than fifteen feet from him, and he presumed the predator could cover the distance in a single bound. He slowly took another look at the branch he was suspended from. It was narrow and protested again at his weight. The sharp movement of his head before, when he saw the leopard, had caused his body to swing a little. There was nowhere within easy reach of him for the animal to land safely, and still be able to get to him.

He knew next to nothing about wildlife, but vaguely recalled Catherine telling him that lions hunted by sight and sound, rather than smell, and that they were more likely to be attracted to prey that was moving. Hence, people on safari in the bush were always told to stay still if they came across a lion. To run was to encourage the beast to give chase. He wondered if the same principle held true for leopards. He risked another slow glance over his shoulder. Ordinarily he would have been impressed by the beauty of the beast, the bunched neck muscles, the snow-white fur beneath its chin and chest, the black rosettes encircling the golden fur on its flanks, the pink triangular nose. Now he was just plain terrified.

'Nice kitty,' he whispered. The leopard emitted a rasping noise, like a sharp saw cutting through wood. 'Fuck,' he said.

The cat started to move, backing its way down the branch to the main trunk of the tree.

Bryant slowly moved his hand to the canvas holster at his waist, unbuttoned the flap and drew out the heavy Webley revolver. In the distance he heard a sound the same as the one the leopard had just made, the sawing cough. Two of them, he thought. Great.

The leopard ran down the trunk of the tamboti tree it had been resting in, rushing headlong towards the ground, then landed silently at the bottom, its four paws raising tiny clouds of dust. It looked up at Bryant, then lowered itself so that its belly was nearly touching the dirt. It started to move and Bryant lost sight of it.

He hoped the animal was leaving and that his movements had scared it out of the tree and sent it on its way. He looked down between his legs and saw he was wrong. It slunk along the ground to the base of the tree he was hanging from. He drew back the hammer of the pistol with his right thumb and raised his arm to a firing position.

The leopard craned its neck and then stopped at the metallic click. It looked up at the dangling human and, in a blur of black, white and yellow, was in the tree before Bryant could let loose a shot. It surged up the trunk, paw over paw, scaling the vertical surface effortlessly, but on the opposite side to the human.

Bryant swung wildly in his harness, to try to take aim, but all he saw was a flash of dappled fur. He fired anyway, the crash of the bullet sending a flock of birds squawking noisily out of the upper branches. His movement brought a cracking sound from the branch above him. He looked up and saw it give, too late to brace for the fall.

Leaves, twigs and bark rained down on him as he hit the dirt and landed painfully on his right side. He tried to sit up, but found the air had been knocked from his lungs. His chest protested as he tried to suck in air and stand. He fell to the ground and rolled over onto his back. He looked up at the tree and saw the leopard staring down at him, the annoyance plain on its face. He raised his arm again and fired another shot. The cat, uninjured, leaped to another branch and then eyed him from around the thick trunk. He fired again and then, still gasping for air, managed to stand.

Bugger standing still, he thought. He undid his parachute harness, shrugged it off and started to run. His ankle hurt and the ribs on his right side felt like they'd been kicked by a horse. Every breath caused so much pain that he thought he might pass out from it. Still he ran, stumbling blindly through the descending gloom.

The leopard called again, and was answered with more sawing.

'Jesus Christ,' Bryant gasped as he glimpsed a fleeting shadow off to his left. He looked over his shoulder and saw the first cat bounding down out of the tree. It was coming after him. He half turned and fired the pistol again, but the leopard was running now, all four paws off the ground with each graceful bound. Not watching where he was running, he missed a tree root and stumbled. He fell hard again and cried with pain as his cracked ribs connected with the earth once more. His right arm shot forward as he fell. His palm hit a half-buried rock and the pistol flew from his hand.

The leopard saw its chance and leaped. Bryant rolled

hard to the right and yelled in pain as he felt the claws dig into his back. It was on him now. It stank of feline urine and rotting meat and he felt its hot breath.

The dappled cat straddled him and tried to find the neck, where it could bite down and silently choke its victim. As strong and deadly as it was, the solitary leopard would be unable to fight off a pack of hyenas or a pride of lion if the dying noise of its prey alerted other nearby predators to its plight. Even if its mate arrived after answering its call, the pair of cats would be hard-pressed to defend the kill.

Bryant groped blindly in the dirt. He felt the incredible force and weight of another round paw pinning his left arm. His fingers touched the wooden grip of the pistol. He grasped it and half rolled, this time towards the leopard, until they were facing each other, their eyes barely a foot apart.

The leopard lowered its sleek head and opened its jaws wide, revealing yellowed fangs as long as Bryant's little finger. He thrust the barrel up into the cat's ribs and its eyes suddenly widened in pain and surprise. He pulled the trigger.

The fur, skin and internal organs muffled the sound of the gunshot, but Bryant felt the terrible weight rise off him for a fraction of a second as the force of the bullet lifted the animal. The leopard growled in pain and writhed above him, its claws lashing at him as it tried to escape the burning in its guts. Blood frothed from its mouth and hot red spittle stung Bryant's face. He pushed his free hand up and into the leopard's chest and heaved it away from him. Finally free of the flailing paws he rolled out of its reach and turned. The leopard lunged back towards him, but its steps were less sure than before and each movement caused bright blood to spurt from the entry and exit wounds in its body. It was still a deadly creature, though, and as its forepaws were almost in swiping range of him once again, Bryant lay on his back, held out his firing hand and fired again. The bullet smashed up through the cat's mouth and out the top of its brain. Bryant sagged, his whole body exhausted and protesting with pain, as the animal gushed its last bloody breath beside him.

Bryant's left arm was dripping blood and his back felt wet and ripped from another gash. He sat up and stared at the dead cat. He shook his head. The shock and terror of the last few moments were too much for his pain-racked body to bear. He turned his head to one side and vomited a mouthful of bitter bile. He snapped his head around again, though, when he heard a twig snap.

There, across a small clearing, at the base of a tree, was the second leopard. It looked at him, and then at its dead mate. It sniffed the air and then lowered its body, the same way as the first cat had before pouncing.

Bryant raised his gun hand again, the pistol feeling like a hundred pounds of lead. The foresight wavered as he tried to take aim. He pulled the trigger and the hammer clicked down into an empty chamber. He tried four more times, but the weapon was empty. The leopard readied itself to pounce and Bryant, the fight gone from his body with nearly the last of his strength, drew back his arm and hurled the useless gun at the cat.

The second leopard, a comparatively small female, lacked the confidence of its dead mate and gave a short, sharp yelp as the thing hit its snout. It turned and fled into the darkened bush.

Bryant started to shiver. He drew himself painfully to his feet and stood in the clearing, looking at the dead predator. After a few moments he hobbled to where his pistol had bounced off the other animal, and picked it up.

He tried to think. It would be madness to attempt to find the main road in the dark and he was disorientated now the sun had set. He had no compass on him, but the morning light would be all he needed to guide him. He knew the best thing he could do now was to get a fire going, in order to discourage other predators, and wait for the dawn, when the smoke would hopefully act as a signal to searching aircraft.

There was wood and kindling all around him, and he suddenly remembered the newspaper clipping stuffed in the pocket of his uniform trousers. It would help get the fire started. He tore the double page of newsprint in half and wadded one section into a ball. He'd wanted to read about the fate of Catherine's husband, but he wanted to survive this night in the African bush even more. He gathered a pile of dried twigs and yellowed grass over the paper and pulled his cigarettes and lighter from his pocket.

First things first, he said to himself, lighting a cigarette and drawing deeply. He felt the welcome buzz of nicotine on an empty stomach. The tremor in his hand slowed enough for him to hold the remaining section of newsprint. By the light of the small flame he started to read as he crouched and then held the lighter to the balled paper.

He winced from the gouges in his back and arm and wished he had water to clean the wounds. God knew what bacteria lived on the claws of a leopard. The newspaper article was detailed and he kept the lighter lit in order to read. It had been written some days after the shooting accident, it seemed, and went into detail about the ill-fated buffalo hunt.

The hunter who fired the fatal shot was yesterday identified as Mr Hendrick Du Pleiss, of Vryburg, South Africa, Bryant read. The story recapped the details, which Catherine had once told him, of how the party had gone searching in a thicket for a wounded buffalo. When the wounded animal had charged them, the South African had dropped his rifle and it had accidentally discharged.

He read on. *Mrs Catherine De Beers, an eyewitness to the tragic accident, was also interviewed by police at length. She corroborated Mr Du Pleiss's account of the incident. Visibly distressed on leaving the police station, she declined a request by this newspaper to recount her version of events.*

Not surprising, Bryant thought. He disliked newsmen, considering them little more than leeches who fed on people's misery and swallowed any old guff they were dished out about the war, no matter how inaccurate. According to the English press, Bomber Command had all but pulverised Nazi Germany. Funny, then, how the Germans were still able to field swarms of night-fighters and keep the Ruhr ringed with deadly flak batteries.

He touched the lighter's flame to the wadded second page. He knew how the story ended, but he continued reading. *Mr Du Pleiss could not be contacted by the* Chronicle. *Police said he had been released and would be returning to South Africa at the first opportunity and* . . .

The paragraph was broken in midsentence at the bottom of the page. Bryant looked down at the growing fire and saw the rest of the article slowly uncurling as the flames took hold. There was a portrait photograph of a man.

He crouched close to the fire, its growing heat warming his face. He took a closer look at the picture. He reached out and snatched the paper, burning his thumb and forefinger in the process, then dropped the sheet on the ground and stamped out the flames.

Suddenly the pain in his fingers, and from the multiple wounds he had suffered in the parachute landing and the fight with the leopard, were the last things on his mind.

16

The settlement of Gwaai River, if it could be called that, was about as far away from England as a place could be, but that's what Constable Roger Pembroke was thinking about when the door to the police hut creaked open.

Gwaai River, halfway between Bulawayo and Victoria Falls, consisted of a hotel called, not surprisingly, the Halfway House, a few outlying cattle farms, a forestry officer and a policeman.

Roger looked up. 'What is it?' he asked the elderly African man who stood before him, dressed in tattered trousers and a threadbare white shirt.

'I saw an aeroplane, boss,' the older man said.

'Plenty of them about these days.'

The African ignored the implied insult. He had seen the *murungu* policeman about, passing through his village. He thought the man was too young to be taken seriously, but he knew no other white man to whom he could report what he had seen. 'It fell from the sky, boss.'

Roger sat up straight. 'The crash? You saw the plane come down yesterday?' He'd received a telephone call from Pip Lovejoy in Bulawayo the afternoon before, alerting him to the Harvard's last known position, and advising him that its pilot was wanted for murder. Roger had saddled his horse and ridden ten miles up and down the main road in the hope of spotting smoke, but had seen nothing. Pip, who had a rather attractive-sounding telephone voice, had told him the air force would be conducting a full-scale search the next day. Today. He'd heard aero engines sporadically during the morning, and these had fuelled his daydreams about becoming an ace RAF fighter pilot.

'Yes, boss. I saw it fall. And a man.'

'A man?' Roger opened his police notebook. 'What's your name?'

'Last. Last Mpofu, boss.'

'All right, Last. Tell me again. You saw a man.'

'He flew, boss. Slowly to the earth.'

'Ah!' Roger drew a crude sketch of a stick-figure man under a parachute and held up his notebook. 'Is this what you saw, Last?'

The older man looked at the picture. 'Yes. A parachute.'

Roger frowned. 'Did you go to him?'

'It was dark. There are lion and leopard in the bush, boss.'

'The crash happened early yesterday afternoon. You took your time reporting this.'

'It was a long walk.'

'I see. Well, you did the right thing coming here. Do you remember where it was that you saw the man land?'

'Yes, boss.'

'And the aeroplane. You said you saw it crash?'

'I saw it fall, boss. Not crash. I heard it, though, and saw the smoke.'

This was big news. With a bit of luck he'd get to meet his first pilot – and his first murderer – today. He flipped back through his notebook, past the reports of stolen cattle, a lion attack on a native farm worker, and a drunken brawl in the hotel, and found the entry he'd made yesterday after being advised of the missing aircraft and wanted man. He picked up the telephone and dialled the number he'd written. Shirley, the receptionist, answered and he asked to be put through to Pip Lovejoy.

'Is it about the missing flyer? The murderer?'

'You bet it is. I've got an African chap here who says he saw the plane *and* the pilot come down. He bailed out.' Roger couldn't hold back a smile as he used the air force jargon.

'Pip's out, Roger. I'll pass on a message to her and Sergeant

Hayes as soon as they're back. What's the location?'

Roger silently cursed. In his eagerness to tell someone the news he realised he hadn't gathered enough facts yet. 'Hold on,' he said, covering the mouthpiece with one hand. 'How far away is the pilot? Where did he go down?' he asked Last.

The African looked back over his shoulder and pointed south. 'A long way, boss.'

'Blast,' Roger said aloud. He spoke into the telephone again. 'Shirley, the bloke can't give an exact location, but he's taking me there now. Get someone in a car to head north. I'll leave a cairn of stones with a note under it when we leave the main road.'

He hung up, then unlocked the gun rack behind his desk and took out a Lee-Enfield rifle. 'This man might be dangerous, Last,' he said in answer to the African's inquiring look as he pushed five rounds into the magazine and dropped a second clip into his uniform pocket. 'Let's go.'

Pembroke saddled his police horse and tethered the reins of a second beast to his saddle. When the policeman asked him, Last said he could not ride, so Roger helped him up behind him, onto his horse's rump.

'Hold on, Last,' he said as he dug his spurs in.

Bryant knew he should have waited where his parachute had snagged in the trees and kept the signal fire going to alert searching aircraft to his presence. Twice since he had set off at daybreak he had heard the drone of single- and twin-engine aircraft overhead but had been unable to signal them due to the density of the bush he was walking through.

In time, if he had stayed put, he was sure the rescuers would have found him. However, he had precious little time, if the pieces of the puzzle swimming in his head were to come together in the way he feared they would.

He knew he had landed west of the main north–south road, so if he headed east he would find it eventually. He had no compass, another oversight he chided himself about, but took his bearings from the rising sun. He knew that he had to find someone – anyone – as soon as possible. He would make another signal fire as soon as he hit the road.

He walked as quickly as his injuries would allow. The bleeding from the gashes to his arm and back had stopped, but the pain in his muscles intensified with every step he took. He shook his head to ward off encroaching exhaustion. The sporadic, mournful rasping of the female leopard pining for her dead mate, and his wounds, which made it impossible to get comfortable, meant his sleep had been confined to a few brief dozes by the fire. After the scare with the cats the previous evening, he ensured he scanned the bush ahead and on either side of him. On three occasions he startled small buck – impala and steenbok, he thought – and the first he'd been aware of them was the flash of their tawny bodies in the bush. His eyes were adjusting to the foreign surroundings, though, and he paused when he saw a flicker of movement.

It was an elephant, perhaps a hundred yards away. No more. He marvelled that the huge grey beast could have remained hidden from him at such a close range. However, he was proud that he had spotted the give-away swish of its tail before the animal had noticed him. He felt a soft breeze on his face. He was downwind of the beast, and that had, no doubt, helped him get so close. Slowly he dropped to a crouch and watched it. The sun was riding high now. Bryant checked his watch. It was nearly eight o'clock. It would be harder for him to keep his bearings once the sun reached its zenith. The elephant was standing at the base of a large tree, in the shade. His big ears flapped back and forth like punkah fans. Bryant vaguely recalled reading somewhere that this was how elephants cooled themselves – something about their blood passing through a network of veins in the ears. The flapping cooled the blood, which cooled the elephant. Clever, though the animal was just plain fright-ening this close and on foot. Bryant slowly unbuttoned the flap of the holster on his belt and withdrew the pistol. He was out of ammunition but if the animal charged him for some reason, perhaps the sight of a man waving a hand gun might cause it to have second thoughts. Bryant looked down at the Webley revolver, then back up at the elephant. He shook his head. No chance.

Another movement caught his eye. Another set of ears, but much smaller. The tiny calf emerged from a thicket and passed the bigger elephant. It was so tiny it could have walked under the bigger one's belly. It trotted from bush to bush with the energy that only a youngster could have in such heat. Bryant noticed that its little trunk seemed to have a life of its own, swishing from side to side, and up and down. The baby elephant stopped and sniffed a branch on the ground. The mopani sapling had been stripped clean of its bark, the honey-coloured core of wood all that remained of the mother elephant's latest snack. The youngster nudged it with the tip of his trunk, then gingerly lifted it. He turned back to his mother, proudly holding the new toy aloft, but it fell from his grasp before he could show her.

Bryant smiled. He'd assumed elephants would be born knowing how to use an essential bit of kit like a trunk, but now he realised baby elephants, like baby humans, had a great deal to learn from their elders.

The baby elephant snuffled away from the protection

of its mother, looking for new things to pick up. Head down, trunk leading, it started moving towards Bryant. Beyond the baby he could now see even more animals. Every second, it seemed, he noticed another swish of a tail or the flap of giant ears. He had very nearly walked into a herd of perhaps twenty or thirty. There were more young elephants as well. A breeding herd. 'Shit,' he whispered as the inquisitive baby moved closer and closer. Bryant looked over his shoulder. At least there were no animals behind him. He started to move, backing slowly away from the advancing infant.

He was a flyer, not a bushman. He didn't see the dead branch behind him. It snapped with a crack that might as well have been a gunshot for the effect it had.

The baby elephant squealed, a noise like that emitted from a toy horn on New Year's Eve. Its mother answered, but with a trumpet blast that Bryant felt in his guts. From others in the herd came deep, ominous rumblings, a noise like approaching thunder.

Bryant swore. The mother elephant saw him and started towards him. She had her trunk curled between her tusks and her ears back. It looked like she meant business. He turned and ran, his arms and legs pumping as he tried to gain some speed. He still held the Webley revolver in his right hand. He waved it high over his head, but when he risked a glance over his right shoulder he saw the big cow was gaining on him.

Ahead of him was a dry riverbed. Without slowing he leaped off the edge of the embankment and landed three feet below in thick sand. Instead of crossing to the other side he turned hard left. The river snaked around to the left again, and he followed its course. The elephant came to an abrupt halt at the edge of the watercourse. A cloud of dust rose around her and she bellowed, long and loud. Bryant kept running through the sand, not risking a peek this time.

'Something's spooked those jumbos,' Constable Roger Pembroke said. He swivelled in his saddle to face the African behind him. 'You're sure this is the place?'

'Yes, boss,' Last said.

'Well, let's get off and start looking,' Roger said.

Nearby, an elephant bellowed again. 'She is not happy, boss.'

'How do you know it's a female?'

'Are you married, boss?'

'No.'

Last smiled and climbed awkwardly down off the horse.

Bryant noticed the bush on either side of the dry riverbed was starting to thin out ahead. He slowed and allowed himself to catch his breath and look over his shoulder. The elephant that had been chasing him had given up. He heard a rumbling to his left. 'Fuck,' he whispered.

The bull elephant had been happily scratching his itchy rump against the leadwood tree he usually used for this purpose when he'd heard the matriarch's cries to her baby. The source of the discontent had just come into view. One of the two-legged creatures. He took a few steps towards the human, raised his trunk and flapped his ears wide. That usually did the trick. For good measure he released a mighty blast from the end of his trunk.

Bryant had had enough of elephants to last him a lifetime. He resumed his sprint, charging down the gully. To his surprise, he nearly ran smack into a man-made stone drainage culvert. He looked up and saw the road. 'Thank Christ,' he said. While a road wouldn't protect him from a charging pachyderm or a hungry carnivore, at least it meant he was on his way back to civilisation. The watercourse had brought him back on his easterly track and he had found the main north–south road. He turned right, towards Bulawayo, and started off at a steady jog.

Roger Pembroke slid the .303 from the leather holster on the right side of his horse's flank. Elephant worried him. Always had since the death of his brother when they were both still teenagers. Gored and trampled, and Roger had witnessed the lot. He slid back the bolt and chambered a round. A Lee-Enfield might not stop an elephant dead in its tracks, but a round through an ear was sometimes enough to scare one of the giant beasts off.

Roger patted the horse, which had shifted from side to side after the African's ungainly dismount. 'There, there, girl,' he said. As he grabbed the saddle's pommel he saw a man round the bend in the road ahead of him, running along one of the tar strips.

'Hey!' the man called.

Roger took in his appearance. Right height, right build, wearing air force uniform. He looked dirty and his shirt was ripped and bloodied. He was carrying something in his right hand. A pistol!

'Drop the gun!' Roger called out. He brought his rifle to bear.

Bryant lifted his arm to wave at the mounted policeman. Never in his entire life had he been so pleased to see a copper. The man had called something to him. 'What?' Bryant replied. The blood was still pounding in his ears from his narrow escape from the elephants, which for all he knew might still be on his tail. With his rescue at hand he felt every one of his wounds start to throb in pain, as if his body were telling him it was safe to hurt now.

For some reason the copper was now raising his rifle.

443

Instinctively, he started to raise his hands in a gesture of surrender. Perhaps the man thought he was a spy or something. 'I'm Bryant, Royal Australian Air Force!'

'Stand still!' the policeman yelled.

Bryant heard the sound of twigs breaking in the bush beside him. The bloody elephants were still on his trail. 'I can't stop now!'

'Stand still, Bryant! You are under arrest!'

Arrest? Had he heard right, was the policeman mad? He looked at the mounted copper, the dismounted African, then into the bush to their left. It was the direction Bryant had originally been travelling. He saw the first great shapes in the trees by the roadside. 'Look out on your left!' he called to the men. As he did so, he unconsciously raised the empty pistol in order to point.

The oldest trick in the book, as they would have said in an American film. Roger wasn't going to be fooled. It wasn't the pilot's words that scared him, but his highly charged state and the way he was bringing the pistol up. 'Stop!' he bellowed.

The first of the elephants broke through the trees at a canter. The police horse reared up in fright.

Roger had been aiming at the centre mass of the approaching murder suspect, just as he'd been taught. Best chance of a hit if one aimed at the torso. It was the horse's sudden movement that caused him to jerk his finger accidentally.

The shot spooked the elephant, and the twenty or more animals turned as one and retraced their steps back into the safety of the bush.

Last walked up to the man lying in the roadway. There was blood on his face, his hair and the black Tarmac. The man was motionless. Last looked back at the young policeman, whose face was even whiter than before, and said: 'Ah, but I think this man is dead, boss.'

17

Pip started work early at the police camp. She'd had a rotten night's sleep.

She looked up at the slowly rotating fan above her head. The once white blades were yellowed, the edges encrusted with a fine layer of black filth thanks to years of tobacco smoke. Dirty and smelly, just like the rest of the camp. What was it, then, that attracted her to this life so much? Certainly not the surroundings, or the male-dominated banter that centred on women and blacks, for all the wrong reasons.

Truth. Perhaps that was it. And justice. It sounded trite, when she said it to herself, but that was all she had been looking for, all her life. She wanted truth – in a relationship, and justice. She'd been with two men so far and had neither truth nor justice from either of them.

The harder she thought about it, though, the less able she was to connect Paul Bryant with the crimes he would soon be accused of. Perhaps they would never know the truth about him if he had been killed in the aeroplane crash.

Paul Bryant, a killer? Again, she found she was less and less able to convince herself that her deduction had been correct. Perhaps it was just her emotions interfering. Only yesterday she had made passionate love to this man – the first time in her life sex had been anything other than a painful duty. She had abandoned her body to him and been rewarded. Had he captured part of her mind as well?

But Bryant would hang if he were still alive. And if he went down, it would be the result of her investigations, her deductions.

She didn't know how to feel about Paul right now. She couldn't be pleased that he might be dead, nor could she grieve for him while a cloud hung over his name. She had been devastated to make the connection between him and Innocent Nkomo, and horrified by Catherine's description of him as a violent man, but it just didn't seem to fit with what little she knew of him. She also felt responsible for his decision to fly to Bechuanaland and this brought back a wave of sadness, mixed with anger and frustration that she might never know the truth about a man she had started to care about, that justice might never be served over the death of Felicity Langham.

She had too much time to think. That was the problem. Hayes and four of the spare male officers had taken a car north, to Gwaai River, where they planned on setting up a police forward command post to liaise with the air force ground search team.

Pip opened the investigation file in front of her. She knew the facts of the case, as they stood, inside out, but there was always the chance she had overlooked some detail. She found the report from the constables who had interviewed Felicity's neighbours. The address of Flick's hillside home was at the top of the page.

From the outset of the investigation she and Hayes had both assumed that Felicity had been abducted, or waylaid by her killer during a night out on the town. The subsequent arrest of Innocent Nkomo had only reinforced their initial deduction. Now that they were on the trail of Bryant, someone who knew the victim intimately – the type of suspect Pip had initially favoured in any case – she now believed that Felicity was probably killed in her own home. The evidence of the message summoning Bryant to the house added substance to this theory.

Someone else could sit in the office and answer the telephone. She pushed back her chair, knocking it over in her rush to stand, and grabbed her hat. She stuffed the notebook and pencil into a pocket of her tunic and strode out the door, into the corridor.

'Oi, where are you off to?' Shirley asked after her, disentangling a telephonist's headset from her hairdo. 'You're supposed to wait here, aren't you?'

'Got to check something,' Pip called over her shoulder. 'Back soon.'

Hayes had taken the duty car, a bakkie, so Pip helped herself to a police bicycle. She rammed her hat down hard on her head and straddled the bike. Two male constables walking up the driveway of the police camp called something, but she was already peddling too fast to hear.

She dodged around a Studebaker that was pulling over in Tenth Avenue and then took the right turn into Main Street so fast that the bike was leaning hard over. She rang the bell on the handlebars and an African street cleaner leaped out of her way as she swung left into Twelfth. Once clear of the city centre she raced through the flat dry countryside until she reached the outer suburb of Hillside, where Bulawayo's wealthier citizens escaped the bustle of the commercial centre. This was a community of peaceful whitewashed bungalows and small farms. An oasis of civility in the African bush. How many of Felicity Langham's neighbours, she wondered, had any inkling of what had gone on behind those virginal white walls? Pip pulled on squeaky brakes and dismounted the bicycle before it came to a halt. She leaned the bike against a white-painted picket fence and strode up the stone pathway to the front door.

It was locked. She hadn't thought to inquire as to what had happened to the key. Catherine De Beers owned the house. Pip suffered a moment's hesitation. She was here on official police business, but without a warrant. She looked furtively up and down the quiet avenue, but saw no movement amidst the flowering jacarandas. She walked around to the back of the bungalow. 'Damn,' she said. The rear door was locked as well. She looked around the back porch and saw a stout-handled broom. She picked it up and rapped hard on the glass of the kitchen window. The pane shattered with the second blow and, careful not to cut either her uniform or arm, she reached in and turned the window's handle. Pip was glad no one was around to witness her undigni-fied scramble through the window and up onto the kitchen bench. Once inside she straightened her skirt and replaced her hat.

The house smelled musty, and of something faintly rotten – perhaps perishable food still stored somewhere in the kitchen. She moved to the adjacent lounge room and paused to get her bearings. A chill ran down her back as her stout police-issue shoes clicked noisily on the polished floorboards.

As she walked through the empty house she wondered what had happened on Felicity's last night. What words were spoken? At what point did everything go horribly wrong?

The main bedroom was down the hallway on the right. She entered. Apparently, neither Catherine De Beers nor any of her servants had returned to the house to tidy up or remove anything. Pip breathed a sigh of relief. Now that they had a new suspect she had come back to the house to find something to incriminate him, some forensic evidence that he had been in the house that night – something he had denied during interview.

Again the niggling doubt that she was rushing to conclusions bothered her. Was it right to go looking for evidence to support a theory?

She walked to the bed and took hold of the corner of the top sheet, which lay half on the bed. It felt limp, almost oily, in her hand, not crisp and starched like fresh linen. She sniffed the air. Stale in here, too, but there was a lingering odour as well. Perfume, mixed with perspiration. Bending over, she found the cloying scent was coming from the sheets. She pulled the sheet back further, wondering exactly what she should be looking for.

Hairs, she thought with a mild sense of revulsion. Charlie left them everywhere. In the bed, on the bathroom floor, on the soap. Pip switched on the overhead light then dropped to her knees beside the bed. She lowered her face to the dank sheet and blinked to refocus on the short distance. At first she saw nothing, but slowly, as her eyes adjusted to the light and the scale on which she was searching, she started to see things.

'Aha,' she said. Gently, with her fingernail, she prodded an eyelash. If a person was in a room, anywhere, they most likely left some tiny piece of evidence of their presence. It was no different from following animal spoor in the bush, really. She picked up the lash and held it to the light. A woman's – curled and unnaturally black with mascara. A piece of Felicity Langham.

She thought about Felicity – about her body, to be exact. She was hairless – shaved – where a woman should have had hair. Pip's eyes roved up and down the bottom sheet, moving in a series of longitudinal sweeps, up and down, gradually tracking right to left. 'No hairs,' she said aloud. Not male, or female. No evidence that Bryant had been in the bed. She stood and chewed on her lower lip as she thought.

Felicity had been sexually assaulted, according to the doctor who had examined her. She knew, from her own illicit experience, that Bryant favoured using air-force-issue condoms when making love. Hence, there would be no evidence of that type. However, if he had assaulted her he must have left something of himself somewhere in the house.

She dropped to her knees again and lowered her face

452

to the floor so she could peer under the bed. Nothing. Just dust. She raised herself and found she was next to a bedside chest of drawers. She opened the bottom drawer. Fashion magazines and a box of tissues. The middle drawer yielded something quite odd. A collection of wigs.

Pip sat on the bed and opened the drawer fully. She drew out three wigs, disentangling the intertwined hairs as she did so. The colours were red, jet black and blonde. She fingered the black wig and tried to think why a beautiful young woman would bother with fake hair. 'Disguise?' she mused aloud. 'Or fun?' Was one of Felicity's unusual sexual practices pretending to be someone else? She replaced the wigs in the drawer.

The top drawer, she could see immediately, contained a collection of undergarments – knickers, bras, stockings, suspender belts. Felicity had been found with her wrists bound with a silk stocking. Was there an odd stocking in this drawer which might somehow be shown to match the one on her body? Worth a look. Pip reached in and grabbed a handful of silk. Her fingers brushed something hard. She peered into the drawer and carefully moved a few lacy garments. 'Oh, my goodness!' she gasped.

Inside, though she dared not touch it, was a penis. Well, a pretty damned good replica of one – a large black one, at that. Pip felt her cheeks colour. She nudged it with a fingertip. It rolled easily. Not stone, perhaps wood. Ebony, she guessed.

She'd wondered, when she'd learned of the existence of a relationship between Catherine and Felicity that was more than platonic, exactly what it was that they did in bed together. She was getting an inkling. The thing lay there, staring at her, mocking her professional resolve.

She sorted and counted the stockings again. As she'd suspected, there was an odd number. Not that that proved anything, of course. She would have to gain access to the one that had been used to bind Felicity's hands, and then get an expert in hosiery to compare it with all of the others in front of her now. If the killer had selected the silk to render Felicity helpless, then he would have presumably opened this drawer. His fingerprints would be there.

Pip left the stockings on the bed and wandered out of the bedroom. She made her way into the bathroom. The toilet seat was down, she noticed. She opened a mirrored bathroom cabinet door and surveyed the contents. Make-up, mascara, lipsticks, soap, cotton wool, talcum powder.

It was hot and stuffy in the house, with no windows open save for the one she had broken. She returned to the bedroom, sat on the bed and removed her police-issue hat. She wiped the perspiration from her forehead and ran her hand through her damp fair hair. When she examined her hand she found a single strand, which had caught on a chipped fingernail. She left plenty of evidence everywhere she went, and she wondered why the killer had not. She held the fine golden strand in front of her eyes for a few moments, concentrating on it. Suddenly it hit her, like a jolt of electricity running through her body. 'Blonde!'

She leaned over and flung open the second drawer in the bureau and pulled out the blonde wig she'd noticed earlier. She turned it over, so that she could see inside it.

'Bloody hell,' she whispered.

'Look at this picture!' Pip ordered.

'I am tired of looking at pictures, of answering questions that go around and around in circles,' Innocent Nkomo said wearily.

'You'll bloody well look at whatever I tell you to!' Pip said. The male constable standing in the corner of the room couldn't hold back a smirk. Pip shot him a look. The man held his tongue.

'I have identified the man you wanted me to identify,' Innocent said.

'The man I *wanted* you to identify?' As she parroted the man's words she realised the truth of it. She had gone to Innocent last time with the pictures from the newspaper, blinded by Catherine's words, with her mind already made up. Perhaps she was about to make the same mistake, but the man in the cell was still her best hope of sorting this whole messy affair out. She hated the idea of confirming that Paul was just as evil as Charlie – or worse – so much that she longed now for him to be truly innocent. She'd learned that there had been a call from Gwaai River while she was gone, something about an African seeing an aircraft crash and a pilot parachute out safely. Her heart had leaped, and she had whispered a prayer in the hallway before entering the interview room. 'Please, God, let him be alive, whether he's guilty or innocent.'

Something indefinable – a deeply felt instinct – now told her that if Paul Bryant had survived, he must be innocent. Her doubts had forced her to search Felicity's house, and they might just save a man she couldn't stop thinking about from hanging.

Her relief – if that was the right word – that Paul could be alive was tempered by the fact that Hayes had threatened, by phone, to have her relieved of duty for being absent when the call from Constable Pembroke had come through. She'd heard no more about how the search was progressing.

'Look at these pictures, Innocent. Your life might depend on it.'

'I have been told that so many times I am beginning to think that you people will never let me go free,' he said. 'Who do you want me to identify now?'

If she had been a male constable she might very well have administered him a backhanded slap across the face. Instead she smiled and said: 'Innocent, I don't *want* any particular person identified. I just want you to look at these three pictures of different women and tell me if any of them was the second-to-last customer you sold *illegal* petrol to on the night of Miss Langham's murder.'

Innocent sighed and shook his head. He looked down at the pictures spread on his cell bed. 'I told you, the woman I sold fuel to had fair hair. These women all have dark hair.'

'Yes, I remember,' she said. 'I want you to imagine all of these women with fair hair.'

He looked up at her, puzzled.

'Just look at their faces, Innocent,' she persisted. As with the photos of the men from which Innocent had identified Paul Bryant, Pip had gathered a random selection of attractive-looking women from the pages of the *Bulawayo Chronicle*. She had dug out the dusty, closed file on the accidental killing of Hugo De Beers and, as she'd hoped, found a photo of Catherine De Beers in the story. The caption read: 'Mrs De Beers – grieving widow witnessed her husband's accidental death'. 'Take your time,' she added.

Innocent scratched his chin and pored over the pictures. 'Her clothes were fine,' he said out aloud.

'What? You remember what she was wearing?'

'Not what she was wearing, just that she struck me as being well dressed. I notice these things in a woman.'

Pip nodded, willing him to get on with it.

'I can't be sure,' he said at last.

Pip sighed.

'Tell me which one, and I will say it is her,' Nkomo said, looking up into her eyes, holding her gaze.

Pip was tempted, but she knew that to lead him to pick the woman she had in mind would be circumventing justice, and the law. 'No, Innocent. It doesn't work that way. Take another look. Please.'

He studied the images again. 'There is something about this one that looks familiar, though it is hard with the dark hair.' He crooked a finger around the halo of curls, obscuring the woman's hairdo, then leaned closer over the bed. 'I am not sure, but of the three, this one, I think, is the one.'

Pip looked over his shoulder and saw the picture. The grieving widow.

'Bloody Bryant,' Wing Commander Rogers said.

'Yes, sir,' said Pilot Officer Clive Wilson. He quickened

his step to stay abreast of the Wingco, who walked very fast for an old man. They were making a last-minute inspection of the route the official guests would take to the parade ground, which had been marked out on the Tarmac in front of Kumalo's main hangar complex.

'You're acting adjutant of the base until further notice, Wilson,' Rogers said. 'Keep up, for God's sake, man.'

'Yes, sir,' Wilson said. He had mixed emotions about the temporary promotion from instructor to adjutant. It would mean no time for flying, which he regretted, and paperwork by the ton, which he loathed. However, the adjutant was the one person, apart from the Wingco, who really wielded power on the base. He hoped, though, that the new role wouldn't delay his posting to England.

'The best thing for Bryant now, Wilson, is for him to be dead.'

'Sir?'

'If he was killed in the prang we can at least give him a hero's burial. Better for him and his family *and* the air force for him to go out that way, rather than being arrested and tried for rape and murder.'

'I see, sir.'

'Leaves in the gutter there, Wilson, make a note.'

'Yes, sir,' Wilson pulled out his notebook and wrote. The Wingco shook his head, tutted and pointed at the stray jacaranda blossoms that marred the uniform black of the

Tarmac road from the gatehouse towards the hangars.

They strode briskly towards the hangar, with Wilson furiously scribbling reminders about uneven lawn edges, a stray cigarette butt, and the exterior wall of the airmen's mess, which was in need of a new coat of whitewash. The paint wouldn't even have time to dry before the brass arrived, Wilson thought.

'This place should be *shining* for Field Marshal Smuts and Mister Huggins, Wilson. At the moment it looks like the municipal rubbish dump!' Rogers fumed, pointing out a dustbin with its lid sitting slightly askew. When they walked between two huge hangars, both men held up hands to shield their eyes from the glare of the morning sun on the concrete runway.

'Aircraft, Wilson.'

'Yes, sir?'

'I don't see any aircraft!'

'Um, they're off searching for Squadron Leader Bryant, sir.'

'The prime minister's office specifically said they wanted to see aircraft. There's a film crew following Sir Godfrey from Salisbury to capture all this for a newsreel. I want aircraft, Wilson, and lots of them!'

'Yes, sir. Um, should I call off the search for Squadron Leader Bryant?'

Rogers stopped and stared at Wilson as though he had spoken to him in Swahili. He said, slowly and loudly as if he were trying to convey a message to a foreigner: 'Aircraft, Wilson. Lots of them. Wingtip to wingtip. For the cameras. Would you like me to write it down for you?'

'Um, no, sir. I mean, yes, sir. Lots of aircraft.'

Rogers checked his watch. Zero-nine-hundred. Three hours to showtime. 'Well, don't just stand about, Wilson. You've got painting, edging, litter collection and aircraft to organise.'

'Yes, sir.'

Hendrick Reitz waited in the shade of the aircraft hangar at Isilwane Ranch. There was nothing else he could do.

He sat with his back against the timber wall, two long metal cylinders lying on either side of him like sentinels. But it was he who was guarding them, not the other way around. His Mauser rifle lay across his thighs. He watched a small herd of impala graze at the far end of the grass airstrip. Here was peace, he thought. A forgotten, wild corner of Rhodesia where the war and the killing could have been a million miles away. That would all change in a few short hours, but for now he let the tranquil scene and the sound of the bush birds and insects wash over him.

Reitz was not nervous, or afraid – except of failure. His last mission to Africa had almost gone horribly wrong, and he was determined to make a good fist of this one. It was essential for him to do well, particularly if he were to live out his dream and play a part in the new Afrikaner administration of southern Africa, after Germany won the war.

In the distance he heard the sound of an aero engine. It was getting closer. Reitz stood, the Mauser carried in the crook of his arm, and moved to the edge of the hangar wall. He did not want to be visible from the air, so he stayed in the deep shade and raised a hand to shield his eyes from the morning sun.

A single-engine aircraft. It flew overhead and circled. He recognised the type. A Harvard trainer, same as the one that had landed yesterday. The pilot put the aircraft into a shallow dive and circled again as the aeroplane lost height. It flew away from him, then turned back in a tight, banking manoeuvre.

Reitz fought the urge to step out into the open. The aircraft came in low, flashing across the granite kopje from which he had first observed the ranch on his trek in. The pilot nudged the stick forward, dropping the nose. By the time the Harvard was over the airstrip it was low enough for its propeller wash to flatten the grass. Its shadow raced ahead of it. Despite the low altitude the pilot waggled the wings a little. A herd of impala scattered in a dozen different directions, leaping into the air after every few steps to escape some imagined predator. The strip was left clear for landing. The horses reared and whinnied at the engine's growl and the smell of burned fuel.

Reitz followed the Harvard's track with his eyes and smiled when he saw the pilot slide open the cockpit.

18

'He's alive, but he's off his rocker,' Constable Roger Pembroke said.

'Trouble from the start, and a smart-arse attitude as well. I knew it was him all along,' Harold Hayes said.

The two policemen rode in the open back of a police bakkie, a Chevrolet utility pick-up truck. Hayes had been on his way north, towards Gwaai River, when Shirley had radioed him from Bulawayo, saying that Bryant had been captured but wounded in the process. They'd arrived soon after the shooting. It mattered not to Harold Hayes whether the Australian bastard lived or died, not after what he'd done to that poor girl.

Bryant let out a groan. 'You say he's been talking?' Hayes said to Pembroke. The bakkie was travelling at speed, and Hayes had to speak up to be heard over the rushing of the wind. Still, it was cool in the back, a nice way to travel on a hot morning.

'He was mumbling something about Greece, or someone called Reece. Keeps coming to and then passing out.'

'Not surprising, since you very nearly put a bullet through his brain.' Hayes lifted the bloodied gauze pad on the side of Bryant's bandaged head and inspected the wound for a second time. 'He'll live, though.' The bullet from Pembroke's rifle had creased the pilot's skull, carving a narrow channel through the skin on the right temple but, miraculously, had not fractured bone. The wound had bled profusely and Bryant's face, neck and the collar of his shirt were dark with sticky dried blood. Hayes absently waved a hand over the prisoner to shoo away some buzzing flies.

'I had to put the handcuffs on him as he was quite angry when he first woke up,' Pembroke explained.

'You did the right thing, Roger. He knows the game's up and that he'll probably swing for what he did. He'll be desperate to escape. You weren't to know his pistol wasn't loaded. He was probably going to try to bluff you into handing over your rifle and then kill you with your own weapon and steal your horse.'

'Gosh,' said Pembroke. 'How d'you know this chap's the killer? I read in the paper that you'd arrested an African for the murder.'

Hayes nodded, as though this were a very wise question.

'Well, you see, Roger, just because the man we arrested was African, and had possession of certain intimate items belonging to the dead woman, didn't mean that we ... that I should stop the investigation right then and there.'

Pembroke nodded as Hayes continued his story. He looked down at the battered pilot. When the sergeant had concluded with how he had gotten Innocent Nkomo to identify Bryant from a newspaper cutting, the younger policeman said, 'Looks like he's been in the wars, doesn't it?'

Hayes gingerly lifted the flyer's torn shirt away from the bloodied skin. 'Animal of some sort, or perhaps he did it parachuting. Nasty gouges. Might need stitching. Waste of good medical supplies, if you ask me.'

Bryant had drifted in and out of consciousness, but each time he awoke he wished he hadn't. His head felt like it had been kicked by a horse – several times – and he was nauseated every time he opened his eyes.

Just that small effort of raising his eyelids brought waves of pain, so he tried to keep them shut. After his mind faded to black, the visions came. A kaleidoscope of images – Catherine, Felicity, the face in the intelligence file. Reitz. Hendrick Reitz. The newspaper story about the death of Hugo De Beers. He couldn't tell. In his dreams he saw Pip Lovejoy, in her uniform, walking away from him, on the other side of the young copper with the rifle. Before he could call to Pip the gun went off.

Bryant winced in pain and opened his eyes as he felt the cloth of his shirt pull away from his skin. The movement dislodged a scab of drying blood and opened one of the cuts inflicted by the leopard. 'Leopard,' he said.

'What was that?' Hayes asked. 'Something about a leopard. Man's lost it completely.' He bent so his face was close to Bryant's. 'Don't try to pull the old insanity defence, matey. You're for the court and the rope, if there's any justice in this world. Why'd you do it, eh? Were you on with that poor girl?'

'What? I—'

'No use denying it, you know.' Hayes laid a hand on Bryant's wounded shoulder but, instead of trying to clean or soothe the injury, he leaned forward, transferring his weight onto the prone man.

Bryant screamed. He'd thought the ache in his head was the worst injury he had suffered. 'Get off me!'

'I'll get off you when I damn well please, sonny boy,' Hayes said, leaning further into Bryant.

Roger Pembroke looked away. He'd never been one for roughing up prisoners. 'Sarge, don't you think . . .'

Hayes shot the younger man a look that said, keep quiet, or else. To Bryant, he said: 'You can save us all a lot of time, fly-boy, and tell us the truth, right here and now. I'll make sure you're well looked after when we get to Bulawayo. Of course, if you want to stay silent, I'll find another way of looking after you in the cells.'

'I need to see Pip, Pip Lovejoy,' Bryant stammered. His head was swimming with pain and he needed to throw up.

'You'll stay away from Constable Lovejoy. I don't know what's been going on between you two, but I'm telling you now, China, that you won't see her again. She's out of your league – and I'll not see her end up the same way as Felicity Langham. Now, be a man for a change and tell us the truth. You raped and killed that girl, didn't you?'

'What?' Bryant had no idea why Hayes was accusing him, and hurting him. He lifted a hand to push the fat policeman off him, and then noticed, for the first time, that his wrists were in handcuffs. 'Get these bloody things off me! You've got to stop the parade. Get me to Kumalo!'

'Parade? You're not going to any parade, *Squadron Leader*. You're finished. We know you hid her underwear in that black man's car. You filthy swine.' Hayes still held Bryant down with his hand on his bloodied shoulder. He drew back his other and slapped the Australian hard, across the face, with the back of his hand.

Bryant's ears rang and his eyes rolled back into his

head. He fought the oncoming unconsciousness. 'Wrong person. It's him, you want . . .'

'Him? Him who?' Hayes shook his head.

Bryant tried to make the words come out. He wanted to say the name but had trouble remembering it. 'German . . .'

'Bloody Germans? Trying to tell us you've got shell shock, hey? Doo-lally? I told you, it won't wash with me.' Hayes shook him. 'Snap out of it!'

Bryant closed his eyes and forced himself to remain still.

'I think he was trying to tell us something, Sergeant.'

Hayes shook his head. 'I've seen 'em pull that daft stuff before, Roger. Wounded war hero, my arse. He's no good, this one. A deviant. I ought to put a bullet in his head now and save the courts the time and effort.'

'Meikles Hotel, good day,' the female voice on the telephone said.

'I'd like to speak to one of your guests, please. Mrs Catherine De Beers,' Pip said into the telephone, in the detectives' office at the police camp.

'One moment, please, madam.'

Pip drummed her fingers on the desktop as she waited for the hotel receptionist.

'Are you there, madam?'

The line to Salisbury was scratchy, and Pip had to speak up in order to be heard. 'Yes, I'm here.'

'Who's calling, please?'

'Constable Lovejoy, Bulawayo Police. This is official business. I need to speak to Mrs De Beers urgently.' She made no attempt to hide her impatience.

'I'm sorry, Constable, but Mrs De Beers has not checked in, and I've no record of a reservation for her.'

'Really?'

'Yes, madam. Mrs De Beers often stays with us when she's in Salisbury. I do hope nothing has happened to her, if you were expecting her to be here.'

'No. I mean, I don't know. I'll leave my number, though, and I'd very much appreciate it if you could call me back if Mrs De Beers does check in.' Pip left the phone number and hung up. 'Damn,' she said to herself.

Pip walked out of the office and into the switch room. She asked Shirley, who took off her headset: 'Any word on where they are?'

Shirley checked her wristwatch. 'Last message I had was that they'd picked up the Australian and were on their way. That was about two hours ago. When you were out. Should be back here any time now, I expect.'

'Shirley, can you get a message out to all the radio cars and major police stations between here and Salisbury?'

The other woman frowned. 'Blimey, Pip, you know you

don't have the authority to issue a bulletin like that.'

'I know, but this is really serious, Shirley.'

'I don't know. It could go bad for me, as well as you.'

'I'm worried, Shirley. I don't think I've been in this job long enough to have instincts about policing, but I think I know people pretty well. I need to interview Catherine De Beers.'

'Don't you think you should wait for Hayes?' the telephonist asked.

'He'll laugh off my worries.'

'You've been right about everything in this case so far. That fellow, Nkomo, might have been at the gallows by now if you hadn't persisted. Hayes thought it was an open-and-shut case once I took the tip-off call.'

Pip suddenly thought of something else she'd forgotten to follow up. '*You* took the call from the person who gave us Nkomo, didn't you?'

'Yes, it was on my shift.'

'I never asked anyone about that call. Who was it from?'

'It was anonymous.'

'Yes, but from a man or a woman?'

'A woman. White, by the sound of her. Said she'd heard about the murder and that she'd seen a blonde-haired girl getting into a car driven by Nkomo.'

'You didn't ask how she knew Nkomo, or if she knew who the woman was?'

'She rang off before I had a chance.'

'We need to get that bulletin out about Catherine De Beers, Shirley. She's not in Salisbury, where she said she was going to be. She told me she had made a hotel booking, but she hasn't shown up there and they have no record of her reservation.'

'You think that she . . . ?'

'I honestly don't know what to think, Shirley, and that's the truth. It seems that every time we uncover something in this case, or think we've got the right suspect, it all takes a new turn. Paul Bryant's still a suspect, but there are a whole lot of new questions I need to ask him about Catherine De Beers.'

Bryant's head banged against the sidewall of the bakkie's tray as the vehicle rounded a corner. He blinked.

'Ah, back from the land of nod?' Hayes said. 'Perhaps we can resume our discussion.'

Bryant's head still throbbed and his body ached all over, but his vision wasn't swimming like before. He blinked and saw purple jacaranda blossoms whizzing past over his head. He lifted his torso a little and saw whitewashed houses rusty with red dust. An African woman with mealie bags piled high on her head turned to watch the police truck. They were in the outskirts of Bulawayo. 'Hayes, listen to me . . .'

The policeman lashed out with his foot and delivered a short, sharp kick to Bryant's ribs. 'Sergeant Hayes!'

Bryant gasped with pain, but controlled his anger and said: 'I think there is going to be an attack on Kumalo air base. Possibly today and—'

'Bloody hell. You Australians won't see sense, will you. Keep your fairy stories for the court, Bryant. You won't fool me. You're going straight to the cells and nowhere else. As I said to you before you nodded off, a confession'll do you the world of good right now.'

Bryant sat up a little. He'd had enough of being civil to this oaf. 'For Christ's sake, shut your fat fucking mouth and listen to me! Take me to Kumalo now, and —'

Hayes was sitting at the far end of the truck. 'Guilty or innocent, no one speaks to a policeman that way.' He grabbed the side of the bakkie's tray and lashed out with a violent kick.

Bryant knew his words would goad the policeman to reckless action. He saw the kick coming long before Hayes stood up. He brought back both legs, bending at the knee, and then met Hayes' kick with a two-footed riposte that caught the Rhodesian in the shin and sent him toppling backwards.

'Stop it!' Pembroke screamed. He fished in the bottom of the truck for his rifle.

Bryant rolled onto his side and was able to get onto

his knees. He stood and stepped over the younger policeman. Hayes had landed on his bottom, on the edge of the sidewall of the pick-up, and he flailed about with his hands to find a grip as the truck went around a corner. Bryant saw his moment. He lunged towards the policeman and grabbed hold of the webbing belt that pinched the man's corpulent waist. Hayes windmilled his arms and toppled over backwards. Only Bryant's hand on his belt stopped him from landing headfirst on the roadway. Bryant hauled the fat man upright again and, as Hayes' face reappeared, Bryant smashed his forehead into the bridge of the policeman's nose. For Bryant it was just one more small dose of pain in a morning full of agony, but Hayes yelped like a kicked dog. Tears and blood streamed down his face. Bryant let go of the belt and dropped the policeman back on the truck's floor. As Hayes moved his hands to his shattered nose, Bryant deftly undid the flap on the other man's holster and drew out his revolver.

'Drop it,' Bryant ordered Pembroke, who had finally managed to find his rifle. The constable had been too slow to bring his weapon to bear, and Bryant pointed Hayes' pistol at him. 'I mean it. I don't want to kill you, mate, but, God help me, I'll put a round in your leg to slow you down. There's too much at stake.'

'It's all right. I hear you,' Pembroke said.

Bryant looked around. People on the street were taking notice. A man in a suit was pointing at him and calling something out. It would only be a matter of time before someone flagged the truck down and alerted the driver to what was going on.

'Keys,' Bryant barked, holding up his manacled wrists to Pembroke. 'Stay where you are, fatso,' he said to Hayes, menacing him with the revolver. Hayes cowered in the rear of the truck, his hands covering his broken nose.

'You won't get far,' Pembroke said defiantly.

'Cut the dramatics, pal, and unlock these cuffs. I don't want to get far, you bloody fool, just back to Kumalo to warn them.'

'Warn them about what?' Pembroke asked as he fished a handcuff key from his pocket and leaned forward to free Bryant's wrists.

'I don't even want to imagine,' Bryant said. 'Look, mate, if you see Pip Lovejoy, tell her to meet me at Kumalo. If nothing happens I'll turn myself in again. But, for the record, I didn't kill Felicity Langham. I've got an idea who did, though.'

'Who?'

'Get Lovejoy. I don't have time to explain it all to you. Just out of interest, tell me why you blokes decided to arrest me?'

Pembroke bit his lip. Hayes had explained the chain

of events that had led to Bryant becoming a suspect.

'Haven't got all day, mate. You want the bullet in the leg or the arm? Your choice.'

Pembroke relented. 'You bought petrol from the man who was the original suspect.'

'Petrol?'

'A man called Nkomo. Black marketeer. You left Felicity Langham's personal things in Nkomo's car, it was a set-up.'

Bryant thought about it for a moment and everything fell into place. 'You're right about one thing. It was the set-up of the century.' He looked around him. They were on the main street. The game would be up soon. 'Lie on the floor, face down. And help Hayes do the same thing. Go on, before I shoot you for real.' Pembroke complied.

Bryant shifted to the front of the truck and rapped on the roof of the cab. The driver slowed and checked his mirror. As he did, Bryant leaned around the side and thrust the pistol through the window until the muzzle was planted in the side of the man's head. 'Pull over!'

The man did as he was ordered. Bryant hopped out of the truck and ordered all three policemen to get out. He motioned for them to move away from the vehicle towards a telegraph pole. 'Ring-a-rosie time,' he said to Pembroke. 'Get your cuffs out and join yourselves together, around the pole.'

'You're making it worse for yourself,' the young policeman said. Hayes just shook his head as Pembroke snapped the handcuff on his wrist and then the driver's.

'It'll be a hell of a lot worse for a lot more people if I let you take me in,' Bryant said. 'Keys. All of you. Someone'll find you soon enough. It's a busy town.'

Bryant placed the .303 rifle in the back of the pick-up, climbed in the cab and started the engine. He rammed the truck into gear and the tyres squealed as he did a U-turn. He took a series of turns at speed until he was on the Salisbury Road, heading out of town. He floored the accelerator, pushing the speedometer up to sixty miles an hour. The engine and gearbox whined in protest.

The flat, dull landscape whizzed by. A shadow overtook him and he looked up through the windscreen. It was a twin-engine Oxford trainer, on a short final approach to Kumalo. He was almost there. He checked his watch. It was ten. The wings parade would start in two hours and Prime Minister Huggins would arrive at the base at eleven, in advance of Jan Smuts. He would have to convince Rogers to cancel the parade, send the Rhodesian PM packing and divert Smuts' aircraft to another airfield. There would be time for explanations later. If he were wrong he'd either end up in gaol or stripped of his rank. The wheels skidded as he braked and turned left up the drive to the main gate. An askari called something into the guardroom, then came smartly to attention as Bryant rolled to a stop. He kept the engine running.

Flight Sergeant Henderson stepped from the guardroom and marched smartly to the boom gate. Always immaculately turned out, Henderson looked as if he had stepped from the pages of the air force drill manual today. His uniform was starched as stiff as cardboard, the toe caps of his boots shone like black glass, and the pistol belt and holster at his waist were so white they almost hurt Bryant's eyes. No doubt the extra doses of spit and polish were for the benefit of the visiting brass. 'Call the Wingco and tell him I'm on my way, Henderson,' Bryant ordered.

'Morning, sir. Expected you in the company of a couple of coppers, we did,' Henderson said as he approached the truck. He made no move to carry out his orders. 'I see you've got yourself a police vehicle, though.'

'All a mistake. Open the boom gate, Flight,' Bryant said. He gripped the steering wheel with one hand so hard that it hurt.

Bryant saw Henderson was looking at the Webley revolver on the seat next to him.

Henderson slowly reached for his own holster and began to unbutton it. 'Perhaps you'd like to wait in the guardroom, Mr Bryant, and we'll telephone him from there.'

'I gave you an order, damn it. Open that fucking boom gate!'

Henderson had his hand on the grip of his pistol now. 'Be so kind as to get out of the vehicle, sir.' The African askari was edging closer to the vehicle, from the other side. 'Open the door for Squadron Leader Bryant, Sixpence.'

Bryant floored the accelerator and dropped the clutch. The rear wheels of the police truck spun on the concrete and smoke poured from the burning rubber as they struggled to find purchase. The rear of the vehicle slid from side to side, and then suddenly leaped forward and smashed through the freshly repainted red-and-white-striped boom, shattering the timber. He tore up the base's main road, leaving black skid marks and running askaris in his wake. Somewhere behind him an alarm bell started to ring.

He sped past the orderly room and came to a screeching halt outside Wing Commander Rogers' office. A telephone rang inside. The guardroom had called ahead of him. Pistol in hand, he bounded up the stairs and through the flyscreen door. An NCO dropped a full cup of tea when he saw the wide-eyed, gun-toting Australian.

'Bryant!' Wing Commander Rogers said as he stepped from his office. 'Put the gun down, man,' he said, holding empty hands up to the wounded flyer.

'Sir, you've got to call off the parade. An attack is about to take place.'

'Yes, yes, er . . . Paul. Put the gun down and we'll talk about it.'

'What?' Bryant looked at the pistol in his hand, only half aware he was still holding it.

He lifted it higher and Rogers screamed, 'No!'

'Sir, I'm not here to hurt anyone.'

'Drop the gun, then, Bryant.'

He let his hand drop to his side, but he would not surrender the weapon until he had convinced them all he was not insane or a murderer. 'Sir, I've found Smythe's missing kite . . . I mean, I know what happened to it.'

'Put the gun down, Paul, and you can tell me all about it. Now, what's this about an attack?'

'Germans, sir. A spy, and maybe his accomplice, have got Smythe's Harvard and I'm fairly sure they're going to use it to attack the parade today.'

Rogers frowned. 'Calm down, Paul. We're a long way from the nearest Germans. And as for them bombing us, I really don't see what damage they can do with a Harvard. Now, take a seat.'

'Sir, I'm not mad. I believe the Ossewa Brandwag agent we were informed about, Reitz, has managed to capture an aircraft and will use it to attack the base, and probably Prime Ministers Huggins and Smuts as well. Exactly how he'll do that, I'm not sure, but we *have* to cancel the parade. You'll have three hundred qualified fighter and bomber pilots out in the open, plus aircraft and dignitaries. They'll be sitting ducks.'

'Yes, yes, I'm sure you're right to be so concerned about us all, and our new pilots but, again, I think there's little one man in an unarmed Harvard trainer can do.'

'Belts . . .' Bryant said. 'She needed belts and . . .' It was not coming out right. His head throbbed and he felt nauseous again. His wounds were catching up with him.

'Belts? What do . . . ?' the wing commander said, but he was cut short by the tramp of boots on stairs and the crash of the door opening again. Henderson stood in the doorway, pistol drawn. Behind him, three African askaris armed with .303s were bumping into each other, and their flight sergeant, in their rush to get into the building.

'Drop it!' Henderson barked.

Bryant turned and saw the look of a man itching to fire his first shot in anger. He glanced at the Wingco and noted the condescending look of disbelief on his face. They thought he was mad. Bugger it. They were probably right.

Bryant pulled the pistol's trigger. It was hanging by his side, so the round punched harmlessly through the wooden floorboards and into the dirt below, but the sound of the gunshot in the confines of the building made everyone else jump a foot. He caught a glimpse of Henderson cowering on the floor, and the wing commander staring at him with an almost comical look of bemusement. Bryant jumped up onto the NCO clerk's desk and, arms crossed protectively in front of his face, leaped through the closed window. Glass exploded around him, and he was vaguely aware of yet more cuts on his body as he landed, feet together, in the grass behind the wing commander's office. As he ran, he heard confused shouting behind him.

He sprinted down the laneways behind the administrative buildings until he reached the hangars. Susannah Beattie and her parachute packers, all dressed up in their best air force khaki tunics and skirts, looked up from cups of tea outside their building and stared open-mouthed at the bloodied running figure. He ignored them and wheeled past the maintenance hangar. At last he was on the concrete airstrip. An area in front of the hangars had been roped off and rows of chairs sat under an open-sided marquee. In front of the seat was a raised dais, where Huggins and Smuts would take the salute as the graduating airmen marched past them. Between two hangars, scores of newly qualified pilots milled about, having a cigarette or chatting while they waited to be formed up to march on for a final rehearsal of the parade.

No official guests had arrived yet, but Bryant knew they would soon, so as to be in place when the prime ministers appeared. Huggins would be entertained in the officers' mess before Rogers escorted him out to the dais. Bryant should have been in his best uniform, overseeing the event. Instead he was running from his own men like a fugitive.

The Oxford he'd seen coming in had landed and was taxiing past him. Stretching out in front of him was a line of about twenty aircraft, representative of all the types used in the Empire Air Training Scheme. The Oxford trundled down the line to take its place. Somewhere out of sight, bagpipers tuned their instruments. The wailing notes only heightened his anxiety.

He looked behind and saw Henderson leading a growing posse of armed men. The flight sergeant was calling his name now, and several of the about-to-graduate pilots looked from the askaris and back to him. It would only be moments before he was overwhelmed by eager volunteers. Bryant took a deep breath and started running again, this time down the line of parked aircraft.

The Oxford had pulled up at the end of the line of aircraft, next to a Harvard, whose propeller was still turning as the pilot was allowing the engine to cool, before shutting it down. Bryant stuffed the pistol into the waistband of his trousers, out of sight in the small of his back, and climbed up onto the wing of the Harvard. The blast of hot exhaust snatched at the tattered remnants of his shirt.

The pilot noticed the movement beside him and looked over. He pulled off his flying helmet, revealing a mass of thick black curls. 'What's happening?' he yelled above the noise.

Bryant recognised the man. Costas, a Greek instructor seconded to the air training group from the Royal Hellenic Air Force. 'Get out,' Bryant ordered.

'Paul, you look like hell! You survived the crash, I see. What went wrong?'

'No time to explain, Spiro. Are your guns loaded?'

Costas looked confused. 'Why, yes. I just dropped off my trainee. We were called back from gunnery practice to join this show for the politicians.'

'Get out, I need this kite,' Bryant said.

'You're injured, I don't think you should be flying,' the Greek yelled above the noise of the idling engine.

Bryant looked over his shoulder and saw Henderson and company charging down the airstrip, past the VIP seating. He leaned over the pilot, saw that he had already unbuckled his parachute harness. Bryant grabbed a fist full of dark hair. Costas struggled, swore in Greek and lashed out.

Bryant unhanded him and drew the pistol from behind

his back. He pointed it at the pilot. 'I'm serious, Spiro. Get out. Someone's going to try to sabotage the parade, and I have to stop them. People's lives are at stake.'

Costas nodded and said: 'Watch the temperature gauge, Paul. She's running a little hot.' He stepped down off the wing and walked towards the group of men who were pursuing Bryant. He turned and waved as the Harvard taxied out of the queue, out onto the runway.

'Your friend Bryant,' said Hayes, pausing as he coughed and spat clotted blood out of the police car's window, 'is a flaming madman. He needs shooting.'

Pip ignored Hayes' ranting and directed her questioning to young Roger Pembroke, who seemed a lot more lucid.

She had gone with the car to collect the three stranded officers, where a passing vicar had noticed them from his car, handcuffed to a telegraph pole. They had quickly been freed, and all had started babbling about Bryant's escape. 'Charge him with assault, I will,' Hayes had blurted, blood drooling onto his blue shirt as he spoke.

Pip was seated in the front of the police car, next to a male constable who was driving. Hayes, Pembroke and their driver were squeezed into the back seat. 'Roger, tell me again what Paul Bryant told you to pass on to me,' she said

Pembroke closed his eyes in concentration. 'He wanted you to meet him at Kumalo. He didn't understand why we wanted to arrest him, so I told him that we had proof he had set up Innocent Nkomo. That seemed to register with him, and then he said something about it being the set-up of the century.'

Pip pondered the words. 'What else did he say, Roger? What's got him so excited? He must have known that even if we took him in, he'd be able to explain his side of the story.'

'He told Sergeant Hayes that there was going to be an attack on Kumalo.'

Pip looked at the blood-smeared sergeant. 'What else did he say?'

'Don't know,' said Hayes sulkily. 'He attacked me before I could get more information out of him.'

Pip noticed the way Roger Pembroke rolled his eyes at this comment. She'd wager that it was Hayes rather than Paul who had initiated the fisticuffs. Bryant, unless he had gone completely off his rocker, must have come across more information. She was prepared to reconsider him as a murder suspect, in the light of her latest investigations, but she'd come across nothing that suggested an attack on the base.

'There was something else. Rather odd,' Pembroke said.

'Don't hold back, Roger. What was it?'

'He said to tell you that he'd found his missing aeroplane.'

Odd indeed, Pip thought. Paul had flown to the saltpans to have another look at the area where the dead pilot had been found. Had he discovered another piece of this increasingly complicated puzzle out in that godforsaken wilderness?

They arrived at the entrance to Kumalo to find two askaris dismantling the remains of the broken boom gate and a third hurriedly sweeping red and white splinters off the roadway. 'Go straight through, madam,' one of the Africans said to Pip. 'Flight Sergeant Henderson is expecting you.'

'Is Mr Bryant here, on base?'

'Yes, madam. The last I heard, on the telephone, was that he was trying to steal an aeroplane.'

'Flight line, Tom,' she said to the driver. 'Straight up the road, then between those big hangars. Hurry!'

The police car raced through the air force base and swung onto the Tarmac. 'There,' said Tom, pointing through the windscreen.

Bryant had been delayed because of air traffic congestion. It would have been funny, he thought, except for the circumstances.

Henderson and his ragtag posse of would-be captors

had piled into a tender truck and trundled down the runway after him like the Keystone Kops as he'd taxied the Harvard to the far end. Every now and then the flight sergeant would raise his revolver and point it at the plane. In answer, Bryant would hold his hand out of the cockpit to show he still carried his own weapon. Henderson did not have the guts to open fire on him, he thought. It would only be a matter of time, though, before they realised that the best way to stop him was to block the runway with a tanker or a line of smaller vehicles.

'Come on, come on,' Bryant said as the Oxford touched down at the opposite end of the concrete strip and raced towards him. He knew the twin-engine machine would stop and turn off well before it reached him. The air-traffic controller, a WAAF sergeant, had probably saved his life when she had bellowed at him through the wireless to hold his position. At first he'd thought it was a trick to keep him on the ground so that Henderson could overwhelm him, but then he'd seen the two Oxfords circling.

'Tower, this is Bryant,' he said. Off to his right, the truck carrying Henderson and his men was edging closer. 'Tell that other Oxford to hold. I'm taking off now, whether you give the green light or not.'

'Sir,' the woman's Rhodesian-accented voice was almost

pleading, 'you know I can't give you clearance to take off.'

'People'll die if you don't, Sarah.'

'Look down the runway, sir. Near the hangars. Police have arrived.'

'Too late,' he said. He opened the throttle and released the brakes. The Harvard shot forward. Henderson turned back off the runway and followed the aircraft's progress down the side road.

Bryant looked ahead. The runway was clear. He saw the police car stop, and four figures climb out. One was in a skirt.

Pip took off her hat and waved it in the air, signalling to him.

His speed was nearly thirty-five knots already and he felt the tail wheel start to rise from the concrete. He could be airborne in seconds. The question was, did he trust the policewoman enough to stop now? If she arrested him on the spot and they took him away, the day might end in tragedy. No, he would go it alone.

He could see Pip mouthing something, still waving furiously. Suddenly she dropped her hat and charged out into the middle of the runway.

'Shit!' Bryant said. The bloody woman was going to kill herself. He wrenched back the throttle and stamped on the brakes. He felt the tail wheel drop with a thud.

The Harvard slowed, reluctantly, like a confused horse after a false start. He swerved, and the violent manoeuvre felt for an instant like it might tear off one of the landing gear struts. Pip was getting closer and closer. At last, he stopped, only a few yards from her. The engine still growled. He tore off his flying helmet and yelled, 'Jesus Christ, you very nearly got yourself killed!'

'Get out, Paul! Let's talk about this,' she called back, cupping her hands around her mouth.

He shook his head. 'No way. You sold me out. Why have you turned on me?'

'There's too much to explain. Shut down and get out. You won't be arrested, Paul. We have to talk, though.'

'No dice. You can come with me if you want, but I'm going. This is serious, Pip.'

'That's a bloody understatement,' she said. She looked back. Hayes and other policemen were standing with the air force men, hanging back.

'Last chance, Pip. Either you trust me on this or you don't.'

Could she trust him? She'd slept with him on Sunday and been willing to see him charged and hanged for murder yesterday. She'd gone looking for evidence with which to nail that conviction, but all she had turned up was doubt. She looked into his eyes and remembered the

490

tenderness in them as they'd made love. Paul Bryant was a troubled man. Even though he had hidden the truth from her about his relationship with Felicity and Catherine, he had never lied to her about his own feelings, his own weaknesses.

'Bloody hell,' she swore again as she hitched up her skirt enough for her to get one foot on the Harvard's port wing. She clambered up until she was next to him. He jerked a thumb rearwards, indicating she should climb into the seat behind him. He smiled and winked at her as she nodded her understanding. It was crazy, but she smiled back. She put a foot on the stubby step beneath the rear cockpit, grabbed the rim of the fuselage and heaved herself up and in.

She sat on something uncomfortable and found that the last person in the aircraft had left his flying helmet, which was connected by a lead to the aircraft's radio and intercom, on the rear seat. Pip also noticed that she wasn't sitting on a cushion, but rather a packed parachute. Bryant was pointing to his head and ears with his free hand. She picked up the leather helmet and pulled it on.

'Hear me?' His voice, tinny and slightly scratchy, filled her ears.

'Yes,' she said, unaware that he couldn't hear her.

He turned back and showed her how he was holding

the dangling oxygen mask over his face. He removed it from his face and mouthed, 'Talk into this.'

She placed the rubber mask over her face. It smelled of sweat and something worse. She tried not to think about germs – the least of her problems at the moment. 'OK. Can you hear me now?'

'No worries,' he said. His voice, his Australian accent, was as laid-back as if he were talking about the weather. 'Hold tight, Pip. As I taxi, grab those straps behind your shoulders and pull them in front of you. They connect to a belt across your lap. Buckle up. I'm not wasting any more time.'

Before she was able to grab the dangling mask again and say anything, she found herself pushed back into the uncomfortable seat as he accelerated down the airstrip. Bryant slewed the plane around in a turn so tight that she was thrown against the metal wall of the fuselage. Something sharp dug into her ribs. She was still struggling with the restraint buckle when she felt the rear of the Harvard rise and, suddenly, for the first time in her life, she was flying. 'Oh, my Lord!'

'Nice feeling, isn't it?' he said, turning and smiling at her over his shoulder. Below them, Henderson's vehicle was slowing to a halt in the middle of the runway. Bryant gave the people on the ground a little wave.

'So, what happens next?' Pip asked. She tried to sound

calm and in control, but all of her senses were over-loaded with the excitement and danger of the last few minutes.

'Next we stop a lot of people, including the leaders of Rhodesia and South Africa, from getting killed, I hope. If I'm wrong about all this you can arrest me when we get back on the ground. If I'm not, and we get out of this alive, I'm taking you out to dinner tonight.'

'You are?' she said, but forgot to hold the mask to her face. She still wasn't sure that she could trust him completely or that he wasn't still involved with Catherine De Beers somehow. As much as she wanted him to be innocent, he had a lot of explaining to do first. If she had made the wrong decision, climbing aboard the aircraft, she might never return to Bulawayo alive. She gulped air as the Harvard bounced through some turbulence. Her palms were wet and her heart was racing, and it wasn't because of a fear of flying. She remembered to hold up the oxygen mask this time and said, more businesslike now, 'Do you want to start talking first, or shall I?'

'Ladies first,' he said into the intercom. He pushed the throttle forward, nudged the stick and pointed the aircraft north by north-west towards Isilwane Ranch.

19

The Harvard rolled to a stop outside the hangar beside Isilwane Ranch's airstrip. Catherine De Beers killed the engine. She took off her flying helmet, shook her dark curls free and revelled in the feel of the slight breeze. She climbed out of the aircraft and then jumped off the wing onto the grass.

She looked around her. No one. 'Hello?' she called. No answer. She felt her pulse start to quicken. She savoured the feeling of fear. She liked it.

The hangar door slid open with an ear-jarring screech. It was dark and cool inside. She sniffed the air. The place smelled of oil and fuel, and something else.

There was movement behind her, in the shadows, but she was too slow to turn. A hand was clamped over her mouth and she felt the cold steel point of a knife prick the soft skin of her neck. The other odours she'd caught were from the man who held her – horse, leather and sweat.

'I thought you'd never come,' Reitz said, dropping his knife hand.

'Didn't you miss me, Hennie? Don't you want me now? We've got time.'

'There will be time for that later, God willing. You cut it rather fine,' he said.

She curled her lower lip playfully. 'You had plenty of time for me on your last trip to Rhodesia, and in Windhoek.'

It had been two years earlier, though the memory was as fresh as if it had happened the night before.

His first mission, to contact prominent Ossewa Brandwag members in southern Africa and establish a network of agents sympathetic to Nazi Germany's cause, had taken him as far north as Isilwane Ranch in Rhodesia, to the estate of Hugo De Beers. The millionaire hunter had been a staunch member of the OB in South Africa, before moving north of the border between the wars. Reitz had been told that the old man would surely be supportive of Hitler, and the creation of an independent, Afrikaner-controlled South Africa – perhaps even incorporating Rhodesia after Britain's defeat.

The reality, however, was that De Beers had gone soft. 'I admire old Adolf's views on racial purity, of course,' De Beers had told him over dinner at the ranch, 'but the man's a megalomaniac. I want a proper democracy here, Hendrick, albeit one where the black man and the Englishman will forever know their places. It's bad enough being an outpost of the British Empire, I don't want us simply to swap a king for a führer!'

Reitz had argued, good-naturedly, with the older man throughout the seven days and nights he had spent at Isilwane, but had been unable to convince him. They had hunted during the trip, bagging sable, lion, elephant and eland. On the last day they had gone after a cape buffalo.

A hunt of a different kind had also taken place during that week. Catherine De Beers was not only beautiful, strong-willed and intelligent, she was also diametrically opposed to her husband when it came to the question of whether or not to support Adolf Hitler and the Nazis. Catherine maintained that Africa needed Hitler, a single leader who could unite a continent, as he would do with Europe. Rumours had come out of Germany about the detention of the Jews, a subject that fascinated Catherine. 'To have the will, the power and the courage to cleanse a country, a continent, is just unbelievably brilliant,' she told him on the evening of the first night she came to his room. Reitz represented Germany and the new world order. He was also, he knew, attractive to women. She had circled him over the first two days and nights, like a prowling lioness, then caught him on the third.

The De Beers, he learned, slept in different rooms. Catherine complained that her husband was impotent.

Reitz had learned of many different sexual diversions during his years in Berlin. He had once been to a private club with one of the chemists from his firm, where men and women submitted to pain in order to achieve sexual gratification. He'd been intrigued by the concept but had never participated – as a giver or receiver of punishment. Until he met Catherine.

He wondered if her plan was to seduce him into taking her back to Germany with him. Instead, she asked him to murder her husband.

The arguments about politics and the Nazis continued during the hunting trips, and Reitz was able to convince himself that Hugo De Beers was not only opposed to Hitler's totalitarianism, he was an enemy of Germany. De Beers knew Reitz's real purpose in Africa. All it would take would be a slip of the tongue in the wrong company and Reitz would be arrested and probably hanged as a spy. Reitz had browsed through the Isilwane guest book and noticed the names of prominent politicians and senior military officers who had hunted on his estate. The man was well connected with the colonial government.

Reitz told Catherine, on the seventh night, that he would carry out her request. The next day, during the buffalo hunt, he murdered Hugo De Beers while the man's wife watched. After a night of fiercely passionate coupling – lovemaking was never the right word with Catherine – they travelled to Bulawayo to face the inevitable round of police interviews. He briefly met Felicity, who lived in Catherine's town house, and bedded the pair of them the night before he fled to neutral Portuguese Mozambique.

'What happened to your friend Felicity?' he asked her as he led her out of the hangar's gloom. As far as he knew, Catherine had never told Felicity of his true identity or purpose for being in Rhodesia. If Felicity had been aware he had murdered Hugo, she showed no sign of it at the time.

'She's dead, Hennie.'

'Explain.'

'It happened the night after I got back from Bechuanaland, with the Harvard.'

Reitz remembered his anxious wait under the cruel sun, how vulnerable he had felt squatting in the paltry shade cast by his horse's body, amidst the blinding whiteness of the saltpans, with just the two hired bushmen trackers for company.

He had scanned the empty sky for hours, searching for the Harvard, fearing it might never come or, worse, that Catherine might have been compromised and the

British would instead gun him down.

As they had planned, when the tiny speck finally appeared, Reitz ordered one of the bushmen to lie down, feigning illness, and he took off his shirt and began waving furiously at the approaching aeroplane.

He smiled as he saw the trainer circling above him, bleeding off altitude with every circuit. The ruse had succeeded. In the aircraft, Catherine had persuaded the English pilot, Smythe, who was taking her on her second joy-flight, to land his Harvard.

He carried his Mauser with him to greet them when they landed – there was nothing unusual about a man being armed out in the wilds of Africa – and the pilot's expression of shock when Reitz levelled the rifle at him and ordered him to step down from the cockpit was almost comical.

'Harm this lady and I'll see you hang, whoever you are,' Smythe growled at him.

The boy looked as though he should still be in school. Reitz mocked him with laughter and ordered him to strip.

'Catherine?' the man asked in astonishment as she strode towards Reitz and kissed him quickly on the lips.

'Sorry, James. I really am,' she said sweetly to him. 'But we're going to need to borrow your aircraft for a while.'

Reitz gave the bushmen their orders and the diminutive hunters chased the confused, terrified *rooinek* out into the salt flats, well away from the telltale marks left by the Harvard's wheels on landing. Catherine laughed, loud and shrill, clapping her hands at Smythe's stumbling gait. The last thing the pilot saw before he died was his own aircraft roaring low overhead, the woman he believed he would bed behind the controls waving at him from the cockpit.

It had been Catherine's idea to steal a Harvard, a last-minute solution to a seemingly unsolvable problem created by her crash-landing her own Tiger Moth. She had flown to Windhoek, the capital of South-West Africa, to meet with Reitz, soon after his arrival by U-boat on the Skeleton Coast.

Their plan, hatched through coded messages sent via OB couriers and the German embassy's diplomatic pouch from neutral Portuguese Mozambique, had involved using Catherine's aircraft to deliver a deadly payload onto the parade attended by Jan Smuts and Sir Godfrey Huggins. Her Tiger Moth, a familiar sight over Kumalo, would not have attracted any undue attention until it was too late.

'How in God's name are you going to steal an air force training aircraft?' Reitz had asked, incredulous, in the hotel room where they had rendezvoused.

'I am a woman, Hennie, in case you had forgotten. It's

all arranged, though it took me a little longer to organise than I imagined. The first man I tried to convince to take me up in a Harvard, an Australian, point-blank refused, even after I'd seduced him *and* introduced him to my dear friend Felicity.'

Reitz had shaken his head at her audacity, as well as her use of her body to meet their needs. He remembered clearly how easily she had convinced him to murder her ageing husband. He silently marvelled at the will of the flyer who had resisted her.

'I had a second fish on the hook, a Canadian this time. He resisted my womanly charms – the man was faithful to his little wifey, believe it or not – so I offered to pay him for a couple of joy-flights in a Harvard. He was in debt up to his eyeballs.'

'He agreed?' Reitz asked.

'Yes, and it damn well cost me a fortune, but the oaf crashed at Isilwane on landing the first time he came up to see me, and ended up getting arrested and charged by the air force.'

'Stop teasing and tell me you have organised an aircraft, Catherine. This mission cannot fail – the future of my people rests on it.'

'Calm yourself, Hennie dear. It's all arranged. My third little piggy is a sweet young English boy called Smythe. I've played hard to get with him and I do believe he may be a virgin. He's taken me up once already and he will do so again, at any date and time of our choosing. He's looking forward to his big reward.'

Which, Reitz reflected now, the boy had never received.

After taking off from the saltpans in Bechuanaland, Catherine had flown to a cattle farm not far from the Guinea Fowl training base, near Gwelo, and hidden the aircraft in a disused barn. The farm was owned by the De Beers estate and managed by a Rhodesian named Butler.

She continued her explanation as he led her behind the hangar to where he had stored the two metal cylinders. 'I took Butler's old car back to Bulawayo. I planned on staying the night with Felicity before coming back here to Isilwane. It was the evening that I radioed you, sending you the coded message to say I'd arrived safely and hidden the aeroplane.'

He nodded.

'As I was packing up my set, rolling up the antenna, Felicity barged in. I'd telephoned her at the air force base to tell her I was coming over to stay, unexpectedly, and that I'd let myself in. However, she wanted to surprise me, so she left the base early. I wasn't sure what she'd seen, but she must have been suspicious.'

'Did she confront you about it?' he asked.

'Not straightaway. We had drinks and dinner, and one

thing led to another, as it usually did with us. It was halfway through that she asked me what I was doing with a radio transmitter and receiver. She must have snooped in my suitcase while I was in the bathroom or something. I'd tied her up by then – just like how you used to tie me up,' she smiled. 'Perhaps she felt truly helpless for the first time since I'd known her. She asked me to undo the bindings, to free her, so we could talk.'

'Did you?'

'No,' Catherine said. She stared into his eyes. 'While I had her tied like that I told her everything.'

He shook his head. 'Why, Catherine? Why would you do that?'

'I didn't want to hide anything from her anymore, Hennie. I wanted her to know who I really was – who I've become – and what I stand for. I asked her if she'd help us with the plan.'

'My God, you could have ruined everything,' he said angrily.

'Don't be stupid, Hennie. I was always in charge. I gave her the option of joining us, but she said she never would. She started crying and begged me to let her go.'

'She could have lied to you, told you she was for us, and then run to the British. What would have become of us then?'

Catherine shook her head. 'You didn't know her like

I did, Hennie. She could never lie to me. I'd have seen right through her immediately. I thought that if she wasn't exactly mad about Hitler, she'd at least be sympathetic to our ideal of a world without so many damn blacks in it. I tried to explain to her that we could control their numbers, in the same way that you'd told me about what was really happening with the Jews.'

'That was secret information I entrusted to you, Catherine,' he said, his anger unabated.

'I know,' she shrugged. 'I thought it would sway her, but I was wrong. I knew she was patriotic – joining the WAAFs and all that – but I never knew just how soft she was on the blacks. She told me I was a fool and an evil person if I would even consider killing hundreds of thousands of innocent people. I gave her a chance, Hennie, but she said she'd die before betraying her country. I tried to tell her that her country would be better than in her wildest dreams if Hitler won the war, but then she spat at me.'

Reitz just shook his head again, then said: 'So you killed her?'

Catherine smiled. 'You've killed, many times, haven't you, Hennie, apart from Hugo?'

'Of course. I'm a soldier.'

'But never with your own hands?'

'No.'

Her voice was low and thick as she said: 'I miss her, Hennie, I truly do, but killing her was the most intensely erotic experience of my life.'

Reitz blinked.

'I had to make it look like a man had done it. It wasn't hard. We'd played games, she and I, just like you and I played games, Hennie. But this time it was the real thing.' She opened her eyes and gave a little pout as she saw the shock on his face. 'Aw, too much for you, Hennie? Do you think that men should do all the killing in this brave new world of ours?'

'There'll be enough for all of us before we eventually win, Catherine,' he said. 'I hope you covered your trail adequately.'

She smiled again. 'Oh yes, lover. I certainly have.' She explained how she had planted some of Felicity's things in the boot of the car owned by an illegal fuel dealer. 'It all came together perfectly. I'd also organised for Paul Bryant, the Australian pilot I first tried to get a Harvard from, to collect some fuel from the man and bring it to me when he came up to investigate the crash of the Canadian's Harvard. My fall-back plan, which it turned out I needed, was to point the police towards Bryant.'

'You needed this fall-back plan?' Reitz asked, still not feeling as though they were completely in the clear.

'The police started checking the black's alibi. I paid

the investigating constable a visit and told her some unsavoury things about Squadron Leader Bryant. The way her eyes lit up, I'd imagine he's in gaol and charged with Flick's rape and murder by now.'

Reitz brought her back to the present. 'A man came to the farm, by aeroplane, a Harvard, yesterday. At first I thought it was you, arriving early.'

Now it was her turn to show alarm. 'What did he look like?'

'Stocky, dark-haired. Hard face. He looked, what's the word . . . messy, for a military man.'

'Bryant. Damn.'

'You think he was on to us? You just said he should have been arrested by now.'

'I know, I know.' She chewed a fingernail while she thought it over. 'He was still looking for the Englishman's aeroplane when I last saw him. Also, he was suspicious about ammunition.'

'Ammunition?' Catherine had been up to a lot since their last meeting – too much for his liking.

'Don't look at me with that disapproving scowl. I've got a surprise for you!'

'I can hardly wait,' he said.

'Spare me your sarcasm, Hennie. You'll thank me when you see it. It's the icing on our cake.' She took his hand and snatched up a shovel which had been leaning against a wall of the hangar.

Catherine walked through knee-length grass for a minute or two before exclaiming: 'Here!' She handed Reitz the shovel and said: 'Dig. There, under that stick.'

He brushed aside the twig that had been left in the dirt as a marker and did as ordered. Catherine had carefully removed a patch of long-grassed turf before digging the hole, and he silently commended her thoroughness. The soil beneath the patch was loose and the blade soon clanged on something firm. She dropped to her knees and together they cleared away the last of the dirt from the top of a wooden crate.

'Took me ages to bury this stuff,' she said as she wiped the perspiration from her forehead with the back of her hand.

Reitz watched her out of the corner of his eye as he got his fingernails under the lid of the crate and started to lift. A few minutes ago she had sent an injection of ice water down his spine as she coolly related how she'd raped and killed her best friend. Now she was as excited as a little girl on an Easter-egg hunt.

He couldn't wait until the operation was over. After Ursula's death, and on learning he would be returning to Africa, he had started to think more and more about Catherine. She was the complete opposite of his dead German girlfriend. There was a dark side to Catherine which excited him and, if he were honest, scared him a little, though he sensed that was part of her attraction.

He lifted the lid of the crate clear. 'Where did you get all this?' Reitz stared in amazement at a pile of .303 bullets, their brass casings glittering like gold in the morning light. What made this cache so special was that each of the rounds was slotted into loops on long canvas belts.

'Your secret weapon will take care of the graduating pilots and Messrs Huggins and Smuts, but I'm going to have some jolly good fun using this on the Empire Air Training Scheme's aircraft.'

'Catherine has to be the one,' Paul Bryant said into the intercom in his oxygen mask. Out of habit, he scanned the sky around him for other aircraft. 'She showed me a collection of wigs when I was at Flick's place. Said she'd be whatever colour I wanted her to be.'

'I thought it must be something like that,' Pip said. 'Felicity was a blonde, so I thought it odd that she'd have a wig the same colour and length as her hair. Then I noticed those black strands inside it. It was silly of me to overlook the fact that Nkomo had sold fuel to a blonde woman on the night Felicity was killed. I was thinking that a man must have been responsible for the rape and murder.'

'Logical assumption,' he said in a conciliatory tone,

although he still smarted from the fact that she had been so quick to believe he could have been the killer.

'I'm so sorry that I misjudged you, Paul. I suppose I didn't trust myself not to fall for the wrong sort of man all over again, and that coloured the way I looked for a culprit.'

'I understand,' he said. 'Pip, I'd never treat you the way your ex-husband did.'

'Your turn now,' Pip said. 'Tell me what you've found out and what makes you so sure Catherine is tied up with this German spy. What's his name again?'

'Reitz. I've got the evidence in my back pocket. I'll show you later if we get the chance. I found it while I was rummaging through some junk at Catherine's place yesterday morning – seems like a lifetime ago. I'd worked out that Smythe's Harvard had landed out on the salt-pans and then taken off again. From the air, our search party couldn't tell the difference between an aircraft's undercarriage tracks and vehicle tyre marks. I landed out on the pan, paced out the distances between the various wheel tracks, and then followed them. Smythe landed his kite, but someone else took off in it. I didn't have any firm evidence that Catherine had stolen it, but one thing I did know was that she was prepared to go to any lengths to get her hands on one. The pieces started coming together in my mind, then. There was the crash of Cavendish's plane on Catherine's airstrip. He's a happily married man, and I believe he wouldn't have let Catherine fly his aircraft on a promise of sex, but he had another weakness.'

'What?' she asked. 'No, let me guess – money?'

'Right again. Cavendish is a gambler. Catherine's rich. He wouldn't confirm it, but I'll wager Catherine offered to pay him to let her fly his Harvard.'

'Lucky for him he crashed, otherwise it'd be his body in the morgue instead of Smythe's.'

'Yeah, well, Smythe must have fallen for her. I flew to her place to try to find some evidence that Smythe or his aircraft had been there, though I still had no idea what her plan or motivation might have been for stealing his kite or doing away with him.'

'So what is this evidence that you found at her place?' Pip asked.

'A newspaper cutting – the story about the death of her husband.'

'I found the same story, from the *Chronicle*. I used it to show Nkomo a picture of Catherine.'

'"*The grieving widow*", right?'

'That's the one,' she said.

'Well, you should have checked out the next page. On it there's a picture of the South African hunter who *accidentally* shot old Hugo De Beers in the back.'

510

'Don't tell me . . .'

'Hendrick Reitz. Ossewa Brandwag *stormjaer* and Nazi spy. You've probably got a picture of him on your most-wanted board. I recognised him from a picture circulated to us by the intelligence people. They've been concerned for some time about a possible OB attack on one of our air bases.'

'I'm sorry I wasted so much time trying to get you arrested, Paul,' she said, and he could tell she meant it.

'Don't worry about it. I was set up by an expert. We both were. I don't think my crash yesterday was an accident, either. I think someone – maybe Reitz – sabotaged my kite while I was searching for Catherine. If that's right, it means he's in position at Isilwane and the next phase of whatever the two of them have cooked up is coming right up.'

'How much damage can they do with one aircraft?' Pip asked.

'Plenty,' Bryant said. 'The final piece of the puzzle was the belts.'

'Not trouser belts, I assume?'

'No,' he said, 'machine-gun ammunition belts. The rounds are slotted into long canvas belts, which feed the guns in the Harvard's wing and nose. Cavendish had been on his way to gunnery practice when he stopped by Catherine's ranch. He had a full load of ammo on board, but when we went to fetch the wreckage there were hardly any rounds in the guns. At first I thought that someone – some African poachers, maybe – had stripped the wreck. But that seemed odd, because if it was the work of thieves, why would they leave some rounds still in the guns?'

'So it would seem, to the casual observer, that the guns hadn't been tampered with?' Pip said.

'Correct. You should be a copper. Cavendish couldn't account for the missing rounds, although he had personally checked the guns before taking off. Catherine fobbed me off when I asked her, by saying she had a storeroom full of .303 bullets and that some poachers probably took them. I took her at face value, which was a mistake. True, she had no need of bullets, but what she didn't have was ammunition belts. Smythe had been on a navigation training solo flight, so his guns were empty. Now Catherine's not only got an air force trainer, she's got several hundred rounds of ammunition. With the way Rogers has got the runway lined with aircraft, she could take out a dozen of them with one pass, if she knows what she's doing. If she strafed the parade . . .'

'Horrible,' Pip agreed. 'But even so, it seems that two people with one aircraft and a couple of machine-guns can only do so much damage. I'm worried, Paul, that there may be more to this. What else do you know about this Reitz character?'

'We got a rundown on him at the base as part of an intelligence update. He's a soldier – fought with the Jerries in Spain before the war, then joined the paratroops. Also, he's a chemist. Worked in pesticides, I think.'

'Poisons? Do you think the Germans would use something like poison gas on the base?' Pip asked.

'Dunno,' Bryant said. 'They did during the last war – and so did our lot. Anything's possible. Wiping out today's parade of trainees and graduates would be the same as shooting down about eight hundred aircraft, in terms of pilot losses. It'd be a devastating blow and a big morale boost for the Germans.'

'Smuts and Huggins are going to be there as well – perhaps they're the main target. It wouldn't take much for the Afrikaners in South Africa to rise up against their government if Smuts were assassinated. The Germans have already tried it once.'

'This is getting bigger by the minute,' Bryant agreed.

'How do we stop the parade?' Pip asked.

'Search me. Wing Commander Rogers thinks I'm a lunatic, and your police friends still think I'm public enemy number one. We can't stop the parade, so—'

'We have to stop Catherine and Reitz,' Pip concluded.

Bryant glanced at his watch. 'If they're using Isilwane as their base for an attack, they'll have to be airborne soon. Catherine knows the timings for the parade, as she was on the guest list. Keep your eyes peeled for an aeroplane like this one.' Bloody near impossible, he thought. He looked ahead and out each side of the cockpit. For miles and miles in every direction there was nothing but scrubby brown bush.

The aircraft shuddered and Pip let out an involuntary squeal. 'What was that?' she said, alarmed.

'Relax. Just testing our guns. Should have warned you.'

Catherine and Reitz knelt on the wing of the Harvard. 'There, that's the last of it,' she said as she folded the ammunition belt into the bin next to the machine-gun. Reitz had been able to figure out how to chamber the first round in each belt into the guns, but it had taken them a couple of gos to lay the belts of bullets in their bins. 'Now, what do we do with the bombs?'

'Nothing very scientific there,' Reitz said as he screwed the gun compartment panel shut. 'When I thought we were going to be using your biplane, I looked back to the First World War for a delivery system for the gas. Come, I'll show you.'

When they had finished at the Harvard he led her back to where the two metal cylinders lay in the grass, beside the hangar.

He stood one of the tubes on its end and began unscrewing a cap. Catherine took a wary step backwards.

'Don't worry,' he said, smiling. 'I checked them this morning, while wearing my gasmask. Both cylinders have weathered the journey well, and the contents are in perfect order. There are no leaks, I can assure you.'

'All the same, the sooner we're rid of the stuff, the better,' she said, not moving any closer.

'I agree with you there,' he said.

As he spoke, he reached into the cylinder and slowly slid out what appeared to be a bomb. It had tail fins, like a normal aerial bomb, but the other end was bulbous rather than pointed.

'The fins stabilise it in flight. This,' he added, pointing to a metal ring attached to a pin in the tail assembly, 'arms it. On the outside, it's the same type of crude device both sides used to drop during the first war. The observer in an aircraft simply leaned out the rear cockpit, pulled the pin, which activated a timed fuse, and then dropped it.'

'I'll have to fly low and slow, I suppose,' she said, looking at the bomb but not touching it.

'Correct,' he said. 'As I explained when we met in South West, if you drop it from more than two hundred feet it will arm while still in midair, too high up and, if there is a strong breeze, the gas may drift away before it reaches its target. Ideally we want to drop at a hundred and fifty feet. At that height, the small charge inside the body of the bomb will detonate after four seconds, just before it hits the Tarmac. It will disperse the nerve agent but not allow it to dissipate too much.'

'All right,' she said. 'With luck they'll think a low, slow flight by a Harvard is part of the graduation show. You said one bomb will be enough, right?'

'Yes.'

'To kill eight hundred men?' She sounded dubious. 'I know this sarin stuff is deadly, but that's amazing.'

'The second bomb is a back-up only, in case we are way off target. This agent *is* amazing, Catherine. Just a milligram of sarin will kill a man in less than a minute. The skin will easily absorb it in vapour form. The first symptoms are a runny nose and then difficulty in breathing. Next the victim starts to vomit and then he loses control of his bodily functions. The poison induces convulsions so violent that the victim becomes comatose and can't breathe.'

She said nothing, just stared at the bomb, and then him, in awe.

A far-off drone made them both look skywards. 'Hell,' she said.

'Aircraft?'

As a pilot she was used to searching the sky for other aeroplanes. She saw the black dot before he did. 'Yes, coming from the south, see it?'

'Should we hide?' he asked.

'No, if they're onto us we won't get a second chance to take off. Let's go!'

He worried about her last remark but had no time to challenge her. She had assured him that she had covered her trail. Perhaps Felicity had been able to warn someone else of her discovery.

'So why would Catherine kill Felicity?' Pip asked. They had been talking about Catherine's possible motive.

'There's something I didn't tell you,' he said into the intercom.

'She tried to contact you on the night of her death,' Pip said.

'How did you know that?'

'I checked your comings and goings with the front gate at Kumalo. They told me you'd left the base at some time that night . . .'

'It was about five in the morning, to collect some illegal fuel for Catherine,' he explained.

'Yes, I know that now. Anyway, the duty NCO said you'd also had a message to call someone that night and your Corporal Richards confirmed it was Felicity.'

'I didn't get that message until the morning, until it was too late,' he said. 'God,' he added, 'if I'd got it, I might have been able to save her life, and foil Catherine's plot at the same time. I guess the mess steward didn't try to wake me because he thought I'd be passed out – dead drunk. And normally he would have been bloody right.'

After a while Pip said, 'So it's possible Felicity was not part of the plot, but that she somehow got wind of it.'

'And Catherine killed her to silence her. I could have saved her, Pip.'

'What's to say you would have made it in time?'

He shook his head. 'We're almost there. That's the Deka River below.' He pushed the stick forward and the Harvard started to dive.

Pip felt the aircraft vibrate. 'Going a bit fast, aren't we?'

'I want to jump them – take them by surprise if they're still on the ground. Pip! Look down, one o'clock. There's our missing aeroplane!'

Pip craned her head but saw nothing until he lowered the starboard wing a fraction. 'Got it! Paul, what are you going to do?'

'No one's supposed to be up here today, Pip. That's got to be Smythe's kite, and whoever's in it, is in it illegally. We're at war, Constable, so I'm going to do the only thing I can.'

Pip gripped the sides of her seat as she felt the angle of their Harvard's dive steepen. Ahead of her she saw

Paul pull down the goggles attached to his flying helmet so that they covered his eyes. He fastened the oxygen mask across his face, presumably so he could use both hands, and she copied him.

'Hold tight,' he said, 'this is going to be fast and noisy.'

Below them, Catherine's Harvard trundled down the grass airstrip, gaining speed.

Bryant had to concentrate on everything at once – the target, his airspeed, his altitude. He flicked the switch on the armaments panel to the left of the other gauges to 'guns'.

Pip felt herself being pushed into the seatback behind her and her stomach churned as Paul flattened out a little. She heard the rattle of the machine-guns and felt the airframe judder.

The Harvard filled the sight in front of him and he thumbed the firing button on the stick again, but in an instant the target was gone. He watched his bullets raise puffs of dirt and grass behind the taxiing aeroplane. 'Shit!' he said. He hadn't allowed enough deflection in his aim for the speed of Catherine's aircraft and the fall of his bullets.

'Stay calm, Paul, you can do it,' Pip urged. In truth, she felt absolutely helpless and terrified.

He yanked the stick back into his belly and the Harvard climbed back into the cloudless sky. He kicked the rudder pedal and brought the aircraft around in a steep port turn that he fancied had rivets popping in the wings.

Pip felt nauseated and swallowed repeatedly. She wanted nothing more now than to be back on the ground.

'Damn, I've lost her,' Bryant said. He had only ever fired an aircraft's guns once, before he was kicked out of fighter-pilot school. On that occasion, the target had been a brightly painted wooden panel laid out in the centre of a field. It wasn't moving, but he, like most first-time gunnery students, had missed it by a mile. He took his hat off to the Brylcreem boys in their Spitfires. This was no easy job for a bomber pilot.

Pip's head lolled against the right-hand side of the cockpit, and she wiped a string of drool from her lips. A flash of movement against the unending brown bush caught her eyes. 'There!' she croaked, and the mere act of speaking almost made her throw up.

'Where?'

'Below, right, um; two, no, three o'clock.'

'Good girl!' he said. He rolled the Harvard over on its right side. Pip tore off her oxygen mask and vomited between her knees. Paul sensed what was going on. 'You'll live,' he said to her. I hope, he prayed silently.

Pip wiped her mouth and streaming eyes, and tried to see over Paul's shoulder.

'Got you,' Bryant said as the other Harvard filled his

gun sight. He aimed ahead of Catherine's aircraft, guessing how much he would have to lead her to compensate for the speed at which she was travelling. He pressed the firing button with his thumb, and the aircraft shuddered.

He held his breath, then cursed again as he saw the glowing tracer rounds sail harmlessly to the right of the other Harvard. Catherine had sensed his next move and jinked hard to the left just in time to save herself. 'Damn, she's a good flyer,' Bryant said.

Just end it, quickly, Pip thought to herself. She saw a flash of sunlight glint off the other aircraft's cockpit, to their left. 'She's climbing, Paul,' she forced herself to say.

'I see her,' he said. He banked to the left to try to follow her, but Catherine had started her turn much earlier. He realised she was turning inside him and, if they both kept on the same course, she would end up behind him. He turned the Harvard on its back and pulled the stick into his stomach. His vision started to grey out as the G-forces drained the blood from his vital organs.

'Oh, God, noooo!' Pip yelled.

'Hold on,' he gasped.

Catherine started climbing, but Bryant stayed low and cut his airspeed. Pip revelled in the moment of straight, level flight, but was then instantly alarmed. 'She's above us, Paul. Aren't we sitting ducks like this?'

'That's what I want her to think,' he replied. He put the Harvard into a slow, gentle left-hand turn. Ahead of him, in the distance, he saw Isilwane's airstrip. 'Good,' he said. 'At least we've kept them from flying south.'

'Good plan,' Pip said, 'but look behind us. Here she comes!'

He looked behind and above him and saw Catherine's Harvard enter a steep dive. He held the stick steady, flying straight and level. He moved his hand over the under-carriage lever.

Pip glanced back over her shoulder and screamed. 'She's shooting at us, Paul!' The aircraft juddered and there was a noise like ferocious hail on a tin roof as a neat line of holes was suddenly stitched on their port wing. 'We're hit!'

Bryant was ready for it. He pulled back on the stick, lifting the nose and closed the throttle, slowing their aircraft from a hundred and forty-five to a hundred and twenty knots. The gap between the two aircraft started to narrow. He pulled down on the lever and the Harvard's wheels dropped. The aircraft lurched and bled off even more speed. Pip screamed in his headphones as the nose dropped sickeningly.

Catherine's plane whizzed past them, on the right, close enough for Pip and Paul to see the startled faces of pilot and passenger.

Bryant's left hand flashed across the instruments as he raised the landing gear and opened the throttle again. With his right he pulled the stick into his belly, bringing the nose back up. He was under her now, and slightly behind. Perfect position. He pressed the firing button. He was pretty sure this would be his last burst, so he made it count. He kept his thumb hard down, even after the last of the rounds had left his guns.

'Hennie, I've been hit!' Catherine wailed. The aircraft slipped violently to the right. 'I'm bleeding!'

'Where? How bad is it?'

'Pretty bloody bad,' she retorted. It hurt like hell, and felt like a hot poker had been rammed into her calf. 'Left leg. Hard to keep my foot on the rudder pedal.' Tears filled her eyes as she pushed down on the left pedal in order to straighten the aircraft. 'Can't . . .'

'You *have* to, Catherine. Take the pain.'

'Can't go on like this, Hennie. I have to put her down.' As if to ratify her decision, a jet of oil hit the front of the cockpit and was smeared all down the left side. 'Losing oil pressure now. He must have hit the engine as well. That's it, we're finished.'

His mind raced. The mission was over before it began. Or was it? The other aircraft was still flying. 'Can you call them up, get them on the radio?'

'Don't know,' she said. She was too busy fighting her pain and trying to see out of the smeared canopy to answer him. Paul had peeled off. She wondered if he were out of ammunition.

'Try!' he insisted.

'All right, all right,' she said. She flicked the radio switch, and said, 'Harvard nine-zero, nine-zero, this is Harvard eight-seven, eight-seven.'

Reitz spoke on the intercom-only channel. 'I want you to tell him that you were forced to fly the plane for me, that I'm holding a gun to your head. I'll cut you off halfway through the transmission. I'll fire a shot.'

'I doubt he'll believe me,' she said.

'It's our only chance.'

Catherine radioed Paul and, with a genuine sob in her voice thanks to her wound, explained that she had been kidnapped by Reitz and forced to fly him. 'He killed Flick, too, Paul.'

The transmission ended with a gunshot ringing over the airwaves.

'What do you make of all that?' Bryant asked.

'Pure Hollywood,' Pip said dismissively. 'Look, she's landing now. Gone home to roost.'

They both looked out the right-hand side of the cockpit

and saw the stricken Harvard on final approach to the grass runway on Catherine's property. 'At least they didn't get far,' Pip added.

'Crikey, she hasn't got her undercart down,' Bryant said. 'Her hydraulics must be shot.'

They watched in silence as the other aircraft bounced and then skidded down the airstrip on its belly. The propeller dug deep furrows in the turf before stopping, its blades bent backwards.

'Cockpit's open. She's getting out,' Bryant said.

As they circled, they watched Catherine climb out of the front seat, leap awkwardly from the wing to the ground, and start to hobble away. 'She's trying to get away from him,' Bryant said.

Pip wasn't so sure, but then she saw the man emerge from the rear of the cockpit. 'Looks like he's got a rifle. He's aiming at her!'

Bryant banked hard and dived for the airstrip. It looked indeed like Reitz was drawing a bead on Catherine, who was limping down the length of the airstrip. He lined up on the pair of them and brought the Harvard down until he guessed he was no more than twenty feet above the grass. He had the satisfaction of seeing Reitz dive out of the cockpit, headlong into the dirt, as the hot fumes from his engine's exhaust washed over the Nazi spy.

'We've got to get down and sort this out,' Bryant said.

'Can't you radio for some help?' Pip said.

'I'm the escaped murder suspect, remember?'

'All right, then put me on. I'll talk to the base and see if they can get a message to Hayes.'

'No time for that, Pip. It's us or nobody.' He had circled around and now lowered his undercarriage. He checked his fuel, airspeed and trim. 'Here we go,' he said as the wheels bounced once on the grass, and then settled.

'Can you see Reitz?' Paul asked Pip over the intercom.

'I saw him dash into the tree line just as we touched down. Nothing since.'

'Catherine's wounded. I can see blood on the side of the cockpit. She won't be too much trouble. It's that other bastard I'm worried about,' Bryant said as he applied the brakes. He kept the engine running, in case they needed to get out quickly. 'Stay put, Pip. I'll go and see what she has to say for herself.'

'Not bloody likely!' Pip said. 'You're the only one who can fly this thing. I'm not having you caught in a trap. You stay here and keep the motor running. I'll go see how badly she's hurt. I'll give you the all clear if it looks like Reitz has gone, and then you can switch off.'

He didn't want to put her in any danger, but he couldn't argue with her logic. 'All right, Constable. I guess we're in your jurisdiction now we're on the ground.'

'Too bloody right, as you Australians would say.' She undid her safety restraints and climbed out of the cockpit, relieved to be on terra firma again, even if she did stink of sweat and vomit. She wished she had brought a gun with her. She was going to ask Paul for his, when she saw Catherine De Beers pass out, flat on her face. She jumped down off the wing and ran to the wounded woman.

Pip slowed her pace as she came closer to the prone form: 'Catherine? Mrs De Beers. Can you hear me?'

Catherine rolled over and drew the pistol from the waistband of her jodhpurs. She held it pointed at the policewoman's heart. 'Put your hands on your head. Turn around so Paul can see you,' she said as she painfully raised herself to her feet. She gave a little wave to Paul with her left hand, and smiled broadly as she pushed the muzzle of the Walther into the side of Pip Lovejoy's head. 'Hennie!' she called. She ran her finger across her throat, a signal that Bryant should cut his engine.

Bryant shook his head in anger, then killed the engine. He undid his harness and got out of the cockpit.

'Slowly, Paul. Very slowly. Do as I say and you and your new girlfriend might just live to see another day.'

'Catherine, you can save yourself a lot of trouble and give up right now. There'll be other aircraft, and a police road convoy here within half an hour,' he said.

'Not much of a bluffer, are you, Paul? I can see right through you. Look at the state of you. You wouldn't be here if anyone believed whatever you told them about Hennie and me.'

'Hendrick Reitz?'

Catherine whistled and Reitz emerged from the trees, the butt of his Mauser in his shoulder. 'Take the pistol out of your holster and put it on the ground. Slowly now, there's a good boy.'

He complied, keeping eye contact with her all the time.

'So what happens now?' Pip asked no one in particular.

'We have an aircraft,' Reitz said, motioning with a flick of his head to Bryant's Harvard, 'and now all we need is a pilot. As you can see, mine is injured.'

Catherine carried on the explanation. 'I'm going to stay here with Constable Lovelorn . . .'

'Lovejoy,' Pip said.

'We girls are going to keep each other company, while you, Paul, take Hennie where he tells you to. When you return, after he has done what he has to do, I will free the constable and Hennie and I will fly away into the sunset.'

Pip risked a sideways glance at her captor. Catherine's face looked pale, but she held her pistol in a steady hand. Her eyes were dark and coldly cruel.

'I used the last of my ammo bringing you down. If

528

your plan was to strafe the graduation parade, you're out of luck,' Bryant said.

Catherine smiled. 'Trying to draw me out, Paul? The belts of ammunition I pulled out of Andy Cavendish's aircraft were just icing on the cake. The real surprise is still in our kite. Hendrick, perhaps you should fetch the cargo now?'

Reitz nodded, satisfied that Catherine could keep the man and woman safely under guard. He slung his rifle, jogged back to the crashed aircraft, leaned into the rear of the cockpit and retrieved the bombs.

'You won't do much damage with those little tiddlers,' Bryant said to Reitz. 'You've put a hell of a lot of effort into an operation that will kill or wound a score of pilots, at the most.'

Reitz smiled. He laid down the bombs and then undid the buckle of a small haversack he carried over his other shoulder. From it he withdrew a rubber gasmask, which he held up for Bryant to see.

'You bastard,' Bryant said. 'You're going to poison a bunch of unarmed men, plus a hundred or more civilians and spectators – men and women.'

The smile fell from Reitz's face. 'Unarmed? So what? Soon they'll be dropping bombs on innocent German women and children. Not only are they *unarmed*, they'll never be combatants. You and the rest of the RAF make me sick. You call me a bastard, but you murder innocents in your so-called *area bombing*.'

'No different from what your German mates did to Coventry and the East End of London, Reitz. Anyway, you're South African, aren't you? If you kill Jan Smuts you might start a civil war in your own country. Didn't anyone ever tell you that your lot are supposed to be on our side these days?'

'*My lot* can never forgive the British – and their colonial lapdogs like you Australians – after they murdered tens of thousands of civilians in South Africa. Keep your lies about British fair play to yourself. Smuts is a traitor to my people, Squadron Leader, and it'll be a pleasure to kill him as well as your latest crop of murdering graduates. Get in the aircraft and start it up. You'll take me to Kumalo air base and fly at a hundred and fifty feet above the runway, at a hundred knots. I'm not a pilot, but I can read gauges and navigate from here. If you don't do exactly as I say, Catherine will have no hesitation in dispatching the constable.'

'Don't do it, Paul!' Pip said. 'There are too many innocent lives at stake.'

Bryant turned and looked into her eyes. 'I can't let you die.'

Pip shook her head. 'They'll kill us anyway, Paul.' She looked at Catherine, waiting for her to confirm it.

'You know who we are, and whose side we're on now,' Catherine said, looking from Pip to Paul. 'No doubt you've told the police that Hennie and I were up to something. Whether or not they believe you now doesn't really matter. By tomorrow, Hendrick and I will be famous – or infamous, depending on which side you're on – but we'll also be safely away from Rhodesia. We won't conceal anything by killing you both. But,' she said, turning to Bryant, 'you can definitely save your life, and hers, by doing what we ask of you.'

Bryant thought about it for a moment. 'How are you going to get away, once I do what you want?'

Reitz said: 'When we get back, Catherine will come on board in the back seat with me. We'll leave the woman here, but you can make a call to alert the authorities when we get to where we're going. When we get to our final destination, you'll be released. You have my word as an officer of the Third Reich.'

Bryant shook his head.

'Enough talking,' Catherine said. She motioned for Bryant and Pip to walk ahead of her, into the hangar. Reitz followed them in and, while Catherine kept Paul covered, Reitz pushed Pip up onto the workbench.

Bryant glared at her. 'If you renege on this, Catherine . . . if you lay a finger on her while I'm gone, I'll kill you.'

Catherine laughed. 'Empty threats and idle promises. A typical male. You don't scare me, Paul. But rest assured, if you keep your end of the bargain you'll get your little policewoman back.'

'Come on, let's get this over with,' Bryant said angrily.

'Don't think you have to do this for me, Paul,' Pip said. She felt utterly helpless now, tied and humiliated.

'It's war, Pip,' he said. 'Sometimes you just get caught in the middle of situations where you have to make a decision, and lives depend on it.'

'Blah, blah, blah,' Catherine said. 'This is making me sick. Be gone, the two of you.' She blew Reitz a theatrical kiss and said: 'Hurry, or you'll miss the parade. I'll expect you in two hours. If you're not here in three I'll kill the girl and head for the rendezvous point in the farm truck.'

Reitz nodded, unslung his rifle and motioned for Paul to leave the hangar ahead of him. He pointed with his rifle to the first-aid kit on the floor and said to Catherine, 'Clean your wound and bandage yourself.'

'I'll be back,' Paul said to Pip. She just closed her eyes and tried very hard not to cry.

Outside, when they reached the aeroplane, Bryant said, 'I could fly us both into the ground as soon as I take off, you know.'

Reitz laughed as he climbed into the rear of the cockpit. 'You don't have the guts, Squadron Leader. Catherine told me all about you.'

'Buckle up – I wouldn't want you falling out,' Bryant said.

'Don't worry, I'd already thought of that. Close your cockpit canopy, and don't try anything stupid midair.'

'Or what, you'll shoot me? You won't get far without a pilot.'

The noise of the engine whining and coughing to life momentarily put an end to any talk. They put on their flying helmets, checked the intercom was working, and then Bryant taxied down the grass airstrip.

'Perhaps you should cancel the parade.' Hayes' voice was nasal and his pronunciation was hampered by the blue-black swelling of his broken nose.

'We've been over this before,' Wing Commander Stephen Rogers hissed back at the policeman. They stood outside the Kumalo officers' mess. A pair of motorcycle policemen cruised slowly up the base's main road, a black Bentley gleaming behind them. 'For the last time, man, do you or do you not believe Bryant killed Felicity Langham?'

Hayes gingerly touched his nose. 'Yes, I do. The man's just weaved some story to throw us off the track. He's also clearly unbalanced. Shell shock, I suppose. Look at the way he bailed you up with a revolver and opened fire in your office.'

Rogers nodded. He and Hayes had gone over the information available and nearly convinced each other they were right to ignore Bryant's half-formed, garbled warnings about a Nazi plot. All the same, Rogers had doubled the gate guard and he'd had Wilson siphon off twenty askaris from their ceremonial duties to form a roving perimeter patrol. As an added precaution, he had also ordered the long single line of display aircraft hurriedly reorganised into two ranks, facing each other across the wide taxi-way. If someone – perhaps even Bryant in his deranged state – wanted to attack the parked aircraft from the air, at least they would be spaced out.

'This'll be the end of us if we're wrong,' Rogers muttered.

'Us?' Hayes snorted and swallowed a clot of blood. 'I'm just a copper chasing an armed suspect. You're the one who's decided to carry on.'

'Get out of my sight. You look a mess, and you'll only start people asking questions.' Hayes reluctantly turned his back on the wing commander and walked back to his police car, as the Prime Minister of Rhodesia's limousine and escorts pulled to a halt outside the mess.

Two immaculately turned-out black askaris stepped up to each of the Bentley's rear doors, opened them and saluted.

Sir Godfrey Huggins stepped out of the door nearest the mess, nodded a polite acknowledgement of the salute and said, 'Stephen, how good to see you again.'

Rogers saluted his head of state and shook his hand. 'Prime Minister. I hope your journey was pleasant.'

Rogers led Huggins through the open double doors of the mess, and they were followed inside by the prime minister's military aide-de-camp – a young Rhodesian army captain – and two civilian men in suits. Clive Wilson, in his capacity as acting adjutant, ushered the official party towards a trestle table covered in a starched white table-cloth. African stewards took orders for coffee and tea, and Wilson brought cups to his commander and the politician.

Huggins explained that he had visited the air training base at Gwelo briefly the day before, and spent the night in the nearby town, midway between Salisbury and Bulawayo. 'It's been too long since I was at Kumalo, Stephen. Hard to believe it's two years since I was here for the official dedication of the base.'

Rogers agreed. He genuinely enjoyed the company of Sir Godfrey whom, they had both realised on their last meeting, he had met once before. It had been in England, in 1917, where Huggins was serving as a twenty-four-year-old army doctor. The future prime minister had pulled a Spandau machine gun bullet from Rogers' leg, the legacy of an unsuccessful tangle with a Fokker triplane over the Western Front. Three bullets had already been removed from the fighter pilot's body, but the fourth was lodged dangerously close to his femoral artery, so he had been hurriedly evacuated to Blighty for the attentions of a specialist. Even at a young age Huggins had distinguished himself as a surgeon. Genial was the word Rogers would have used to describe him. With his aquiline features, neatly trimmed moustache and soft voice, he still seemed more the reassuring doctor than the shrewd politician he was.

'Leg still giving you curry?' Huggins asked, noticing Rogers' slight limp as he placed his empty teacup on the table.

'Only when the rains are coming. We've reserved the anteroom in the mess for your meeting with Prime Minister Smuts after the parade. I hope it will be suitable.' Rogers felt prickles of sweat in his armpits. He hated hiding the events of the morning from the country's leader, and prayed he had made the right decision.

'I'm sure it will be fine. Now, tell me about the troubles you've had here, Stephen.'

'Troubles?' Rogers swallowed hard, fearing the prime minister's entourage might somehow have picked up on police radio traffic or some other gossip about the morning's debacle.

'A woman murdered and a pilot killed by blacks across

the border. We do know what goes on in Bulawayo, even though government is based in Salisbury, Stephen,' the PM smiled.

Rogers tried to hide his relief. He hurriedly assured Huggins that the riot in town had been swiftly contained, and that they were expecting a breakthrough soon on the search for the dead pilot's aircraft. The latter was a half-truth, as Bryant had been babbling something to that effect. If the man were captured, Rogers at least wanted an explanation of what he had learned about the fate of Smythe's Harvard.

'The business in town worried me greatly, Stephen. We've had no violence between blacks and whites for decades and I don't want to see a repeat of it.'

'Of course, Prime Minister. Rest assured, the trouble-makers have been dealt with.'

'I don't have to tell you there are some natives who want to flex their muscles politically but I don't want the police or the air force giving them something to protest about. I want peace between the races. Our Africans do all right and the fate of blacks in South Africa will be better if Jan Smuts comes around to our way of thinking as well.'

'Really, how is that?' Rogers asked, grateful that the conversation had quickly swung away from the recent unrest to Huggins' favourite topic, the idea of a union between Southern Rhodesia, South Africa, Northern

Rhodesia, Bechuanaland and Nyasaland.

'A United States of Africa, I think it should be called,' Huggins said, after outlining a plan that had received regular coverage in the press. 'With all of the British colonies united in one new nation, still tied to England, we can ensure that all the blacks get a fair deal, and the British model of development and industrialisation is spread throughout the continent. We'll be a force to be reckoned with.'

'I can't see the Afrikaners being too pleased about it,' Rogers said. 'Do you think Field Marshal Smuts would be able to convince South Africans they'll be better off under such a union?'

'It's essential he does. Unless South Africa's white population can be absorbed into a greater, English-speaking fraternity, I fear the Smuts government will eventually fall prey to Afrikaner nationalism. Also, Jan Smuts is a player on the world stage – he has Churchill's ear – and he'll be a powerful advocate for our proposed federation if we can win him over.'

Rogers nodded in agreement. Despite South Africa's remoteness from Europe and world affairs, Smuts was a respected international statesman who had served as a member of the British war cabinet in the first war and played a role in the formation of the League of Nations. Although now in his seventies, he was reputed still to be ambitious, and no doubt saw himself as playing a role in carving out the new order if and when the allies prevailed in the current conflict.

'The Germans know how important Smuts is – look at how they tried to bump him off in '41. By the way, Stephen, I read a report in the car on the way over of a possible threat by the Ossewa Brandwag to the air training scheme. What do you make of that?'

Rogers coughed. 'Nothing to it, I'm sure, Prime Minister.'

'Excuse me, Prime Minister, sir,' Clive Wilson interrupted. 'We've just had a message from Field Marshal Smuts' aircraft. They're on time and will be landing in half an hour.'

Catherine walked to the hangar door and checked her watch. They'd wasted a lot of time with the dog-fighting and sorting out Bryant and Lovejoy, but she was sure Hennie would arrive at Kumalo in time to deliver his deadly payload with maximum effect. The graduation parade would last the best part of an hour – she had been to similar functions before. They should arrive overhead within the last ten minutes.

She savoured the thought of the hundreds of new pilots, bursting with pride, turning their faces skyward as the unannounced aircraft arrived. That Afrikaner traitor, Smuts, and Godfrey Huggins would no doubt think it was all part of the show – the grand finale. The wing commander and others from the base would be confused, perhaps alarmed, but it would all be over before anyone had time to react. A mass of writhing bodies shaking themselves to death within minutes.

Another forty minutes or so after the raid and Hennie and Paul would be back at the airstrip. From there they would fly to the abandoned farm near Gwelo, quickly refuel, and then fly on to neutral Portuguese Mozambique. Hendrick would contact a Nazi agent in the capital, Lourenço Marques, and passage to Germany on board a U-boat would be arranged for them.

Back inside, she sat on a stool, gingerly removed her riding boots and unbuttoned her pants. She inspected her leg. Her jodhpurs were soaked with blood, but the bleeding seemed to have stopped. She washed the wound with saline solution, flinching again at the pain. Once cleaned, it looked little worse than a deep cut, though the skin was burned on either side of the gouge.

She ripped open the cover off a shell dressing and discovered it was a bulky cotton pad with bandage ties attached. She found a foil packet of antiseptic powder, tore it open and sprinkled it over the bloodied flesh. She pressed the pad onto her leg and then wrapped the bandage around it. With difficulty, because of the bulki-ness of the dressing, she pulled her pants up again and buttoned them. She felt a little dizzy, so she dragged the stool close to the workbench and sat down. Her face was only inches from Pip's. She smiled.

'Why, Catherine?'

'Ah, I was wondering how long it would take to get around to that.'

'You're a fixture at Kumalo, almost one of them. How could you turn on your friends like this? How can you see so many of them murdered?'

'We're weak, Philippa. You and me. Our people. We've colonised this country, yet we don't have the strength to do what's needed. We hide our occupation, our subjugation of the Africans, behind a thin veneer of civilisation. We talk of educating the blacks, of improving their lot. Why? Because it makes our lily-livered colonial masters back home in dear old England feel good about themselves. They can take their cut of all the crops, the gold, the tin, the tobacco that comes out of Rhodesia, but they don't want their profits tainted with any thoughts that we, the whites, aren't being anything short of jolly decent to the blacks.'

Pip found it hard to follow the logic. 'So, you don't like the British because they expect us to treat the Africans in this country fairly?'

'Fairly? There's nothing fair about the way the average black lives in this country. Ever seen a rich one? Ever seen one who wasn't a criminal who owned more than the shirt on his back?'

Pip shook her head. 'No, I suppose not, but what's your point? You don't want to have to look after the black population, and I don't imagine that if Hitler ruled Africa he'd be very fair on them.'

'Oh yes, we'd be fair on them. When the Führer rules Europe, and the Afrikaners rule South Africa, we'll ensure that the blacks that remain are well employed – in the mines, on the farms and in our households – and that they are fed and clothed adequately.'

'Those that *remain*?'

'Now you're getting the idea, old girl,' Catherine said, leaning even closer to her. 'How many blacks are there on this continent? Millions, Pip. Absolutely bloody millions of them. And what do most of them do? Sit on their arses and tend a few miserable goats or a patch of pathetic mealies. The productive ones – those that contribute something to the economy – do so because they're employed by us whites.'

'Some people value their traditional way of life,' Pip said defensively.

Catherine laughed. 'They'd be better off dead.'

The words hung in the stuffy, greasy-smelling hangar. The tin door pinged as the sun warmed it. It would be like an oven inside soon. 'Better off dead?'

Catherine went on: 'There are too many of them, Pip. Too many for what we need – too many for their own good. Sooner or later God might take a hand – strike them down with some mysterious plague, or famine might reduce their numbers – but in the meantime they're nothing but a burden on the rest of us. There is a solution, Pip.'

'My God,' was all Pip could say.

'Open your eyes,' Catherine said, picking at Pip's closed eyelids with her fingers.

Pip recoiled from the shock of Catherine's touch. There was madness in the other woman's eyes. 'You don't mean . . .'

'You've heard the rumours coming out of Germany – about the way Hitler's treating the Jews? Yes, we all have. Stories about those concentration camps, where they're worked to death and not fed?'

'Yes, of course,' Pip said.

'Well, those stories aren't just allied propaganda, Pip. In fact, the situation is far worse – or better, depending on what you think about Jews.'

'How could it be much worse for them?'

'Hendrick told me some things. I probably shouldn't tell you.'

Pip knew if Catherine were going to tell her some monumental German state secrets, it probably meant that she had no intention of letting her live.

Catherine smiled, a contented smirk, like she'd just savoured a mouthful of chocolate ice cream on a hot day. 'They're killing them, Pip. The Germans are killing the Jews. Not by the hundreds but by the thousands. By the train load, in fact. Hennie's company was involved in finding the solution – the way to exterminate an entire race. They use gas, Pip. It's just amazing. Think of it – having the will to reorder society, to remove those who are a burden. To cleanse a nation, to create a better world in the process.'

'No!'

'Oh yes, Constable Lovejoy. It's working in Europe, right now, even as we speak. It's an industry over there. You know, they even have uses for the corpses – skin tanned as leather, hair used to stuff pillows, all sorts of things. It could work here, too, Pip. It would work here. Only it'd be Africans we'd be ridding ourselves of. Think of it – an Africa just for the whites, just for the strong.'

'That's unthinkable! My God, what kind of monsters have you fallen in with? How could a human being do that to another?'

'Hah! Spare me the liberal moralising, Pip. In a sense, what Hitler's doing is no different from what mankind has been doing for centuries. It's just that the Germans, in their efficient, industrialised manner, are much better at it than anyone before. The British did their best to wipe out the Irish, through occupation and starvation. The Australians killed off all the Aborigines in Tasmania. And it's not something we whites have a monopoly on. The Matabele pushed out the bushmen from this part of Rhodesia, and their cousins, the Zulus, despatched thousands of Africans from other tribes – and some whites – when they were at their peak last century. Don't blame the Germans for simply being efficient at killing.'

'Why did you murder Felicity, Catherine? She was your lover.'

'In war we make sacrifices. I gave her the chance to join Hendrick and me and she rejected me.'

Pip saw the complete lack of emotion in Catherine's dark eyes. 'You're going to kill me, aren't you?'

Kenneth Ngwenya raised a hand to his eyes to shield them from the sun's glare and watched in amazement as the two aeroplanes chased each other across the sky. The sound of gunfire had taken him by surprise – he had only just realised that was what it was. There was a dogfight taking place above his father's kraal.

His father was lying on the grass-filled sacking that served as a mattress on the earthen floor of his hut. Kenneth drew a deep breath as black smoke began pouring from the engine of one of the aircraft. He

watched it disappear behind the trees in the direction
of the landing strip that belonged to Isilwane Lodge. The
second aircraft, which seemed to be undamaged, circled
and descended towards the airstrip as well.

Soon after, once he had checked on his father again
and told him he was going to investigate this strange
happening, he heard an engine being revved. One of the
aircraft – presumably the undamaged one – lifted from
the treetops ahead of him. He started to run.

Bryant dragged the Harvard into a steep, reluctant climb,
fighting for as much height as he could, as quickly as
possible. Behind him Reitz said: 'We have to drop the bombs
from low altitude, remember? Why are you climbing?'

'Let me fly the bloody aeroplane, all right? We'll make
better speed at altitude, but if you want this flight to
take another half an hour . . .'

'Very well,' Reitz conceded. He'd held the rifle up
during take-off, in case Bryant tried anything, but now
they were airborne he saw no need to keep the pilot
covered. The tip of the barrel of the weapon rested near
Bryant's right shoulder, on his seatback.

When Bryant reached three thousand feet, he levelled
off and started to turn.

'What are you doing?' Reitz asked.

'We took off to the north, into the wind. I have to turn

us around to head back to Bulawayo. Unless you've changed your mind and want to fly to Germany.'

Looking out the left side of the cockpit, Reitz saw Isilwane Ranch, the airstrip and its hangar below. He returned his gaze to the instrument panel in front of him. As a trainer, the Harvard had dual controls. The stick between his legs moved when Bryant touched it, as did the rudder pedals on the floor. 'I've found the compass, Bryant, and my navigation is good. I know the heading to Kumalo, so don't try to deviate.'

'*Jawohl*,' Bryant said mockingly. They crossed the granite kopje. In a couple of minutes they were out of sight of the ranch.

'It's hot up here, with the sun coming in through the front. I'm going to get some air,' Bryant said, reaching up for the cockpit release. He lowered his hand when he felt the cold metal of the rifle's muzzle dig into the soft skin behind his right ear.

'You'll keep your cockpit closed and, while you're at it,' Reitz said, loosening his straps and leaning forward, 'you will also rebuckle your restraint.'

Bryant muttered a curse to himself. The spy had guessed the first ruse he tried. He had envisaged leaping out of the cockpit and leaving Reitz to crash.

'Take your hands off the stick and your feet off the pedals, Bryant.'

'Now I know you're crazy. This aircraft needs constant attention – it's been designed to teach pilots to fly the hard way,' Bryant replied.

'Just do as I tell you.'

'All right, but get ready to jump.' The Harvard lurched as soon as Bryant removed his hands and feet from the controls, the nose dropping sickeningly.

Reitz let the rifle rest on Bryant's seat again and grabbed the stick. The aircraft swayed from side to side as he overcorrected one way and then the other, but after a few seconds his hand and feet were working in unison and the trainer settled back into the straight and level flight. He turned to bring the compass back onto the original heading. 'I might not be able to land and take off, but I've been in enough Luftwaffe aircraft to know how to fly one of these things.'

'Very impressive,' Bryant conceded. On Reitz's order, Bryant took control of the aircraft again.

'If you try another of your little stunts, Bryant, I'll shoot you in the head. I'll still be able to bomb the parade and find my way back to Isilwane. Once there I'll try to crash-land. I'm prepared to die for my cause. Of course, if I do lose my life, then so will Constable Lovejoy.'

Like a light being switched on and off midair, the sun glinted on the bare metal wings of the South African

DC-3 Dakota as it lined up on final approach to Kumalo air base.

Wing Commander Rogers scanned the wide expanse of sky with fighter pilot's eyes, praying he would see nothing else. A murmur of excitement rippled across the crowd of two hundred guests seated below the raised official dais where Rogers sat next to Sir Godfrey. 'Shall we, Prime Minister,' Rogers said. His bad leg, which shouldn't have been giving him trouble for another two months, felt shaky under him.

The two men, followed by the prime minister's aide-de-camp, walked down the steps onto the Tarmac, past a rank of white mechanics and ground crew who had drilled for several weeks to function as Jan Smuts' guard of honour. Spit-polished boots slammed into the ground as a warrant officer called them to attention. At the command 'Pre-sent arms!' their rifles were held out in front of their bodies in a salute to the Rhodesian leader.

The Dakota bounced once on the runway with a squeal of rubber, then settled and flashed past the crowd. It turned and motored slowly back to where the massed ranks of pilots stood ready to march onto their graduation parade. Two askaris pushed a wheeled set of steps up to the rear door, which was swung open by a crewman. The Kumalo band struck up 'God Save the King', as the familiar, gaunt figure of Jan Smuts appeared.

Rogers still searched the sky, albeit discreetly, as Sir Godfrey Huggins moved forward to the bottom of the steps.

Smuts, with his distinctive white goatee beard and moustache, high forehead and receding snowy hair, stepped down and shook hands with his counterpart. A field marshal in the South African army as well as his country's PM, Smuts was dressed in khaki dress uniform adorned with the red collar tabs of a senior officer and four rows of campaign ribbons. As the honour guard crashed to attention and presented their arms again, Smuts drew himself to his full height, placed the pith helmet he had carried under one arm on his head, and returned their salute.

'So good of you to agree to visit us,' Huggins said as they passed the guard.

'My pleasure, Sir Godfrey. I do like a good parade, and I am sure your Rhodesian Air Training Group will not disappoint. And such a perfect African day it is for this historic occasion.'

'Shoot me,' said Bryant into the intercom.

'What?' Reitz replied, his finger tightening on the trigger of the rifle.

'I can't do it, Reitz. I won't be party to the death of two heads of state and hundreds of my men, and I don't want to live if Catherine kills Pip Lovejoy.'

'Shut up and just fly the aeroplane, Bryant. You could have refused on the ground. You're a coward. You'll do what I say and, when it's done, you and the woman can go hide with your shame. You want to live.'

'I'm letting go of the controls now.'

'No, Bryant, grab the stick, you idiot!' The Harvard's nose immediately dropped, and they entered a dive.

Instinctively, Reitz grabbed the stick with his left hand and pulled back, but his first attempt to keep the wings level failed and the aircraft yawed steeply over on its left-hand side.

Bryant reached up with his right hand and grabbed the barrel of the Mauser, yanking it violently towards him. The movement forced Reitz to jerk the trigger and a round exploded inside the cockpit, drilling a hole through the front windscreen. Air hissed through starred glass and Bryant's right ear rang with pain. He held onto the hot, smoking barrel with one hand and used his other to release and roll back the pilot's cockpit canopy.

'Let go!' Reitz yelled, his feet frantically working the pedals to steer the Harvard as he tugged back on the rifle from his end. Reitz felt resistance on the stick as Bryant tried to wrestle control of the aircraft from him. He fought back for an instant, using his left hand, then realised he would have to release the controls if he were going to be able to retrieve the rifle from the Australian and chamber another round. It was a bolt-action weapon and he would need both hands to recock it.

'Given up on your flying lessons, Reitz?' As Bryant spoke, he increased the throttle setting and pulled back on the stick until the nose was up, thirty degrees over the horizon. Once there, he centred the stick then snapped it fully over to the right.

Reitz let out a scream as the aircraft flipped over on its back. 'Stop!' G-forces pushed him into his seat and made his arms feel as though they were encased in lead. He struggled, unsuccessfully, to chamber another round into the Mauser's breech.

Reitz had stowed the two sarin bombs under his seat. When Bryant had first released the stick and the Harvard had dived, one of the bombs had rolled forward between his legs, coming to rest against the rudder pedals. As the Harvard reached the top of its roll, the bomb flew past Reitz's face, a tail fin scratching his cheek before it came to rest on the inside of the closed canopy over his head. 'You'll kill us both!' Reitz had not retightened his restraint straps after leaning forward to check on Bryant earlier, and he hung now below his seat, the straps the only thing stopping his head crashing into the canopy.

Once the wings were level with the horizon, Bryant calmly moved the stick to slightly left of centre and then back to the central position, so they were flying level, but still upside down.

Bryant looked in the rear-view mirror and saw Reitz, one arm dangling, trying to retrieve the evil-looking bomb, which still rattled and rolled against the glass, just out of reach. Bryant gave another vicious tug on the Mauser and felt it come free of the Afrikaner's grasp.

Like Reitz, he knew he needed two hands to load the weapon. He chanced letting go of the stick and dragged the long rifle across his body. He worked the bolt, pulling it rearwards.

Having lost his weapon, Reitz gave up trying to recover the bomb and reached awkwardly for the control column. Unsure what would happen upside down, he pulled the stick hard back towards his groin.

Bryant gasped as they entered a steep dive, inverted. He knew he needed to get a hand back on the stick, but one was not enough to regain control. He let go of the Mauser and, with the aircraft still upside down, the weapon sailed past his face and was snatched away into the sky by the slipstream.

Bryant heard a bounce and a clatter above his head and looked up just in time to see the bomb slide towards him with the changing angle of the dive. Reitz struggled clumsily with the stick and the deadly device suddenly dropped into Bryant's lap. He winced in pain as the snub-nosed mass hit him. 'Shit!' he said as he looked at it sitting there.

Bryant fought against the crushing forces of gravity as the brown bushveld raced up to meet them. He took a breath and held it hard in his chest, trying to stop all his blood draining from his torso to his legs. Still, he felt his vision starting to grey out. 'Help me . . .' he gasped, hoping Reitz knew what he meant.

Reitz, too, was being forced back into his seat as they entered a vertical dive. Summoning every reserve of strength in his arms he slowly reached out to grab the stick. He grasped it and pulled back, adding his effort to Bryant's. The Harvard whined and vibrated around them, protesting audibly at the terrible strain of the manoeuvre, reluctant to let the men save her.

Bryant felt his head clearing, his sight returning as the unbearable pressure started to ease. He saw clearly the detail of individual dried, dying leaves on a tree in front of him, and was convinced they were too late. God help Pip, he prayed.

Then they were level, the same leaves brushing noisily along the bottom of the fuselage as they screamed fast and low across the trees. Bryant needed altitude and he brought the nose up again, searching for the road below as he did.

Freed of having to help save the aircraft, Reitz, his face

red with rage, undid his restraints and half stood in the rear cockpit. He reached around the seat in front of him and locked his fingers around Bryant's throat.

'What . . .' The protest faded on Bryant's lips as he felt his windpipe being crushed. He glanced down at the altimeter. They were at nine hundred feet. Not high enough, his mind registered as he fought a losing battle for breath.

'I am going to kill you!' Reitz screamed. He knew Bryant would have to release the stick to try to claw the hands from his throat, but Reitz was certain he could kill the Australian and then quickly regain control of the aircraft.

Bryant kept one hand on the control column and, with the other, punched the release buckle on his restraint straps. He looked at their height again. Eleven hundred feet. He felt his vision fading once more. With his free hand he grabbed one of the tail fins and lifted it up, so the blunt nose was cradled in his lap again. He hooked a finger into the pin at the centre of the tailpiece and yanked it out.

Reitz craned forward, trying to see what the other man was doing. Wind from the bullet hole in the windscreen and the open front cockpit stung his eyes, but he knew Bryant was up to something.

Grinning, despite the pain in his throat, Bryant held up the pin and dangled it, from the ring, in front of Reitz's eyes.

'No!' Reitz screamed. He let go his grip on Bryant's neck and tried first to reach across the other man, to get to the bomb.

'Die!' Bryant croaked, his voice weak with pain. He rolled the bomb off himself, onto the floor, pushed the stick forward, then let go of it. The Harvard started to dive again.

Reitz fell back into his seat and tugged on the control column, trying to arrest the dive. The only thing he could do was to try to roll the Harvard again, to get rid of the deadly cargo, whose fuse whirred unheard on the floor in front of the pilot's seat, way out of his reach. Having unclipped his harness to get his hands on Bryant's throat, he was no longer attached to his parachute either.

Bryant allowed himself one last glance at the wide-eyed terrified face behind him as he stood on his seat and vaulted out of the cockpit, into the rushing slipstream outside. As soon as he knew he was clear of the tailplane he wrenched the ripcord. They were back below safe jump altitude, so it would be a fast, dangerous ride down.

Reitz yanked the stick over to the left and the Harvard slowly started to roll.

Bryant heard the explosion as his parachute deployed, and swung around under the silken canopy in time to see smoke streaming from the open front cockpit.

Reitz screamed in fear and frustration as he tried to yank open the rear cockpit cover. He had finally realised, too late, that there was no way he could shake out the first bomb, and that the mission was doomed. All he could do was save himself. The explosion was not enough to destroy the Harvard, though the controls were suddenly slack, as the charge had severed cables and shattered gauges. Far more dangerous was the payload that the small blast had released. He fumbled with the parachute harness straps.

Most of the sarin was sucked out of the aircraft, along with the smoke from the detonation, but as Hendrick Reitz finally released the rear sliding canopy a mist of remnant vapour hit him full in the face. He slumped back down into his seat – paralysed by the realisation that hit him, as surely as if he had been felled by a bullet. One drop, he knew, was all it took to kill a man.

His agonised screams died on the wind.

20

Kenneth Ngwenya put his hand over his mouth as he peered through a crack between two of the rough planks in the hangar's walls. Catherine De Beers, his father's employer, had a knife in her hand and was standing over the body of another woman who was tied down on a workbench.

He had no idea what was going on here, but he had finally been able to coax from his father the truth about who had hit him. It was not a man, but the woman standing with her back to him. She had struck her feeble though devoted servant with a riding crop over some minor incident involving an unlocked gate. His father had said the madam had been acting increasingly strangely in the preceding week.

Kenneth had never harmed a woman in his life, but he seethed with rage over his father's treatment. He had been fully prepared to report Mrs De Beers to the police, but it looked very much like a policewoman's skirt that her captive was wearing. How was he to know, however, that the prisoner was not a wrongdoer herself?

What he saw next, though, galvanised him into action. Catherine De Beers leaned over the woman, slipped the blade of the knife under one of the buttons on her captive's blouse and, with one deft movement, sliced it off. The woman screamed. Kenneth had armed himself with a spade, which he had found beside a freshly dug hole behind the hangar. He strode through the open door of the hangar, swung back the shovel and slammed the flat of the blade into the back of Mrs De Beers' head, just as it appeared she was about to terrorise the other woman with another knife stroke.

'Are you all right, miss?' Kenneth Ngwenya asked the obviously relieved woman.

'Oh, God, thank you, whoever you are,' Pip said, fighting back tears.

'I am Kenneth Ngwenya. My father works for Mrs De Beers,' he said as he laid the spade against the bench. 'I don't think things are as they should be here at Isilwane.'

'That's the understatement of the century. Untie me, quickly. Before she comes to. I'm a policewoman, and Mrs De Beers is guilty of murder, along with plenty of other things!' Catherine had tired of waiting for Reitz to return, and Pip feared she was about to become the woman's next victim.

'Hurry, Kenneth!'

'I am trying.'

'The knife! She dropped it when you hit her. It must be on the floor somewhere, along with her pistol.' Catherine had laid her pistol on the workbench when she'd pulled out the knife, and both weapons had fallen to the floor when she had staggered against the bench before collapsing.

Kenneth bent over and looked around Catherine's prone body.

'Here is the knife,' he said, beaming as he stood. He started sawing at the ropes binding Pip's hands. The razor-sharp blade sliced smoothly through the strands and in less than a minute her wrists were free.

'Give it to me. I'll do my ankles. You look for Mrs De Beers' pistol, please.'

Kenneth dropped onto his hands and knees, his head under the workbench, and began searching in the shadows.

Pip hacked at the ropes around her legs. She needed to get Catherine tied up as soon as possible, and to make her way to the house. 'We need to get to the telephone, as quickly as we can.'

* * *

Tears filled Catherine's closed eyes, but she willed herself to stay silent. When she regained consciousness she heard a man's voice close to her. An African.

She heard him crawling around on all fours like the animal he was, searching for the pistol, but she had already located it. Ever so slowly, she reached out with her right hand. Her fingers brushed the grip of the Walther. Thank God, she thought. She grabbed the pistol and rolled hard to her left and started to sit up. Her head rang with pain from the blow to the back of her head and her vision swam.

Pip was sitting up on the workbench, swinging her freed legs over the edge. Catherine blinked and aimed at the swimming image of the policewoman, pulled the trigger twice.

The first bullet sailed wide, but the second punched through Pip's upper left arm. Pip screamed but didn't fall. She regained her balance, jumped off the bench and delivered a vicious kick with the toe of her heavy police-issue shoe into Catherine's bandaged leg.

Catherine howled like a cat and her vision went grey. She pulled the trigger blindly again.

Pip turned and sprinted for the sunlight. 'Run, Kenneth!'

The schoolteacher hauled himself to his feet. He saw the lady in the uniform running for the doorway, and

Mrs De Beers raising her hand, aiming the gun. He lunged from out of the shadows, throwing his body in front of her.

Outside, Pip heard another gunshot and the immediate thud of a falling body.

21

Bryant felt as though his heart and lungs were about to explode from his chest. He'd never run so far in his life. It was only the thought of what Pip might be going through that kept his legs going, stride after weary stride.

He'd checked his watch and done a quick calculation as soon as he hit the ground. He had landed hard, but his body was running on adrenaline and fear, so the pain from his many injuries barely registered. On take-off he'd taken the Harvard north of Isilwane to cut the distance he'd have to fly from the ranch before bailing out. He'd lied to Reitz about the wind. There was hardly a breeze, so he could have taken off in either direction.

Though it had seemed to take an eternity to free himself from Reitz, he reckoned he had flown for two minutes until he'd disappeared from view of the lodge, past the granite hills. A hundred and fifty miles an hour equalled two and a half miles a minute. He was five miles from the ranch – at least.

Five miles hadn't sounded like a lot, but he'd never run more than three during air force physical training. His feet burned as blisters formed on his heels and soles.

He was unarmed. That was a problem. Catherine had at least one weapon – the pistol – and she wouldn't hesitate to use it. He'd have surprise on his side, and that was something.

Sweat poured from his body, staining his tattered shirt and filling his eyes. When he wiped a hand through his hair it came back sticky and red with blood oozing from the wound on his temple. He was painfully thirsty and he'd had virtually no sleep in the last twenty-four hours, unless one counted intermittent bouts of unconsciousness.

He crested the granite-capped rise and coughed a ragged, 'Thank God,' as the ranch came into view again. He followed the road almost all the way to the homestead, then turned off on the airstrip track. Halfway to the airfield he allowed his pace to slow to a shuffle, in order to catch his breath and make a plan.

Three shots, in fairly quick succession. He started to sprint again, drawing on a hidden reserve of strength and breath. Another shot rang out.

* * *

Catherine hobbled into the light and brought her pistol hand up to her eyes to shield them from the glare. Her leg burned with every step and her head still pounded a tattoo of pain. She blinked twice and saw Lovejoy running across the runway, a bloodied hand to her shoulder. 'Stop, Philippa! You won't make it.' She turned and looked down at the young man. He writhed on the ground, a hand clutched over his stomach, blood oozing between his fingers. He'd be dead soon enough. 'I won't even waste another bullet on you.'

Pip didn't look back. She kept running. Her hand seemed to be getting wetter and wetter. She guessed her increased heart rate was pumping more blood out of her damaged shoulder and down her arm. She fought back tears and forced herself to keep moving. The gun fired again, though she had no idea how wide of the mark the bullet went. The important thing was that it missed.

'I'll get the dogs, Philippa. They'll drive you to the river and I'll kill you there!' Catherine stopped, steadied herself, raised the pistol and supported it with her left hand in order to take better aim. She held the foresight on the middle of the running woman's back and squeezed the trigger.

The shot hit the ground directly behind Pip, inches from her heel. She felt a spray of dirt pepper the backs of her calves. She glanced over her shoulder and saw Catherine standing still, both hands extended as she took aim again. Catherine had aimed too low, not allowing for the bullet's fall. Her second shot would probably not miss. Pip zigzagged to the left, then the right, and risked another glance. She heard the crack of the pistol again and a bullet rushed past her right side, where she had been a split second ago.

Catherine took aim again, then noticed the furrowed grass in front of Pip. She held her fire and yelled instead. 'Paul!'

Pip instinctively looked back over her shoulder. She saw only Catherine, looking down the barrel of the pistol and grinning. Her left foot suddenly met nothing, where there should have been grass. She fell headlong onto the ground.

Catherine staggered along, favouring her injured leg. She'd noticed that Pip was heading straight for the same hole that had destroyed Andy Cavendish's undercarriage. Pip hadn't seen it, and had either fallen into it or tripped on the furrows made by the Harvard's shattered landing gear, fooled by her bluff.

Pip tried to stand, but fell. Her ankle was badly damaged. Twisted, if not broken. She tried again, but it was no use. She started to crawl.

* * *

566

Bryant was alarmed when he heard his name called. He dropped to the ground, seeking refuge in the long grass and braced himself for the shot he thought would surely follow. Instead there was silence. He looked up and saw that Pip had fallen. Catherine was hobbling across the runway.

He had circled around the hangar, sticking to the tree line. Close to him, just a short dash away, was the wreck of Sergeant Smythe's Harvard – the aircraft Catherine and Reitz had crashed. Catherine was looking away from him now, still limping towards Pip. He stood and sprinted across to the aircraft. When he reached it he climbed onto the wing, put a hand on the hot metal of the fuselage and vaulted into the pilot's seat.

Tears of anger and frustration rolled down Pip's cheeks. She had been so close to getting away. If only she had disarmed Catherine, it would have all been over. Or would it? She wondered what had happened to Paul.

'Stop crawling, you pathetic little bitch,' Catherine said. She stood behind Pip, the pistol levelled at her back.

Pip stopped, rolled onto her side and looked up at Catherine. 'You're sick, Catherine. Your vision of the future is a nightmare.'

Catherine laughed. 'You and your kind will give Africa

away in the end, surrender it to the blacks.'

'There are more of them than us, Catherine. But I think we can all live together, even if you don't.'

Catherine shook her head. 'The new Africa starts today, Philippa. With you. Before we can rid ourselves of the useless blacks, we need to weed out soft, liberal whites. Your kind.' She raised her hand until the pistol was pointing at Pip's forehead.

'I'd rather die than live in your world, Catherine.'

'All right, then,' She laughed and took up the slack on the trigger.

'Catherine, drop it!' Paul bellowed.

She spun around, raising her free hand to her eyes, searching for the location of the voice. 'Where's Hendrick?'

'He failed his first flying lesson.'

'Come out now, wherever you are. If you don't show yourself on the count of three, I'll kill Philippa. One . . .'

'Drop the pistol, Catherine.'

'Two . . .'

'Stay where you are, Paul!' Pip cried. She sat up and started to crawl towards Catherine.

'Down, Pip, stay down!' he yelled.

Pip dropped and lay on her back. She looked up at Catherine, silhouetted against the sun, and prayed it wouldn't hurt too much. At least Catherine's plot had been foiled.

'Three!'

Pip shut her eyes and heard the deafening thunder of gunfire. Not one bullet, but a storm of them, filling the air above her. She shrieked as Catherine's body fell across her injured ankle.

Paul leaped from the cockpit and ran through a fog of lingering cordite smoke. He'd had no idea where the rounds from the Harvard's two .303 Browning machine-guns would fall. He'd hoped the fusillade would be enough to shake Catherine. He hadn't expected to hit her.

But he had. 'Pip, are you all right?' he said as he grabbed Catherine's lifeless wrist and pulled her body away.

Pip fought for breath. 'I'll live, Paul, I'll live. There's a man been hit, over by the hangar. His name's Kenneth.'

'Kenneth?' Bryant bent over her, put an arm under her knees and one under her neck and lifted her, like a child. 'We'll go check on him now. You're safe, Pip. I won't leave you again.'

They paused to look down at Catherine. A stream of bullets from one of the Harvard's guns had caught her in the stomach, almost severing her torso from her legs. She stared skywards, eyes wide in shock.

'The gas?' Pip asked.

'One bomb's gone for sure, along with Reitz. The air

force will have to search for the wreck of the Harvard. I hit the ground before I saw it crash.'

'It was a nightmare, Paul, what they had planned for Africa.'

'Well,' he said as he carried her back across the runway, towards the hangar, 'their dreams are over now.'

EPILOGUE

Four weeks later

For a time she allowed herself the fantasy that they were a normal couple. The semblance of married life and domestic normality they had enjoyed were an almost dreamlike counter to the nightmarish few days over which they'd first met.

The bullet wound in her arm was healing well, but it was a constant reminder that things had never actually been normal for them at all.

'Hello?' he called, and she heard the front door creak open.

'You've been busy again today,' he said as she rose on her toes to kiss him. She wrapped her arms around his neck and he held her close for a few moments longer.

'Well, Enoch did most of the painting. He's a star considering he's only recently recovered from pleurisy.'

Enoch Ngwenya had come to work for Pip on the farm as a general handyman. The old man had been more than happy to turn his back on Isilwane, which had been thoroughly searched, with no result, for any evidence that might indicate Catherine De Beers was working with any other enemy agents.

'The place looks so much bigger and cheerier in light colours,' Paul commented approvingly, walking through the latest freshly painted room. Long gone, on a bonfire, were any photos or remembrances of Pip's dead husband or his family. 'I stopped in on Kenneth today. He's recovering well, for someone who took a bullet in the guts. The doc says he'll be fine in time.'

'Thank God for that. Any news on the missing bomb?' He had told her the air force and police were organising yet another search for the crashed aircraft and its payload, having yielded nothing on two previous sweeps of the approximate location Paul had supplied.

'Nothing. It's a big area of bush to search, and there were no reports from any landowners in the area of smoke or fire. It's a worry if that bomb survived. Who knows where it might end up.'

Pip hoped the hideous device was never found. She wanted no more reminders of the past, just a future to look forward to. They had said their goodbyes, together, to Felicity Langham, Pip laying a dozen red roses on the grave, while Paul stepped back, solemnly, and saluted the deceased airwoman.

Though still on leave while her injury healed, Pip had been given a promotion to acting sergeant, on the basis that she reveal nothing of the plot by Reitz and Catherine to commit mass murder at the graduation parade. As far as the official report went, the one that was released to the newspapers, a German spy had been uncovered by the police and killed while trying to escape. The government had decided to quash the release of any information about poison gas, in case it sparked mass hysteria. Reitz's mission, according to the propagandists, had been to set up an Ossewa Brandwag cell in Rhodesia, and he had failed.

'So, other than that, how was your day?' She moved to the sideboard and opened a beer for him.

'Thanks,' he said, accepting the drink. 'You know, I can't wait for work to end at the base each day, to get back out here to the farm. It's bliss. I can see myself as a gentleman farmer one day.'

She frowned. They were not married, although they lived as though they were. They had agreed to put off talk of their future until they knew where the air force would next send Paul. Wing Commander Rogers had survived, barely, as base commander at Kumalo, but both he and Paul had agreed it would be best if Paul moved on, to serve under someone else.

Although not his wife, Pip knew Paul intimately enough to read his moods. 'You didn't answer my question. You've got news, haven't you?'

He walked outside, and she followed him through to the courtyard where he had sat that first time, when she had heard of Charlie's death. 'Sit down, Pip.'

He told her of the posting order that had come through, to a pathfinder squadron in England, equipped with twin-engine Mosquito bombers. He would be flying fast, ahead of the massed bomber streams, dropping flares to light up their targets. It was dangerous work, reserved for the best pilots in the command. He would leave for England in two weeks' time.

She was silent for a while as she sipped her drink. 'You told me they would give you the posting of your choice, Paul. I thought you might move to another base near Bulawayo, or at least still in Rhodesia, maybe as commanding officer. You said you'd never leave me.'

He looked at the ground, then into her eyes. 'There's work still to be done, Pip. I'm a pilot, not a bureaucrat. I've got to do this.'

Tears streamed from her eyes. 'I know.'

The first of the Dakota's two engines coughed to life with a belch of black smoke. It was time. He set the duffle bag down on the Tarmac, turned to her and took her hands in his. They were both in uniform, Pip having returned to work at the police camp the week before.

'It's time,' she said, taking a deep breath to help ward off the tears, for his sake. He kissed her.

'Pip, you know you don't have to wait for me. I might ... well, you know, it's not over yet. The war, I mean. The odds are ...'

She knew what he was trying to say, and she wanted to silence him before the fear overwhelmed both of them. As much as she wanted him to stay, she knew he couldn't, not if he were going to remain the man he'd become again. She put a finger to his lips. 'There are still people like Catherine De Beers and Hendrick Reitz out there, Paul. I don't think we'll ever be completely free of them, but I'd hate to live in their world, a world without hope.'

The odds of him surviving another operational tour were not worth contemplating. But Pip had given him something he'd not had in a long time.

'Hope,' he said, then he kissed her goodbye for the last time.

By any measurement, the Empire Air Training Scheme was a massive undertaking. More than 37,000 Australian pilots and other aircrew were trained under the scheme during World War Two, including 583 who undertook instruction in Southern Rhodesia (now Zimbabwe).

Fifty of those Australian servicemen are buried in Zimbabwe, in Bulawayo, and at the other major training centres, Gweru and Harare (formerly Gwelo and Salisbury).

The fact that at its peak the Empire Air Training scheme was producing 50,000 graduates a year in Rhodesia, Australia and Canada says as much about the efficiency of the training as it does about the horrific losses suffered in the allied air forces, particularly in bomber command.

As in other countries that went to war, women played a vital role on the home front in Rhodesia, freeing up men for military service by taking jobs as policewomen, railway workers, parachute packers, aircraft fitters and mechanics and a host of other occupations hitherto reserved for men.

There is one woman buried in the RAF/military section of Bulawayo Cemetery, a Rhodesian Leading Aircraftswoman. Of course, there is no suggestion she met her fate in the same way as Felicity Langham; however, when I first visited the graveyard, with the rough idea of the book in my mind, this discovery was enough to raise the hairs on the back of my neck.

The information about the Ossewa Brandwag (OB), its membership and rituals, largely came from *For Volk and Führer* by Hans Strydom, a factual account of Operation Weissdorn, in which the former South African heavyweight boxer Robey Leibbrandt, trained by the Germans as a spy, attempted to assassinate Prime Minister Jan Smuts in 1941. Leibbrandt was the inspiration for my Hendrick Reitz.

The idea for an OB attack on the Empire Air Training Scheme came from a brief reference in a book called *A Dream's Reality*, by Kelvin Hayes, DFC, an excellent first-hand account of life as a wartime RAAF fighter pilot. Mr Hayes, who was trained in Rhodesia, talks of base security being increased one night because of fears of an OB raid.

While we might think of weapons of mass destruction as a relatively modern concept, I was surprised, as some readers may be, to learn that sarin gas, the lethal substance used in the Tokyo subway attack, was indeed invented by the Germans prior to World War Two. Fear of reprisals and like attacks by the allies caused the Germans to hold off ever using it.

I am grateful to a number of sources and individuals for my research into the Empire Air Training Scheme, and life in 1940s Rhodesia.

In Zimbabwe, I would like to acknowledge the help of the Bulawayo city hall historical collection; the staff at the Zimbabwe military museum; and the British South Africa Police (BSAP) collection, at Gweru.

Mrs Esme Stewart, of Bulawayo, provided a wealth of written and anecdotal information about her years as a young woman during the war. It was a conversation with this delightful lady that prompted me to write the book in the first place.

Nick and Alison Jones, of Sydney, and Alison's mother, Dorothy Crombie, kindly provided additional information about life in wartime Bulawayo. Dave Munro and former BSAP officer John Bennett helped me with several questions about police uniforms and equipment.

Isobel 'Scotty' Wrench read the draft manuscript and provided invaluable suggestions, as well as information about Sir Godfrey Martin Huggins, former Prime Minister of Southern Rhodesia.

The Royal Australian Air Force museum at Point Cook, in Victoria, gave me a valuable starting point for information on the AT-6 Harvard aircraft and the Empire Air Training Scheme.

Thanks also to Jeff Mueller, of Sydney, who took my wife, Nicola (who, at five foot two, made a good Pip Lovejoy stand-in), for a memorable joy flight in his immaculately restored Harvard as part of our research. Jeff read and corrected early drafts of the flying scenes, and also came up with the means of sabotaging a Harvard, as employed by Hendrick Reitz in the book. You can see his Harvard at www.australianwarbirds.com.au

Ace aerobatics pilot, fellow author and good friend David Rollins helped me navigate Paul Bryant through some gut-wrenching aerial manoeuvres. If you liked this book, you'll love his work. His latest is *The Death Trust*, also published by Pan Macmillan.

Don Caldwell-Smith, of Lindfield, Sydney, a wartime Lancaster pilot in the Royal Australian Air Force, kindly took the time to answer my many questions, and provided me with anecdotes and books which added immeasurably to my research on bomber command and the men who served in it.

The Nanton Lancaster Society in Canada, which houses a Lancaster bomber, provided advice and copies of original flight manuals to give me some tips on what could go wrong with an aircraft's landing gear, and how Paul Bryant would go about landing his stricken kite.

Sheila Bunnage from the Freedom of Information Cell at RAF Headquarters Personnel and Training Command, at RAF Innsworth, UK, provided historical information about wartime air force protocols relating to funerals.

As is and always should be the case, if I've got something wrong, it is due solely to me, and not to any of the individuals who have helped me, or sources I have drawn upon.

In Zimbabwe, my thanks go to Sally, Dennis and Liz, and Don and Vicki for being great friends and fantastic hosts.

As usual, my daydreams would be nothing more than that without the support and input of my wife, Nicola; mother, Kathy; and mother-in-law, Sheila, who all read early drafts and gave full and frank advice (it gets fuller and franker with every book) and constructive feedback.

Thanks, too to my editor and publisher at Quercus Books, Katie Gordon and Jane Wood, and to their sales and publicity people in the UK and South Africa. Finally, if you've got this far then thank you, you're the one who counts most.

AFRICAN DAWN

Tony Park

**Spanning fifty years and three generations, African Dawn
is the breathtaking story of three families, their dark secrets
and violent threats**

Southern Rhodesia: 1959. Natalie is ten years old when she is
kidnapped by guerrillas. Bloodied, terrified, and beaten at the
hands of her captors, her life is saved by a young soldier.

Thirty years later, Natalie returns to her homeland,
now Zimbabwe, and becomes embroiled in the dangerous
world of rhino conservation. Hunters are making a fortune
on the black market, and now the survival of the
black rhino is at stake.

Natalie and her family must fight – not only
to save Zimbabwe's rhinos, but to save themselves.

Quercus

1

Southern Rhodesia, 1959

Makuti learned to swim almost as soon as he learned to walk. He didn't know that he wasn't born to enter the water; he just followed his mother in and did what she did.

The rain had been falling all his short life. Makuti couldn't know it – how could he – but it was not supposed to be like this. It was not meant to pour down so heavily from the skies, at this time of the year. It was not natural.

His first steps were in the mud and he tried as best he could, on his short legs, to keep pace with his mother who was terribly stressed. She walked in circles and Makuti's path was made harder because he had to lift his little feet in and out of the ever-deepening footprints his mother was pounding into the sticky slime.

When she stopped abruptly, Makuti skidded and

bumped into her legs. He fell over and, instead of scrambling to his feet, enjoyed the peace of lying there for a moment, wallowing in the cloying mud. When he tried to stand, he slipped and rolled some more, and found that he enjoyed it.

His mother turned and looked down at him. She snorted and stamped her foot. He dragged himself upright again – the brief moment of play over.

Makuti was hungry. Although he was already walking, it would be some time before he was weaned – such was their way – so he sought out the solace and nourishment of his mother's teat. She brushed him aside and, hurt, he stumbled and sloshed after her. The rain started again and spattered his back. He was tired, hungry and cold.

His mother shook her head. She was starving too. The ring of their forlorn footsteps grew shorter each day, as the rain continued to fall and the river continued to rise. In the days before she had given birth, Makuti's mother had exhausted herself climbing higher and higher up a hill, which had now become an island. Although they were safe from the rising waters up here on this rocky outcrop, there was nothing to eat and the new mother was half-crazed with hunger.

Thunder rolled down the valley and lightning ignited the night sky. Makuti's mother walked to the floodwaters' edge and waded in. And Makuti, not know-ing any better, plunged in joyfully behind her and started to swim.

'Bejane!' Paul Bryant raised a hand to shield his eyes from the glare of the morning sunshine on the still waters. The lake was the same molten silver as the hazy sky and it was virtually impossible to discern the horizon. Paul pulled the battered pair of binoculars from their worn leather case to see what fourteen-year-old Winston Ngwenya was pointing at. 'Well spotted, Winston. It's a rhino all right.' 'There are two.' Paul moved the focusing wheel and saw the youngster was correct again. Bobbing behind the first horned head was a little dark blob. 'A calf.'

'Ah, but the mother will be trouble, *baas*.'

'Dad, let me see.'

'Steady, George!' Paul lurched as his son inadvertently shifted the outboard engine's tiller in his haste to catch sight of the swimming black rhinoceroses, but regained his balance. He smiled to show George he hadn't meant to chastise him, just to warn him.

George set the throttle to neutral and the wooden dinghy slowed. Long-limbed and angular, with his father's height and his mother's blonde hair, George had the awkwardness of adolescence and the promise of manhood competing for control of his every move and word. Paul smiled as he handed his son the binoculars.

Winston, kneeling at the bow, reached out a hand to steady his friend, but George brushed it away. 'I'm fine.'

It was amazing what a difference a year could make, Paul thought. Winston's body was filling out quickly and he was almost a man. His voice was breaking and his movements around the boat were self-assured and confident. Bryant thought of the African boy as a second son, almost. He was the firstborn child of his good friend Kenneth, who taught in the black township of Mzilikazi, on the outskirts of Bulawayo, back home in Matabeleland.

Kenneth and his wife, Patricia, had two more children after Winston, a girl and a boy, Thandi and Emmerson. All three of their children were healthy and strong, which was something to give thanks for.

'I see them, Dad,' George said. 'Too bad Mom can't be here.'

Paul nodded. He, too, wished she were here with him, instead of back on the farm, way out near the Bechuanaland border.

'Go, Paul. For God's sake, please go – you're driving me bloody mad,' she'd urged him. They'd tried for a second child after George had been born, back in 1946 after Paul had come back from the war, but Pip had miscarried. Then, thirteen years later, at the age of thirty-nine, she had told him the news that she was expecting what the Afrikaner farmers living in Rhodesia called a *laat lammetjie*.

This, however, was no late lamb. It was a tiny human life that Philippa was carrying. Paul had been adamant that Pip should stop work around the dairy and spend more time indoors resting. They'd had fights over it, but she'd stood up to him, telling him that she would not live her life in fear – not even of another miscarriage. He'd seen in her the same fierce independence and stubbornness she'd shown as a volunteer policewoman during the war, when they'd first met.

When the call had gone out from the Rhodesian Game Department in the early days of Pip's pregnancy for volunteers to help with a massive operation aimed at saving wildlife stranded by the rising waters of the newly created Lake Kariba, they had gone as a family to camp near the growing but still primitive township that had sprung up near the dam construction site.

The three of them had known bugger all about how to save wild animals from drowning when they'd arrived five months earlier, but since then they had learned how to corral and drive impala, kudu and waterbuck into the lake, then shepherd them towards the mainland. They had plucked deadly mambas and irate cobras from waterlogged trees and rescued a host of smaller creatures then transported them by boat to the new banks of the swelling Zambezi River.

One thing Paul had learned from his time working as a volunteer on Operation Noah, as the rescue operation had been dubbed, was that every animal could swim. The problem was that some could not swim as far as others. The rescuers' hearts had soon hardened to the sight of the bloated bodies of dead buck that hadn't made it, or half-eaten remains of animals that had literally fought each other to death.

Earlier in her pregnancy, Pip had come out most days on the boat for an hour or two at least, and proved herself as able and fearless as any of them. Paul was sick with worry about the baby sometimes, but Pip was happy to pull on his old wartime pilot's goggles and a pair of motorcycle gauntlets and pull a mamba from a tree, or sit in the boat cradling a soaking, shivering baby baboon whose mother had drowned.

Paul had lived in Southern Rhodesia since the end of the war. He'd had few family or prospects to encourage him to return to his native Australia and he'd fallen in love with Pip in 1943, when he'd been based at Khumalo airfield, near Bulawayo, as the adjutant of an aircrew training base. When he'd returned to Africa after being demobbed in 1945, he'd realised he'd also fallen for the continent.

There was a wildness of spirit in Africa that had once existed in Australia but was fast disappearing. Out here, in the wilds of Rhodesia, things were very different. Life was harder in Africa, and it had to be lived on the edge. As such, people seemed to enjoy things more, and live for the day.

Paul had taken Pip back to Bulawayo and the family dairy farm after their first month with Operation Noah, at the same time that George was due to return to school. But as the next school holidays approached, George pleaded with his parents to be allowed to return to Kariba to help out again with the relocation of animals. Paul did not want to go without Pip, but she all but ordered him to take their son back to the growing lake. Paul had been reluctant to leave her alone and heavily pregnant, but if he'd learned one thing in the past sixteen years it was that his diminutive Rhodesian wife was not to be disagreed with. He'd left with George and Winston, promising to be back in plenty of time for the birth, which was still not due for another month.

'Look, Mr Bryant, she is going the wrong way,' Winston said.

Paul saw he was right. 'Head for that island, to the left, George. We've got to try and drive her towards the mainland.'

George nodded, his face set with concentration. The

quickest way to the rhino would be to come close around a trio of dying trees that marked what had once been the top of a hill. As they closed on the trees Paul joined Winston at the front of the boat, and both peered ahead looking for submerged trunks that might ground them or tear the bottom out of the boat, which had been designed for waterskiing and fishing rather than rescuing animals.

'Stick!' Winston called, pointing off to starboard. George swung the tiller and the boat glided past the dangerous obstacle.

Paul scanned the nearest tree. 'There's a cobra up there. Make for it, George.'

As George turned again and cut the throttle, allowing the boat to coast up to the top branches of the drowning tree, all three of them looked down at the bottom of the boat to protect their eyes from the potentially blinding venom. Paul took off his Australian Army slouch hat, a souvenir of his war days, and put on his old flying goggles. He reached for a steel pole whose end had been fashioned into a u-shaped hook. Winston cried out and wiped his bare shoulder as a jet of venom lashed his skin.

'Come left,' Paul said. He placed a hand on Winston's neck to stop the boy from looking up, and ducked sideways as the cobra reared in the branch and spat another jet of milky venom towards him. Droplets spattered the goggles' right lens and burned his cheek. Paul reached for the snake. It pulled back and then struck, lightning fast, at the pole, but Paul was able to trap its head against the waterlogged trunk of the tree. 'Pass me the bag, Winston.'

His head still bowed, Winston raised the hessian bag to Paul then took hold of a nearby branch to secure the boat, while Paul grabbed the pinned snake behind the back of its head and thrust the writhing, hissing reptile into the sack.

'Can we go for the rhino now, Dad?'

Winston looked up and laughed at George's deadpan remark.

'Head for the rhinos, George, fast as you can,' Paul said.

Philippa Bryant exhaled and leaned against the hot metal of the Chevrolet *bakkie* as the young African man loaded her paper bags full of groceries into the rear of the vehicle. 'Thank you, Sixpence,' she said, and handed him a few coins. 'Are you all right, madam?' he asked. 'Fine, thank you.' She forced a smile and he walked back into Haddon and Sly. She was actually far from fine. She felt hot, fat, tired and thoroughly sick of being pregnant. She and Paul had been ecstatic about having another baby – at the start – but now she found herself moodily alternating between being annoyed and terrified. It had been many years since her last miscarriage, yet being pregnant again had reopened her old wounds and poured salt into them. At the same time she was full of nervous hope for the baby that kicked inside her.

She regretted ordering Paul to take George to Kariba for the school holidays. She wanted to be there with them, or, if she couldn't have that, she wanted them both back at the farm. Now.

Pip opened the door of the car. 'Bloody hell.' She realised she'd forgotten the bread. She was terribly forgetful these days, and remembered it as a symptom of her first pregnancy. 'I'm too old to be pregnant,' she said out loud as she walked slowly back into the department store. She felt like crying when she found the bakery had just sold its last loaf. Dejected, she turned and headed back out into the street. There was a bakery a block down Fife Street.

The sight of purple jacaranda blossoms cheered her a little. She knew from her time as a volunteer policewoman that this city of Bulawayo sometimes lived up to its Ndebele name, as a place of slaughter. She'd been involved in a couple of murder investigations and several cases of rapes, stabbings and beatings. She herself had been a victim of domestic violence at the hands of her first husband, before she'd met Paul. Fortunately, Charlie had died during the war. Fortunately for him, that is, because she'd decided after a couple of years as a volunteer constable that she would have had him arrested on his return from duty overseas, war hero or not. She knew that the orderly grid of wide, clean-swept streets and the impressive, stately public buildings of Bulawayo were, in some cases, just a façade of order. Pip had seen the grubbier side of the city – the blood, vomit and sewage in the streets of the black townships, and the seamy private lives of the outwardly upstanding members of the white community.

Pip only came to town once every month or so, to shop for what she couldn't grow or make herself. It was a chore at the best of times, but on her own and carrying another person in her belly it really was no fun at all.

'Howzit, Pip?'

She looked up and saw Fred Phipps touching the brim of his hat. Fred farmed in the same district as she and Paul, and they ran into each other at parties once or twice a year. The Bryants and the Quilter-Phippses weren't close friends, but they got on fine. Fred had played in the same rugby team as her first husband, Charlie, and Pip often sensed that he disapproved of her marrying Paul. Word had gotten around town during the war that she and Paul had become an item virtually as soon as she had heard of Charlie's death. Pip didn't care, and she had told anyone who bothered to listen that Charlie had been a bastard, despite receiving a posthumous Military Medal for his actions in the desert in North Africa.

'Fine, Fred, and you?'

'Fine, fine. You must be due soon, hey?'

Pip nodded, and her head felt heavy. She was sick of being asked the same question. 'A month.'

'Sharon's due any day. I'm just busy in town getting some things for when I have to fend for myself on the farm.'

Pip smiled and felt a genuine warmth for the man. She'd heard, ages ago, but had since forgotten, that his wife was pregnant. 'Please give her my best, Fred.'

'I will.' He paused and cocked his head. 'What's that noise?'

Pip heard shouts, and more rhythmic noise, like singing, coming from around the corner. She started walking in the direction of the sound, and Fred, who had been walking in the other direction, turned to follow her. Pip reached the closest corner and saw a group of about forty African men and women holding placards. One read, *Down with unfair bus fares*.

'Bloody *munts*,' Fred said.

Pip turned and looked at him. 'What's all this about?'

'Probably tied up with the bus fare protests in Salisbury. A friend of mine in the police told me they've had to crack a few kaffir skulls up there because the *munts* are complaining about some increases in the UTC bus fares. I mean, why should we whites be subsidising their bloody travel? If a bus company needs to charge more to make ends meet, then who are they to object?'

Pip frowned. Very few African people owned a bicycle, let alone a motor car and for most of them the bus was the only affordable way to travel. Now that Fred mentioned the Salisbury trouble she did remember reading somewhere that the fare hike meant some Africans were paying up to twenty per cent of their meagre wages on bus tickets.

'Come on, Pip,' Fred said, putting a hand on her arm. 'We'd best get you away from this mob.'

She shrugged off his touch, then turned and gave him a smile to show him she meant him no offence. All the same, Paul was the only man she wanted touching her. And she could look after herself. 'I'm fine, Fred. I'm only going to the bakery.'

Fred looked past her, at the crowd. The group was well dressed – the men in suits and the women in neatly pressed skirts and blouses. A few were singing, and two of the men were walking up and down the street handing out pamphlets of some sort. Most of the pedestrian traffic was white people and they uniformly ignored the Africans and their handouts. A white man stopped to berate the group and tell them to go back to the bloody trees they'd climbed out of.

One of the men handing out flyers had his back to Pip, but he looked very familiar. When he turned around she saw it was Kenneth Ngwenya. Pip ignored Fred's panicked warning cry from behind her, looked both ways, and walked across the street towards the protesters.

'Kenneth!'

The tall Ndebele schoolteacher turned and smiled. He closed the gap between them. 'Hello, Pip, how are you?'

'I'm fine, and you?' He nodded and told her he was well. 'Is this what you do in your school holidays, organise civil disobedience?'

He chuckled. 'It's a peaceful demonstration. The bus companies are holding people to ransom. There have been big demonstrations in Salisbury and I, as an interested community member, wanted to show my support for the people opposed to these increases. We're calling on all African people to boycott the bus services until the companies drop their prices again.'

Pip knew that Kenneth was much more than an interested community member. He was a member of the Southern Rhodesia African National Congress, the dissident pro-black-independence organisation headed by

Joshua Nkomo. As a native-born Rhodesian, and the descendant of one of the members of Cecil John Rhodes's Pioneer Column, part of Pip bridled at anyone – African or white – wanting to destabilise the Rhodesian political scene. Rhodesian Africans, in her opinion, were better educated and better treated than any other blacks on the continent. There was agitation for majority rule in countries to their north and Pip, like most other whites, feared what might happen if Britain were to make a blanket decision to give independence too soon to people who were not prepared or educated enough to rule a country themselves. She liked Kenneth, although she found his wife, Patricia, surly to the point of being objectionable. Pip got the feeling that the woman disliked all white people. Kenneth, however, was like Paul – he took people as he found them. Paul often had Kenneth over to the farm for tea or went fishing with him after church on Sundays.

Pip wanted to ask Kenneth more about the demonstration, but their conversation was interrupted by the clanging of a police car's bell. They looked down the street and saw two patrol cars speeding towards them. The cars skidded to a halt and four officers got out of each vehicle, drawing truncheons as they strode towards the protesters.

'Break it up. This is an illegal gathering and you are

hereby ordered to disperse,' called Chief Inspector Harold Hayes from the head of the group. Pip cringed. She hadn't seen the bull-necked policeman for years. Hayes had been a sergeant during the war and Pip had been partnered with him for a while. He was an inept, racist bully, and proof that many people in uniform were promoted far above their capabilities simply because they hung around long enough. 'You, move away from that woman!'

Hayes was pointing his truncheon towards Kenneth, but Pip could see the overweight police officer hadn't recognised her yet. 'Chief Inspector . . .'

As Pip started to walk around Kenneth, he put out his arm, as if to tell her not to involve herself. At the same moment two of Hayes's young British South Africa Police constables bolted ahead of their commander, obviously ready to break up the gathering by force if they were given the slightest encouragement.

The protesters had stopped their singing and chanting and looked at each other for guidance. Some stood defiantly facing the oncoming police, but two younger men and a woman started to flee. One of the men, perhaps a student, was looking back over his shoulder at the advancing constable as he ran, and as Pip moved out of Kenneth's protective reach, the man collided with her and she fell over backwards, hitting the ground hard.

'No!' Kenneth yelled.

'He's kicking her, sir!' one of the junior constables cried out as the young man's legs became entangled in Pip's and he dropped to one knee beside her. The policemen raised their batons and charged.